Praise for Anna Kashina

*"Epic fantasy readers will love this action-packed a
dventure of elite warriors and romance!"*
Amy Raby, USA Today Bestselling author of the
Hearts and Thrones series

*"Assassin Queen continues to thrill and titillate with its
heady blend of fantasy romance and battle arts. Sometimes
swordplay is foreplay, a kiss can be a debilitating blow, and
the battle of the sexes spills onto the battlefield."*
J. M. Sidorova, author of *The Age of Ice*

*"A very promising new writer with a lot of originality, an exciting
story, a well realized background, and vivid writing."*
Poul Anderson, author of *The Broken Sword*

"Mixing the best elements of folklore...with modern fantasy"
Publishers Weekly

*"Anna Kashina has created a magically enthralling world of
extraordinary warriors – female ones, too! – bound by extreme
codes of honor, scholars dedicated to preserving ancient mysteries,
and crew of stalwart heroines and heroes. Set against a sweeping
political backdrop of warring kingdoms and religious faiths, the
books of The Majat Code hit that sweet spot of excellent world-
building for fantasy readers and a poignant romance payoff in the
end. Love this series!"*
Jeffe Kennedy, author of *The Twelve Kingdoms trilogy*

*"Kashina's talent for conveying complex ideas quickly endows her
characters with instant depth."*
Cowering King

By the Same Author

The Majat Code Series
Blades of the Old Empire
The Guild of Assassins
Assassin Queen

The Princess of Dhagabad
The Goddess of Dance
Mistress of the Solstice

Anna Kashina

SHADOWBLADE

ANGRY
ROBOT

ANGRY ROBOT
An imprint of Watkins Media Ltd

Unit 11, Shepperton House
89 Shepperton Road
London N1 3DF
UK

angryrobotbooks.com
twitter.com/angryrobotbooks

An Angry Robot paperback original,
2019

Copyright © Anna Kashina 2019

Cover by Alejandro Colucci
Set in Meridien

ISBN 978 0 85766 815 8
Ebook ISBN 978 0 85766 816 5

Printed and bound in the United
Kingdom by TJ International.

9 8 7 6 5 4 3 2 1

To My Family

BETRAYAL

Gassan heard the shouting from all the way down the narrow stone passageway leading to the entrance of the serai. A woman, her voice raising to a near-scream and eventually dissolving into sobs. He broke into a run, noting in passing the slanted crescent of the waning moon peeking in through the narrow window overhead. Not the average hour to expect visitors in the Daljeer command center, disguised as a scholarly hall.

The door at the end of the curving passage stood ajar. Gusts of cool night air washed through the entrance hallway, filling it with the scents of desert rosemary and creosote. As Gassan skidded around the last bend, he caught a view of the moonlit path outside, winding to the city down below. Dark shapes loomed along it, outlined against the white sand. Boulders? Odd. Just yesterday, when he arrived here from the empire's capital for the celebration of the Sun Festival, the path had been clear. He peered closer, a chill creeping down his spine as the objects began to take shape.

Bodies. Dear Sel.

His mind jerked into a heightened state of alertness, taking in the details of the scene much faster than he could possibly process them. People rushing back and forth at the serai entrance ahead. A woman crouching on the doorstep leading outside, clutching a bundle of rolled-up cloth to her chest. Half a dozen bodies lining up the path outside, visible through the open doorway. The gleam of the dead soldiers' armor, their dark red cloaks shifting in the wind. *Red cloaks. Sel almighty save us all.*

The logical part of Gassan's mind told him he couldn't possibly see it right, not from this distance. But the other, panicked part kept nagging him with the same urgency as the woman's sobs. From here, he couldn't see the cloaks' style or fully make out the bronze-gold patterns on the dead soldiers' breastplates, but his imagination painted the rest as clearly as if he were standing up close. The one-of-a-kind gear worn only by the Royal Challimar Redcloaks, the elite unit that personally guarded the queen.

Gassan darted forward, to the crouching woman. *Not the queen, thank the prophets.* She looked twice the age – in her forties, at least. Torn strands of gold beads glittered in her disheveled hair, her jeweled slippers far too ornate and impractical for a run through the sands. A noble? A high official of the royal court? Gassan forced away the guesses, not nearly as important right now as the immediacy of her need. He knelt by the woman's side, edging out a young Daljeer girl who was making vague moves around the woman, clearly with very little clue of what to do.

The woman's clothes and hair were soaked with blood. Gassan hoped it wasn't all her own. His eyes glossed over the long scratch at the base of her neck – not life-threatening despite its ugly look – down to a deeper stab wound below the collarbone, oozing with slow but steady gushes of blood. *Cursed Irfat.* He wasn't sure he could possibly do anything about that one. Not with all the distance she ran here from the royal palace, likely after she incurred the wound.

Gassan reached forward to pry the bundle the woman was clutching in her arms, as if it was more precious to her than the life seeping out of her. She held on for a moment longer, then released her hold, meeting his eyes with plea.

"Protect her... please... she is the only one left now..."

Her? What in three hells is she talking about? "Keep still." Gassan handed the bundle to the Daljeer girl still lingering behind him, then ripped his medicine bag off his belt, fumbling for bandage and disinfecting liquid.

"The imperial soldiers are coming..."

"Imperial soldiers?" Gassan frowned. The kingdom of Challimar was under the empire's protection. Their queen was about to sign a treaty that would give Challimar full province status in exchange for relinquishing their ancient succession claim. What could this richly dressed woman, escorted by the royal guards, possibly fear from the imperial soldiers?

"Betrayed..." the woman's voice faltered and grew stronger again under Gassan's urgent gaze. "The treaty... was a trap. Our queen ..." The woman gasped, her mouth opening and closing like that of a fish thrown ashore.

"Don't talk," Gassan snapped, clasping a fresh bandage to her neck while his other hand ripped open her cloak to reveal the mess inside. *Cursed Irfat.* For the first time in his healer's career he felt helpless – made worse by the fact that no matter what, he couldn't possibly show it.

The woman's pale lips twitched. "Don't bother with my wounds, Daljeer... Just listen... The queen... the royal family... the Redcloaks... they're all dead ... The only one left... my queen..." She gasped, her eyes rolling to stare at the passage just past Gassan's shoulder.

For an eerie moment it seemed to Gassan as if these words were directed not at him but at someone standing there in the shadows, but he had no time to wonder. The woman was getting delirious, another bad sign he couldn't possibly ignore.

"Save your strength," he said. "You can tell me all this when you recover."

Her lips twitched into a ghostly smile. "I said, listen, you stubborn man... My life is not important right now. The imperial soldiers... They will come after me. No matter what, they must not find her... Our savior... When the time comes... She can set things right... I..." She didn't finish her sentence as her entire body went limp.

Damn it, no. Not on my watch. Yet, even as the thought raced through Gassan's mind, he knew there was nothing he could possibly do. Not even with his healing skill, already famed within the Circle despite his relatively young age of thirty-five.

He lowered the woman to the floor and turned to the Daljeer girl standing behind him. She held the bundle the dying woman had brought in gently, her arms curved around it, rocking it. *Protect her. Damn it.* "Is this...?" Gassan's skin prickled as he saw the girl's slow nod.

"Yes. A baby."

Bloody hell. "A girl, I assume."

The Daljeer girl briefly lifted the baby's wrappings, then nodded as she tucked in the loose cloth. A distant smile played on her lips, oddly calm amidst the havoc around them.

"You don't need to concern yourself with this baby, Dal Gassan," she said. "We have everything we need in this serai to take care of her."

Gassan rose to his feet so fast that he felt lightheaded. "It's not the taking care of her that I'm concerned about right now. It's the imperial soldiers, who I assume will arrive here shortly to look for this woman and her charge." His eyes drifted to the limp shape on the floor. At least the imperial soldiers could no longer harm the woman, whoever she was. *Imperial soldiers.* His mind simply refused to enfold it. Young Emperor Shabaddin was known for his cruel, volatile temper, but a power grab like this exceeded everything the Daljeer feared when he had ascended the throne. The Challimar treaty took years to negotiate. And now, all this intricate work was laid to waste on a tyrant's whim.

One way or the other, Shabaddin was going to pay the price for it someday. There was no telling, though, how many innocent people would pay it first.

He turned back to the Daljeer girl. She stood very still, her eyes unfocused as she clutched the bundle to her chest. An understandable shock, given the girl's young age. Still, being stationed in this serai, the center of the Daljeer's southern operations, meant she was not only a highly promising scholar, but also someone Gassan could trust implicitly – an important commodity right now.

"What's your name?" Gassan asked.

"Mehtab."

Only now did Gassan notice the shade of her eyes – light brown with yellow-orange speckles, like a spray of molten gold. *Desert-kissed.* Not so rare in these parts, even if to a northerner like him it continued to look like a marvel. Up in Zegmeer and Haggad, men swooned over Chall women. Many would certainly fall head over heels for one like Mehtab. Her face looked so classic – not exactly beautiful, but timeless and majestic in its elegant lines. For some reason, it seemed vaguely familiar, as if bearing resemblance to someone he'd seen before. He wasn't certain where the feeling came from, but he was sure he would remember her if he saw her again.

"Mehtab," he said. "When the imperial soldiers come, I need you to disappear, and keep this baby safe. I'll follow you after I take care of some things, and take her off your hands."

An odd expression shifted Mehtab's features, playing in the downturned corners of her eyes and mouth. Resentment? Scorn? Unlikely, given that the girl should have no reason to object to his words. He realized now that she was not as young as she seemed, maybe twenty-five? In the flickering torchlight he couldn't quite tell. He frowned, then stepped away as he realized he was staring.

"Find the nearest hideout and stay there until the imperial soldiers are gone," he said. "Feed the baby. I'll find you."

"Don't worry, Dal Gassan. I'll take good care of her."

Gassan nodded. He knew he should feel nothing but relief at the fact that Mehtab was here to help with at least one of the problems that had been dropped on their heads so unexpectedly. He should focus on dealing with the more immediate threats, like the imperial soldiers who were making their way up the winding path to the serai gates – as well as the longer-term repercussions of the Challimar coup.

He wondered about the story of the baby girl, entrusted into their care so dramatically. Obviously someone important. If only he had time to ask the dying woman any questions at all. And now it was up to him to work out this mystery, as well as to find the best way to keep the baby girl safe.

The dying woman's words stuck in his memory. *When the time comes she can set things right…* He didn't like any of the guesses that came to mind. He hoped Mehtab didn't hear all of it, or at least wasn't informed enough to put the ends together the way he did.

The failure of the treaty left the royal family of Challimar the only power that could possibly challenge Emperor Shabaddin's right of succession and take over his throne, when his time came. This right had been the biggest contention point in all the negotiations over the last few years. Was this why His Imperial Majesty had been so keen to kill them all?

And could it be that the baby, so mysteriously delivered into the Daljeer care, was the key to enforcing this right and taking control of the imperial succession?

He heard soldiers approaching along the path outside, shouting orders as they walked. The Daljeer scrambled to get out of their way. Gassan turned to the place where Mehtab had been standing moments ago, relieved to see her gone. He heaved another breath of cool air, its fragrance now tinged with smoke from distant fires, then slipped away too, down another long passage. He could do no good by staying around any longer, except to identify himself as the healer who had tried his absolute best to save a potential enemy of the empire fleeing from justice, and the only man who heard her dying words.

It was a comfort to know that no matter how hard they searched, the soldiers would find nothing, and would eventually have to leave the serai alone. The Daljeer Circle was good at building secret chambers and nooks that could easily hide a battalion, not merely a small child. Assuming that Mehtab knew her way around the place – a certainty, judging by her confidence – the baby was safe for now. Barring unforeseen circumstances, this little girl was going to survive and do well in the Daljeer's care.

It was the next steps that worried him more.

Present day

TRAINEE

Naia paused at the edge of the practice range, looking across it toward the distant mountain crest. Its jagged ice peaks, highlighted at the edges by the rose gold of the rising sun, gleamed, as if adorned by precious jewels. She narrowed her eyes, then turned to look the other way, over the rooftops of the city below. Quiet, just like everything here, enjoying the last hour before the start of the day. Her last one on these grounds, if her trainers got their way.

She reached for her gear – then froze, as she caught a movement in the shadows of a deep side archway.

An intruder? Unlikely. The Jaihar stronghold, located in the very heart of the busy city of Haggad, trained the top blademasters in the empire. This place was better protected than the emperor's palace itself. No sane person would ever sneak in here with bad intentions.

Of course, there were always the insane ones.

The thought barely formed in her head when the low hum of a flying dagger cut through the stillness. Her body reacted on its own as she dove. Not away from the blade – which was probably the smartest thing to do – but toward it. Time slowed for an instant, then returned to its normal flow as she snatched the dagger by the hilt and clenched it in her hand, watching her attacker step out of his hiding place toward her.

Anyone less experienced would probably think of him as an enemy right now. Naia knew better, though. The way he'd aimed – off to the side, so that the dagger couldn't possibly hit her unless she purposely flung herself into its path – told her that the stranger never intended to harm her. This was a test. She saw a confirmation of it in the man's broad smile, in his nod of approval as he crossed the grounds in measured steps and stopped in front of her.

She took her time to look him up and down.

He was probably in his fifties, and very fit, for an outsider. His plain clothing – a loose shirt and ankle-length pants, girded with a large bulky belt-bag and covered by a dusted brown thawb – suggested a lower class occupation. Most traders and workers in the city wore similar outfits, well-worn and devoid of any decorations or jewelry. Yet, the way he held himself – with an air of superiority, as if used to people bowing to him – didn't match the image at all. She had no idea what to make of him.

"Impressive," the man said, then held out his hand in a commanding gesture, palm out. An order to hand him back the dagger.

Well, she would have, if he asked nicely. But she was damned if she was going to be patronized by an outsider. There were plenty of men on these grounds to do the job.

She ignored his waiting hand, moving slowly and deliberately as she turned the dagger in her fingers to look it over. Noble steel – reasonably balanced, its double-edged blade polished to mirror-smooth perfection, its simple but elegant hilt carved with an emblem. All the telling signs of its owner's high standing, despite the shabby clothing he chose to wear. She took another moment to examine the carving – two curved lines meeting at an angle, like a crude depiction of a flying bird. It seemed vaguely familiar, but she couldn't quite recall what it meant.

She kept his gaze as she bent down and placed the dagger on the pavement between them.

The stranger's face stretched in surprise, but his twitching lips betrayed a smile, one she didn't quite expect. He held in place for another moment, then lowered his hand.

"How did you learn to do this?" he asked.

"By watching my superiors," she said.

He grinned. "I was referring to the dagger catching."

"So was I." *Mostly.* She couldn't help a grin in response. Despite his obviously high standing, this stranger seemed surprisingly easy to talk to.

"I believe I might have neglected to introduce myself," he said. "You may call me Dal Gassan. I am on my way to see your headmaster."

"*Dal?* You're a *Daljeer?*"

"I thought you recognized the emblem, didn't you?"

Naia glanced at the dagger, still lying on the pavement between them. She was recalling it now. The curved lines didn't depict a bird, but the contour of an open book seen from the side. The Daljeer were known for their scholarly activities, as well as hospitals and schools that served everyone, regardless of their ability to pay. Every city had a Daljeer serai for the poor.

The last thing she expected for a Daljeer was to seek an audience with the Jaihar Headmaster. Or to throw daggers with this kind of a skill.

"I never realized the Daljeer were so proficient with weapons," she said.

Gassan laughed. "Come now, you can't possibly call this proficient. Not at your level. How about another test?"

Before she could respond, he whipped out a whole pack of daggers and hurled them at her, one by one.

Naia could tell that, just like last time, he was trying to avoid targeting her directly, but at this short distance it didn't really matter. The challenge was simply too hard to resist. She reached out toward the flying blades and caught all of them in turn, stacking them neatly into her hands.

"Six." Gassan nodded approvingly. "At a very close range. Now, this has to be impressive, even for you."

"Only as a party trick."

Gassan frowned. "Why?"

Naia swallowed. The last thing she wanted was to discuss her situation with an outsider. Yet, it was hard to hide the resentment in her voice. The best of her peers were already training on the upper grounds, hoping for a chance of attaining an elite Jai rank. She – well, she would be lucky to leave here with a Har cloak, if she earned any ranking at all.

"Never mind," she said.

"Is it really that bad?"

She briefly looked away. Never before had she felt so tempted to share her story with anyone at all, let alone someone she'd just met. Gassan seemed different somehow. He was looking at her so intently, as if she mattered. She knew she shouldn't be falling for a trick like this, but was there really any harm in telling him just a little more?

"I'm about to be expelled," she said.

"Expelled?" Gassan's frown deepened. "Why?"

"I… I got into a fight."

"I thought fighting is what you are supposed to learn here,

isn't it?"

"I attacked a trainer."

"Oh." Gassan regarded her thoughtfully. "I'm sure you had your reasons."

"It doesn't really matter, does it?"

"It would, to me."

Because you are not a Jaihar. She swallowed. Past deeds couldn't be revoked, not that she had any regrets. "Well, it doesn't. Not in my case."

"What's so special about your case?"

"Nothing." She guessed it was part of the problem too. If she showed enough promise, her superiors might have tried harder to salvage her situation.

Gassan leaned closer.

"There are many things that could go wrong in your life," he said quietly. "But I can think of only one that matters. Losing faith in yourself. You must never do that."

Naia's eyes widened, but before she could respond, his expression changed again, as if an invisible shutter had clicked into place to cut off the emotions inside. Three hells, this man was like the foothill weather, his moods flipping too fast to follow.

"I'm afraid I have to go," he said. "It's almost time for my audience with your headmaster."

Naia nodded. "Goodbye, then."

"It's been a pleasure."

A pleasure. It was, even if the realization in itself was surprising. She looked at his dagger, still lying on the pavement between them, feeling mildly guilty. It couldn't have hurt her that much to show some courtesy and just hand it to him, could it?

"Likewise," she said.

"I hope we'll meet again."

Me too, she wanted to say, but she kept her silence as she watched him pick up his dagger and stride away toward the archway on the other side of the grounds.

Only now did she realize that, despite introducing himself, he never asked her name. And now, even if he wanted to find her again, he wouldn't know who to ask for. A part of her wanted to run after him and tell him. Another, more reasonable part, told her to forget the whole thing. She was about to leave these grounds for good. Chasing after strangers was the last thing she should concern herself with.

She strode to the weapon stand and grasped the heaviest two-handed sword, plunging into a battle routine that left her sweaty and breathless in just a few moves. She didn't slow, though. With luck, she still had time to exercise herself to exhaustion before the day even started, so that she could forget everything that happened on the training grounds today.

CONFRONTATION

Naia lowered her sword and flexed her tired muscles. In less than half an hour she had managed to all but forget her encounter with the Daljeer. And now, the start of the training day was upon her, which meant that for the rest of it she was not going to enjoy any peace. As she glanced around the training range, rapidly filling with people, she noticed a group of young men about her age, watching her from a distance safe enough to stay out of weapon range, but not to afford any privacy.

"Trying to build up some manly muscles, Naia?" the nearest one said.

Naia sighed. She knew this group, the cocky youngsters who had too much trouble with the fact that she nearly always beat them in practice. Their jabs didn't normally bother her, but today she wasn't in the mood.

"Leave me alone," she said.

The speaker squared his shoulders, stepping up closer so that their height difference – about a head and a half – seemed even more impressive. "Or what? Are you going to beat the crap out of me, like you did with Har Ishim? Oh, wait. He's the one who beat the crap out of you, wasn't he?"

Hesitant laughter echoed around them. Naia looked away. Following the formal inquiry, Ishim, the Har trainer responsible for all her troubles, had recently been reassigned to a distant Jaihar compound. Everyone here knew it was her fault.

"Get lost." She turned away pointedly, taking unnecessary care to slide the sword she'd practiced with back into its slot at the stand. But her tormentors simply wouldn't take the hint. In fact, they shuffled closer, fanning around until she couldn't possibly pretend she wasn't aware of their attention.

She sighed. Dear Sel, why couldn't they just leave her alone?

"So, what *did* happen between you two?" another young man asked. He sounded friendlier than the first one, but Naia knew better than to take the bait.

"None of your bloody business."

The laughter around them became louder as more people approached them from the direction of the trainees' quarters.

"Come, now," the speaker insisted. "You can tell us, Naia. We're all friends here. What did Ishim do to you? Did he, um, grab your feminine parts?"

Blood rushed into Naia's face. She was surprised at the speed of her own reaction. As she swung her arm at the speaker – the biggest and strongest of the lot – she didn't expect his block to seem so clumsy and slow. In her altered state of mind, everything around her seemed to stall, giving her plenty of time to calculate every step, to slide between his blows without letting him land any of them.

It felt as if she barely had to touch him to overbalance him, sending him down to the ground. He landed flat on his back, looking up at her in disbelief.

Naia let out a breath. Time around her slowly returned to its normal flow, the wind shifting her short hair, sweeping an unruly lock over her face. She tossed it back, watching her opponent scramble up to his feet and retreat toward his suddenly quiet comrades.

Silence descended on the group around her, their awed expressions making Naia feel uncomfortable. This had to be yet another way to make fun of her, but she couldn't quite tell where this was going.

"Are they really planning to expel you?" The trainee who spoke sounded genuine, as if this was a real question. He was also younger, definitely not one of her usual tormentors.

"I believe so, yes," Naia said.

The young man shook his head. "This isn't right. They should have set you up for a proper evaluation with the Jai."

"Right," a tall girl said from the back of the group. "Naia's too good to be expelled. Maybe the headmaster–"

Several senior trainees around her lowered their heads. Their resigned looks spoke without words. The headmaster would be highly unlikely to overrule the Har trainer's decision. Not in the case of a trainee who hadn't even undergone a formal Jai evaluation.

Naia noticed a change of mood in the group, the trainees' sympathetic glances cut short by the sight of an approaching man. *A trainer.* None other than Har Valmad, the head trainer on the lower grounds. Ishim's best friend, at least in the Har's very loose definition of the word.

Three hells. It had to be her luck that out of all the trainers to show up first on the grounds today, Valmad would be the one.

The group around her rapidly scattered away. She willed herself into calmness as she watched Valmad stop in front of her, his beady eyes running over her from head to toe, as if trying to find a fault in her appearance and gear. He frowned as his gaze fell on her lowered hand, and she raised it belatedly, pressing it to her chest with an open palm in a formal Jaihar salute.

"Up to your tricks again, are you?" Valmad asked.

Naia only shrugged. There seemed to be no reason to engage in this conversation at all. Not when the outcome was more or less decided anyway.

Valmad's gaze drifted to the trainees she had been talking to, suddenly so busy with their warmup routines on the far side of the range that Naia wondered if they were going to fall over with effort.

"Care to explain what happened?" he said.

"Nothing important, Har Valmad."

"You've just knocked a young man to the ground."

He asked for it. She knew this line of argument would only make her situation worse. She continued to stare at him, blank-eyed.

Valmad's face twitched into a malicious grin. "Well, if anything, it only reinforces the decision we've just reached about you. We're expelling you without a rank."

"Without a rank?" She knew it wasn't a good idea to show surprise, but she couldn't help it. Even though she'd always known this was a possibility, deep inside, she never believed it. Her skill was far superior to everyone else's on these grounds – including some trainers by now, even if Valmad probably wasn't aware of it.

"You seem surprised," Valmad said.

"I am, Har Valmad. I believe, with my skill, I've earned a Jaihar cloak."

"It isn't about your skill. Your advanced level makes it worse, actually. People like you should never be trained to fight at all. You are volatile and temperamental. Training you any further would pose a danger to your peers – and to the regular citizen, once you leave these grounds." Valmad glanced at the trainees again. "The scene I just witnessed is yet another confirmation."

Naia continued to stare. She knew how much Valmad hated her for what happened with Ishim, but all the other Har trainers couldn't possibly have gone along with him, could they? They all knew what really went on, even if no one was willing to volunteer the information.

She was most certainly *not* volatile and temperamental. Well, perhaps she did tend to get confrontational far too easily, but it wasn't *all* her fault, was it? Not when it came to fights, at least. Why couldn't her trainers see it?

"I'd like to formally appeal this decision," she said.

Valmad shrugged. "Don't bother. Your appeal will be denied. On my authority as the head trainer on these grounds."

Naia held his gaze. Taking a swing at him suddenly seemed more tempting than she liked.

"You will surrender your gear," Valmad said, "and leave the training area immediately. Stay around, though, until the headmaster formally approves our decision. Later today, I expect."

Later today. Naia blinked. She had expected to leave these grounds formally ranked. Anyone of her skill deserved a Jaihar cloak and a steady guard job somewhere in the empire. Expelling her without any rank at all meant committing her to a life of hardship and humiliation. Worse, there didn't seem to be anything she could possibly do about it. But even as she lowered her eyes in resigned silence, her encounter with Gassan came into her mind. This wasn't the worst that could happen to her. The worst would be to lose faith in herself. She couldn't afford to do that, no matter what.

Working as hard as she could to complete her training had been the focus of her entire existence up to now. Yet, did she truly have a place here, among the people who put obedience so far above compassion and normal human decency?

She was surprised at the way her resentment receded as soon as these thoughts swept through her head. She squared her shoulders as she met Valmad's gaze.

"There is at least one good thing about your decision, Har Valmad," she said. "It means I won't have to ever see you again. I consider it a bonus."

Valmad's brow furrowed, his burly neck flaring up with pink splotches. If they continued this conversation, these spots would soon cover his whole face, fusing into a uniform red color by the time the discussion elevated to a regular yelling session. He appeared to have decided against it, though, as he looked at her for another long moment, then turned and strode off the grounds.

Naia took her time to strip off her gear and return it to the stand, piece by piece. The grounds around her sank into silence, all the trainees watching her frozen-faced. Many of them, even the ones who constantly pestered her, had to be feeling bad right now. None of it mattered, though. Not anymore. All she could think of was finding a nice, quiet place where she would not have to talk to anyone at all.

GAMBIT

Gassan looked down at the shatranj board, encrusted with an alternating pattern of ebony and ivory squares. He was playing the black, and his opponent – Arsat, the Jaihar Headmaster – had already laid carnage to his suite, leaving only two pieces besides the shah: a tall swordsman and a small, delicately carved pawn. On the opposite side of the board a much more impressive white pair – a priest and an elephant – protected the secure corner where the white shah stood in relative safety.

Arsat's face, tanned to a deep brown that sharply contrasted with the white curtain of his shoulder-length hair, bore a serene expression that betrayed none of his thoughts. The man's top Jaihar training made him so much harder to read – and so enjoyable as an opponent. Gassan had a weakness for a good shatranj game, and these regular visits with the Jaihar Headmaster were a treat that made the job of mediating the complex business dealings between the Jaihar Order and the Daljeer Circle more pleasurable than they had any right to be.

He leaned forward and picked up his swordsman, placing the piece halfway across the board on the crossroad of two diagonal black lines. Arsat responded almost instantly, moving his priest in a sneaky pattern to block the swordsman's advance.

Gassan smiled inwardly, while keeping his face impassive. He knew Arsat's style, and counted on exactly this response. The man played with the brutality and strategic sense that left no doubt of why he occupied his high post. To head the Jaihar, Arsat not only had to belong to their top, Shadowblade rank, but also to prove himself a superior leader that held together some of the most complex threads governing the affairs in the empire. Yet, with careful plotting, one could upset this balance – just as Gassan was about to do.

He picked up his pawn, hovering it over the board for a dramatic moment before placing it right into the middle of the white defenses. "Shahmat."

Arsat raised his eyebrows.

Gassan let his smile surface, leaning back in his chair to allow himself a full moment of enjoyment at the look of surprise on the senior blademaster's face. His shatranj matches with Arsat tended to get exhausting at times, as appropriate when facing an opponent of equal skill. This was why a clean and painless victory like this felt especially rewarding.

Arsat's long, deft fingers moved slowly and deliberately as he reached over and lifted up his shah piece to lay it down on its side, signaling defeat.

"I am not familiar with this gambit," he said.

Gassan's smile widened. He had worked the gambit out in his head on the way here, and he was glad to see how well it worked in practice. Shatranj players tended to focus on the more powerful pieces and often underestimated what one could do with a simple pawn.

"It's a new one," he said. "I've been looking forward to trying it out, before I could introduce it to the shatranj players at court."

Arsat briefly inclined his head. "Your visits here are always a pleasure, Dal Gassan."

Gassan shifted in his chair. It was time to come to the main reason for his visit, but despite the calming effect of a good shatranj game, he still couldn't quite settle his racing thoughts. Seeing the girl on the training grounds stirred up memories of that night, seventeen years ago, in the Daljeer's Challimar serai. *Naia.* He'd chosen the name himself, but until now he didn't have a chance to see how well it suited her. In ancient Aramit, the language that used to dominate these lands before the Chall and the Zeg rose to power, the word "naiah" meant "lost" – befitting, for someone of her hazy origins. For the past seventeen years, Gassan had been digging as deep as he could into the events at Challimar, but even with his nearly unlimited resources he was unable to learn anything at all about the girl's lineage, or the reason that the Challimar queen's closest protectors chose to risk their lives to bring her to the Daljeer.

Placing her with the Jaihar was part of the plan of keeping her safe. It seemed appropriate, especially after her caretakers had spotted her unusual affinity for weapons. The Daljeer in Haggad kept an eye on her, and reported to Gassan regularly, but he had never seen her in person until today, when his Daljeer informants had told him about the trouble she was in with the Jaihar Order.

Whoever this girl really was, someone with her talent, someone important enough for the high-standing Chall to risk their lives, surely deserved better than being expelled from the Jaihar Order for a minor case of insubordination?

"Just before I came to your audience chamber," Gassan said,

"I met an unusual trainee on your lower grounds."

Arsat's gaze flickered, showing that Gassan's casual tone didn't conceal the importance of the topic. "Unusual, how?"

"She has an exceptional talent with weapons. Yet, as I gathered from a brief conversation with her, she is not considered for Jai training."

"The Har trainers surely have their reasons." Arsat shrugged. "Perhaps she simply isn't good enough?"

"She caught six throwing daggers at a close range, in under a second."

The headmaster measured him with a long look.

Gassan waited. The Jaihar normally gave outsiders like him no credit at all when it came to evaluating anyone's weapon skill. But the headmaster knew better. Gassan saw evidence of it in the length of the pause, even if Arsat chose not to show any other reaction.

"Catching daggers is not something the Har teach on the lower grounds," Arsat said.

"That's what I thought. As a matter of fact, she did not look as if she was familiar with the exercise. This makes the skill she showed even more impressive, doesn't it?"

"What's this trainee's name?"

"Naia."

Arsat let out a sigh. "Oh, *her*."

"You know her?"

The headmaster pointed to his desk. "Her case was submitted for my attention last night. It's rather long, so I only had a chance to take a brief look so far, but it doesn't very promising, I must tell you. The Har trainers recommend expelling her from the Order, effective immediately."

"Do they now?"

"You don't seem surprised."

"Well." Gassan held a pause. "She *did* mention serious problems with her superiors."

"Did she mention attacking her trainer?"

"She did, yes. We didn't get into her reasons, though."

"Her reasons don't matter. The fight got ugly, and very violent. This girl, Naia, suffered injuries so grave that, following her recovery and the formal inquiry into the matter, we had no choice but to reassign the trainer involved to another compound. The other Har on our lower grounds didn't take kindly to it."

"Weren't these grave injuries she suffered punishment enough?"

Arsat shook his head. "Not nearly, no. Her insubordinate behavior is simply incompatible with our chain of command."

Gassan looked away. He was willing to bet there was more to Naia's story – if only because, despite their best efforts, Gassan's informants in Haggad had been unable to find out anything about it at all.

"Isn't there anything to be done for her, Jai Arsat?" he asked.

The headmaster frowned. "Is there any special reason for you to care?"

Several, but none of them suitable for the purpose of this conversation. Gassan smiled. "Only the fact that she is very talented. Her trainers choose to downplay it for some reason, and she is deeply aware of it. She also seemed very level-headed, at least to me. A reasonable person, willing to own up to her mistakes. I couldn't speak for the Jaihar, of course, but in the Daljeer Circle we would have found a way to evaluate her more thoroughly before signing off on a decision that would ruin her entire future."

Arsat paused. Gassan waited. The silence itself was encouraging, the way it stretched on and on, like it sometimes did when Arsat was working out a difficult shatranj move in his head.

"Very well," Arsat said. "I will look further into her situation. With no guarantees, of course."

"Of course, Jai Arsat. Forgive me for taking so much of your time with this minor matter. The reason for my visit here is different, and much more important on the great scale of things. I traveled here from Zegmeer to show you this." Gassan fumbled in his robes and handed Arsat a tightly rolled scroll.

The headmaster opened it and read through it slowly, his face betraying no emotion at all.

"This is a report from the top Daljeer physician that treats the imperial family," Gassan said.

Arsat's eyes hovered on the densely packed lines of the spidery writing that covered the entire page. "I'm afraid I am not familiar with some of the medical terms here."

"I apologize. The document was prepared for internal use. It appears that His Majesty suffers from a rare progressive condition that will be certain to claim his life in a matter of a few years."

"How few, exactly?"

"Three or so."

Arsat cocked his head, looking at him thoughtfully. "Are you referring to a naturally occurring condition, Dal Gassan? Or is this sudden ailment manmade?"

"A natural one, of course. I've always believed that the manmade ones are more within the Jaihar's expertise."

"Not the ones that take three years to work, no."

Gassan leaned forward and carefully rolled up the document,

tucking it back into a deep pocket of his robe. "Picking up on a conversation you and I had at some point, I felt this illness could be our window of opportunity."

Arsat stiffened. "Hardly. Death by an illness would be no better than an assassination, the course of action we decided against seventeen years ago."

Seventeen years ago. Gassan remembered that conversation as vividly as if it had happened yesterday. And yes, at that time, he would have agreed with Arsat. But he had learned a lot since then.

"Death by an illness, progressing slowly and visibly in the months preceding the end, gives everyone a chance to prepare," he said. "You can count on every province ruler, every high noble and every member of the High Council, to be in the palace when it happens."

"So what?"

"So that a succession contest, if evoked, has an actual chance of being backed up by a majority vote."

"A *succession contest?*"

"Yes. A plausible alternative to the bloodshed and chaos that would erupt if the emperor were to die suddenly."

Arsat kept very still, his eyes trailing to the distant mountain view visible through the window. Gassan had a good idea what was going through the headmaster's head. This fear of chaos was the reason they had originally decided against drastic measures like this, no matter how despicable Shabaddin's actions had been, no matter what losses both Gassan and Arsat personally suffered in the wave of the Challimar Royal Massacre. The headmaster's own brother died in the aftermath, as well as a few of the Daljeer scholars Gassan had been looking up to. The decision to stand back and rein in their anger had not been easy.

Would they truly get their chance for a redemption, after all these years?

"How exactly do you plan to do it?" Arsat asked.

Gassan smiled. The excitement rising in his chest resembled the one he felt a few days ago when he'd first thought of the new shatranj gambit. And now he was about to uncover a real-life version of it, or as close to it as one could play out with the powers involved.

"The ancient succession tradition requires all the imperial princes and rulers of the provinces to pledge allegiance to the official heir."

"A formality, no more."

"Not if one of the province rulers claims succession rights and challenges the official heir."

Arsat frowned. "Impossible. All provinces are under a treaty, which precludes them from putting a succession claim forth."

"All except one."

"You can't mean…"

"I do." Gassan held a dramatic pause. "The kingdom of Challimar."

Arsat leaned back in his chair, his long fingers playing with the hilt of the dagger at his belt. A black blade, one of the distinctive signs symbolizing his Shadowblade rank. Gassan found himself absorbed in watching the movements, fast and precise above what seemed humanly possible.

"Am I the only one here," Arsat said, "who sees a problem in the fact that the entire Challimar royal family was killed in a massacre?"

"Yes and no. The massacre happened before their queen had a chance to sign away her succession rights. This means, if a member of the Challimar royal family were to miraculously survive…"

"…which didn't actually happen."

"But if it did, no law would prevent this heir from putting a claim forth."

"No *written* law, perhaps. But there's also the cutthroat law, the one Shabaddin uses so widely at court. How long do you think this newly discovered heir of Challimar can actually survive in the imperial palace?"

"Longer than you think, if this heir, purely coincidentally, also happened to be a Jaihar-trained blademaster."

Arsat shifted in his chair again. His fingers resumed their dance, even though now they were moving almost too fast to trace.

"Very well," he said at length. "Supposing a plan like this does have merit, what would you do once the succession contest is evoked?"

"We will stack the vote to ensure our candidate's victory. I'm certain many council members would be more than happy to back up anyone who challenges the current order of things. Once this is settled, and Shabaddin's immediate heirs are out of the way, all our candidate would have to do is pass on the crown to an heir of our choice."

"Which is?"

"It could be anyone at that point, assuming that this person carries at least a measure of the imperial blood."

"You'd be hard pressed to find anyone decent from Shabaddin's bloodline."

"We have three years."

Arsat nodded. His eyes briefly trailed to the dramatic skyline of the distant mountains out of his windows.

"Back to your Challimar heir, then," he said. "How are you going to convince anyone that he's the real thing?"

Gassan smiled. "It all comes down to storytelling, something our scholars are exceptionally good at."

"You can't get far in politics by telling stories."

"You can, if they are the right ones. Imagine, for instance, a tale that goes like this. A dark night descending over the Challimar royal palace. The queen and her family, summoned urgently to the throne room where the assassins are waiting. She has a premonition about this late-night visit from the imperial envoys, so before rushing to follow the summons, she entrusts her lady chamberlain with a precious bundle: her newborn child. The lady takes an elite unit of the Redcloak guards to deliver the baby to the Daljeer serai outside the city walls, where she knows they would be offered sanctuary with no questions asked. She succeeds, but, along with all the guards, dies of the wounds they've incurred while fighting their way out of the palace."

"Fascinating," Arsat said. "But a bit too wild."

"It's the truth."

"The *truth*?"

"The episode I've just described actually happened – at least its public part, give or take some minor details." Perhaps not so minor, given that Gassan could find no evidence whatsoever that the queen bore a child, or was even pregnant at the time. Her love affair with her guard captain made pregnancy a possibility, but there was simply no evidence of it.

The scene in the Challimar serai surfaced in Gassan's mind with frightening clarity, down to the smells – creosote, tinged with a faint, metallic scent of blood. The lady chamberlain's rugged breathing. Her words. *Protect her... No matter what, they must not find her… When the time comes… She can set things right…* Seeing Naia this morning added one more piece to the picture in his head, so perfect that his skin started to prickle as he thought about it.

"What exactly do you mean by the public part?" Arsat said.

"The lady chamberlain, along with the Redcloak guards, did deliver a baby to the Daljeer. I was the one who met them at the doors. I treated the lady's wounds – unsuccessfully, to my dismay. I also took charge of the baby and helped to hide it from the imperial guards."

Arsat's eyes widened. "What happened to this baby?"

"She is safe, at least for now. The Daljeer have kept watch over her all these years."

"*Her?*"

"Yes. All the better for my story, since the royal succession in Challimar goes through the female line."

"And you have proof of her identity?"

"Unfortunately not. However, given that she exists, it would be easy enough to start the rumors. The actual girl we found doesn't even have to factor into this." *Even though it would be so perfect, wouldn't it?* Gassan forced the thought away.

Arsat leaned forward over the table. "So, you want me to find a girl among our trainees, about seventeen, whose blade training would enable her to defend herself against the empire's worst?"

"Do you have one in mind?"

"Not at the moment, no."

"We could think more broadly, at least for now. Rumors can be twisted. Age, for one, doesn't have to be precise. Gender, too. Any plausible survivor would be guaranteed to ignite rumors."

A man fitting the bill would be far easier to find among the Jaihar. Gassan was sure that Arsat had at least a few warriors that could play this role. But he simply couldn't stop thinking about Naia. She had the talent to be trained for the role, he was sure of it. She was also of the right age and appearance – not to mention the possibility that she was actually the real thing. But his instincts told him this wasn't the right time to bring it into the conversation. Arsat would likely take issue with the fact that none of this had been disclosed to him when Naia was first brought into his Order for training. Gassan couldn't afford to risk jeopardizing his ally's trust at this vulnerable moment, or appear as if he was piling up the stakes to manipulate the Jaihar's rigorous process of trainee evaluation. He had to let the Jaihar play this part out on their own, before suggesting her candidacy at all. Which meant, for the moment, he had to act as if she didn't even exist.

"Very well," Arsat said. "I think the Jaihar Order can work on finding a warrior you need."

Gassan's lips twitched into a grin. Dethroning Shabaddin and his dynasty had been personal to both of them in many ways. But the excitement he felt, one also reflected in Arsat's face, had nothing to do with these old ghosts. It was all about the pleasure of playing a good match to achieve a clean victory.

"Give me a few days," Arsat said.

Gassan nodded. "Of course. I'll need some time too, to research the possibilities. It would be good, though, if by our next meeting you put together a list of candidates. Young warriors who have some acting talent would be best. Once we make this choice, we should begin the training as soon as we can."

"The *training*?"

"There are many essentials this person would need to learn to impersonate Chall royalty. Language, history, traditions – as well as royal manners and bearing. I intend to provide a special Daljeer tutor, chosen from one of our top scholars."

"What about appearance?"

"Appearance?"

"Resemblance of the royal family members. They all had a particular eye shade, didn't they?"

"The 'desert kiss', yes. Many Chall have it, actually. The feature can be quite subtle, visible only at a close range. It would be a bonus, but it's not strictly necessary." Once again, Gassan's thoughts trailed back to Naia. When he saw her this morning, her eye color gave him an extra shock. Dark amber, with a fiery rim around the iris, like rain clouds lit up by a late sunset. The shade seeped into her hair too, a deep mahogany tint that graced only the very few. Despite her tomboy looks, she could be so perfect, if cleaned up and dressed in Challimar royal garb. He forced down this thought before it had the danger of surfacing in the conversation.

Arsat's fingers twirled around the hilt of his dagger again, then came to an abrupt standstill. "I'd like to share this plan with the senior members of the Jaihar command."

"As long as they are sworn to secrecy."

"Of course. It may also be advisable to keep the head of the Jaihar Imperial Dozen informed, at least in broad terms."

The Jaihar Imperial Dozen. Twelve of the Jaihar elite under the command of one of their top blades, whose ceremonial duty consisted of serving as the emperor's personal bodyguards. After the emperor's death they would go into a brief hiatus, stationed at court but not formally sworn to service. It could make them valuable assets to the plan.

"Closer to the time," Gassan said. "I assume it will be Jai Elad?"

"No, actually," Arsat said. "Jai Elad's term at court is nearly over. His replacement for the next four years is leaving for Zegmeer very soon."

"Who?"

"Jai Karrim."

"Oh." Hard as he tried, Gassan didn't quite manage to keep the distaste out of his voice.

"You've heard of him, I see," Arsat said.

"I have, yes." *And not in a good way.* Well, to be fair, the rumors left no doubt about the man's blade skill, reportedly exquisite, even for a Shadowblade. This wasn't the part Gassan had such problem with, though. The talk that bothered him came mostly from the court ladies, who tended to turn misty-eyed whenever Karrim's name came up. Gassan wasn't privy to what the man actually did to feed these rumors, but assuming they had at least some substance to them, Karrim wasn't the kind of man Gassan preferred to deal with, especially for a plan of this magnitude.

"I don't suppose you can reconsider this choice, Jai Arsat," he said.

The headmaster's face hardened. "He's the best we have. In fact, the best we've seen in years on these grounds. His recently earned title of our top blade is but a small testament to his superb blade skill."

"It's not his blade skill I'm worried about."

"What then?"

Gassan sighed. Arsat had to know what he was talking about. The fact that the headmaster was feigning ignorance meant that the choice was not up for discussion.

He tried, anyway.

"He seems a bit young."

"He's twenty-five."

"My point exactly."

"His combat experience and command qualities more than make up for it. Did you hear about his assignment in Scinn?"

"More than once, in fact." More than a dozen times, probably, each account blown so much out of proportion that Gassan knew better than to believe any of them.

Arsat nodded. "There you have it, then. As for his age, he will be twenty-eight by the time your plan sees action – prime age for a warrior. By that time, he will be intimately familiar with the affairs at court."

I have no doubt of that. Gassan suspected Arsat's wording to be deliberate, but the fact the headmaster said it with a straight face didn't seem very helpful. He sighed. Admittedly, he had only seen Karrim once, even if that meeting left him utterly unimpressed. The man looked so unremarkable for the kind of a reputation he had. Even though Gassan knew that blade skill was about much more than the size of one's muscles, he simply couldn't match the image to all the rumors. Was this the real reason for his negativity?

"Jai Karrim has my full confidence," Arsat said. "Above all, I value his unconventional thinking and his ability to make good decisions on the spot. There is no one I'd rather have at the post when our game is played out."

Our game. The ownership with which the Jaihar Headmaster referred to the plan, the hidden excitement in his voice, resonated in Gassan's heart. They were about to play a game that could end decades of injustice and torment for many in the empire, including those at the very top. Sel knew, Arsat's own stakes in this game were high enough to put his very best into it. If the headmaster was willing to trust Karrim with all this, perhaps Gassan should feel better about the choice.

"Very well," he said.

"I promise, Jai Karrim won't disappoint you. Just make sure things go smoothly on your end."

"I will, Jai Arsat." Gassan rose. "See you in a few days."

Before he walked out of the room, he saw Arsat reach for the dossier on his desk. Naia's. Gassan hoped that the headmaster had taken his words to heart, that he was going to give the girl another chance. The idea that she could be the one to play the role he had devised continued to inflame his mind. He forced these thoughts down, for now.

SECOND CHANCE

When Naia heard the echo of footsteps at the entrance to the back courtyard, she refused to feel even remotely interested to know who it was. Whoever wanted to see her right now would be most likely to gloat or offer sympathy. She wasn't in the mood for either. Best to remain unnoticed, so that the strangers would leave as soon as possible. Just to make sure, she crept deeper into the narrow gap between the piled crates holding scrap metal and spare pavement stones, so that the newcomers, whoever they were, would not be able to see her at all.

The footsteps drew closer. Two men, treading with a special kind of sure-footedness that came only with the top blade training. It seemed as if their boots – by the sound of it, made of the finest soft leather – barely touched the stone pavement while striding in her direction. Not trainees then, they all made such a ruckus as they approached, even the very best ones. Not the trainers either, or so she guessed. The ones she was familiar with tended to have heavier steps.

Even in her despairing stupor, she felt curious. What could high-ranked blades possibly come looking for here, in this deserted courtyard used mostly for storing broken gear?

The footsteps slowed and came to a halt in the middle of the courtyard. A rustle of their feet on the stone told her that the newcomers paused, then turned, as if getting ready to leave. If she kept to her hideout just a little longer, they would depart and leave her alone. To her surprise, she realized that if she allowed this to happen without even learning who it was, she would never forgive herself afterwards.

She shifted against the wall, leaning out of her hiding place – and froze.

The two men in the center of the courtyard stood statue-still, their graceful stance betraying their combat skill. Naia didn't need to see the color of their cloaks – black, with a faint silky sheen – to know who they were. The Jai blademasters from the upper grounds. It was the color of their cloaks' underlining that made her skin creep with a chill she hadn't experienced in a very long time. A deep, suffused gray that made a man almost invisible in the dark, if wearing this cloak inside out. *Shadowblades.* The Jaihar Order only had a few warriors of this top rank, held so far above the others that trainees like Naia could never hope to see any of them up close.

Shadowblades.

Now that she knew their rank, she realized that they could have easily approached her without making any sound at all. The sound of their feet on the stone had been purposeful, to make sure they were heard. Which meant that they knew someone was hiding here, and wished to make their arrival known to whoever it was they were looking for.

Her heart skipped a beat. She refused to follow the thought any further as she scrambled to her feet and stood upright, hurriedly running her hands over her clothes to dislodge the worst of the dust.

She willed herself not to show any emotion under the men's scrutinizing gazes. It was damn hard, especially after she recognized the one in front – with a second's delay that made the effect so much worse. This older man, his flat mask-like face covered with a fine meshwork of old scars, could only be one person. Jai Surram, the headmaster's right-hand man, in charge of all the training in the Jaihar Order.

Her hand belatedly flew up to her chest, pressing against it with an open palm in a formal salute. She wished they would say something to explain their presence here, but neither of the men seemed in a hurry to break the silence. Surram's dark eyes studied her appraisingly, as if set on dragging every bit of her insecurity out into the open. Perhaps he was doing just that, but she was damned if she was going to give in to it.

"You are the one called Naia, I presume." Surram's deep voice rolled through the small space with deep echoes. The loose stones piled at the top of the nearest crate stack rumbled in response, as if about to roll down in a minor avalanche. Of course, the senior blademaster was probably used to addressing hundreds of people lined up on the training field, not one stray girl who could find nothing better to do than hide from her peers in this deserted courtyard.

"Yes, Jai Surram." Naia swallowed, aware of how her own voice sounded so weak in comparison.

"We are here to speak with you," Surram said.

Naia blinked. How did they know where to find her? More importantly, why? The idea of their Order's top men coming here to speak with her seemed beyond ridiculous. To the best of her knowledge Surram almost never left the upper grounds

at all, except for the formal events at the main arena, where
the lower ground trainees like her could glimpse him from the
distance of the back rows. Even if, for argument's sake, he truly
wished to see her for whatever reason, he could have easily sent
his attendants to fetch her. Why come here, and bring another
Shadowblade along? She waited, knowing that trying to say
anything right now was a really bad idea.

Surram nodded briskly, as if the mere fact of her silence had
just yielded some important information he was looking for.
"I believe you are aware that your case is being decided by our
headmaster right now."

"Yes, Jai Surram." Dear Sel, why couldn't she make her voice
roll as effortlessly as he did?

"Before finalizing his decision, Jai Arsat asked me to look
further into your situation."

He did? Naia blinked, unsure what to say. She hated the way
her heart fluttered with hope at Surram's words. Luckily, he left
her no time to wonder as he stepped back, his eyes darting to
his silent companion.

"This is Jai Hamed."

Naia saluted again, trying her best not to gape. Hamed
looked much younger than Surram, a Shadowblade on active
duty. His narrow eyes watched Naia impassively, without
betraying any of his thoughts.

"Jai Hamed will test your skill now," Surram said.

Naia frowned. Did Surram mean a weaponry test? This
couldn't possibly be right. Someone of Hamed's skill could
easily kill with a flick of a hand. Nothing she had learned so
far on the lower grounds, even by watching her superiors and
practicing after hours, could possibly counter that.

Her gaze darted between the two men, searching for any hint

of a doubt in their calm faces.

"We'll make it fast," Surram said. "I don't have much time."

Naia expected him to describe the test, but no explanation ensued. Focused on Surram, she barely caught the moment Hamed moved his hand, drawing a set of blades from the sheath at his belt. He flung them at Naia in a single pack – or so it appeared. In her heightened state of alertness, she could actually see them flying in a string, as if connected end to end. She heard them cutting the air as they approached, silken and smooth like a lash of wind.

She had no time to adjust. Yet, miraculously no time seemed necessary to do what she needed. Guided by all her senses, she reached out to snatch the blades out of the air one by one. Not quite fast enough for all of them, tough. She missed two, and was too slow on the last one, grabbing it by the blade instead of the hilt. Its sharp edge bit into her skin, the pain jerking her back into the normal flow of time.

She blinked, hearing the two blades she missed clatter to the pavement behind her. The rising breeze felt cool on her flushed skin.

Four out of six. Is this what they wanted me to do?
Did I pass or fail?

She raised her eyes to the two Shadowblades, trying not to look too anxious as she watched the men exchange a glance.

"Most trainees at your stage would have tried to avoid the daggers, not to intercept them," Surram said.

Naia kept his gaze. "I assumed you wanted me to catch them. Didn't you?"

Surram's frown sent a chill down her spine. "Did anyone teach you how to do this?"

"No."

"How did you learn it then?"

"I practiced on my own," she said.

"Why?"

"Because I hoped it could be useful someday." *Like today, when two of our Order's best came here to test me on this skill, of all things.* She thought back to her encounter with Gassan, to the fact that this was also the exact test he used. Was this a new fashion? Or did Gassan's conversation with the headmaster somehow trigger Surram's visit today?

She followed the thought further, trying to read anything at all in Surram's stern face. Whatever drove the senior blademaster to seek her out, it didn't really matter. All that mattered right now was whether or not she had done well. She had no idea at all. Surram continued to watch her impassively, while Hamed stepped forward and retrieved his daggers, sheathing them at his belt in such a fast, fluid move that she couldn't help but stare.

"You will report to the upper grounds tomorrow morning," Surram said. "I will send a Glimmerblade to collect you at precisely seven o'clock. Dress for a training day."

"Yes, Jai Surram," Naia heard herself say. *Upper grounds. A Glimmerblade. Dear Sel.* It probably meant good news, but she was too overwhelmed to feel any joy. Besides, Surram could be summoning her tomorrow for an entirely different reason. She had seen too many ups and downs in her life to celebrate before time. She stood, dumbfounded, pressing her bleeding palm to her chest as the two Shadowblades turned and left the courtyard.

DISCUSSION

Karrim stopped at the door leading into the headmaster's audience chamber. The sounds of heightened voices left no doubt of an ongoing argument inside, several men speaking at once, as if trying to silence each other. He glanced at the saluting Glimmerblade guards at the door, their restrained looks telling him more than words. The argument had been going on for a while. And by the sound of it, it wasn't about to end any time soon.

Karrim considered his choices. He could pretend he didn't receive the headmaster's summons and walk away, to come back at a later time. Or, he could go ahead and step into the hellstorm going on inside. The choice seemed obvious, yet, just as he was about to leave, the sound of a raised voice carrying through the door paused him in mid-step. That singular voice, barking like a hound on a trail, could only belong to one man. Valmad, the Har training master from the lower grounds.

Valmad was the last person Karrim ever expected to cause a disturbance in the headmaster's chamber, if only because of his inferior rank. Valmad was also easily the last person Karrim ever wanted to see again, his own memories of the lower grounds training too painful even after nearly eight years. He probably should leave after all, but his curiosity got the better of him. Something that brought Valmad to near-hysteria in front of the headmaster had to be worth listening to.

He winked to the Glimmerblade guards and stepped into the room.

The minor crowd gathered in front of the headmaster's chair sank into an abrupt silence as he approached. All of them wore ranking cloaks, flipped to the inner side that emphasized the formal nature of the gathering. Inadvertently, Karrim's eyes sought out his own rank – Shadowblades, the soft gray of their cloaks making them nearly invisible even in plain daylight. There were two – Hamed and Surram – standing notably apart from the rest of the group. They didn't speak, but something about their postures made them look smug, as if they knew they were behind all the ruckus. This was getting more and more curious. Karrim saluted the headmaster and took a place beside them.

Valmad's face contorted into a pained grimace at the sight of Karrim, as if the man had just swallowed a spiky mountain plum. Karrim suppressed a smile. Apparently, their memories of each other were mutually unpleasant, which left Karrim mildly comforted by the fact that he presently outranked Valmad by a very long shot.

"Glad you are here, Jai Karrim," Arsat said. "We would greatly value your opinion on a difficult matter of a lower grounds trainee."

"A lower grounds trainee?" Karrim frowned. To the best of his knowledge no trainees ever merited a discussion of this magnitude, unless they were surely headed for a top blade rank. This obviously couldn't be the case here, since the discussion

clearly concerned someone in the Har's charge. His curiosity
was piqued, even though he knew better than to show it.

"This trainee's situation is most unusual," Arsat said. "The
Har trainers have reached a decision to expel her from our
Order without any rank. However, despite considerable
character flaws, this trainee apparently shows exceptional
promise with weapons. We are trying to avoid a mistake."

Valmad's face developed red splotches. "Her promise with
weapons is exactly the reason she should be expelled as soon as
possible, Jai Arsat. If someone as unruly as her is trained, she'd
be a danger to the public."

She. The fact that this was a girl really shouldn't change
anything. Still, added on to Valmad's agitation, it made Karrim
even more intrigued.

"What exactly has she done?" he asked.

Valmad opened his mouth, but Arsat spoke before he could
respond.

"She attacked her trainer. Physically."

"Oh." *Good for her.* Karrim did his best to hide the smile.
These fights did happen from time to time, but they were
normally hushed up. What could have possibly happened here
to blow this one so far out of proportion?

"You may well laugh, Jai Karrim," Valmad said. "But I'll tell
you right off. This girl has no business being a Jaihar. She'd put
us all to shame if we give her a formal rank."

"I assume there's another side to this story, or else we
wouldn't be having this discussion."

Again, as Valmad opened his mouth to speak, Arsat answered
first.

"There is another side indeed," he said. "By an improbable
coincidence, Jai Surram and Jai Hamed chanced to be on the

lower grounds this morning and ran into the girl. They were quite impressed with her blade skill – enough, in fact, to bring it to my attention. Of course, during the encounter, they did not have a chance to gather much about her character. However, based on this brief meeting, Jai Surram feels she may deserve a second look."

An improbable coincidence indeed. Karrim looked at his fellows in rank curiously. It was nearly impossible for Surram, a man at the very top of the Jaihar's command, to run into a lower ground trainee by chance. Even less likely would Surram feel impressed enough by anyone to overrule the Har trainers' decision. Karrim and Surram rarely saw eye to eye, but the girl's situation was clearly far more complex than it seemed. Besides, Karrim had to admit he felt a nearly subconscious inclination to side with anyone who could put such a look of annoyance onto Valmad's face.

No harm in poking the hive even more, was there?

"This changes everything, of course," he said. "If Jai Surram feels she needs to be evaluated, I fail to see why this is even a discussion at all."

Valmad's face, already uniformly pink, lit up with deeper patches of crimson. "I have close knowledge of the girl, Jai Karrim, and I can tell you with absolute certainty. She is not fit to be a Jaihar."

"This doesn't change the fact that you cannot have a say over Jai Surram." Hell, Karrim had never imagined he would back up Surram in an argument.

"This situation is very delicate," Arsat said. "Attacking a trainer is a grave offense, regardless of the circumstances. No amount of skill could erase something like this from a trainee's record."

"Perhaps a heartfelt apology would suffice?"

"This is no time for mockery, Jai Karrim." Valmad pursed his lips.

"It's more complicated than that," Arsat said. "Even if we forgive the incident – which would be very difficult, given Har Valmad's strong feelings in the matter – she already lost too much time compared to her peers that have been accepted to the upper grounds. She may be past the age to be trained."

"How old is she, exactly?"

"Seventeen."

A year or two behind. A lot, for someone striving to be a Jai. But if she managed to impress Surram in what was likely to have been a very brief meeting, there may still be hope for her.

"It all depends on how good she is," Karrim said.

"Exactly, Jai Karrim. I was hoping, as the top Jaihar blade, you could perhaps offer us your unbiased opinion?"

Karrim looked at the headmaster in disbelief. Had he just been asked to evaluate a problem trainee from the lower grounds?

"What do you want me to do?" he asked.

Arsat shrugged. "Whatever you see fit, Jai Karrim. Test her blade skill. Spend some time with her. Look into her situation in any way you can. I'm giving you a day. I hope, at the end of it, you can come up with a formal recommendation that would break this tie."

Try as he might, Karrim could see no irony in the headmaster's face, a fact that made the whole situation seem even more ridiculous. He should refuse, he knew. But against his better judgment, he found himself nodding his head.

"Of course, Jai Arsat," he said. "Anything I can do to help."

"You can't be serious, Jai Arsat," Valmad protested. "Jai

Karrim's time is too valuable to waste in this way."

Karrim looked at Valmad curiously. The Har trainer's continued insistence, even when faced with such high authority, made no sense whatsoever. Valmad appeared to have an agenda, one he seemed adamant to keep out of this conversation. The idea of learning about the girl was becoming more and more appealing.

"I appreciate the concern, Har Valmad," Karrim said. "But this would be no trouble at all."

THE CHALLIMAR EXPERT

Gassan settled into a deep armchair by the lit fireplace, cradling a hot, steaming mug between his palms. The plantations to the west of Haggad produced some of the best tea in the empire, including this dark, smoky sort, tinged with the natural flavors of honeyweed and rose. Few people in the lower lands ever learned to appreciate it – perhaps because no one could afford it in enough quantities to bring out its full flavor. He took a long sip, inhaling the hot, fragrant vapor.

His companion, a thin, elderly woman with bushy gray hair no headscarf could possibly confine, looked at him knowingly. Zhemirah, the head of the Haggad serai, was famous for her tea, as well as her brutal political sense – both qualities putting her very high in Gassan's book.

"How was your meeting with the girl, Naia?" Zhemirah asked.

Gassan set his tea on the table.

"She's very talented, from what I could tell in the little time we had. I hope the Jaihar give her a chance."

Zhemirah nodded. "I regret we couldn't give you any more information. Something about the trouble she is in is very hushed up. I have a feeling that even the Jaihar command doesn't know what went on between her and the Har."

"Jai Arsat promised me to look into her situation," Gassan said.

"Good, but possibly not good enough, at this point."

"If not, she will become our responsibility again. We must find her a place among the Daljeer."

"Fair enough." Zhemirah reached for her own tea, a green persimmon blend in a delicate semi-transparent bowl. A wisp of its scent drifted Gassan's way, sweet and fragrant like exquisite perfume. "What about the affairs at court?"

"I think I have an idea for a potential candidate for the throne," Gassan said. "His name is Halil, Shabaddin's son by one of his concubines."

"It would take work to elevate a concubine's son to the status of an imperial prince."

"True. But at this point, people at court are very motivated to cut corners."

Zhemirah took a long sip from her cup, briefly closing her eyes to enjoy the balance of scents. Gassan sipped his, no longer scalding hot, but every bit as flavorful. Zhemirah's talent to brew tea was almost like a magic power. No matter how hard Gassan tried, he could never achieve the same result.

"What is he like, this Halil?" Zhemirah asked.

"He's eighteen. An uncharacteristically nice young man, given his bloodline."

"Nice isn't exactly a favored quality for ruling the empire. Besides, eighteen is a bit young, isn't it?"

"He'll be twenty-one in three years." Gassan sighed. "We don't exactly have a lot to pick from."

He didn't blame Zhemirah for being hesitant. He had been

searching all this time for any of Shabaddin's relatives who wasn't a raving maniac or an imbecile, but even with these low standards, Halil seemed to be the only one to stand out among the rest.

"What about the Jaihar?" Zhemirah asked.

"Jai Arsat promised his full cooperation in finding and preparing the warrior we need. On our side, I volunteered to provide a Daljeer tutor who could teach this warrior Challimar ways. Someone we can trust implicitly. Do you have anyone in mind?"

Zhemirah smiled. "Fortuitously, our Circle's topmost Challimar scholar happens to be visiting my serai. As it turns out, our library has some unique history books worth traveling here for."

"Good." Gassan took another sip of his tea. "I'd like to meet this scholar as soon as possible."

"I'll send for her right away." Zhemirah stepped to the door, opening it to speak to someone outside.

After a few minutes the door opened again, letting in a tall, majestic woman, wrapped head to toe in a garnet-colored abayah and headscarf.

Gassan's heart skipped a beat.

Mehtab.

He hadn't seen this woman for nearly twenty years, after their brief encounter on a very busy night at the Challimar serai. Yet he recognized her at once. For a moment, the mere sight of her transported Gassan back to that night. *Desert rosemary and creosote.* These smells washed over him now, real, as if he were there once again. Or was it the scent of her perfume?

She hadn't changed much from the way he remembered her to be. Her classical face looked younger than her years, set with a pair of desert-kissed eyes that gleamed like molten gold in the flickering light from the fireplace. Just like back then, he found himself staring, his skin prickling as she measured him with a slow appraising glance.

"Dal Gassan. You haven't changed one bit." Her voice was low and soft, a perfect match for her appearance.

Gassan took a breath, settling his senses. "Likewise. It's Dal Mehtab now, I presume."

She briefly inclined her head, her lips curving with a slow smile. "You do remember me."

"I said I would, didn't I?"

He could sense no tension in her voice, yet her eyes spelled it clearly – the burden of memories they both shared, the dark events that bonded them to each other. It was as if the years in between never happened, as if they had only parted for a very short time. *Our topmost Challimar scholar.* She seemed too young to fit the image. Still, it had to be true. This woman was Chall, likely born and raised in Challimar before joining the Daljeer. She was probably also a talented scholar. She could easily have spent the seventeen years that passed since they first met learning everything about Challimar.

"I had no idea you two knew each other," Zhemirah said.

It took Gassan a surprising amount of effort to break the eye contact with Mehtab. "We met seventeen years ago, in Challimar."

Mehtab's lips twitched into a mysterious smile. Gassan had an odd feeling he was being evaluated. Even stranger, he felt nervous about it, as if failing her test was a distinct possibility that somehow carried long-term consequences to his plans.

"Dal Gassan and I met on the night of the Challimar Royal Massacre," Mehtab said.

Gassan looked at her searchingly. He never spoke about the baby after he'd taken her off Mehtab's hands and put her in a foster home. The very few Daljeer who knew about Naia kept their silence. Did Mehtab ever mention it to anyone? He knew he couldn't possibly ask her, not until they were alone.

"I'm told you might be in need of my Challimar expertise, Dal Gassan," Mehtab said. "I am honored."

She didn't look honored, not exactly. Her proud demeanor was quite different from what Gassan had grown to expect from his subordinates. Did she hold herself like this all the time? Or was this attitude reserved specifically for Gassan's sake? It didn't really matter, even though Gassan didn't like feeling this unsettled in the presence of someone he was likely going to work closely with.

"I appreciate your help, Dal Mehtab," he said. "Your expertise on Challimar would be invaluable for an assignment I have in mind."

"What assignment, exactly?"

"I will tell you, in due time. For now, I need detailed information about the Challimar royal line. Especially the more recent branches of the royal family."

"How recent, exactly?"

Gassan heaved a breath. "I'd like to come up with a plausible member of the royal family who might have theoretically escaped the Royal Massacre."

Mehtab's eyes hovered on him thoughtfully. Was she guessing what he wasn't telling her? Or did she merely enjoy maintaining this knowing look, as if she was a step ahead of him?

"As it happens, I might have an answer for you," she said. "Let me bring in my research notes." She left the room and returned minutes later, carrying a satchel full of scrolls. Her hands moved deftly as she cleared the tea cups off the table and unrolled one of the scrolls over the tabletop.

"This is the Challimar royal family tree, going back forty-two generations," she said.

Gassan stared. The list of names seemed endless, all of them written in neat rows, connected by arrows, drawn out all the way to the bottom. From what he could tell, the writing also continued on the back. The idea that someone would have produced a document this detailed as part of their scholarly research seemed dizzying.

"I doubt we'd need to go back this far," he said.

"Let's start at the very top then." Mehtab's long fingers smoothed out the tiniest crinkles in the document – carefully, as if handling a precious piece of art. "The massacre. That night, Emperor Shabaddin's guards executed Queen Tajeerah, her consort and guard captain Assam, her aunt Zuleidab, and her two younger cousins, Zuleidab's children, aged twelve and fifteen. One could envision a plausible scenario for each of them to have survived."

"If I am not mistaken, their bodies were recovered and buried, and this information has been widely circulated."

Mehtab inclined her head. "Correct. However, one could imagine someone who may not have been present in the palace for unrelated circumstances. Say, the queen's newborn child, sent away to safety under care from a trusted member of the court?"

Gassan met Mehtab's eyes, feeling a jolt of power surge through his body as their gazes locked. Just then, he knew with a strange certainty that she had never told anyone about the baby girl they rescued.

"Go on," he said.

"Many Daljeer know about the lady chamberlain's flight

to our serai that night," Mehtab said. "Some saw her carry a baby-sized bundle in her hands when she ran up the path to our doors – an observation that was later dismissed as a myth, since the bundle was never recovered. Yet, it would be relatively easy to restart these rumors and speak of, say, a baby girl smuggled from the palace by a loyal servant of the queen."

"Perhaps a boy?" Gassan did not mean for this to sound like a test of her memory. He was merely being cautious in considering all the possibilities. The Jaihar men greatly outnumbered their women, making it far easier to come up with a suitable male candidate.

"Perhaps. But I assume your reason for asking me all these questions is not purely theoretical, is it?"

"What do you mean?"

"You are looking into presenting someone as the Challimar royal heir, aren't you?"

Gassan hesitated. If Mehtab were to become his aide in carrying out his imperial succession plan, he would have to tell her everything, sooner or later. True, he'd want to first know for certain if he could trust her. But what better guarantee could he possibly have than the fact that they knew each other for nearly twenty years, that Mehtab had faithfully kept the secret they shared for all these years? He would be hard pressed to find a more trustworthy person within the Daljeer Circle.

"Yes, I am," he said.

Mehtab smiled. "In that case, let me show you something else." She unrolled another scroll, much smaller than the first one, and pushed it over the table to Gassan.

Gassan glanced down at it. It appeared to be a poem – a translation, judging by the way the rhythm did not always flow as perfectly as expected. "What is this?"

"An old Challimar legend. It tells about Princess Xarimet, a desert-chosen who will come in Challimar's darkest hour and raise the kingdom to glory."

Gassan ran his eyes down to the end of the page. By the looks of it, the poem was probably written a long time ago, even if the translator put in some modern terms – like the empire, which he was sure didn't exist in the times the kingdom of Challimar had been so set on glory and dominance.

"I fail to see how a legend this old could possibly be relevant," he said.

Mehtab smiled. "To make people believe that an heir of Challimar is alive, you need to ignite rumors."

"So?"

"The legend of Xarimet is still popular. If you as much as hint that the baby smuggled from the palace could be the legendary Princess Xarimet, all the Chall would unite around her and create a wave that would be hard to stop."

"It's hardly this simple."

"Why?"

"I am preparing this person to be a decoy. A fleeting participant, who would step aside and disappear once the succession is over. It would be hard for someone as famous as Xarimet to just disappear, wouldn't it?"

"If you are talking about a power takeover in the empire, this is the least of your concerns right now. You need someone who would succeed, in the first place."

A power takeover in the empire. In addition to being perceptive, Mehtab certainly had a point. Gassan looked at the scroll again.

"This description of Xarimet appears to be very specific. Beautiful and young, with desert-kissed eyes." He looked up.

The person in the scroll could have been Mehtab, twenty years ago. For certain, her eyes had the kind of fire that would inspire legends and songs. If not for her age, or lack of any blade training whatsoever, she could have easily been the one.

"People would see her only from afar," Mehtab said. "Not close enough to make out the details of her eye color. Any young woman could be trained to hold herself appropriately enough to create the right impression."

Gassan sighed. He knew in his upcoming conversation with Arsat the idea of a young woman was most certainly going to become a contention point. Unless they used the real one, of course – a possibility he didn't want to entertain just yet.

"I'll keep this in mind," he said. "But let's prepare for other possibilities, just in case."

"Other possibilities?"

"Another branch of the royal family, perhaps?"

Mehtab's shoulders stiffened just briefly, then relaxed again as she glanced down at her scroll. "Queen Tajeerah was rumored to have a sister, Selhath, who disappeared as a child under mysterious circumstances. It is a possibility, but in my opinion, a very remote one. No one has heard of her since, so she is presumed dead."

"Wouldn't that be a bonus to our plans?"

Mehtab shook her head. "If alive, Selhath would be in her middle years now – not someone a top Jaihar warrior could easily emulate."

"Perhaps her child then?"

"Possible. But not as promising as Tajeerah's child would be, given all the rumors that are already surrounding the Challimar Royal Massacre."

Gassan nodded. "Agreed. Still, I would appreciate it if you

keep all options in mind. Bring the details to me as soon as you are done."

The woman's lips twitched again. "Of course, Dal Gassan."

"I'm glad for this opportunity to work with you, after all these years."

Her gaze wavered, her heavy eyelashes throwing deep shadows that briefly highlighted the dramatic lines of her cheekbones. "So am I, Dal Gassan. I look forward to working together." She bent down to gather the scrolls from the table, then nodded and exited majestically through the door.

Gassan sat for a moment watching her go.

"How well do you know her, Dal Zhemirah?" he asked.

"Not that well," Zhemirah admitted. "According to the reports, Dal Mehtab is quiet, but very dignified. A superb scholar. Well-loved by the locals at her serai, apparently."

"The locals?"

"Her superior in the Challimar serai, Dal Bakhum, says many people from the city visit her all the time."

"*Visit* her? Why?" The Daljeer scholars spent most of their time in libraries and archives, which made them far less popular with the locals than, say, healers or teachers. It was rare for any scholars to receive personal visitors.

Zhemirah shrugged. "Apparently, because of her knowledge of Challimar history and traditions. People come to her to consult about their ancestry, or to learn the details of some of the rarer holiday celebrations."

Gassan nodded. This was unusual, but made sense. Ever since Challimar had been brought to its knees by the Zeg, the Chall people tended to put a lot of value into ancestry and traditions. This trend had greatly intensified in the past two decades of turmoil that followed the destruction of their royal family. And of course, this was yet another quality that made Mehtab so instrumental to his plans. She could easily use her local connections to spread rumors.

"I need you to do me a favor," he said. "Send someone you trust to the Challimar serai to gather Dal Mehtab's research notes and personal belongings. Have them brought to my attention, to the serai in Zegmeer."

"*Personal* belongings?"

"Yes. I will write a note to Dal Bakhum to aid our messengers in finding everything we need."

Zhemirah didn't respond at once, cradling her tea cup in her hands.

"Dal Bakhum may consider this a gesture of distrust," she said.

"Dal Bakhum will consider it a service to our cause. He'd be a fool not to."

"Do you have reasons not to trust Mehtab?"

Gassan shifted in his seat. "Not in particular, no. In fact, I trust her more than anyone else I have so little personal knowledge of."

Trust was a luxury a man in his position simply couldn't afford. Besides, Mehtab was too close to the events he was building his plans on.

EVALUATION

The Glimmerblade sent to fetch Naia to the upper grounds was dazzling to look at. Tall and broad-shouldered, he projected the confidence of a man who expected his presence to cause a major stir, although he seemed somewhat deflated by the sight of the small courtyard at the back of the kitchens, adjoining the horseback riding field, where Naia was told to wait for his arrival. The air here was perpetually infused with the stench of manure, mixed with the equally potent smells of onions and stale cabbage – the main garnish for nearly every dish served in the lower dining hall. Anyone should be embarrassed to let the Jaihar Order's finest come here on official business. She secretly wondered if Valmad and the Har purposely set it up this way.

The servants and kitchen hands paused in their tasks, watching the Glimmerblade approach her with a mildly surprised look on his face. Her salute, a palm to her chest, seemed inadequate for the occasion, her best training leathers shabby next to his gleaming cloak, flipped to the silvery side to indicate the fact that he was on official Order business. He did not offer his name, which was just fine. After today she was probably never going to see him again.

Walking in his wake across the training range, Naia felt uncomfortably aware of the continued silence around her, everyone watching with frozen faces. She kept her chin high, willing herself to look calm, as if being escorted to the Jaihar upper grounds by a Glimmerblade, in response to the summons from Jai Surram himself, was a perfectly ordinary thing.

A group of Har trainers crowded at the side of the field, prominently away from the path Naia and her guide took to the upper grounds. She spotted Valmad among them, keeping to the back, averting his eyes when she glanced in his direction. His grim expression seemed fit for a funeral. Naia took it as a positive sign. If she was headed for trouble at the upper grounds, Valmad would probably look happy right now, not dismayed.

The door within the massive gate ahead swung open to admit them and closed behind them with a deep thud. Inside, the entrance courtyard was lined with armed guards, their cloaks light gray on the underside. Quickblades, a lower Jai rank responsible mostly for the internal security. They watched Naia with unreadable expressions as she walked through their gauntlet. No greetings were offered or exchanged, but it still felt refreshing to see no hostility or challenge in their faces – such a change from the antagonism she left behind on the lower grounds. She vowed to herself that, no matter what, she was not going out there again. After Surram's test, which she was certain she was going to fail, she would leave this stronghold and never return.

Her Glimmerblade guide led her through another narrow gateway to an open training area, which looked very similar to the one she had just left – except for being cleaner, obviously better maintained, and almost entirely devoid of people. Those exercising on the far side did so in much smaller groups. *The Jai trainees.* Naia's eyes were inadvertently drawn to their moves, graceful and precise like an elaborate dance. More than ever, watching them made her feel delusional. How could she have ever seriously hoped to become as good as any of them?

She expected her guide to stop here, but the Glimmerblade led her on, through another gateway, into a small courtyard deeper in the compound, adjoining the back of the tower-like building she assumed to be the headmaster's hall. He pointed to the grassy area at its side and left, without giving her any further instructions.

Naia stood for a moment, watching his retreating back. She didn't feel too worried. Someone was going to come for her soon, she was sure of it. Someone who was probably going to tell her this was all a mistake and she had to leave after all. To distract herself from these thoughts, she looked at the stand near the wall, holding an array of practice blades in every possible size and shape. *Dear Sel.* She had never seen this kind of wealth.

The blades beckoned her, better crafted than any weapons she had ever seen before. She quickly glanced around. No one seemed to be coming for her yet. Would there be any harm if she took a closer look? She reached for the nearest pair – and froze.

Was someone standing right behind her? Someone who wasn't there just moments ago?

She spun around, suppressing a gasp at the sight of the lone figure, just a few steps away from her. *A Shadowblade. Dear Sel.* He wore no cloak, but even without it, he left no doubt. No one else could have possibly approached her like this, without making any sound at all.

She did a poor job of hiding her curiosity as she looked him up and down.

He wasn't exactly handsome – or even that muscular, at least judging by the visible parts. Yet, something about him arrested the eye. His lean form had a way to fill the space with its powerful presence, his light, graceful stance leaving no doubt about his superb blade skill. She guessed, even with his unremarkable build, very few on these grounds could stand up to him in a fight. In fact, as this realization settled firmly into her flustered mind, she finally started to realize who this was.

Except that he couldn't possibly be.

Like with Surram yesterday afternoon, it took her moments – not to recognize him, but to convince herself that he was truly who he appeared to be. Her mind had difficulty with the very idea of matching his features, those she had previously seen only from a distance, to the real man. *Jai Karrim. Three hells.* The top Jaihar blade, standing so close that she could touch him if she reached over – not that she would ever dare to do any such thing.

She blinked, half-expecting him to disappear, but he was still here, solid and real. And, oh, more attractive than she ever realized. His eyes, greenish-gray, unnaturally light compared to the usual brown and black everyone here tended to have, shone like gems in the setting of his tanned face. His intent gaze made heat rise into her cheeks. Hastily, she looked away to the thin line of a scar, crossing his left cheekbone to the outer corner of his eye – a final confirmation of his identity. She'd heard so many stories about this scar, the token of the impossible battle he won on his very first assignment in Scinn.

Dear Sel, she must look like an idiot, gaping at him for so long without saying anything at all.

"Jai Karrim." Her voice came out husky, totally inappropriate for greeting a senior. Belatedly, she straightened up and pressed a palm to her chest, even though she knew the salute couldn't possibly make this situation any less awkward.

"At ease," he said. "Naia, I assume."

"Yes." She continued to stare, even though she knew it would be a really good idea to start acting more normal right now.

He frowned. "Anything wrong?"

Naia swallowed. "Yes. I mean, no. I just… I didn't expect to see you, Jai Karrim. Not up close." She bit her tongue, wishing she'd done it before she ever opened her mouth.

Karrim's frown deepened, but instead of the anger the expression implied, she had a distinct impression he was holding back laughter. The way his lips twitched drew her attention to their perfectly sculpted shape. *So sensual.* She quickly turned away, but not before she caught his knowing look that sent a new wave of heat into her face, all the way to the roots of her hair. Irfat's hells, was he baiting her on purpose? Or was he really finding her reactions amusing?

"Our headmaster sent me here to evaluate you," he said. "You're having a bit of a problem with your superiors, or so I was told."

You have no idea. Well, this probably wasn't true. More likely, Karrim knew exactly what was going on, which made it even more surprising that he was here at all. She itched to ask him about it, but she quickly decided against it. No reason to question her luck, especially since it was so unlikely to last.

"Um. Yes," she said. "I am. I mean…"

Karrim nodded. "We'll talk about it later. For now, let's do some practice. Choose your blades." He gestured with his chin toward the weapon stand.

My blades. Right. Naia tried to look natural as she ran her eyes over the array in the stand. Karrim offered her no guidance, so after a moment's hesitation she lifted out a pair of scimitars she had been eyeing earlier, weighing them in her hands. Perfectly balanced, of course. Their edges were blunt, as expected for practice swords, but it seemed like nothing a day in the smithy wouldn't be able to fix.

Karrim stepped past her, casually graceful as he picked up two short daggers from the very front row. Unimpressive, insofar as anything here could be described this way, a highly inferior choice against the scimitars she now held. Mesmerized, she followed him to the flattened area in the center of the courtyard.

"Show me what you've learned so far." Karrim squared off to her and raised his daggers in a defensive hold.

Inviting an attack. She spun her blades as she advanced, opening with the head-on she'd become famous for on the lower grounds.

She expected – if not to hit him, at least to engage him in the fight. But nothing like this happened. Despite the close range, Karrim simply shifted out of her way without touching her or using his weapons at all. For an eerie moment it seemed to her that he was immaterial, made of air, even though she knew this couldn't possibly be true.

Naia pressed the attack, putting all her ability into moving as fast as she possibly could. She thought she'd be able to match him now – or at least do better than before. But Karrim shifted styles too. He turned, sliding between her uselessly flailing blades without making contact. *Like a ghost.* Surely he wasn't one, but she had yet to find any proof that he was real, and not an illusion conjured by her overactive mind.

His blades. Focus on his blades. She could sense the steel of his daggers, calling to her. She honed in on the feeling, reaching toward them. He evaded, but she pursued, relying on her senses rather than sight.

When their blades finally clashed, the sound rang out loudly through the courtyard. Karrim stepped forward, suddenly solid, and far more powerful than anyone she'd ever faced. His moves seemed too fast to follow as he raised his daggers, twisting them around the length of her scimitars, as if their steel somehow became flexible, like rope. He slid them along the edges of her blades with a long, drawn-out sound – a half-screech, half-moan that echoed with a tremor all the way down her tiring arms. His daggers twisted again, a short move that somehow rendered her weapons useless in her hands, spinning them in a movement contrary to her frantic efforts to control them. She lost her grip – first her left hand, then her right, helplessly watching her blades fly away from her, as if anxious to get as far from her as possible.

Before she could go after them, Karrim stepped up and crossed his daggers over her throat, pinning her in place.

Naia froze. Karrim's face was very close to her, his eyes filling her vision, his face calm, mask-like. *Dear Sel, he isn't even out of breath.* Her own breath came out ragged, far too uneven for the short fight they had had.

Even for her level, she made more mistakes in this fight than she had any right to. But none of these thoughts compared to the realization of how ridiculous it was for her to strive for a Jai rank. As she stood in front of Karrim, locked in his hold, trying and failing to calm her labored breath, she dragged the thought through her mind. Was she cut out to do this?

Karrim kept his hold a moment longer, then lowered his daggers and stepped away, tossing them back into the stand. She searched around with her eyes until she spotted her scimitars in the grass lining the edge of the courtyard. Shakily, she picked them up and returned them to the stand too. The skin of her throat itched, even though she knew that Karrim had pressed too lightly to do any damage. Still, the memory was going to stay with her for a long time.

"Tell me how it felt," Karrim said.

She frowned, unsure of what he was asking. Did he mean, disappointing? Disastrous? To her surprise she realized that none of these definitions matched the sensations she experienced in this fight. Despite how tired she was, she wanted more. She wanted to cross blades with Karrim again.

"Eye-opening," she said.

Karrim nodded, as if he expected exactly this answer. "I sensed a change, during the fight. Tell me what happened."

"You mean, when you disarmed me?"

"I mean, when you were able to engage me."

She nodded. She knew the moment he was referring to, when she extended her senses to his blades. "I couldn't target you, so I targeted your blades instead. The steel. Once I focused on it, I was able to follow it... Does this make any sense?"

It was unnerving to see Karrim watching her so intently, without being able to say if he was pleased or disappointed.

"Jai Surram told me you can catch daggers, despite the fact that no one trained you to do it," he said. "Is this the trick you always use?"

She hesitated. She never thought of it in these terms, but now that he mentioned it, she realized that the feeling was indeed exactly the same. Sensing the steel.

Did this ability make her abnormal?

"I have no idea," she said. "Sorry."

For a moment, Karrim's gaze became distant, as if his

thoughts trailed away before returning back to the conversation.

"Want to try again?" he asked.

"Yes."

This time Karrim didn't try to evade or disarm her. *Toning down to match my level.* She appreciated it. More, the enjoyment she felt as he matched her moves, blow by blow, without overwhelming her, made her forget about feeling tired.

As soon as the feeling settled, Karrim started to pick up the pace. In her new state of mind, she was able to extend herself to match as he pressed on slowly through a series of blocks and attacks that increased in difficulty. Testing her limits. This was what he was here for, after all. But there was more to it too. Through these moves, he was also teaching her, and she did her best to absorb everything.

She had never faced an opponent as enjoyable as he was. No matter what happened to her after today, she was always going to cherish the experience, the way the touch of his blades on hers empowered her too, as if lending her a part of his skill. No words were necessary in the cocoon of power that enclosed them. Nothing mattered but the unity they had.

When Karrim finally stepped away and lowered his blades, she felt disappointment, a sense of withdrawal, as if suddenly deprived of support she had come to rely on. She knew she was sweaty, panting from the exertion she rarely experienced even after a very intense practice, but that didn't matter at all.

She wanted to continue, to learn more. *To experience his closeness again.* She forced back this last thought, so inappropriate that her cheeks warmed with a blush even though she knew he couldn't possibly read her mind.

Karrim kept his silence as he replaced his blades in the stand. He looked distant, thoughtful. Disappointed? She knew that wasn't it. Could it be that he'd felt it too – the bond, the enjoyment? Most likely, she'd never know, and it was all to the best. It was utterly inappropriate to think this way of a man who stood so far above her that she had no chance to see him up close again after today.

She had always known she wanted to be a Jai, but until today she had never realized what it truly meant. And now, after a brief glimpse at the kind of skill she strived to achieve, she felt as if her life had acquired a new purpose. One way or the other, she was going to do everything in her power to learn to fight like Karrim. This was a goal truly worth living for.

"How did it feel this time?" Karrim asked.

The blades. He means the blades. Now that they were no longer fighting, it was so much harder to think straight.

"Good," she managed, then blushed, aware that her response was even more ambiguous than his question.

The sun seemed higher in the sky than she remembered it to be when Karrim showed up. The shadows of the tall courtyard walls receded toward the tall building of the headmaster's audience hall on the far side. Its windows gleamed in the sun, deflecting any possibility of seeing inside.

"Anything else?" Karrim said.

She knew she was still blushing, but she couldn't possibly do anything about it. "I've made a lot of mistakes."

The muscles around his eyes crinkled with a smile that didn't quite make it to his lips.

"True. But what do you think was the worst one?"

"The worst?"

"Yes."

"Um. Losing sight of your left hand when you tried to disarm me?"

He shook his head. "Think broader than your blade technique."

"Broader?"

"Yes. Everyone makes mistakes, especially in an uneven fight. This wasn't why you lost so badly, though."

"Does it have something to do with how superior you are?" Dear Sel, when was she going to stop this habit of blurting out the first thing that came to her mind?

Karrim's lips twitched. "It does have to do with that, yes. But not in the way you think."

"What do you mean?"

"Before you even raised your blades, you'd already made a decision you were going to lose. The rest was truly up to minor errors and technicalities."

Her eyes widened. She *did* know she was going to lose. This was *Karrim,* for Sel's sake. Yet, she also knew this was a training match where he would likely control his skill to give her a chance. Did she truly commit to a defeat before the fight even started?

"Being a Jai," Karrim said, "is all about balance. Without it, your blade technique, however superior, is meaningless. Before you can go through any further training, you have to make sure you have it in you. As I understand it, your trainers have this doubt, don't they?"

She hesitated, thinking of a proper response. Her problems with the Har were about much more than balance – or this was what she had thought, up until now. Could it be that, with the right balance, the prize had been within her reach all along?

"What can I do to improve, Jai Karrim?" she asked quietly.

He held her gaze. "You have to find a way to believe in yourself. Truly believe, without any reservations. Only then would you have any chance of succeeding."

Naia stared. *Believe in yourself.* Karrim couldn't possibly know what Gassan had said to her during their recent encounter, about losing faith in herself. Both of them were right. If she wanted to succeed, she had to find her own balance. She had to *believe*, truly believe inside herself that she was good enough to do it.

"Can we try again?" she asked.

Karrim's face lit up with a quick smile as he nodded and gestured to the training floor.

ARRANGEMENT

The windows in the headmaster's study afforded a perfect view of the entire upper grounds. Gassan paused near the one that overlooked the private training courtyard adjoining the back of the building, watching Naia and Karrim talking down below.

Now that he had the opportunity to observe Naia without interruption, he felt even more determined. Her looks seemed perfect for the part, give or take some minor details. It wasn't just about her desert-kissed eyes, or the mahogany tint to her dark hair that could be accented so well with the right kind of dyes. There was something else about her. Was it the way she carried herself – with a special inner dignity that could easily pass off for a natural regal bearing within the right setting? Watching her down below, he could picture her in the role so well it made him uneasy.

The girl nodded to Karrim, then picked up a weapon and followed him to the training floor. For an instant, Gassan's thoughts wandered as he watched them fight, their moves so fast and powerful that it took his breath away. Gassan was no Jaihar, but he knew a thing or two about inborn abilities. This girl had the potential to become one of the best, even if her superiors chose to make it unreasonably difficult for her. More, he was beginning to realize that, even if she didn't pass whatever trials the Jaihar Order had in store for her, she would be a perfect candidate for this task.

Perhaps, instead of insisting on this evaluation, he should have allowed the Jaihar to kick her out? Picking Naia off the streets after being expelled from the Order would have restricted her allegiance to the Daljeer alone. But he knew it wasn't a productive thought. He needed the Jaihar Order to put their full weight behind his plan, even at the expense of all the extra trouble.

He turned to Arsat and his three top men, looming in the depths of the chamber like silent shadows. Their ranking cloaks made them nearly invisible even here, in broad daylight – perhaps because they also sat so still that they appeared inanimate. He glanced over them, reflecting the way their titles mirrored their looks, so different from one another: Surram the training master large and burly, Ilhad the combat master lean and wiry, Dahib the weapons master tall and stooping, probably the oldest of the three. Gassan couldn't guess any of their thoughts from their impassive faces. Shadowblades remained unnerving even in their older age.

"Well?" Arsat said.

Gassan stepped away from the window. "Thank you for following up on my request regarding this trainee, Jai Arsat."

The headmaster exchanged a glance with Surram. "I hope you understand that this informal session with Jai Karrim doesn't mean she is going to qualify for Jai training."

"Of course."

"Nor is this really relevant to today's meeting." Arsat pointed at the stack of parchments on his desk. "At your request, we've collected the information about each of the Jai warriors and trainees within your specifications. Our Order's seniors are here to answer questions about any of them, in case my knowledge isn't sufficient." He glanced at the other senior blademasters.

Gassan nodded. He knew the other men's presence here had nothing to do with his potential questions about the pile on the desk, ridiculously large to go through, even if they had the whole day. Arsat was using this opportunity to make sure the members of his command were appraised of the plans first hand – a natural precaution, given the stakes. If the meeting was happening on Daljeer territory, Gassan would have done the same.

"Let's start with the Shadowblades," he said. "If you have anyone even remotely suitable."

Again, the Jaihar blademasters exchanged a glance, but this time it was Surram who spoke, his powerful voice rolling through the chamber.

"I'm afraid we don't, Dal Gassan. Most of our Shadowblades, regardless of age and other qualifications, have been on at least one assignment public enough to put them at risk of being recognized."

Gassan sighed. This was true. Nobles and high officials, who had enough gold to hire the best of the best, valued Shadowblades above the rest. Each of these top warriors had probably been to court at least once. Most had the tendency to spawn gossip, even if not quite on Karrim's scale.

"The only exception is Jai Hamed," Surram said. "He has spent the last four years almost exclusively in our stronghold."

Jai Hamed. According to the rumors, the man was being groomed as Surram's successor, who would take over the training master's post when the time came. A good choice, from what Gassan remembered of Hamed – a quiet, efficient man, competent but definitely lacking the glamor essential for impersonating royalty.

"I was hoping for a younger candidate," he said.

Surram nodded. "You also prefer a woman, I believe." His lips twitched in distaste, mild yet recognizable. The Jaihar resented gender distinctions, priding on equal training – even if, for entirely natural reasons, many of their top warriors tended to be male.

"I do," Gassan said. "Merely because of the matriarchal traditions of succession in Challimar."

Surram's eyes darted to the window overlooking the training grounds, then returned to the pile of parchments on the headmaster's desk. "This constraint, on top of your age requirement, significantly limits the possibilities among our ranked warriors."

"What about trainees?" Gassan avoided looking at the window, even though he knew his line of thought would still be too obvious to the Jaihar seniors.

Surram frowned. "Before we consider this route, I'd like you to take a look at one candidate I have in mind. A female. Her name is Jai Layath – twenty-one, a recently ranked Glimmerblade, who has not yet been on an assignment outside the Jaihar stronghold. As an added bonus, she does have a measure of Chall blood, including a lighter brown eye color that, I understand, may be desirable in this case. Given how well she fits your requirements, I took the liberty of arranging for her to lead the archery practice today, so that you could take a look." He pointed to another window on the opposite side of the room.

Gassan stepped toward it, mesmerized by the scene below.

He was unaware of the existence of this practice area, located at the very back of the upper grounds. The long, hollow space was surrounded by walls on three sides, so tall that they almost entirely blocked the sunlight. The effect was like looking into a fish tank from the top – except that this fish tank held air rather than water, making everything that happened in there plainly visible to the observers from above.

Gassan spotted an array of archery targets at the distant end. Some of them were quite elaborate, suitable only for very advanced kinds of practice – like the ornate snowflake shape hanging off a pole on a very thin chain, swaying in the breeze.

He paused, watching the twenty or so people stringing their bows on the side proximal to the headmaster's hall, close enough for a good view.

"Is one of them a woman?" he said, then bit his tongue. It was not in his nature to be so tactless, especially with important allies. Still, he was finding it hard to contain his surprise.

"Jai Layath is the one all the way on the left," Surram said stiffly.

Gassan narrowed his eyes to see better. The lean, muscular warrior Surram indicated looked no different from the rest. The same short hair, cropped closely to the scalp, common for those who put convenience above appearance. The same broad shoulders, burly neck, and square line of the jaw – perhaps even more pronounced than in many of the males around her.

He looked closer. He was certain Layath was superb with weapons. She certainly looked more fluid, and competent, than the warriors next to her. Yet, it would be difficult to match her to the image of Xarimet from old texts, one that was beginning to take root in Gassan's mind.

"I have no doubt Jai Layath will perform brilliantly," he

said. "But I believe for this assignment physical resemblance to the members of the Challimar royal family is more important than the weapon and leadership skills. I'd like to consider some additional possibilities."

"Well," Surram said stiffly. "If you feel this way, we are left only with male candidates, I am afraid."

Not necessarily. Gassan glanced out of the first window again, where Karrim and Naia looked deeply absorbed in a complex sword routine. "Are you telling me you have no other females, not even trainees, to consider?"

"No one advanced enough, no."

"Perhaps we should give more consideration to that trainee, Naia?"

It took a closer look to catch the glance Arsat exchanged with Ilhad, the combat master. It was no coincidence Naia was here today, training with Karrim in full view from the headmaster's windows. Arsat was keeping this possibility open, even if Surram seemed opposed to the idea.

"I thought the whole point of our meeting was to find you a candidate who is proficient with weapons," Surram said.

"It is." Gassan looked out of the window again. True, Naia was not nearly as good as Karrim – or even Layath – yet there was something about her that continued to hold his eye. The Jaihar seniors were bound to see it too, even if they chose to downplay it, for whatever reason.

"She seems to have promise, at least to my untrained eye," he said.

Surram pursed his lips. "Given her shady past and very explicit recommendations to the contrary from her immediate superiors, it would take more than promise in her case."

"At the very least, could we wait and see what Jai Karrim

says about her after the session today?" Hell, Gassan never thought he would be appealing to Karrim's authority. The man had ruffled more feathers at court than the Raj rebels delivering their ultimatum. In Gassan's book, this alone took Karrim far out of the range of trustworthiness. Yet now, seeing the Jaihar seniors' stiff expressions, Gassan couldn't help wondering if Karrim was exactly the kind of man he needed to help his case.

"Jai Karrim was asked to give his opinion on her potential," Arsat said. "But we can't expect him to resolve all her other issues in one day. Besides, even if he deems her worthy of further training, there are no guarantees. Her head trainer, Har Valmad, would gravely oppose any decision in her favor."

And you, as the headmaster, can overrule him any time you wish. Gassan was enough of a player to see when an opponent had a few moves up his sleeve. Arsat didn't give away much in his gestures, but there was still plenty to go on, such as the way Arsat's voice tended to trail at the end of each statement, betraying a hint of a hesitation. Gassan waited out the long pause as the men around him exchanged glances, then stepped closer to the window to watch the display below.

Karrim's style was spectacular. For a moment, watching him made Gassan almost forget his purpose here. *Naia. Yes.* She wasn't a match for Karrim, not by a very long shot, but the fact that she was down there right now, spoke volumes. Gassan knew Karrim couldn't be using his full ability with her, but even so, the way Naia seemed to anticipate his moves just a fraction of a moment before they came, the way she was able to keep up with every step of the complex routine, seemed remarkable.

He turned back to the headmaster. "I'd like to add her candidacy to your list, Jai Arsat."

"No." The word came from Ilhad, the combat master, his

voice surprisingly low, whisper-like. Gassan felt a chill at the insinuating sound.

"Why not, Jai Ilhad?" he asked.

"Because you still haven't told us all the details, Dal Gassan," Ilhad said.

"What makes you think so?"

Ilhad smiled – or at least Gassan assumed so. The grimace that stretched the man's parched face had nothing joyful in it.

"Many subtleties, Dal Gassan," he said. "The most glaring one, at least to me, is the fact that you seem to believe this girl, Naia, to be better suited for the job than the others. There has to be more to it, isn't there?"

Gassan sighed. He had underestimated this man, probably because he'd never had any dealings with him before. He supposed, if the Daljeer were choosing to partner with the Jaihar for the long haul, he couldn't afford to keep secrets from them anymore.

"She's the real one," he said.

"The real one *what?*"

"The actual child delivered to the Daljeer on the night of the Challimar Royal Massacre."

The pause stretched so long that for a moment it seemed to Gassan that none of the Jaihar were going to speak at all.

"When exactly were you planning to tell us that?" Arsat asked at length.

"Right after I made my decision."

"A *decision?*"

"Yes. After what I've just seen, I am convinced that this girl, Naia, would be perfect for the role."

"What made you think so at this particular moment, if I might ask?"

Gassan knew he was playing with fire right now. The Jaihar seniors were bound to take it very hard that he had chosen to conceal this information until now. Yet, Gassan was sure that once they got over their initial reaction, they would understand. Now that his decision was formed so clearly, he couldn't take any more chances. He needed to lay out the entire plan, and face whatever questions they had.

"Have you ever heard of Princess Xarimet of Challimar?" he asked.

The senior blademasters exchanged glances.

"Is this the time for a lesson in ancient mythology?" Arsat said.

"Bear with me." Gassan felt impressed. He knew that the Jaihar blademasters received extensive education in history, languages, and traditions of the surrounding lands. The headmaster had to be one of the best in that too, to achieve his high post. Still, Gassan was surprised that something as obscure as the legend of Xarimet had been included in this education.

He took out the scroll he received from Mehtab and unrolled it over the desktop. The Jaihar seniors leaned over it, running their eyes through the lines.

"It's just as I remember it," Arsat said at length. "Somewhat archaic, even in this translation. Is there a reason for bringing it up?"

"Apparently, this legend is still very popular among the Chall."

"Fascinating, I'm sure."

Gassan shook his head. "Aren't you amazed how well this girl, Naia, fits the description?"

Arsat frowned. "Don't tell me this is part of the rumors you want to create. If it is, we might still reconsider this whole arrangement." His eyes trailed to the window.

Gassan looked too. Naia was standing at the side of the practice floor, her face flushed and sweaty, her short hair disheveled. Not much of a princess right now, but if one were to see though all her rough layers, the words of old songs came all too easily to his head.

In the empire's darkest hour she'll come,
Her eyes and hair kissed with the desert sun,
Her footsteps as swift as the desert breeze,
Her voice clear like ice that makes hatred freeze.

Her compassion and wisdom will show us the way,
Guide us past evil that led us astray.
She will bring the empire back to glory once more –
Chall and Zeg, Raj and Scinn, close like never before.

She's our rightful heir, maiden born to command,
To unite all the people, to rule all the land.
Through love and justice, under Sel's grace,
Xarimet is our savior, our future, our faith.

"You don't actually believe she is the real Challimar heir, do you?" Arsat said.

"What I believe doesn't really matter, does it?"

"It does, to me."

Gassan shook his head. "I have no idea who she is, or why she was brought to us on that night. What I do believe, though, is that with these origins, with her looks, she has the potential to ignite rumors like no one else."

Arsat pursed his lips as he looked through the window again. Yet, he didn't say anything as he watched Naia and Karrim circle around the small practice space. Gassan took it as a good sign.

"What about the members of the imperial family?" Arsat asked at length.

"What about them?"

"Prince Ramaz and his brothers would do everything in their power to rip her identity apart."

"They won't be able to. Not if the Daljeer put all our resources into building up her story."

"The lore I remember describes Xarimet very explicitly." Arsat stepped to the bookcase behind his desk and reached to a higher shelf to pull out a small leather-bound tome, flipping through the age-yellowed pages until he found the right spot.

Gassan watched him with interest. He had seen a similar edition in one of the Daljeer libraries. It was a rare one, containing the more complete version of Challimar history than anything found in the more official chronicles. To the best of his knowledge, only few of the editions remained.

"Here," Arsat said. "This translation is less literary than yours, but the meaning is clear. *Xarimet, our savior, blessed by the desert sun. A maid young and beautiful, yet more powerful than any man. Her eyes hold Sel's fire. Her voice can charm snakes. Everyone follows her.* This girl, Naia, is a bit of a stretch, isn't she?"

Gassan continued looking out of the window as he listened. His skin crept as he fit all these features Arsat read out onto Naia's appearance.

"Not as much of a stretch as you think," he said. "With work."

"Too much work."

Less than with Layath. Gassan forced his eyes away from the window. "There's an advantage to the fact that Xarimet is a legend, Jai Arsat. No one knows for sure what she should look like. No one even knows her exact age, for that matter. I'm certain our scholars can train almost any young girl to fit the part."

All three blademasters were staring through the window now. Naia and Karrim were talking. She looked flustered at whatever he was saying, her body angled awkwardly as if she was having trouble maintaining her composure in the conversation. Here and now, it was indeed hard to picture her as a legendary princess with undisputable rights to challenge royal succession. Yet, Gassan could also see the other side of her – the powerful, fearless side that she'd shown so plainly during their encounter two days ago.

"If you ask me," Surram said, "no matter how much you train her, this girl couldn't possibly fool anyone. You'd be better off with Jai Layath. She has superior leadership skills, and one certainly couldn't dispute the 'more powerful than any man' line. I'd like to see any man at court try to take her on." He chuckled.

Gassan had the good sense to keep his reaction to himself this time. "I am certain Jai Layath is a great warrior, but it's all in the presentation, Jai Surram – something the Daljeer are very good at. Besides, Naia has the advantage of her origins. They give the rumors we intend to spread the kind of authenticity that would be difficult to achieve with anyone else."

"You seem to be set on her," Ilhad said.

"Now that I've familiarized myself with some of the alternatives, I tend to feel she is our best option, yes."

"And if she doesn't qualify for Jai training?"

"This is of course something only the Jaihar could decide," Gassan said. "But from what I've seen so far…"

Ilhad smiled. "You were impressed, I know. Many outsiders are. But catching a few daggers and holding up through a training match are not the feats anyone on these grounds would consider surprising in someone her age. Most of her peers are far more advanced by now."

Gassan begged to differ, but it didn't seem productive to mention it. Instead, he reached into his deep pocket and took out a small bag of gold, placing it on Arsat's desk.

Four pairs of eyes narrowed, watching him. Gassan could guess at least some of their thoughts. The gold was sufficient to hire a Shadowblade, a sum that took this conversation to an entirely different level.

"This gold," he said, "is an advance, for whoever your Order decides to put forth for the task. I want to stress, however, that even more than weapon ability, this person must possess many other qualities that come with the role. I hope my willingness to pay this much upfront without any guarantees is yet more evidence of how serious the Daljeer are about the whole thing."

Arsat glanced out of the window toward the training grounds. "Naia will undergo the most thorough evaluation. Both with Jai Karrim, and – if she continues on with her training – at the time of her possible ranking. I cannot guarantee the outcome, so I just wanted to make one thing clear right now. The Jaihar Order will not stake its reputation on a problem trainee for an assignment of this caliber. If you are set on her and no one else, you must hire her at your own risk, by putting down a sum of gold that equals the price of a Shadowblade bodyguard. This doesn't count the gold you brought today."

Gassan held back his smile, feeling relieved. Of course, the Jaihar were all about gold, which made perfect sense right up to the point when it didn't. This girl would have been kicked out of the Order if he didn't show up with his highly unusual request. And now, before even finalizing her fate and that of the assignment, Arsat was asking him with a straight face to pay through his teeth for her.

"Of course, Jai Arsat." He glanced at the bag of gold on the table. "But I must add some conditions of my own."

"Such as?"

"If you decide to expel her after all, you will send her to the Daljeer."

"And if we accept her to the Jai grounds?"

"She starts her training for the assignment tomorrow, even though you must tell her nothing about it. I will send our best Daljeer tutor to assist you."

Arsat locked eyes with his fellow blademasters, then nodded slowly.

"Agreed."

CHALLENGE

Naia barely noticed the moment when the sun slid behind the distant foothills, flooding the courtyard with long, deep shadows. Karrim signaled the end of the fight and she lowered her blades, realizing only now how heavy her limbs felt after a full day of training.

During the day, she felt so absorbed that she forgot to even think about what came next, or the fact that she was also being formally evaluated. Karrim made everything she had previously learned with such difficulty seem so easy. In just one day he had shown her more tricks and techniques than she ever remembered learning before. More than that, Karrim's confidence and calmness, the quiet interest in his eyes as he watched every step of her progress, made her feel important. She had never felt so good around anyone, on or off the training floor.

She stifled her regret as she returned her blades to the stand. She should probably be asking him about the future, about his opinion of her. But she didn't want to say anything that could potentially bring their time together to an end. Starting tomorrow, this encounter would probably seem distant, like a dream. She wanted it to last as long as it possibly could.

"Want to go out into the city with me and get something to eat?" Karrim asked.

Her eyes widened. Was he inviting her to spend more time together? It didn't seem possible, yet Karrim's expectant gaze confirmed that he was waiting for an answer. Besides, after all the impossible things that had already happened to her in the last two days, she should really know better than to question her luck.

"Yes," she said.

Karrim's nod in response looked casual, as if there was nothing to it. "Good. Let's go then."

She felt surreal as she followed him to the side gate.

The street, winding downhill in front of them, looked completely unfamiliar. She had never been to this part of the city before. As she walked beside Karrim – a shadow, barely visible in the gathering dusk – she realized that if she lost him now, she would probably have a hard time finding her way back to the gate they had exited through. Of course, she was not worried about being lost in the city she grew up in, but this part of it was so different from the Haggad she knew, the residences behind the walls on each side taller and more expansive than the honeycomb-like dwellings common in the lower areas of the city, their roofs sinking into the luscious greenery of the orange and persimmon trees that probably took a fortune to water.

Karrim didn't talk as he strode purposefully ahead, and Naia was just fine with it. She needed time to gather her thoughts. At the very least, she should really shake off the surreal feeling – as if she was dreaming, about to wake up in her cell-like room in the lower trainee quarters. None of what was happening right now could possibly be real, but right now, it really wasn't her place to judge.

She recognized the area now. The street ahead of them ran straight into the open-air market that stretched for blocks and blocks in each direction. This place, famous for its street food but lacking the comforts of the inns and taverns in the more upscale Lantern District, was Naia's favorite, even though she could rarely convince any of her fellow trainees to come here with her.

Rich smells of spices and roasting meat hit her nostrils as she and Karrim pushed their way past the stalls. The place sizzled with activity. Men rushed around the flaming stoves, handing out skewers of roasted lamb, coal-baked cactus pears, spiced sausages, sand shrimp, and deep-fried scorpions. Further on, the more exotic-looking merchants wearing pancake-flat Scinn turbans sold flatbreads, smoked snakes, figs, and peacock meat. Naia didn't realize until now how hungry she was.

She reached into her thin belt pouch for the coins she'd saved up from her trainee allowance, but Karrim stopped her with a short gesture.

"My treat," he said. "If you don't mind."

Naia hesitated, then nodded her acceptance. She knew she probably shouldn't allow a senior to pay for her, but this entire day with Karrim was already strange enough not to worry about something as minor as that.

They spent the next hour or so wandering around the stalls, tasting everything their eye fell on. Karrim was such a fun companion, showing her his favorite dishes and some of the more exotic things she had never tasted before. Only his challenging gaze could possibly force her to try a scorpion, deep-fried in oil straight on the skewer, incredibly life-like.

Once she'd convinced herself to take the first bite, she liked the meat, fresher and more tender than the shrimp that were in such a high demand here, its rich flavor rivaling some of the best dishes she'd ever tried. Her favorite, though, was peacock – an outrageously expensive morsel cooked in exotic spices and served in a fleshy bowl-like leaf of a water azalea, a local delicacy down south. The same merchant sold skewers of lamb and quail, the more affordable alternatives. They spent extra time by this stall, laughing and daring each other to try the things Naia would never have eaten on her own.

After they had their fill, Karrim bought a large jug of cactus pear cider and led the way to a small courtyard at the side of the plaza, empty, despite the turmoil in the street. A burly man guarding the entrance nodded to Karrim with silent acknowledgment and stepped aside to let them through.

The secluded area inside was separated from the street by a picturesque wall of vines. A few empty tables here were artfully arranged around a fountain, trickling with a coolness so welcome after the hot day.

It was so quiet here, away from the bustle of the main street on the other side of the gateway. The light of the rising moon mixed with the more intimate flame of the oil lamp hanging off an ornate hook right over the table. Naia took a deep breath of its fragrance – sandalwood essence – as she settled into her chair, sipping the sweet, bubbly drink from her cup. It was by far the best cider she had ever tried, its spices balanced just right to add up to an exquisite bouquet.

In all the times she had been to this market by herself, she'd never had a meal as enjoyable as this one. Some of it was the food, but it would never have been the same in different company. She didn't want to think of the fact that any moment now this magical time was going to come to an end, like a fairy tale too good to last.

She had never met anyone like Karrim before. No one she felt so at ease with, no one who matched her in so many ways. In a normal life, she could perhaps have been tempted to pursue a relationship with him. But nothing like this was possible between Jaihar warriors. Especially not between a superior and a trainee. After tonight, she should stay away from Karrim, if she had any sense. Chasing these feelings, even in her head, couldn't possibly lead to anything good.

Looking was allowed, though, as long as she kept these thoughts to herself. She used this opportunity to the full, watching him over the rim of her cup as she sipped her cider. He looked so graceful as he curled up in his chair, slim and powerful like a mountain jaguar. So perfect.

Dear Sel, when would she ever learn to cast her sights only at things at least remotely available to her?

"I can never thank you enough," she said. "For everything you did for me today. Starting with the training, and ending with this delicious dinner."

He grinned. "Many in your place would have preferred a more formal meal."

"Probably true. Many around here don't know any better."

His grin widened. Naia smiled too. She knew she shouldn't be getting too comfortable with him, but she simply couldn't help it.

"I still have a few questions, though," Karrim said.

"Questions?" She paused. Karrim's face, while still friendly, shifted imperceptibly. He looked more formal now – a sharp reminder that, despite the casual atmosphere, she was still being evaluated.

His eyes were in shadow as he looked across to her. "What really happened between you and the Har?"

The Har. Of course, no matter how well their training session went, it was naïve to think that Karrim was going to leave the topic alone. He'd even warned her about it, when he first showed up. Naia sighed. No matter what she did, it all came back to that incident with Ishim.

"I assume you've read the reports," she said stiffly.

"Actually, no."

"You didn't?" She looked at him in disbelief.

Karrim shrugged. "Reports are a waste of time, if only in the way they tend to omit all the important details."

"What makes you think so, in my case?"

"Experience." He kept her gaze. "I'd like to know your version – unedited, if possible."

"There's nothing much to know, really. I attacked a trainer. We had a fight. He beat me up – badly enough to get into trouble. The Har blamed me for the whole thing. And rightfully so. It was all my fault." She paused. The mere mention of the incident echoed through her limbs with phantom pain that had been haunting her since her recovery. Months ago, long enough to erase the worst of it in her mind – but not her body.

"Do you really feel this way?"

Naia kept his gaze. She did. Taking responsibility for her actions was one of the most important lessons she had learned during her time with the Jaihar.

"Yes," she said.

"Try again."

Her gaze wavered. "I... I don't really remember what happened. I had a concussion."

Karrim let out a short laugh. "Do you really think I will stop

90

asking, if you claim a memory loss? Come, you should know me better by now."

Naia didn't know him better. In fact, Karrim was the hardest person to read that she'd ever met. Like now, when his friendly smile sent a chill down her spine. She thought of this morning, when his angered frown made her feel as if he was holding back laughter. It was the opposite now. Behind his calm façade, he was furious, and she had no idea why.

"I… I remember hitting him," she said. "The rest was a blur, really, until Har Valmad arrived and pulled us apart. Around that time, I passed out. That's all I can recall."

"I assume you had a reason to attack him, important enough to risk the consequences."

"My reason doesn't really matter, does it?"

"It depends."

"There is no excuse to attacking a superior," she said.

"There isn't, no."

"Why are you asking me then?"

"For several reasons, none of which matter if you don't tell me the truth."

"Do you believe I am lying to you, Jai Karrim?"

"No. But you are withholding information. You don't trust me, and I don't blame you. We've only just met. However, getting to the bottom of your story would be really important in my conversation with our headmaster tonight, with long-term repercussions to your future. So, I hope you'll forgive me for refusing to take your reluctance for an answer." Karrim turned and raised his hand to signal the guard standing by the courtyard's entrance. The man bowed and stepped outside.

Only now did Naia think of the fact that this courtyard, probably a choice place for many patrons buying their dinner at the market, had remained empty all this time. She recalled the knowing looks Karrim exchanged with the guard when they first walked in here. Did Karrim bring her here on purpose? Did he do anything in advance to arrange for privacy, so that he could have this conversation with her?

And if so, what did his signal to the guard mean just now?

Before she could wonder any further, new movement at the courtyard entrance announced the guard's return. Not alone. Naia's eyes widened as she saw the young woman walking past him to the table, dressed in Scinn fashion in a hooded gray abayah over narrow blue pantaloons.

No. Dear Sel, no. Naia slowly rose to her feet. *"Tami."* The words came out in a half-whisper.

Karrim nodded, as if this reaction somehow revealed an important piece of information. "I thought you two might know each other."

Naia spun around to face him. "Bloody hell, Jai Karrim. Was this really necessary?"

Karrim looked up at her, a half-smile twitching the corners of his mouth. He looked smug – or so it seemed to Naia in her anger-distorted state. She clenched her fists, then relaxed them slowly, knowing that no matter how tempting it seemed, she would never be able to land a punch against someone of his skill.

She turned to Tami. "You don't have to be here, or say anything you don't want to. You can leave any time."

The girl shook her head. "No. I *want* to be here, Naia. Jai Karrim asked me to come."

How the hell could he possibly do that? Naia dismissed the useless thought. "You can't–"

"Yes, I can," Tami said firmly. "It's all right, Naia."

Naia heaved an exasperated sigh. "No, it's not. He's a Jaihar senior – the last person you should be talking to right now."

"It's my decision, isn't it?"

Naia's eyes narrowed. Tami couldn't possibly understand everything she was risking by telling her story to a top-ranking Jaihar. Karrim had no right to force this meeting. None at all.

"I had no idea you were in such trouble because of me," Tami said.

"I'm not, really." *I'm in trouble because of my own shortcomings.* Such as attacking her superiors when they got out of line. *Karrim, damn it.* Was she going to add another offense to her already impressive record by lashing out at the Jaihar's top blade?

She could feel Karrim's gaze on her, but she refused to turn and look. She could also sense his smile, smug and triumphant, as if he had called her out at a difficult match and won. Her fist itched to swing at him, to erase this smile off his face. He was way out of her league, but it suddenly seemed so tempting to put this knowledge to the test.

"You have no bloody right to do this, Jai Karrim," she said. "Tami is a free citizen, not your subordinate."

"You are correct. Tami is here of her own free will."

"Because she has no idea of the trouble you are putting her into."

"I don't intend to put anyone into any trouble."

Naia heaved a long breath as she finally turned to face him full-on. Slowly, so that she wouldn't do anything rash. "With respect, what happened between me and Har Ishim is none of your business."

"It is, actually." His smile returned, more annoying for the fact that she could do absolutely nothing to erase it off his face.

"Our headmaster has formally charged me with looking into your situation."

"Did he order you to question Tami too?"

"No."

"Right."

"I can see how your superiors may tend to have a problem with your temper," Karrim said. "Remember what I told you about balance?"

"What about it?"

"It tends to come in handy in situations like this. I find it a great help at times when it may be a good idea to at least consider a possibility of thinking with your head."

"What the hell are you referring to?"

"I'll tell you when you calm down."

"I'm not—"

"Naia," Tami said. "You should listen to Jai Karrim. He is a good man. He's helped many servants before. I trust him. Why can't you?"

Naia looked at the girl. A part of her was aware that she was being unreasonable. She should at least consider the possibility that Karrim meant well, that he wasn't doing this to harm anyone. But she was not ready to think this way just yet, or even give any further thought to the implications of Tami's words.

"What exactly do you hope to achieve by this, Jai Karrim?" she said.

Karrim settled deeper into his chair, like a spectator taking his seat for a show. "I hoped seeing Tami here might jolt your memory."

It did. In fact, it worked far too well. In Naia's unbalanced state, the mere reminder made her head throb. Sounds around her receded as she submerged into the flow of memories.

"Hey, you! Kitchen servants are not allowed into the trainers' hall. Who the hell are you anyway?"

"My name is Tami, Har Ishim. Please forgive me, I didn't know…"

A slap, ringing loudly through the suddenly quiet hall. A whimper, then more slaps, coming in rapid succession. A thud, followed by the rustle of a body skidding over the floor.

"Don't, Har Ishim, please, no!"

A scream, so piercing that it hurt the ears.

Sounds. Only sounds. Why can't I see anything at all…?

"Naia, are you all right?" Tami's voice cut through the haze in Naia's head.

No, I am not. Naia blinked, slowly unclenching her fists. Her heart was still pounding. Karrim. It was all his fault. Except that when she raised her head to meet his gaze, instead of the mockery she expected to see in his face, she saw emotion – one she couldn't quite place.

"That bad, eh?" he said.

Naia didn't bother with a response. Whatever she had to say on the topic was none of Karrim's business anyway. Except that Tami was talking to him right now. Bloody hell, she had been talking all this time, and there seemed to be nothing Naia could do to stop her.

"Har Ishim often beat servants for the slightest misdeeds," Tami said. "Mostly men, and most of them got away with only a bruise or two. We all tolerated it, because of the Jaihar pay. But that day…"

That day. Naia swallowed. Never before did Ishim raise a hand to a girl, or looked as if he was about to kill her. Naia was the only one around. There seemed to be no choice but to step between them, to catch his swinging hand. To hit. She remembered it so well – the surprise when her blow came through, the crack of his nose under her fist, warm moisture seeping between her clenched fingers, its sickening, meaty scent. *Blood.* The memory made her gag as she trailed her attention back to the conversation.

Karrim was on his feet, Tami talking to him in her quiet, rushed voice. *Telling him the whole story. Damn it. She has no idea what she's doing.*

If Karrim learned that Naia attacked Ishim over a servant, if he told it to the Jaihar command, Valmad was going to ruin the life of every servant on the lower grounds. They all depended on the Jaihar pay. No way Naia's career with the Jaihar could possibly be worth the damage. *Damn* Karrim, for forcing the story out.

She needed to do something right now, to stop Tami from ruining her own future.

In Naia's distorted state, the solution seemed obvious. She stepped forward and grabbed Karrim's shoulder, spinning him around to face her as she swung her fist at him.

She didn't quite catch what happened next. Karrim's body seemed to have lost substance as it melted out of her grip. Her blow met no resistance at all as she swung past his face into thin air, causing herself to overbalance. His hand came out of nowhere, closing over her wrist – solid again, hard like a shackle. She tried to pull free, but the movement only got her tangled in her own limbs that suddenly seemed to follow Karrim's bidding instead of her own.

He spun her around to plaster her back against his chest, her shoulder echoing with pain as he twisted her arm behind her. She knew he could easily snap bones if she tried to resist, so she eased the pressure, relaxing against him. He eased his pressure too, not allowing her any freedom of movement, yet not causing pain anymore.

She felt too aware of his body against her back, warm and toned with every sculpted muscle. He had his arm around her too, his hold intimate, like an embrace – no better for the fact that he also had her trapped, powerless to move at all. She hated the way her body reacted to his closeness, as if driven by a mind contrary to her own. Her quickening breath had nothing to do with exhaustion, heat pooling at the base of her spine as he shifted against her, a conflict of sensations that left her weak and disoriented. *He is doing it on purpose, damn it.* Even with this knowledge, she couldn't possibly distance herself from these thoughts, especially when he leaned forward to her ear until she could feel the warmth of his breath on her skin.

"If you want to tell me something next time," he said quietly, "you can just say it. No need for getting physical."

Physical. Naia clenched her teeth. It did get too physical all too quickly, all in the wrong way. Worse, with the way he held her – one hand on her wrist, still twisted behind her back, the other lying steadily against her throat, each finger over a key pressure point – she could easily end up crippled, if she moved. Dear Sel, she was so far out of her depth right now. Karrim could do so much worse to her than any of the Har trainers.

This was a good moment to stand down and admit her defeat. But the way her body was betraying her right now, reacting to his closeness in such a contrast with her mind, angered her too much to care about reason. She relaxed her muscles, aiming to make herself as heavy as possible, then kicked backward at his kneecap as she threw her weight sideways to overbalance him.

She didn't have a serious hope of succeeding, even though she felt she had to try. It was more realistic to expect that, with the grip he maintained on her, he would simply dislocate her shoulder, bringing on the pain necessary to snap her out of her sensual stupor. Of course, he could also use his other hand to press at her throat and force her to pass out. Importantly, both responses would bring this encounter to a speedy end, something both Naia and Tami needed very badly right now.

But Karrim didn't do any of these things. In Naia's disoriented state, it seemed to her as if he merely opened his embrace and released his hold, letting her slip out of his arms and down onto the cobbles. There might have been a moment when she tried to balance herself, when his foot came out of nowhere to kick her legs from underneath her, but she wasn't quite sure. All she remembered was the pavement coming up so fast that she barely had time to protect her face with her arms before smashing down messily onto the ground.

She lay there for a few moments, panting, too ashamed to turn and look at Karrim standing over her. For now, she made no attempt to rise. Not until she caught her breath. Not until she had a chance to quiet the rage, still roaring inside her. She knew if she stood up just now, she would feel too tempted to go at him again, and he might injure her much worse this time. But deeper down, it wasn't the fear of injury that kept her down, but a sense of wrongness about the whole thing.

She couldn't prevent Tami from talking to Karrim – not if the girl wanted to, for whatever reason. But in her attempt to interfere, by allowing her anger to take over, she had just attacked another one of her seniors – this time, not a Har, but someone of a far higher standing. Worse, even in her anger she knew that Karrim was the only man among the Jaihar who'd shown her compassion and kindness, who had actually been trying to help. He had been her only hope out of the situation she drove herself into – and now she had just cut off that hope forever.

As she finally rolled over and looked up into his face high above her, she tried to read her future in his expression, but couldn't guess anything at all. *It's all about balance,* he'd said to her earlier today. Balance, the one thing she clearly would never achieve.

"Do you need help getting up?" Karrim asked.

She looked away, then sprang to her feet, taking extra time to straighten out her clothes and brush off the dust.

"Why don't you sit down?" Karrim said.

Naia remained standing, keeping her gaze past his shoulder, on the line of the distant rooftops. If she met his eyes right now, she'd probably cry – or slide into another fit of rage that would make things even worse. Besides, no matter what she said right now, it couldn't possibly improve the situation in any way. Best to keep her silence and get this over with.

"Please, Naia," Tami said. "You have no reason to be so upset. Jai Karrim is a good man. All he wants is to clear your name."

Too late for that. Naia swallowed. The best she could do would be to go back to her quarters right now and pack her very few belongings, so that she could leave the Jaihar stronghold forever. Or maybe she shouldn't even bother with the packing. She didn't really own anything worth saving.

For the moment, though, she felt too shaky to move. Even though she knew that Karrim had consciously avoided injuring her, she still needed time to recover. Her shoulder ached from the way he twisted her arm. She probably had bruises too, both from his grip and from hitting the cobbles as ungracefully as she did. No one who made these kinds of mistakes could possibly qualify for Jai training, or have any right to carry a Jaihar rank.

She wished everyone would just stop looking at her right now.

"Please forgive Naia, Jai Karrim," Tami said. "She is hot-headed, yes, but she has a good heart. She was the only one brave enough to stand up for me. If it wasn't for her, Har Ishim would have killed me that day. He looked so mad…" She stopped as she met Naia's gaze.

Naia swallowed again. Tami, pleading on her behalf, felt worse than accepting the consequences of her actions. The serving girl had no reason to apologize for her. It was all Naia's own doing.

Slowly, steadily, she turned and met Karrim's gaze.

"I am sorry for attacking you, Jai Karrim," she said. "It was foolish of me. I guess your plan worked. You've exposed me for what I am."

Karrim raised an eyebrow. "And what is that, exactly?"

She wanted to retort, then stopped when she realized it was a genuine question. "Speaking in your terms, I am unbalanced, I guess."

"Is this what you choose to be?"

"What do you mean?"

He shook his head. "No one is born with balance. You have to find it in yourself. But first you must choose to do so."

"But I…" She hesitated. How could Karrim possibly say it, after everything that had just happened?

"Are you trying to convince me you are unfit to be a Jai?" Karrim asked.

Naia swallowed. "No. I mean… I am trying to convince myself, I guess. After what happened, I don't see how it can possibly be otherwise."

Karrim shrugged. "It's your choice, of course, but let me present it in another light, for argument's sake. Just now, you drew the fire, because you thought Tami was in trouble. As I gathered between the blows we exchanged, something very similar happened with Har Ishim, didn't it?"

Naia's gaze wavered. "He was going to kill her."

"So I understood, yes."

"Back then, I couldn't think of a better thing to do."

"What about now?"

"What about it?"

"There had to be a better thing to do than attacking me. You had to know I was going to win."

Naia's gaze wavered. "I wanted Tami to stop talking, before she said something that could ruin her life."

"Tami is an adult."

Just barely. Naia looked at the girl. Tami was seventeen, Naia's age, but she looked much more fragile and defenseless. It seemed natural to assume the role of a protector to her. Still, Karrim was right. Naia knew when she raised her hand to him that he was going to defeat her easily. She'd assumed this with Ishim too, and it didn't stop her either. Did the balance Karrim was talking about mean stopping herself from doing what she believed was right?

"You still had no right to bring Tami here," she said. "Do you know what the Har trainers would do to her if this story comes out?"

"Hard as it may be for you to believe it, I do. I've trained on the Har grounds too. Ishim wasn't there at the time, but Valmad was personally in charge of me at one point."

"He was?" Naia's eyes widened.

"Don't think you are the only one who ever suffered at their hand."

"You should see what I mean, then."

Karrim shook his head. "I've hoped, after the day we spent together, you would be more trusting of my judgment. Of course, that was before you decided to kick my butt. I expect your famed temper often gets in the way of common sense, doesn't it?"

My famed temper. She kept his gaze, noting the play of shadows on Karrim's face, the smile that twitched his lips but didn't quite reach his eyes. He was still angry – and for a good reason too.

"I've made some inquiries about you at the lower grounds," Karrim said. "All the servants are nothing but grateful to you for standing up to Har Ishim, down to the fact that the incident, however harsh, led to his reassignment. They all regret what happened to you. Which is why Tami was glad for this chance to come here and help set things right."

"By putting herself into danger?"

"By telling her side of the story to someone she trusts."

"Why would she trust you?"

Karrim laughed. "You haven't been listening, have you? Of course, you've been too busy going around using your fists to solve all your problems."

Before Naia could think of an appropriate answer, Tami stepped forward.

"Jai Karrim is not like the rest of the Jaihar," she said. "He never betrays anyone's trust. He's helped many servants and city folk in the past. Why don't you just talk to him, Naia?"

"Good idea," Karrim said. "Unless, of course, you'd rather have another tumble."

His direct gaze made her blush, bringing on all the wrong memories. The play of his muscles against her back. The warmth of his breath on her skin. Damn it. He wasn't even that handsome. What was it about him that made her skin tingle from his mere glance?

"All right, Jai Karrim," Naia said. "Let's talk. Assuming there's anything left to say."

"There is, actually. I still don't understand why this incident with the Har got so blown out of proportion that they are insisting on such a harsh punishment for you."

"Oh, I don't know. Because I tend to attack people for no reason?"

"I doubt it."

"You do?" She stared. What the hell was he trying to say?

Karrim shrugged. "From what I've seen, you do seem to be good at justifying it, at least in your head."

"Fine. Go ahead and laugh."

Karrim regarded her thoughtfully. "Tell me about the fight again."

Naia ran her hand over her face. "I really don't remember much. I was too angry, I guess. My first blow blooded Ishim's nose. I was surprised it came through, actually. He looked surprised too. He must have hit me in return, the blow that caused the concussion, but I don't really recall. It all happened too quickly before Har Valmad rushed in and broke us apart."

"Oh, he did more than that," Tami said.

Naia and Karrim both turned to her abruptly.

"Har Valmad held Naia while Har Ishim hit her," Tami said. "Again and again. That's why she passed out. They were beating her so badly. I started screaming. Then the other trainers showed up…" Her lips trembled. "At the inquiry, Har Valmad questioned me himself. I said I didn't remember anything. I had no idea I was putting Naia into even more trouble by not coming forward. I was so afraid…"

Naia blinked, her head flooding with memories again. *"Stupid… stupid… stupid girl." Thud… Thud… Thud… Each blow jolted though her body like fire. "Enough, Ishim." "No, not yet. I want her to remember what it means to attack a trainer. I want them all to know, damn it." "Ishim." "Want to hit me again, huh? Stupid…" "Stop it, you'll bloody kill her." "Stupid… stu…"*

And then the scream, so piercing that it felt as if her head was about to splinter into pieces. Or was it the blow to her head, the trainer's heavy boot connecting with her skull as she fell on the floor?

Naia pressed her hands to her ears.

All this time Valmad had been making her life a living hell, plotting to expel her. Was he covering up for his best friend? Or was he worried about his own skin?

Karrim's face looked cold and distant as he spoke. "Thank you for coming here and telling me everything, Tami. This means a lot."

Tami nodded. "I am so glad to be of help, Jai Karrim. If you want me to tell this to the Jaihar command…"

Karrim shook his head. "It won't be necessary. Just go back to your work and don't worry about anything. I'll handle the rest." He nodded his dismissal and Tami backed out of the courtyard, briefly squeezing Naia's hand before she left.

Naia stood in the middle of the courtyard staring after her. Now that she remembered more about the incident, she didn't feel surprised. Strangely, this new knowledge fit everything she knew, putting the finishing touches on the story that had been, up to now, too hazy in her memory.

She understood now why Valmad always acted so affronted around her after the incident, as if every one of her actions and words was a personal offense. He felt *guilty* about what happened to her, and this guilt made his anger toward her so much worse.

"So, what are you going to do now, Jai Karrim?" she asked.

Karrim's eyes hovered on her thoughtfully. "I'd like to finish my drink. I hope you'll join me." He stepped toward the table. After a moment, she followed, lowering into her chair.

"I'm so sorry for attacking you, Jai Karrim," she said. "I've acted like a fool. I can see now that I don't deserve to be a Jaihar."

He sipped his drink, then lowered it, looking at her over the rim of his cup. "You seem to be curiously keen on throwing away your future."

Naia's eyes widened. Was this what she was doing? What the hell was Karrim trying to say to her?

He reached forward and set his cup on the table. "Remember what I told you about balance?"

"Yes."

"Part of this balance is learning to live with the decisions you make, to stand behind them. You tend to second guess yourself a lot, to blame yourself for everything. This attitude only leads to more mistakes."

"Mistakes?"

"I'm certain many in your place would have attacked Ishim. I also understand the concussion, not remembering what happened. But most in your place would have done more in their own defense. You had to know it was his bloody fault. Did you?"

Naia lowered her head. Of course she knew. It was just that somewhere between the pain of lying in the hospital bed without any idea if she was ever going to be able to hold a blade again, and Valmad's incessant yelling, she seemed to have lost the sense of it.

"I did," she said.

"Good. You could have said so at the inquiry."

"I did what I thought was best."

"For Tami, yes. And you're bloody lucky Ishim was sent away. It could have been the other way around."

"The other way around?"

"They could have cleared him and let you take all the blame. I'm sure Valmad wanted it this way. They could have expelled you right away, and left Ishim to continue doing his worst – at least until he actually killed someone."

Naia opened and closed her mouth wordlessly. Karrim was right. She hadn't thought through all the possibilities, not at all.

"So, here's a lesson for you," Karrim said. "If you choose to act, you should also find your balance in living with the consequences. All of them, not just the ones that first spring to mind."

He took a long sip from his cup. Silently, she followed suit.

REVELATIONS

Karrim didn't speak again until the jug of cider was empty and the moon rose higher in the sky. Naia didn't want to break the silence either. It was comfortable just to sit next to him, enjoying the calm confidence he emanated. So unfair that after today she and Karrim were probably not going to see each other again. She realized with surprise that this thought bothered her even more than her future with the Jaihar Order. But it was useless to think about it too much, when she couldn't possibly do anything about it.

She startled from these thoughts as she realized Karrim was watching her, his quiet, sideways glance instantly sending her on alert. How long had he been looking at her like this? More importantly, how much could he guess of what was going on inside her head?

Balance. Right. The best thing she could do was stop second-guessing herself.

"I assume by now you must've made your decision on my case," she said.

He shifted in his chair. "No, actually. Simply because my

decision at this point is actually up to you."

"What do you mean?"

"Instead of asking me what I think about your potential, you should really be questioning yourself right now. Is being a Jaihar truly what you want?"

Naia raised her eyebrows. Of all the things he could have said right now, this was the least expected. "I fail to see how what I want could possibly matter."

"See? You tend to let others make important decisions for you. You should learn to take the initiative, if you're striving to become one of the best."

"But…"

"But what?"

Naia heaved a breath. "With everything on my record, after the way I behaved today…" Her voice trailed off as the full meaning of what he was saying finally reached her head.

Karrim leaned closer. His gaze mesmerized, calm and intent all at the same time.

"When I first met you today," he said, "I saw a talented trainee, who loves her blade fights and is not afraid to speak her mind and stand up for what's right. It took me a while to understand why, with these qualities, you are willing to let others decide what happens to you. Do you want to achieve a Jai rank or not?"

She frowned. "Of course I do."

"Why?"

"I…" She hesitated, knowing that her words right now were going to be really important. It had to be the truth, even if it may sound laughable. "I want to learn to fight like you… Even though I know it's impossible."

"See? You're selling yourself short again."

Naia shook her head. "No, I'm not. You must know how special you are. When we fought today… I never felt this way before. This feeling, the ability to experience it any time I want, is worth everything."

This couldn't possibly be good enough. The enjoyment she felt with a blade in hand couldn't be the reason to strive for a Jai rank. Karrim probably expected her to be speaking about honor, about serving on assignments for the empire's elite. Yet, if she wanted to take his advice, she had to learn to speak from her heart, however outlandish it seemed.

She expected him to laugh, to mock her for her words. Instead, his gaze lit up with a strange recognition, as if encountering a kindred spirit. Could it be that he felt this way too? Could it be that his own reason for becoming the Jaihar's best had nothing to do with all these other considerations?

Karrim held her gaze for another moment, then nodded. "That's all I wanted to know."

"What are you going to do?"

"Speak to our headmaster tonight – hopefully, to clear you of all charges."

She stared. "Are you *forgiving* me for attacking you?"

A quick grin slid over his face. "Well, I did act like an ass at some point, didn't I?"

"Well… maybe a bit, yes."

"I might have done the same in your place."

"You would?" Her eyes widened.

"When I was young and stupid, yes. But even then, I would have probably given more consideration to our difference in skill."

"But…"

His grin widened. "Do you actually think you are the first

Jaihar trainee ever to raise a hand to a senior?"

"I am not?" Naia stared.

Karrim shook his head. "Our Order raises the best warriors, by teaching them combat and control. These skills, however, don't always come hand in hand. By now I expect you know which one is the harder one to learn."

"Control." Well, it was certainly true, in her case. If she was always in control, she probably would have handled the situation better – with Karrim, for sure. Probably with Ishim too.

"Right."

Karrim glanced up at the sky. Naia looked too. It was getting late, definitely past the usual bedtime in the trainees' quarters.

"Time to go." Karrim rose to his feet and gestured to the courtyard entrance, letting her go in front of him.

As they passed the guard, Karrim handed him something Naia didn't quite see. Payment, she assumed, for affording them privacy for the whole evening. Another thing Karrim did for her, above and beyond his regular duties. Would she ever be able to repay him for all that?

"Thank you," she said.

Karrim smiled. "Don't mention it. I hope today's meeting was worth it."

It was. The thought of everything he did for her filled her with warmth. This warmth stayed with her all the way, past the market stalls, up the meshwork of winding streets and narrow alleys adjoining the back of the Jaihar upper grounds.

Karrim stopped before the last bend of the street that, as she now remembered, would bring the stronghold into view. It was so dark here that she could barely see his shape, the oval of his face, blending with the shadows.

"We are about to reenter our grounds," Karrim said. "After

we do, we'll have to go our separate ways. If I'm successful in my conversation with the headmaster, I expect you to be transferred to the upper grounds as soon as possible, but I have no control over any of it. I wanted to ask you to be careful."

"Careful?"

"The Har. If they learn that you got your memories back…"

Naia swallowed. If she ran into Valmad after what she'd learned today, she would have serious trouble speaking to him with any level of civility. Of course, she also realized acting any differently around him could lead to nothing but trouble, both for her and for Tami – as well as, probably, for many other servants.

"I will be careful," she said.

"Good."

"Jai Karrim…"

He looked like he was about to resume his walking, but he stopped and turned around to her. Readily. She swallowed.

"I… I just wanted to say that no one has ever done as much for me as you did today. I'll never forget this, whatever it's worth."

He laughed. "I haven't done anything yet, have I?"

She shook her head. "I know how precious your time is. The training session alone was worth a lifetime, but you've also done so much more. You've gone above and beyond what is imaginable, to help me out – despite the fact that all I did in response was act like an ass. I don't think I could ever find a way to thank you enough."

She still couldn't see his face in the darkness, but somehow she could tell that he was no longer smiling.

"You don't have to thank me," he said. "If I manage to clear your record, this would probably be the worthiest thing I've done in a very long time."

On impulse, she stepped forward and hugged him, burying her face in his shoulder.

He stiffened, then slowly relaxed. His arms moved hesitantly, closing over her, easing her into his hold.

It seemed so natural, their bodies molding so perfectly as if they belonged together. The warmth of his toned body, even through the clothes that separated them, made her skin tingle. She knew that holding this embrace any longer was utterly inappropriate. But she simply couldn't find it in herself to move away. Worse, she seemed to have lost control of her body that insisted on snuggling even closer, turning her face up so that she could smell his skin, a faint scent of spring water and sun-baked sandalwood. She inhaled deeply, feeling dizzy with it.

Dear Sel, no one's closeness, no one's touch, ever made her feel so good before.

What in three hells am I doing?

Karrim was keeping so still, probably shocked at her bold move, unsure how to react without making this situation any more awkward. But even if he was attracted to her too, he would never act on it. And neither should she. If this went any further, there would be hell to pay.

Even with this knowledge, it took all her effort to find the strength to step back, to keep her breath even, so that he wouldn't notice how it quickened at his closeness. She had to maintain at least a pretense that this was just a friendly hug of gratitude, for it could never be anything more.

"Thank you, Jai Karrim," she said. "Thank you for everything."

*

Karrim struggled to quiet his agitated senses as he and Naia walked back to the Jaihar Stronghold side by side. What started as a simple assignment to look into a trainee's situation ended up an experience so overpowering on so many levels that he was having trouble sorting it out.

From the moment he saw Naia, he felt spellbound – not only by the raw power of her talent that shone though, despite the steady abuse she must have suffered on the Har grounds – but also by how similar she seemed to the boy he had been at her age; perhaps outwardly more confident than her, but no less confused on the inside. The first words she spoke to him, the first blows they exchanged, resonated with him on so many levels that it seemed almost frightening. This connection made it easier for him to understand her, to unravel all the layers surrounding her unusual situation. But it also made it so much harder to keep his distance.

The way his body reacted to her didn't help either. She wasn't a conventional beauty, by any means – flat-chested and skinny, even if delicately built – but the attraction he felt for her went so much further than looks. She was a ball of contrasts – both vulnerable and strong, honest and elusive, unpolished yet more elegant than the finest court ladies he'd ever seen. Her tomboy looks betrayed a measure of conscious effort toward going around unnoticed by the opposite sex – probably essential for someone striving to succeed on these male-dominated grounds. But when she flung herself into his arms just now, he also sensed the fire beneath it. Holding her made his head spin with the possibilities he knew he was never going to allow to play out, even in his head. She was still a child, for Sel's sake – or very nearly so. And he was her superior. The mere fact he was having these thoughts right now made him a bastard with no right to go near her at all.

He didn't trust himself to speak, or even stay too close to her, as he led her back to the side gate of the upper Jaihar grounds, where they parted in plain view of the gate guards, with no more than a few polite words. He could sense her confusion around him – yet another reason to run away from her as fast as he possibly could. After he spoke to Arsat tonight, after he made sure she was going to be all right on her own, he should do his best to forget the whole thing.

It was late, definitely past the hour the headmaster was expecting him back with a report. Yet, when Karrim approached the headmaster's hall, he was not surprised to see the lights inside. The Glimmerblade guard swung the door open to let Karrim into the study, where Arsat was sitting at his desk, deeply immersed in a pile of scrolls in front of him.

He raised his head abruptly as Karrim approached, looking at him with narrowed eyes as he gestured toward the visitors' chair on the opposite side of the desk.

"How did it go?" Arsat asked.

Karrim lowered into his seat, running his fingers over the carved wooden armrests. Despite preparing for this conversation, he was still having trouble finding the right words. "Somewhat unexpectedly, I admit."

"How so?"

"Naia is very talented," Karrim said. "I cannot tell for certain, but I believe she may be gifted with inborn iron-sensing."

Arsat's eyebrows rose, an uncharacteristic display of surprise from the senior blademaster. Karrim expected it, though. This kind of inborn talent was rumored to grace only the very best. Karrim himself had achieved this quality through hard training, which made him even more awed to see someone who apparently came upon it with no effort at all.

"What about her level?" Arsat asked.

"It's uneven. Her technique needs work. But not as much as you'd expect for someone at her stage. In my assessment, with the right training she'd be able to do well on the Jai grounds."

Arsat nodded slowly. "What about her situation with the Har?"

Karrim heaved a breath. "It's not all that it seems, actually."

"How so?"

"Naia had a very good reason to attack Ishim. Perhaps good enough to forgo the usual considerations about subordination."

"Can you be more specific, Jai Karrim?"

"She believed she was saving a life. I think she was probably right."

Arsat's eyes trailed away. "Are you implying that her actions have likely prevented a murder?"

"Yes. And there is more to it, I'm afraid."

"*More?*"

"Valmad is deliberately making her take the fall for it, to cover his own ass."

Arsat cleared his throat, a sharp reminder that the common way people talked on the training range didn't apply to the Jaihar command. Karrim didn't feel guilty, though. It was either this or swearing, which he knew wouldn't be nearly as effective.

"Once again, Jai Karrim, I'd like to ask you to be much more specific." Behind his cold façade, Arsat seemed surprised – a rare sight to encounter twice in the same conversation.

"I spent some time yesterday evening questioning the lower grounds servants," Karrim said. "Eventually, I was able to find one of them who was present at the incident. A young serving girl, too frightened during the official hearing to give out any information at all."

Arsat's eyes narrowed. "Go on."

"Apparently, Har Ishim's tendency to beat servants was well-known, but generally overlooked."

"It certainly never came to my attention."

It took close knowledge of the headmaster to notice the way his eyes very briefly flickered as he spoke. *Bending the truth.* Not something Karrim would ever understand, but a relief for the purpose of this conversation. If Arsat knew about the problems with Ishim, Karrim would have to spend much less effort to convince him.

"None of the servants wanted to lose their jobs over it," he said. "Everyone tolerated it, until one day when Ishim crossed the line."

"What happened?"

"He attacked a serving girl for inappropriately entering the trainers' hall. Naia was nearby and overheard him beating the girl to death. She felt she had no choice but to interfere."

"Why didn't she mention any of this during the inquiry?"

"To protect the servant. With a good reason, I believe."

"Still, it was her duty to tell us everything she knew."

Karrim shook his head. He knew Arsat understood, even if he would never say something like this out loud. "She chose to take the fall, rather than put someone's life at risk. It's true that she could have probably handled the inquiry better, but these things tend to be very hard to navigate. I might have done the same in her place."

Arsat measured him with a long look. "You mentioned Har Valmad's involvement."

Karrim flexed his fist several times, trying to still the rising anger. "Ishim didn't beat her so badly on his own. Apparently, he was having trouble besting her, until Valmad arrived and held her up. They would have killed or crippled her if the servant she saved didn't scream for help."

The pause stretched even longer this time. Karrim couldn't read any reaction in the headmaster's face, but he could guess it nonetheless. He had the same reaction when he'd heard this story earlier today. Arsat's shock was relieving, actually. The headaster probably expected dirty play, but he didn't expect *this*.

"This is a grave accusation, Jai Karrim," Arsat said.

"Yes, I am aware of that."

The headmaster twitched his fingers around the hilt of his ranking dagger, a habitual motion that used to leave Karrim awestruck when he was still a trainee. The fact that he could now do this too didn't make it any less impressive.

"What do you think I should do, Jai Karrim?" Arsat said at length.

"Strip Valmad of ranks and kick him out of here. That's what I would have done, at least."

Arsat shook his head. "I can't. To take this kind of an action against a trainer, I need solid proof. The word of one serving girl is not enough."

"Naia remembers what happened."

"Do you really want her to testify?"

"No."

"I thought so."

Karrim sighed. "At the very least you should clear her record and begin her Jai training immediately. You should also take extra precautions to keep her out of trouble. If the Har learn that she got her memory back…"

"Don't worry, Jai Karrim. We will protect her. Starting tomorrow, she will be safely in the Jai charge."

Karrim heaved a sigh of relief. *Starting tomorrow.* The best possible outcome, given the circumstances. Before he left for

Zegmeer, he was also going to put in place some precautions of his own, to make sure Valmad and his cronies never got to Naia again.

"Are you going to do anything about Valmad?" he asked.

"I'm afraid I can't."

Karrim shook his head. "People like him have no business training anyone, let alone our youngest trainees who really deserve better."

"It's more complicated than you think, in Har Valmad's case. I believe it safer to keep him close by. Who knows what he is capable of without the Jai oversight?"

Karrim's eyes narrowed. "You think this way of him, and you still leave him with the authority to do his worst?"

"For the most part, he does his job."

"He is also known to destroy lives. Naia is not the first, I presume."

"Perhaps not, even though she is probably the first one with this much promise. It tends to be more complex with others. As the head trainer, Har Valmad rarely trains anyone personally, but I tend to see his zeal as an important character test. Not everyone is cut out to be a Jaihar."

Karrim glanced away. This kind of thinking was one of the many reasons he never found the idea of joining the Jaihar command even remotely appealing.

"Naia is," he said. "With the right training, she can become one of our best."

Arsat nodded. "Thank you for being so thorough with her evaluation, Jai Karrim. I am glad that your findings can remove a dark spot from a promising trainee's record."

Following Arsat's gesture of dismissal, Karrim rose and saluted again, then strode away through the door.

In the past day, he'd learned more about the darker side of the Jaihar Order than he ever cared to know. He supposed his shock at these revelations made him no better than the youngest trainees, too naïve and trusting to have any business in politics. If only everything was as simple as a blade fight, where one could rely entirely on skill.

He hoped Naia would become a great Jaihar – and that, once that happened, she would continue to be happy with this choice. Karrim had done everything he possibly could for her. And now, it was in both of their best interests to forget the whole thing as soon as he could.

He knew it wasn't going to be easy.

A NEW TUTOR

Naia narrowed her eyes, watching a group of people walk toward her across the grounds. This was the first day of her Jai training and she didn't yet know how things were supposed to go, but she was fairly certain this wasn't the kind of a group that would normally start off a trainee like her. Well, perhaps she wasn't that surprised to see Jai Hamed among them. He was the training master's right-hand man and one of the top Jaihar involved in her evaluation. But what was Dal Gassan, the man she met on the lower grounds a few days ago, doing in his company? Or the veiled woman by his side, dressed in an abayah of the deepest garnet color Naia had ever seen?

She turned to her new trainer – Omar, an elderly Glimmerblade she was assigned to this morning – but saw no surprise in the man's calm expression. Did he expect this kind of a greeting party? Did he know what this was all about? She knew there would be no chance to ask as the newcomers approached and stopped in front of them.

"Jai Hamed." Naia saluted with her palm. "Dal Gassan." She lowered her hand, looking at him with a half-question as her gaze trailed to the Daljeer's silent companion.

"You look surprised to see me," Gassan said.

"I am." Naia regarded him curiously. She still wasn't sure how much of a role the Daljeer played in the recent turn of her situation, but she had no doubt he had a hand in it somehow. It seemed too coincidental to see all her troubles magically resolve right after she met him. He must have talked to Arsat about her. Which implied that this man was far more influential than she realized.

"I believe I owe you a debt of gratitude, Dal Gassan," she said.

The Daljeer grinned. "I have no idea what you mean. I'm here at your headmaster's request." He pointed to his companion. "Allow me to introduce Dal Mehtab, our Circle's foremost expert on Challimar."

"Challimar?" Naia's eyes briefly darted to Omar and Hamed, only partially reassured by their continued lack of reaction.

"Your headmaster felt that, given your Chall origins, it would be beneficial to give you extra schooling in Chall ways. He asked the Daljeer to provide a tutor, so Dal Mehtab is here to offer her services."

My Chall origins. Until now, Naia wasn't even aware of them, not so explicitly, at least. She looked at the woman curiously. Her thin veil looked more like protection from the sun than a means to disguise her face, carved in bold, elegant lines. Her eyes, visible above the veil, had a peculiar color – honey-yellow, with speckles that made them gleam like gold.

Naia had never heard of anyone here being trained with a personal non-Jaihar tutor. On top of the fact that she already had her very own Jai-ranked trainer, this was beginning to seem more and more odd. Was this all because Karrim put in a good word for her? Or was this something all Jai trainees had to go through at some point? Somehow, she doubted that.

"Dal Mehtab will be giving you lessons on a regular basis," Gassan said. "As permitted by your other duties."

The older woman unclipped her veil, letting it fall to the side of her face to reveal the part previously half-hidden. She looked remarkable, her skin nearly unblemished, her age guessable mostly by the knowing expression in her eyes, rather than any faults in her appearance.

She stepped closer, reaching out to Naia's face and freezing her hand an inch away as she saw Naia's hesitation.

"Your hair," the woman said. "It's so beautiful. You must grow it out."

Must? Naia frowned. Was her Daljeer tutor going to have a say in how she looked? She glanced at Hamed and Omar, curious at their impassive expressions, as if the request was perfectly normal and ordinary.

"I will wear my hair the way I please," she said.

The woman laughed, a rich melodious sound that made Naia want to listen to it more. "Let's leave this discussion for later, shall we?"

Naia shrugged. It didn't seem like a good idea to engage in an argument right after they met, in front of her superiors – especially over something as trivial as a hairstyle. She focused on the woman's voice instead, so soothing and comforting. Mehtab softened her consonants as she spoke, and sang her vowels in the way only desert dwellers could do. *Do I have to learn to speak like this to become eligible for assignments in Challimar?* Up until now, Naia tended to believe that her weapon training was her main challenge. But now she started to realize that there was a lot more to it.

"I look forward to our lessons, Dal Mehtab," she said.

The older woman's smile faded. "And here is your first one, my dear. A true Chall never tells a lie outright, without a good reason. Not to a person you've just met."

She turned and walked away.

Naia stared at the woman's retreating back. She felt taken aback, yes, but also strangely refreshed. No one here talked like this. And yes, now that Mehtab brought it up, she did admit that the polite phrase she just said was indeed a lie. Well, she was curious to see what these lessons were about, but she didn't look forward to them, not exactly. Not if they were going to involve discussions about her hair. She tended to cut it short, even if, between trimmings, it could occasionally grow out to neck length.

Now that her new tutor had walked away, though, this odd reaction made her realize that these lessons could indeed prove interesting – provided that she hadn't messed up her chances for tutoring. Mehtab certainly piqued her curiosity. Naia found herself wondering if one day she could learn to hold herself with the same kind of allure.

"I didn't mean to offend her, Dal Gassan," she said.

"Don't worry." Gassan's face retained its easygoing smile, but the way his eyes trailed to watch the Daljeer woman betrayed his surprise. "Mehtab is just fine."

I hope so. The idea of taking lessons with Mehtab was beginning to seem more and more appealing. Anyone who could bring this absent-minded look to Gassan's normally confident face had to be worth learning from.

"I do look forward to my lessons with Dal Mehtab," Naia said – and added with a smile, "This isn't a lie, in case you're wondering. Not anymore."

Gassan's eyes hovered on Mehtab, who was walking away in slow but steady steps, without showing any intention to turn back. "I'm glad to know that. I will make sure to check on your progress when I'm in Haggad next time."

Without waiting for a response he turned around and hurried after Mehtab. Hamed exchanged a brief nod with Omar and followed.

Naia stood for a long moment watching them. Too many questions flooded into her head. She chose the easiest one, the one she expected Omar would have at least the slightest idea about.

"Why is Jai Hamed following them, Jai Omar?" she asked.

The trainer shrugged. "The headmaster feels it necessary to keep an eye on the Daljeer."

"Why?"

"It's always a good idea with outsiders who are allowed to roam freely on our upper grounds."

"Still, this seems unusual, doesn't it?" Surely the Jaihar had plenty of errand men, far more suitable for the job than one of the Order's top elite.

Omar grinned. "Just as well that Jai Hamed was here when this woman acted up. No one would believe me if I told the story – not without a backup."

Naia looked at him thoughtfully, warmth spreading through her at the thought that this man was going to train her from now on. His easygoing manner was so different from the barking and yelling she had gotten used to on the lower training grounds. Just standing quietly at his side made her feel so calm.

"Is this kind of scholarly training common for a Jai?" she asked.

Omar shook his head. "Not that I know. But I've learned

during my years here that our headmaster never does these things without a very good reason. I'd make the most of it, if I were you. Personal training by one of the Daljeer's top scholars is a rare opportunity."

Naia nodded. Something in his tone suggested there was more to it than met the eye. But she knew she may not be able to learn what it was for quite a while.

Gassan caught up with Mehtab at the edge of the grounds, near the gateway that led off into a quiet city street. The woman turned as she heard his approach, her entire figure emanating a special calmness that he was beginning to find just a tiny bit annoying.

"Any reason for running away like that?" he asked.

Mehtab smiled. "I didn't run away. I merely left, after I realized there was no point for further conversation."

"Is this one of your famed Chall ways? To walk away without warning?"

"In this case, yes."

Gassan looked her up and down. Everything about Mehtab was not what he expected. This feeling, as he now realized, had pursued him from the very first time he saw her on that fateful night seventeen years ago. She held herself as if she was in charge – which definitely hadn't been the case back then, and shouldn't be the case now, when Gassan, her ultimate superior, was around. Perhaps it had to do with the Chall traditions too? In the matriarchal society of Challimar, did women act like superiors by default around any man, the way Zeg tended to do the opposite?

"Why did you have to start the conversation by talking about her hair?" he said.

Mehtab frowned. "Only a peasant would cut her hair so short."

"Or a warrior."

"I thought you wanted me to train her to be something else."

Gassan sighed. "With everything else we are facing, isn't this detail somewhat minor at the moment?"

"Every detail matters," Mehtab said.

Gassan continued to study her curiously. He could probably send for another Chall tutor to train Naia, one more obedient and predictable. But, despite Mehtab's insubordinate behavior, the woman knew her job better than anyone else, he was sure of it. However hard it was to deal with, insubordination was at the core of any interactions between the Daljeer. For high level scholars there could be no other way but constantly testing each other's limits and exposing each other's incompetences, even if they normally did it in a more respectful manner. This consideration ended up reassuring him the most. If Mehtab had any hidden agenda, wouldn't she do her best to be as easy as possible to deal with?

"I still think walking away just now wasn't necessary," he said.

"You are training this girl to be able to impersonate royalty. A royal princess would do no less, when faced with a newcomer. I wanted her to remember that. I am sure she will, after what just happened."

"Of course she will remember. You've accused her of lying."

Mehtab shook her head. "Not exactly. Naia is dealing with a lot of change in a very short time. She has no idea where she stands with everyone right now. She needs boundaries, so that she can develop the confidence that comes with the role. Among other things, she must remember never to twist the truth merely for the fear of being impolite."

"Establishing these kinds of boundaries seems like a strange way to encourage confidence."

Mehtab glanced past him to Hamed, who was standing so still that Gassan almost forgot about the man's presence.

"Why don't you ask Jai Hamed? Would trying to convince Naia that she could trust me be more effective?"

Gassan turned to the Shadowblade too, surprised to see a half-smile briefly shift the man's normally impassive face.

"Dal Mehtab has a point," Hamed said. "To the Jaihar, trying to convince someone of your value is a sign of weakness. An abrupt departure like this would likely show Naia that Dal Mehtab deserves her full respect. She will also know that next time there's no need to pretend where Dal Mehtab is concerned. It should make their future conversations easier."

Gassan looked at him for a moment, then turned back to Mehtab, who was watching him smugly. Clearly, despite dealing with the Jaihar for nearly thirty years, he still had a lot to learn.

"Very well," he said. "I will trust you on this one, Dal Mehtab."

"Thank you, Dal Gassan."

"What's next?"

The woman's full lips twitched into a mysterious smile. "I will wait for Naia to settle into her training routine before showing up again."

"This would cost us some precious time."

"My goal is to start slowly. Just a few pointers here and there, before moving on to the extensive sessions back in the serai. This girl still has a long way to go."

"Exactly. This is why I felt we couldn't possibly spare any time."

Mehtab's lips twitched. "You still don't trust me, Dal Gassan."

"If I didn't trust you, you wouldn't be here."

"This assurance seems half-hearted, at most."

"It's as much as anyone could ever get from me, I'm afraid. Which means, among other things, that you can't possibly remain so enigmatic about your plans for the girl."

"No enigma, I assure you, Dal Gassan. It's just that the kind of training Naia requires has to do with more than knowledge. Before she can even begin to grow into the role, she must learn balance. The kind that will come only after she progresses with her Jai training."

Gassan glanced at Hamed standing beside them, surprised to see acknowledgment in the man's gaze. He'd heard about the Jaihar balance, yes, but it never came up in a conversation with his own subordinate.

"How do you know so much about Jai training, Dal Mehtab?" he asked.

She shrugged. "I've been to Haggad before."

"So have I."

"But you probably didn't stay in the city much, did you?"

"No." *And neither should you, if you came here on Daljeer business.* The Daljeer serai was admittedly not the most comfortable accommodation, but it served well, especially when time was as precious as it always tended to be.

Mehtab smiled. "On occasion, my research on local customs took me to the city taverns. Those closest to the Jaihar Stronghold tend to be the ones Jai trainees visit in their off time. One can learn a lot about them merely by sitting quietly and watching."

Gassan receded. He knew what she was referring to. One

could always distinguish the Jai trainees by the way they held themselves, with the calm dignity of those absolutely certain of their value. For an inexplicable reason, it continued to bother him that Mehtab showed so much knowledge about this. He should be nothing but glad at this extra evidence of her competency, shouldn't he?

"Very well, Dal Mehtab," he said. "I will let you do it your way – for now, as long as we continue to get results."

Mehtab bowed. "You won't be disappointed, Dal Gassan."

That remains to be seen. Gassan hid the thought behind a nod. "I hope you encounter no further obstacles in getting to know Naia. As soon as you start regular training sessions with her, I'll need weekly reports, sent to my attention in Zegmeer. You might also receive additional instructions from the Circle's headquarters, which may, if requested, be shared with the Jaihar command." He glanced at Hamed, once again standing perfectly still. It would have been better to act without the Jaihar supervision, but given that Naia was one of their own, it was probably fair.

He hoped none of the parties involved would mess things up.

AN OLD TALE

"How can my training possibly have anything to do with my hairstyle?" Naia asked.

Mehtab's smile in response would have seemed unbearably patronizing, if Naia didn't feel so intrigued. Today was their first lesson at the Daljeer compound, and nothing about it had been what she'd expected, starting with the sight of Mehtab's luxurious chamber, set with expensive rugs and fancy but comfortable furniture, and ending with the older woman's apparent preoccupation with Naia's hair. Mehtab went as far as releasing the string that held back Naia's short ponytail, to let her mahogany tresses spill freely over her neck.

Naia was *not* going to grow them out, no matter what this strange woman said. In fact, she was long overdue for a haircut.

"You'll see," Mehtab said.

Naia shook her head. "I won't. This isn't going to happen."

Mehtab didn't respond as she reached into a drawer to bring out an ornate box.

"For our lessons," she said, "I want you to wear this." She flipped the box open, bringing out a necklace.

Naia stared. The necklace didn't look like any jewelry Naia had ever seen before. Wide and collar-like, it was made of dark yellow metal, shaped like two wings that met in the center to hold a faceted yellow-green gem.

"You want me to wear a *necklace*?" This had to be one of the most unusual requests one had ever posed to a Jaihar.

"Yes."

"Why?"

Mehtab sighed. "Our lessons would go a lot easier if you stop questioning every small thing I ask of you. Go ahead, try it on."

Naia took the necklace, surprised at how heavy it was, despite the delicate metalwork. Definitely not gold. She had never seen this kind of metal before.

"It's crafted of imlar," Mehtab said. "A rare metal that has the ability to attract iron and steel. Watch." She drew a pin from her hair, bundled at the back of her head, and tossed it up into the air.

Naia gaped as the pin abruptly changed its path and leapt toward the necklace, latching onto it length-wise.

Mehtab laughed at her stunned expression. "Now, pick up the pin and give it back to me."

Naia reached for it, surprised at the amount of force it took to pry the pin off the ornate metal surface. She could feel the pin shift and twitch in her hands as she gave it back to Mehtab, who tucked it into her hair again.

"Imlar ore used to be mined in Challimar, centuries ago," the older woman said. "The mines have now been depleted, making these imlar objects more precious than jewels."

Naia shifted the necklace in her hands, admiring the craftsmanship, the elegant lines weaving into wave-like patterns that seemed to come alive if she stared at them long enough.

She supposed she should be asking how Mehtab came to possess such treasure, and why it was necessary for Naia to wear it for her lessons. Instead, her eye was drawn to the gem, shifting with a deep yellow-green fire.

"Imlarite," Mehtab said. "A precious stone occasionally found in the imlar mines. People refer to them as Challimar diamonds. The one you're holding is nearly flawless, but small in comparison to the one I have here." She folded away the tall collar of her abayah to reveal a large stone resting in the cleft between her collarbones, held by a plain metal chain around her neck. This stone was less transparent and had an irregular shape, but the fire playing inside it had a palette much richer than the one Naia held in her hands – like a rainbow, gleaming in the sparse room's light with many different colors.

The question Naia was about to ask froze on her lips as she felt the daggers on her belt move, as if suddenly coming alive. She hastily raised the necklace away from her belt, feeling all her weapons shift and settle back into their inanimate state.

Mehtab chuckled. "This much imlar in one place is bound to affect your weapons. If you allow them to touch the necklace, the steel would hold the memory of it for a while and your blades would become attracted to each other, distorting their movements when you use them."

"Do they ever craft blades out of imlar?" Naia asked.

Mehtab shook her head. "Imlar is too soft to make an effective blade. But it has other uses. Challimar craftsmen used to mix imlar into their best steel, creating armor that could deflect and alter the paths of the enemy blades."

"If it's that effective, how come no one has ever heard of it?"

Mehtab grinned. "I can see that you would make a great Jaihar. Only your top warriors have this tendency to think of their knowledge as absolute."

Naia didn't respond. She did tend to believe that the Jaihar knew everything, even if the Order's elite didn't necessarily share their knowledge with lower-ranked warriors. But, put this way, it did seem categorical to say that no one had ever heard about imlar. Clearly the Daljeer did, or Mehtab wouldn't be telling her these things right now.

"Imlar was banned centuries ago," Mehtab said. "Ever since the Succession War."

"'Banned' doesn't mean it's not around anymore, does it?"

Mehtab's grin widened. "You have a wicked mind, don't you?"

"Wicked?" Naia echoed Mehtab's grin, feeling a strange closeness to the woman. She did not mean her question as a jest, but it felt so nice – and so unusual – to have someone to share a smile with.

Maybe it was all right to follow her new tutor's suggestion and grow out her hair – at least for a while, until it got annoying.

"Most imlar pieces were confiscated and melted down, stored somewhere in the dungeons beneath the emperor's palace," Mehtab said. "But some items did survive. Like this necklace, for instance. Here, let me put it on you."

The cool metal settled around Naia's neck, Mehtab's deft fingers clasping the lock at the back. The necklace lay heavily over Naia's collarbones, fitting as precisely as if the artisan who crafted it had the exact measurements to work with. She closed her eyes briefly, enjoying the feeling of smooth metal against her skin, the calmness it brought. She knew she would have to take it off eventually, but she could definitely get used to wearing this piece.

"Was this necklace ever used as armor?" Naia wasn't sure

what prompted the question. The delicate workmanship made the idea seem odd. Yet, the weight of the metal, the way it lay so comfortably over her upper chest, did make her feel strangely protected – not only by shielding her from a direct blow to the area of her neck, but also by the fact that its effect on metal was likely to divert any blade within range.

Mehtab nodded slowly. "In a way, yes. This necklace you are wearing is one of those given to every Redcloak guard of the royal Challimar unit, as protection and a symbol of servitude. The Queen wore a full imlar bodice – as an ornament, and a symbol of her power. It has been known to avert a blade or two throughout Challimar's long history."

Inadvertently, Naia's hand flew up to touch the necklace again. "How did this necklace come into your hands?"

Mehtab shrugged. "Many Challimar treasures ended up with the Daljeer. Our Circle studies them, trying to decipher their properties and use. Common folk believe them to be magical, but for most of the artifacts we examined so far, each of their properties has a natural explanation. Since I will be teaching you everything about Challimar, I felt it was a good idea to bring one such piece along."

"What about the stone you are wearing?"

Mehtab's fingers ran over the large stone at her throat, now once again hidden by the tall collar of her abayah. "This one is a family heirloom. It holds mostly sentimental value. As you can see, it's far less transparent than precious imlarite, and the necklace it is set into is far less ornate. It's of no use to anyone but me."

Naia nodded. Mehtab's voice was so soothing. She loved the woman's lilt, the rich accent of a true desert-dweller. The conversation sent her into a relaxed state she hadn't experienced for a very long time.

"And now, let me tell you a story," Mehtab said. "About a great kingdom that once reigned over the desert sands."

Following her gesture, Naia settled into the pile of sitting pillows next to the lit fireplace. The heat licked her cheek, making her entire body tingle with warmth. If only her lessons with the Jaihar could be so relaxing.

"Is this the story of Challimar?" she asked.

"Yes. But you will hear it told differently in your other lessons."

"Why?"

"Save your questions for later. The kingdom of Challimar was the first to be created, a chosen nation destined to rule the others. It was beautiful, inhabited by people whose eyes carried the golden light of Sel's sun within them. Their birthright as Sel's chosen put them above the barbaric tribes that inhabited the rest of the lands."

Naia frowned. "This is not how Challimar is portrayed in the official chronicles."

"No," Mehtab said. "It is not."

Naia watched her curiously. Mehtab's face lit up as she spoke, as if the subject was deeply personal to her. She vowed not to interrupt again, wondering at the emotion her new tutor put into the experience – as if she was teaching Naia something sacred.

"The people of Challimar were peaceful," Mehtab went on. "They knew no war and put all their strength into scholarly knowledge, learning everything they could about the world. They invented medicines and cures unlike anything the lands around them ever knew. They developed technology: ships that could traverse the desert sands, shields that were light and portable and yet could protect their people from sandstorms. They learned to gather water from the dry desert air, and planted gardens that turned each of their cities into an oasis, an island that graced the dune sea like a beautiful and priceless gem."

Naia watched the flames as she listened, falling into the rhythm of Mehtab's melodious voice. Its fable-like tone evoked images in her mind. Sand ships travelling the desert, their sails filled with the wind. Rich and beautiful gardens, rising among the dunes. People walking unhurriedly among the lush greenery, enjoying scholarly conversations as they bathed in Sel's divine light.

"How did the barbaric tribes feel about this?" she asked.

Mehtab smiled. "You catch on quickly, don't you? Yes, the barbarians. They envied Challimar's greatness. They sent envoys to steal its scholars' inventions and medicines. They built kingdoms of their own, putting all the stolen knowledge to use. And, as they did all these things, they also worked on building up strengths of their own. Weaponry, that enabled them to fight and gain power."

"Long term, this seems like a losing situation for Challimar, in your story," Naia said. "Tactically speaking, of course."

"Now you are talking like a Jaihar – the special tribe of barbarians, who stole one of Challimar's most prized inventions, now long lost. These barbarians learned to infuse their blood with iron, so that they could bond to their weapons and become the best fighters of all."

Naia's eyes widened. "Is this true?"

"If you believe the old texts, yes."

"But how is that possible?"

"Like many others, this secret has been lost. If anyone knew how to do it, we would all be in trouble right now, wouldn't we?"

"I don't know. Would we?"

"The ancient texts," Mehtab said, "speak of elixirs one could take to increase the iron in the blood. Taking this elixir made warriors faster and more agile than regular humans. It also made them more responsive to weapons. It was said that such warriors could sense steel, control their blades like an extension of their own limbs. The best of them also had the ability to anticipate their enemies' weapons in a fight. I assume these are the feelings you can relate to, right?"

"Yes, but how…" Naia paused. Mehtab's tale sounded outlandish. Yet, the feeling Mehtab described, the ability to sense steel, did sound eerily familiar. Naia had never given it a thought before, but everything Mehtab said just now, however unusual, made perfect sense.

"The elixir was invented as part of Challimar's attempts to defend themselves against the lesser nations," Mehtab said. "They created an elite guard unit, the Ironbloods, all of them magically enhanced to make them capable of defeating any normal warrior. In Challimar they wore red cloaks, so that they could be easily recognized."

"The Redcloaks," Naia said. "The Challimar royal guards."

Mehtab nodded. "Yes. Even though now, thanks to the emperor who ordered the Challimar Royal Massacre, they are extinct too. With the secret lost, only the Jaihar now remain to propagate this warrior ability."

"Propagate?"

"Yes. This ability can be passed on to your children. This is how, despite the lost secret of the elixir, the Ironbloods still live on – no longer exclusively Chall, no longer serving the queen, but just as capable in battle – or more."

"But the Jaihar warriors don't marry or have children."

"They don't marry, no. But the matter of having children is more complex than that. Surely you are aware of how the Jaihar encourage their trainees to explore sexual liaisons?"

Naia nodded. She knew, even if she found the idea far less compelling than the other trainees tended to. "The purpose of this has nothing to do with bearing children. This is just one of the possible ways to develop one's physicality."

Mehtab smiled. "Is this what they've been telling you, girl?"

Naia didn't respond. What she knew from the Jaihar made sense. And she did try it, once. The memory was shameful, the fleeting pleasure definitely not worth all the talk. During the entire encounter, no one ever mentioned anything about procreation. Mehtab had to be wrong about this – understandable, for someone non-Jaihar.

She felt affronted when the older woman leaned over and patted her arm.

"You have a lot to learn," Mehtab said.

Naia shook her head. "We are all warded against pregnancy. Even when I went out and, um, explored a liaison with a man, I knew I wouldn't bear children."

Mehtab nodded. "*You* wouldn't. A pregnancy would most certainly ruin your training, which is why the Jaihar girls receive their wards without even a discussion. It is different with the male trainees, though. While all of them are warded against disease, they tend to retain their fertility."

"But the girls in the taverns..."

"...are richly rewarded if they bear a Jaihar child. Why do you think they are always so eager for the experience?"

Naia thought about it. She always assumed the girls' eagerness had to do with the way the Jaihar men tended to be so good-looking and skilled, an irresistible combination for the type of women interested in such things. She had never realized there were other considerations involved.

"How do you know all this?" she asked.

Mehtab smiled. "I am a Daljeer scholar, one of the best at what I do. Of course I know."

Naia glanced away. All this talk about exploring their bodies. Was it a way the Jaihar Order took advantage of the fact that bodily pleasure and procreation normally went hand in hand, ensuring their warriors' experience and enabling the supply of new warriors all at the same time?

"Do the Jaihar descend from the Challimar Redcloaks, then?" she asked.

"Not exactly, no. The Jaihar warriors descend from those barbarians who stole the elixir and took advantage of it. This was how your Order originally formed, when a group of warlords sneaked into Challimar and took hold of a large supply. The ability they gained was inferior to the original, but the Jaihar perfected it by training, molding themselves into warriors far beyond anything Challimar ever had. They were also the ones who destroyed the original texts detailing the elixir's recipe, so that no one else could ever do what they did. That was the time our kingdom's demise really began."

Our kingdom. It was odd to hear Mehtab speak this way, as if this ancient history was deeply personal to her, as if the Chall blood she and Naia shared made them special. Somehow it was easy to believe Mehtab's words, though. While the Jaihar Naia knew were nothing like barbarians and warlords she'd read about in the chronicles, their stronghold was still dominated by this kind of mentality.

"With time," Mehtab went on, "the Redcloaks' blood diluted

too much, so that the top-ranked Jaihar always bested them in battle. This was why, when seventeen years ago it came to Challimar's last stand, they were so easily defeated."

"Were the Jaihar the ones fighting for the emperor that day?" Naia never thought of the Jaihar as executioners. But she supposed this did not differ that much from the assassinations the top Jaihar were rumored to perform for the imperial family and the nobles. The Challimar Royal Massacre was nothing but an assassination on a larger scale, if one thought down to the bare facts.

"No one knows," Mehtab said. "The details of that event have been erased from history. The only fact is that the royal family and all the Redcloaks were exterminated that day. The palace library, containing the knowledge of centuries, was looted. And now, all Challimar's scholarly secrets, all the technology that was invented in the old days, is credited to the Zeg."

"I'm certain the Zeg must have invented some of that technology too."

"Not on the same scale. Much of their technology is for the purpose of killing or dominating others. The kingdom of Challimar at its height stood for entirely different values. This was how they originally lost their dominance. Once the barbarian tribes around them became stronger, they led an attack on Challimar and conquered it, turning it into a province."

Naia sat up straight. "You are speaking about the Succession War."

"Yes."

"At that time, the Zeg weren't exactly barbarian tribes. Not by a long shot."

"They were, compared to Challimar. But in the end force always tends to win. You, as a Jaihar, should know that well."

Naia didn't respond. The Jaihar were known for their refined weaponry and high level combat skills that made them different from everyone else. Calling them barbarians, the way Mehtab tended to do, was similar to comparing fine jeweler's tools to a stonemason's hammer. But, by her own admission, Mehtab's story was just a story. At least Naia chose to think of it this way. She didn't know Mehtab at all, except for observing the older woman's tendency toward unpredictable behavior. For all she knew, Mehtab might snap right out of her semi-entranced state any moment now and call it all a joke.

"After they lost the war, the Challimar people were forced to give up a lot of their inventions to their new rulers," Mehtab said. "This was how the Daljeer were able to become such advanced healers, and how the Jaihar acquired their weapon crafting techniques."

"They are all using these achievements to help others," Naia protested.

"Perhaps. But it doesn't mean it was all right to steal them in the first place."

Naia wasn't so sure. But it seemed pointless, at the very least, to bring it up in this conversation.

"This happened ages ago," she said. "Have the people of Challimar been holding a grudge all this time?"

"Not a grudge. A memory. It's important to understand where many of the common things we all take for granted come from, isn't it?"

"I suppose it is." *Especially since none of this information ever seeps into the official chronicles.* Naia wondered at the way she felt inclined to believe Mehtab's words, even if this went against everything else she had learned. Perhaps it was the power in the older woman's voice, as if Mehtab herself was fully convinced of everything she said?

"And then came a time when people started talking," Mehtab said. "About Challimar rising again. About the way the Chall people were blessed by Sel. About the Challimar queen being the rightful ruler of all the lands, even if the Zeg male succession traditions tried to reduce her birthright to a mere ceremonial role. They formed a movement, aimed to restore the kingdom to greatness. They vowed to kill every Zeg, every Raj, every Scinn that ever walked these lands."

Mehtab's voice sounded different now, stronger, more forceful. For a very brief moment it seemed as if she believed these convictions, the idea that many people in the empire had to die. Naia peered closer, reassured to see Mehtab's face soften with a smile. Strange how the play of shadows from the fireplace could alter one's perception.

"Is this when the emperor ordered the death of the Challimar royal family?" she said.

Mehtab looked her square in the eyes. "No one knows what truly happened that day. Or rather, no one remembers. Nearly everyone who witnessed the event has been wiped out, save for the closest advisors of the emperor who helped orchestrate the whole thing. Even the warriors that carried out the emperor's orders were killed later on."

"Really?" Naia didn't know about this at all, yet Mehtab spoke of it with such conviction as if she truly knew.

Once again, the shadows from the fireplace shifted around Mehtab's face, highlighting her nose, the hollow of her cheeks, the deep shadows around her eyes. For a moment she looked like a different person, one that Naia didn't recognize.

"How do you know so much about it?" she asked.

Mehtab shrugged and shifted in her seat, her face falling into full shadow then coming into light again, calm and familiar. "Like I said, Naia, this is all just a tale. One that I felt you should know, but shouldn't take too seriously at all."

THE COMBAT MASTER

Naia lowered her blades, watching a man walk toward her across the field. Her heart quivered as she recognized his singular gait – so smooth that he appeared to be gliding over the ground. Jai Ilhad, the combat master.

Despite training on the Jai upper grounds for nearly a year, she still wasn't quite sure about this man's role in the Jaihar Order, except for the fact that his post was so high that even the headmaster rarely made any important decisions without his approval. Everyone she knew always pulled up to attention when Ilhad was around, even the senior Shadowblades. Her trainer, Jai Omar, standing by her side, stiffened visibly. Naia saw no surprise in his face, though. Clearly, he expected Ilhad's visit, even though he obviously didn't see fit to warn Naia about it.

Ilhad's nod in response to her salute looked more like a downward glance, with no movement in his head at all.

"You will be training with me today," he said. "Follow me."

His voice, deep and low, crept straight into her gut. She felt angry at herself for this reaction. After a year on the Jaihar upper grounds she should be able to counter such a blunt attempt at intimidation, shouldn't she?

Ilhad did not speak or acknowledge her presence in any way, until they came to a secluded area at the back of the stronghold, a walled-in courtyard adjoining a tall, faceless wall of the rear guard tower. Naia looked around curiously. She had never been to this place before.

"You may leave your blades over there." Ilhad gestured to a small stand near the courtyard's entrance. "You won't be needing them today."

I won't? Naia knew better than to question this order as she tucked her blades neatly into the narrow slots. She kept glancing at Ilhad out of the corners of her eyes. Up until now, she had never seen the combat master up close, but everything she knew about his dangerous reputation went well with his gaunt, heavy face. Was it because of the injuries that prevented his facial muscles from moving? Or was it all about control, a trained ability to conceal every emotion?

Standing in front of him without her blades made her feel vulnerable. Perhaps it had to do with the rumors that surrounded this mysterious man. After all this time on the Jai grounds, she no longer felt the same awe she used to feel at encountering any of the Order's elite superiors, but it was hard in this case not to feel just a little intimidated.

"I've heard you're making good progress," Ilhad said.

"Am I?" She blinked. The information was news to her. Omar, who had been training her up to now, rarely expressed either praise or disapproval, keeping all his comments to the specifics. She found it comforting, but she also realized that it gave her very little in terms of comparison to other trainees.

Ilhad's eyes narrowed. "With blades, yes. It doesn't really matter for today, though. We will be reviewing other weapons, ones you may not be as closely familiar with." He gestured to the stands at the back of the courtyard.

Naia approached, barely able to contain her curiosity. These stands seemed very different from the ones she had gotten used to seeing on the regular training grounds. Tall and expansive, they held every possible type of weapon she could imagine, from long staffs and halberds to small spiked balls on chains, hanging loosely without any visible handle. She reached over and lifted one, surprisingly heavy for its size.

"What are these?" she asked.

"Orbens."

She rolled the unfamiliar word through her head as she ran her hand along the length of the chain, thin and flexible like a rope. Ilhad watched her silently, until she lowered her hand and turned to him.

"They are very tricky to fight with," he said. "Or to defend against. I'd leave them alone for now." He pointed further down the stand. "Let's start with something more straightforward. The staffs."

Naia swallowed. Her build, lighter and slimmer than most of the other trainees here, made staffs an additional challenge. Of course this referred to the heavy full length ones, all the way at the end of the stand, rising at least two heads taller than she was. She was marginally better with the shorter and lighter ones, and actually enjoyed the kind that flexed, making the fight all about calculation and technique. She reached for one of those, but Ilhad's brief shake of the head stopped her. His eyes pointed to the end of the row. Right.

Naia tried not to betray her hesitation as she reached over and took one, selecting the smallest out of the lot. She could tell from the way Ilhad's eyes hovered on the stand that the choice didn't escape him. He didn't comment, though, as he reached over and took another staff, heavier and longer than hers.

Dear Sel, is he going to fight me himself? Ilhad was a man in his advanced years, definitely past his prime. Yet, in his own time he had been a legend in the Jaihar Order, his unmatched skill leading him to his current post. She was probably going to get her butt kicked very badly, no matter what she did.

"Attack me," Ilhad said.

Naia grasped her staff mid-grip. She expected Ilhad to match the move, or at least raise his weapon, but to her surprise he didn't do anything at all. He just stood there, leaning on his staff as if it was a walking stick, as if he needed it for support. His defenseless look made her hesitate. She had to remind herself that she'd just received a direct order from a senior she couldn't possibly disobey.

She raised her weapon and took a swing, aiming at his left, unprotected side. She committed enough strength to land a blow, yet also balanced it enough to pull back if he did something unexpected. Even so, she nearly missed the moment Ilhad shifted weight, tilting his staff into her path. Clashing into it felt like running into a wall at full speed. Only the fact that she was at least marginally prepared saved her from tumbling over.

She regrouped without changing stride, redirecting her attack to his other side, aiming low. This time, she didn't see Ilhad move at all. It felt more as if his staff just evaporated from her path, causing her to stumble – slightly, yet too much for the opponent she was facing. His blow came from an impossible direction, the tip of his staff connecting to the back of her legs just below the knees in a neat move that seemed far too slow and showy to fall for. Her feet flew out from underneath her, the ground coming up hard to meet her back.

Damn it.

She hated staffs, bulky and heavy, lacking all the neat elegance of the blades. But this fight with Ilhad sharply reminded her that no amount of fancy bladework she was learning made for a complete training without covering all the basics. Not if she strived to become one of the best.

She heaved a few breaths, then sprang to her feet.

"What did you find the most challenging just now?" Ilhad asked.

"I didn't know what to expect."

Ilhad nodded, as if something in her words answered an important question in his mind. "Expectations, yes. It's a problem for you when no blades are present, isn't it?"

"Yes, it is." Naia was surprised. She had never thought about it. Blades felt natural to her. Staffs didn't. Surely there was nothing complicated about it, was there?

"Let's try again," Ilhad said.

She nodded and stepped into position opposite him again.

She did better this time – at least in terms of staying on her feet. The improvement had little to do with technique, though. Mostly, unlike the first time, she felt more ready to face the unexpected. Still, after a series of thrusts and lunges, narrowly avoiding being knocked down several times, she managed to miss the moment Ilhad's forward thrust caught her under the wrist, twisting her staff right out of her grip. As its free end swayed out, Ilhad caught it in his off hand, pinning both staffs end-first into the ground and crossing them over her chest as he crowded her into the wall. A lock that could crush her ribs if he chose to press any harder. The thought didn't help at all.

She panted as she pressed away from him, unsure of what to do. Did he expect her to acknowledge defeat, or attempt to salvage the situation? She felt so utterly exhausted, made worse by the sight of Ilhad's unperturbed face. Dear Sel, he was probably sixty, at least. How could he still fight like this at his age?

She was recalling more rumors about him now. This man had a special talent for spotting weaknesses – even those of the top-ranked Shadowblades. This was why he took such effort to familiarize himself with everyone's combat styles. She supposed she should be flattered that she deserved his special attention, but she also realized that sparring with him was not all about training. With every blow, she was exposing her weaknesses to him, ones that later on could be used against her.

Ilhad held her in place for a moment longer, then lowered the staffs and stepped away.

"Let's try something different now." He pointed to the stand again, indicating a pair of sticks connected by a short chain. Naia frowned. She knew this one – nunchaku, a street weapon everyone always looked down upon, one almost never used on the main training grounds.

"But… this is a weapon for thieves and thugs," she said.

Ilhad's face remained still, but she could sense his scorn in the set of his shoulders, in the way his eyes narrowed slightly as he looked back at her.

"Did it ever occur to you that thieves and thugs may be choosing it for a reason?" he asked.

"Um… poverty?" It seemed plausible, at least. Everyone knew how expensive good blades were, even those that most warriors on the Jaihar grounds took for granted. She assumed a good pair of nunchaku would be much easier to make. Now that she looked at their perfectly polished wood, though, she started to have her doubts.

"I hope you didn't get the impression that the Jaihar skill is all about technique."

"Isn't it?" Naia frowned. If it wasn't about technique, what had she been doing here all this time?

"Technique is important," Ilhad said. "But not nearly as important as strategy and tactics. The weapons in this courtyard are all about that. As the next part of your training you'll need to familiarize yourself with every one of them."

"Every one?" Naia looked at the stands. There were dozens of different weapons here. How could she ever hope to even try every one?

"As part of your ranking," Ilhad said, "you would most certainly be asked to fight without rules, to change tactics and make quick choices between a multitude of weapons at your disposal. In these kinds of fights, the winner typically emerges based on wit and experience. Technique alone cannot carry you through."

Naia looked at the weapon stands again. If this was a test she was going to face at some point, she'd definitely need to learn everything she could about them.

Ilhad picked up a pair of nunchaku and tossed one to her. She barely had time to grip it when he swung his, a stick on a chain flying off his hand at an odd angle she completely didn't expect. *Aiming at my knees.* The realization came too late. Her feet tangled as she dodged, sliding from underneath her. She barely had time to regroup as she landed on her side, clutching her weapon uselessly in her hand.

Ilhad watched impassively as she scrambled up to her feet.

"Does anything about this defeat seem familiar to you?" he asked.

Aside from reinforcing my knowledge that you can kick my ass again and again? She did her best to keep resentment out of her voice. "I am not sure what you mean, Jai Ilhad."

"Remember our staff fight?"

"Yes."

"The way you fell, the first time?"

"Oh." He was probably referring to the way he knocked her feet from underneath her both times, even though she still didn't understand what he was driving at.

Ilhad straightened out his nunchaku to hold them out at full length. "You can think of them as a staff. One much more your style, short and flexible, with steel in it. A weapon like this would enable you to cut corners, literally. Incidentally, the orbens you asked about earlier are an extension of the same technique, only even more advanced."

Naia straightened out her own nunchaku, looking at them thoughtfully. She'd never thought of them this way, but strangely, the more she digested this new information, the more it made sense. Nunchaku were nothing like a staff, but when she tried to think of them as one, their seemingly disorderly movement acquired new logic, new sense.

"Here," Ilhad said. "Let me show you how they move."

She watched him go through a series of swings that seemed far too complicated for something she could ever achieve. He was moving slowly, giving her time to appreciate the technique. She did her best not to gape.

"With nunchaku," Ilhad said, "finesse and precision are no less important than with the blades. Perhaps more. Now, try for yourself."

She nodded, using her nunchaku to imitate the routine he just showed her, first slowly, then with accelerating speed. It was awkward at first, but once she realized the logic of it, the way each movement seemed to flow naturally into the next, it felt surprisingly good. As she lowered her hands and looked back at Ilhad, she caught approval in his gaze. Or did she only imagine it?

"Can we try again?" she asked.

Ilhad nodded.

This time, as he advanced on her, Naia no longer felt as helpless as before. Trying to emulate the movements he had shown her, she could feel the weapon acquire new power in her hands, the thick wooden rods snaking their way between his. More complex than with any straight weapons she had ever wielded, but once she got into the rhythm of it, it felt no less enjoyable.

When Ilhad lowered his nunchaku and stepped away, she felt a brief pang of regret, then excitement as she looked at the wealth of weapons they hadn't yet approached. *Dear Sel, before I am done with my training, would I truly be able to master every one?*

"You are relying too much on your instinct," Ilhad said. "Your natural ability has carried you this far, but it's not going to be enough if you don't extend yourself."

My natural ability. Naia raised her eyebrows. She didn't realize she had one. She showed promise, yes. She was able to catch up with her peers after only a couple of months of training and was ahead of many of them by now. But it was all because of hard work, not any special ability she had – wasn't it?

"I am not sure what you mean, Jai Ilhad," she said.

"I am referring to iron-sensing. It makes you better than average with steel. But every time we choose a weapon where steel doesn't predominate, you feel lost, don't you?"

Naia stared. Iron-sensing, the quality that came to the top

Jaihar after very intense training. Did she have it already? Was this why a staff, all-wood, was one of her worst challenges?

Ilhad nodded as he watched her. "You may have heard of my role in our Order, to identify warriors' strength and weaknesses. Your natural iron-sensing is both. It's your strength in a blade fight. But with a weapon like a staff it can become your handicap. Think of it as you go through the rest of your training here."

She didn't have time for a response before Ilhad raised his weapon again and gestured to the training floor.

DREAM

"You look tired," Mehtab said.

Naia hesitated. For the last few days she had been spending extra time on the range, sneaking to Ilhad's practice area during her breaks to try out some of the weapons there. She wanted to take full advantage of her lesson with Ilhad and go through everything he showed her while it was still fresh in her memory. Today had been especially exhausting, as she tried to emulate the movements of the staff in a number of flexing weapons. By the time she finished her day and made it to Mehtab's quarters, she felt so tired she could barely stand up straight.

Mehtab watched her knowingly. "Why don't you sit in this armchair and relax? Close your eyes. I will sing you an old Challimar song."

Naia nodded gratefully, sinking into the deep, soft seat. She stiffened, then relaxed as she felt Mehtab's fingers untie the string holding up her hair – now reaching down past her shoulders – and lower something heavy and cool against her skin. The necklace. She wasn't sure why Mehtab insisted that she wore it every time, but it did help the relaxation somehow.

She felt a pleasant void in her head as she wore it, so that Mehtab's soft words could sink in deeper, etching into her memory with no effort at all.

"I will sing to you of Xarimet," Mehtab said. "The legendary Challimar princess."

Her voice rose, surprisingly clear and powerful for the softness with which she usually spoke. She sang in an unfamiliar language, its strange reverberating consonants softened by the music. They flowed, blending into words that somehow bypassed Naia's consciousness, until she felt as if, without knowing the language, she could understand the song. Or maybe she was just making up her own words, based on Mehtab's stories, to the rhythm of the music?

Challimar, reigning over the sands.
Challimar, the Sel-blessed land.
Challimar, a beautiful dream.
I will defend you with my life.
Challimar, betrayed and destroyed.
Challimar will rule once again,
Led by our true queen, Xarimet,
Born from the ancient royal line…

Naia was aware that she couldn't possibly understand this song, but in her dream-like state this knowledge didn't seem to be important at all. Or perhaps she was already asleep, imagining it all?

Challimar, reigning over the sands…
I will defend you with my life.

She could almost hear the sound of the shifting sands, feel the heat of the desert sun on her face, its light penetrating her closed eyelids to fill her vision with a deep crimson color. *Blood...*

Our iron blood will rise like a tide,
And bring our enemies to ruin...

She was definitely dreaming now – or rather, day-dreaming, shifting realities, part of her still sitting in Mehtab's soft chair, another part far away, in a large hexagonal hall, its numerous windows on all sides overlooking a lush garden and the sands beyond.

Challimar, a desert gem,
Cradling Sel's divine light within...

She was seeing it as a bystander would, from the side of the room, her vision partially concealed by a layer of silky, semitransparent cloth. A veil? She was also rocking, as if someone was cradling her in their arms. The sight of a woman standing in the center of the hall made her heart stir with warmth.

My mother...

Where did that thought come from?

It was a peaceful scene, yet she couldn't escape a sense of danger lurking just under the surface. It tensed up the postures of the people lining the walls – some of them Chall, wearing royal yellow livery, some Zeg in their purple imperial colors. It infused the air, fragrant with rosemary and creosote, with a subtle tinge of steel. It enveloped the woman and the man in the center of the room – a Chall and a Zeg standing side by side. They were arguing, their abrupt gestures sending ripples through the hall and beyond.

The man stepped away. The woman moved to follow, then abruptly changed direction to approach the place where Naia stood – or was held and cradled like a baby by someone she couldn't quite see? *The veil. Am I a baby watching the scene from my wrappings?* The thought seemed odd, alien – as if purposely inserted into her head – yet it somehow clicked all the pieces into place. The awkward angle that shielded part of the hall from Naia's view. The warmth of the woman's hands, tucking in her wrappings. The rhythmic rocking that faltered as the scene in front of them rapidly changed pace. *Dear Sel, is this my childhood memory? Am I watching an actual scene from my past?*

The thought didn't have time to form in her head when the room exploded with weapons, all the guards whipping out blades, turning on each other. Through the windows, Naia could see dark shadows in the gardens outside, moving in through the gates and archways, laying the grounds to ruin. The regal woman reached forward, her movement cut short by a blow from the nearest guard. *Mother. Dear Sel, no!* Naia had no idea where this thought came from, and she no longer cared. Tears streamed down her cheeks. Screams echoed around her, blood streaming over the veil covering Naia's face, filling her vision, drowning out all the images with its deep red color. *Iron. So much iron, going to waste.*

Naia gasped and opened her eyes.

In the semi-dark room, the glow of the fireplace in front of her seemed unnaturally bright. Its heat settled over her like a blanket, licking her face, invasive like an unwanted touch. She shrank away from it, sinking deeper into the pillows at her back. Mehtab's song had stopped – a long time ago, it seemed, for no matter how hard she tried, Naia couldn't possibly recall any sounds.

She started when she realized Mehtab was sitting close by, at the side of the fireplace, so still that she looked like one of the carvings on the fireplace's frame.

"I… I must have fallen asleep," Naia said.

Mehtab smiled. "You certainly did. Looked like you needed it too."

"I guess so." Naia couldn't help feeling uneasy. She had never had a dream as vivid as this. It felt so real, down to the metallic smell of blood that still clung to her nostrils. She touched her face, relieved to find that the slick moisture coating it was just sweat, not the blood and tears she imagined.

"I had a strange dream," she said.

"Tell me about it."

"I… I think I was a baby, watching my mother get murdered."

"Dreams are a strange thing," Mehtab said. "Do you remember your parents?"

"No. The Jaihar trainees are chosen from abandoned children and orphans."

"Or children willingly given up for training."

Naia glanced away. She knew some parents did that, in exchange for the gold the Jaihar promised to those whose offspring achieved a high rank. She didn't blame those families. Many of them had too many mouths to feed. At the very least, Jaihar training, even for the lower ranks, ensured regular meals and a roof over one's head, as well as a steady guard job for the rest of their lives.

She had never been told how she ended up in the Jaihar Order. Most trainees came from orphanages, or had been donated anonymously by their families. In any case, it didn't seem to matter, did it?

"The woman who got killed," she said. "She was a queen, I think."

"What did the place you saw look like?"

"A very bright room. Hexagonal, with many windows looking out into the garden. It was lined with guards, both Chall and Zeg. They seemed unarmed at first – and then some of them took out concealed blades and killed everyone else."

"Except the emperor."

Naia's eyes widened as she remembered the dark-eyed Zeg man she saw talking to the woman. He seemed to be the one in charge. "Was that the emperor?"

"His Imperial Majesty, Shabaddin Selim. Or so I assume, from the scene you are describing. Did you take a good look at him?"

"Yes. Young, richly dressed. In my dream, I thought of him as an ally. But when he ordered the attack, I…" She paused, unsure how to continue. The vision she saw didn't make sense, no more than the conversation they were having right now.

"Is this how it really happened?" she asked nevertheless.

"What?"

"The Challimar Royal Massacre."

Mehtab took time to respond, her eyes fixed on the play of the flames. "Some say so. Others speak of the betrayal happening outside the royal chamber. No one knows for sure, though. Only one thing is certain. Challimar's royal palace was laid to ruins that day, the queen, her closest kin, and all her loyal guards, slain. No one escaped."

Naia hesitated. "Before I fell asleep, you were going to tell me about Princess Xarimet. Was she in this dream somewhere?"

Mehtab glanced away. The shadows folding over her face briefly showed an odd change of expression. Was it regret? Triumph? Sadness? It shifted away too fast to tell.

"Dreams are an odd thing," Mehtab said. "Some say they reflect reality, each an experience you've once lived through. Others say they have no meaning at all. In this case, your dream might have been inspired by my song, even though you probably couldn't understand the words. I'm afraid I don't have an answer to you beyond that."

Naia nodded. It was useless to engage in any guessing. The Jaihar trainees were kept carefully away from any possibility of learning about their true parentage. In most cases, even the Jaihar seniors had no idea. Most definitely, though, if anyone here was aware of any connection between Naia and the Challimar Royal Massacre, she would probably have been brought up as someone important, not a problem trainee who nearly failed even a Har ranking.

"Tell me about Xarimet," she said.

Mehtab shifted in her seat. "Remember when I spoke to you about those who want to restore the old glory of Challimar and lay everything else to ruin?"

"Yes." *The fanatics.* They were always around, in one form or another. She even heard of crazy religious sects who worshipped Irfat instead of Sel. She supposed there was no avoiding the fact that some of the Chall would think so categorically about the nation who drove their once-great kingdom to ruin. The only thing that still made her uncomfortable about this was the lingering uncertainty on where Mehtab stood with regards to all this. Every time she talked about it, she seemed so involved...

"There are legends out there," Mehtab said. "'Prophecies' they call them, even though prophecies are impossible, of course. They say that one day a great Chall princess will be sent by Sel to lead Challimar to victory. She will be both an Ironblood and a direct descendant of the royal line, combining her birthright as the heir to the throne with the most cherished Chall ability of bonding with imlar. There are many legends and songs about her, telling of her arrival in the kingdom's darkest hour, of how she will challenge the tyranny that oppresses her people to unite and save everyone. These legends precede Shabaddin and his dynasty, but just recently more and more people are starting to talk about them again."

"How old are these legends you speak of?" Naia asked.

"Many centuries old. Why?"

"Challimar's oppression by tyranny, if you can call it that, is relatively recent. Many centuries ago, Challimar was the strongest of all the kingdoms. How could people be singing about oppression that long ago?"

Mehtab's face relaxed into a smile.

"You are a good student," she said. "You've been learning well, to spot the discrepancy. And yes, the fact that the legend of Xarimet is that old is amazing, isn't it?"

The street outside the Daljeer serai looked unusually crowded. As Naia paused at the edge of the small plaza, trying to think of a faster way back to the Jaihar grounds, she noticed many eyes following her with an interest that made her uneasy. She quickly glanced over her appearance and gear. Was something out of place? It didn't seem so. Why then were they all watching her?

It took another look to see that many people here had an odd eye shade, richly speckled with various shades of gold. *Desert-kissed*. Was this some sort of Chall gathering?

She tried her best to ignore them as she stepped into the

crowd. She expected the people in front of her to part and let her through, but no one seemed in a hurry to get out of her way. Worse, as she tried to squeeze between them, they backed off into tighter rows that left the space around her empty, but made it impossible to proceed.

Naia stopped, aware how she was now a center of a small crowd that left her with no place to go. People facing her didn't seem hostile, but they all had a detached look about them, the kind she had seen before in the faces of pilgrims gathered for prayer. Their gazes held reverence as they watched her every move, as if she were some sort of religious relic.

Her mind raced.

Should she try to talk to them?

Should she fight her way through?

She turned to the nearest man, wearing a pale blue thawb and a headscarf that indicated his affiliation with the city temple. He looked middle-aged, with an air of authority around him that suggested he was someone of influence.

"Is there a problem?" she asked.

The man's lips trembled, his eyes widening in disbelief, as if he were being addressed by the Holy Prophet himself.

"No problem, um, my lady," he stumbled.

Naia's eyes widened too as she stared at him. *My lady?* Did this man really just address her this way, despite her Jaihar training leathers, despite the array of weapons she wore that should have left absolutely no questions about her occupation?

Was he delusional? Or perhaps this was some sort of madman parade?

"Let me through," she said.

The crowd in front of her parted instantly, but the people in the back pressed in, making the obstacle even denser than before.

Naia hesitated, seized by a rising alarm. Should she try to retreat back to the Daljeer compound? Her eyes darted in that direction, finding the way blocked just as decisively as the one in front. Should she try to command, or reason with them, again? It seemed hopeless, with the way everyone was looking at her with detached expressions, as if entranced. What was she going to do? She couldn't possibly fight unarmed citizens. Yet, barring that possibility, she couldn't move anywhere at all.

The crowd pressed on, leaving her less and less space. Hands were reaching out to her, as if determined to – what? Touch her? Rip away a piece of her clothes? Her flesh? She lowered her hand over the hilt of her dagger, wondering if wielding it sheathed would give her the necessary leverage. She really didn't want to harm anyone here. Perhaps if she leapt on top of the crowd, she could run over their shoulders and heads and climb onto the nearest building before they had a chance to pull her down? Or should she try to snake under their feet?

Just then, she heard a commotion on the other end of the crowd, the sounds of argument rippling through. Heads turned, shifting the attention away from her.

Relief washed over her as she saw the crowd parting before a group of men wearing Jaihar leathers. She was about to rush toward them through the gap, then stopped as she saw the nearest man's face. *Valmad. Three hells.* Several Har trainers walked beside him – probably out for a drink in the city.

She hadn't talked to any of them since she'd learned about the exact role Valmad played in her fight with Ishim. The last thing she needed was to face him right now, when she was alone and he had several trainers likely to back him up in a potential confrontation.

Her eyes darted the other way, searching for an escape route, but the crowd behind her was even thicker. The encounter seemed inevitable, so she lifted her head and walked forward, straight toward the Har.

Valmad stilled as he saw her, his face slowly lighting up with a pinkish red color. As Naia attempted to side-step him, he shifted too, his burly shape decisively blocking her way.

"Look who is here," he said. "A Jai wannabe."

Naia took care not to look hostile. Valmad had six trainers with him, all the bad sort. No matter how much she had learned in the past, if a fight erupted, they were going to win. Off the Jaihar grounds, with no one else to intervene, this could end really badly for her.

She lifted her chin. "I'm on my way back to the stronghold, Har Valmad." *And I don't have to answer to you anymore.* She kept in the last thought as she looked at the trainers gathering behind him, the sight of their familiar faces echoing with a hollowness into her gut. All of Valmad's cronies, certain to take his side if the situation erupted out of control.

"Let me through," she said.

Valmad smirked. "Why don't you ask your countrymen here to part for you? They seem helpful, don't they?"

My countrymen. Never before had Valmad referred to her Chall origins. Naia looked at the human wall around them, staring at her with expressions that made her doubt they were fully aware of the conversation. They were keeping their distance, but not dissipating, leaving her in a confined space with too many Har.

"So, the Jai didn't kick you out yet?" Valmad said.

Naia squared her shoulders, measuring him up and down with her eyes. If he was going to challenge her, she should think of ways to confront him effectively. She could probably take him down with a quick blow – if she acted fast enough to surprise him – but it was still too close of a call. Worse, such an attack would leave her open to the others, who would most certainly overpower her, no matter what.

What would Karrim do in her place? The thought seemed far-fetched. No one in their right mind would challenge Karrim to a street fight, if only because of his reputation.

"No," she said. "My training's going well, in fact. I am learning a lot about combat."

She didn't mean for it to sound like a threat, just a reminder that her skill now was much better than before. Yet when she saw Valmad's lowered hand clench into a fist, she realized that her words had just brought the situation one step closer to the edge. His gesture evoked the worst of her memories from *that* day, when she got into a fight with Ishim. The pain. The blackout. The agony of waking up in a healers' sanctuary and living through the recovery, the longest two months of her life. Her muscles tensed up as she flexed her arms, ready to act at the merest sign of danger.

"You think you are better than us, don't you?" Valmad stepped closer, so that she could smell the drink on his breath.

Well, this kind of a state would probably make him an easier opponent. But it also made the fight even more likely. She looked away, considering a leap over the crowd after all, and saw a movement on the other side, a group approaching them from the opposite direction. Her eyes widened when she recognized Tami, surrounded by a group of young men.

Tami smiled as she saw Naia, pushing her way forward until she and her companions surrounded Naia in a tight ring. On purpose or not, this move placed them directly into Valmad's path, with both Tami and Naia safely out of the Har's way.

165

Naia let out a breath. No matter how drunk, Valmad would be unlikely to attack a civilian – or a whole group of them in this case. He'd likely recognize Tami, though. She hoped it wouldn't create more problems for the girl.

"What are you doing here, Tami?" Naia said in a half-whisper.

"We were just passing by." Tami's eyes drifted to her companions. "On the way to the Merchants' Hill. Why don't you come with us?"

Naia threw a restrained glance at the Har, watching her tensely. The crowd of fanatics around them receded, as if seeing Naia in new company had successfully dispelled whatever it was that possessed them to pursue her in the first place.

"Sure, thanks," she said.

Tami placed a hand on her arm as she maneuvered past the Har, keeping inside the ring of young men. Over her shoulder Naia saw Valmad shuffle in indecision, watching their retreat.

No one spoke again until they were walking along a side street, the young men still surrounding them on all sides, like a unit of bodyguards.

"I appreciate the rescue," Naia said. Her glance, encompassing all of them, was answered by many smiles and nods that reinforced her certainty that this meeting was not accidental. "I would love to know, though, how you all happened to arrive at the plaza at this particular time."

Tami shrugged. "Simple. When Jai Karrim learned about what Har Valmad did to you, he mobilized many around the city to keep an eye on you."

Naia's eyes widened. "He did?"

"He cares about you."

No, he doesn't. Naia looked away. Tami couldn't possibly

know these things. Still, warmth washed over her at the mere suggestion.

Even from afar, Karrim continued to watch over her. She owed him everything. She couldn't even begin to think of how she could ever repay him.

They turned a corner and walked into the busy area on the outskirts of the market.

"I, um, I think I can make it the rest of the way without escort," Naia said.

"We'll walk you back all the way," Tami said, her quiet but authoritative glance answered by nods from the young men around her.

Naia frowned. When did Tami acquire such power? This was certainly a big change from the timid young girl she remembered. "I don't think that is necessary."

Tami laughed. "Oh, yes, it is. In case you're wondering, my father is in charge of the city militia. He feels indebted to Jai Karrim for helping me out and protecting other servants from the Har. The least we can do is return the favor by making sure you are safe. Jai Karrim certainly wouldn't take it well if something bad happened to you."

Naia didn't respond. She knew that this simple statement shouldn't seem so meaningful to her.

It had been a year since she spent her one single day with Karrim, and she still couldn't stop thinking about him. She should do her best to forget all about him as soon as she possibly could.

GRADUATION GIFT

Mehtab was smiling, the mysterious gleam in her eyes revealing that the older woman had a surprise in store. Naia felt intrigued. After three years of tutoring, nearing the end of her training, it should be time for Mehtab to run out of surprises, but the older woman kept proving otherwise.

As Naia walked in, Mehtab pointed to a small crate tucked into the corner, one Naia did not notice until then.

"What is it?" she asked.

Mehtab batted her eyes conspiratorially. "Think of it as a graduation gift."

"A gift?"

"One you probably won't be able to keep, but yes." Mehtab propped the lid open, revealing a layer of lush yellow silk piled inside. Before Naia could ask a question, she pushed the cloth aside, its shimmering waves spilling over the top of the crate onto the floor.

The object she held up caught Naia's full attention.

It looked like a delicate lace bodice, except for the way it held the form stiffly, as if unable to bend at all. Other clues betrayed its make too – the metal glint, the tremor in Mehtab's arms, straining from holding up its weight, the familiar wing-like patterns that resembled the necklace Naia wore for her regular lessons. She found herself longing for the bodice, for the calm she was somehow certain it was going to bring if she was allowed to don it – the same kind of calm she always felt when she wore her necklace. She reached for it, and Mehtab stepped forward and put it into her hands.

"The Challimar queen's imlar armor," Mehtab said. "I also have the wrist and leg guards that go with it. Here." She stepped back toward the crate.

Naia shifted the bodice in her hands, admiring the delicate metalwork, the patterns that made the ornate piece, despite its weight, appear like an elaborate jewelry item.

"Try it on," Mehtab said.

Naia looked at her in disbelief. "Really?"

"Why do you think I went to all the trouble? It looks as if it'll fit you just fine."

It did. As Naia clasped the breastplate on, its weight enfolded her naturally, fitting every line, every curve, every unprotected space, as if it were crafted for her. Well, perhaps her breasts didn't quite fill out the chest area, but it was close enough. She felt powerful as she donned it, more so than she had felt before in her life.

Mehtab handed her the wrist and ankle guards, wide bracelets that closed around her limbs, adding a pleasant measure of weight. Naia closed her eyes briefly, enjoying the feeling.

"And now, the necklace." Mehtab's voice came from behind, soothing and soft.

Naia kept her eyes closed, enjoying the familiar feeling of the necklace settling over her chest. A calm, like one she had never felt before, filled her.

Mehtab laughed. "You look like you are enjoying it."

"I am."

"This was the purpose of my gift. But before you fully give in to the feeling, I want to show you something else."

She held out a flat, elongated box, about four feet in length. As Naia watched, Mehtab pushed the lid open.

Inside was a set of blades.

Naia stared.

Their hilts were carved of ivory, or something very much like it, their flowing patterns making Naia feel a strange longing to hold them in her hands. And the blades...

Shorter than her regular swords, they were made of semitransparent yellow material that looked like no metal Naia had ever seen. Peering deeper into them, she could make out some sort of darker core, a rod that ran along the entire blade's length to the tip.

"They're made of reinforced imlarite stone." Mehtab's voice rang with hidden pride, as if she had personally participated in crafting them.

Naia heaved a long breath. Mehtab referred to these stones as precious. The one in Naia's necklace was no bigger than a thumbnail, yet Mehtab always handled it with the care that spoke of its high value. These blades, three feet long and half a palm wide, were not nearly as transparent or radiant, but the stone they were carved from – a single piece, as far as Naia could tell – had to have been enormously large in comparison.

"They must be priceless," she said.

"They are. Only a few of these blades were ever made. Yet, you can see that the stone is not nearly as clear or flawless as the one set into your necklace, nor does it have the fire of the one I wear. This variety of imlarite, partially reinforced by the imlar ore infused into it, was never valued for jewelry, but could be crafted into other objects. These blades feel just like regular metal – perhaps heavier, but no less versatile."

Naia reached out and ran her hand along the blades' smooth surface, then felt the edge, razor-sharp like the best steel weapons she handled. She wanted to draw back, but her hand inadvertently continued on, to the flowing line of the hilt. She closed her fingers around it, enjoying the way it fit into her palm, smooth and responsive as if it belonged in her hold.

"Try them out," Mehtab said.

Naia picked the swords out of the box. They felt heavier than she expected, but their perfect balance made up for it. After a few experimental swings, wielding them seemed as natural as her regular blades.

"Go on," Mehtab urged. "Do one of your routines with them."

Naia looked at the older woman. Was there some extra eagerness behind Mehtab's tone, or was Naia only imagining it? She hesitated, longing to do as Mehtab asked, yet held back by this extra emotion she couldn't quite place.

"How did you get them?" she asked.

Mehtab shrugged. "The Daljeer possess many Challimar artifacts. I had our scholars trace these and bring them here."

"Why?"

"So that I could show them to you."

"Isn't this a lot of trouble to go to, for my sake?"

Mehtab glanced away briefly. "It's not just for your sake, actually. It's for the benefit of the Daljeer too, even though I am not at liberty to give you any further information. You will learn it all, in due time."

"And when is that, exactly?"

"After your ranking, perhaps?"

Naia nodded. All her trainers believed her to be ready. More than, judging by the tasks she was being given lately; from Omar's obscure hints, she suspected they would be setting her up with the kind of tests that could potentially qualify her for the top. She didn't dwell on it too much, so as not to get her hopes up, but she was definitely going to do her best.

"In any case," Mehtab said, "I felt it would be appropriate to let you try these out before the end of our sessions here."

"The end?" Naia raised her eyebrows. She had a very definite idea about the amount of training needed to complete her Jaihar ranking, but she never thought about her lessons with Mehtab coming to an end. In fact, while the older woman was teaching her a lot about Challimar, these lessons were so unlike any of Naia's regular training that she had come to think of them as leisure, the rare time when she could relax and let go. Besides, Mehtab was one of the few women Naia had ever spent any time with. The affectionate warmth she expressed from time to time evoked longing for this kind of love – motherly, the type Naia had never experienced before. Naia had come to crave and cherish these interactions.

Mehtab laughed. "You look forlorn."

"Well, if I can't see you again–"

"No one said that. I'll still be here. In fact, there's a distinct possibility we may be spending even more time together after you're ranked."

"More?"

"Like I said, I am not at liberty to tell you anything right now. So, why don't we just do our best to make the most out of today's session? Try to move in this armor, with these blades.

After the trouble I've gone through to get them here, I would love to see them in action."

Naia had almost forgotten she was still wearing the armor. It felt so comfortable, despite the extra weight. She raised the blades, flipping them both backward parallel to the arms, so that as she moved she would not feel as constrained in the confines of the room.

She did a simple routine, one that took only a few minutes but enabled her to test the blades' full capacity. They were so perfectly balanced it was easy to forget that these were in any way different from the normal weapons she used on the practice range. After a few more steps, their weight settled into her hold so well that she could anticipate them with every muscle. Odd how she could sense these blades, made of stone, just as well as she sensed regular steel. Even better, maybe. Was it because of the imlar infused into them? Or the fact that imlarite was akin to it?

She felt regret when the routine came to an end. Her breath was slightly uneven, but for the life of her she couldn't remember exerting herself enough to achieve it. The blades seemed to have some extra effect on her – calming, like the imlar armor and necklace she was wearing.

She turned to Mehtab, the older woman's dazed look telling her the routine she just did must have been impressive. By this stage in her training, she was used to this reaction from observers, even some of the Jai trainers on the upper grounds. But it was still odd to see someone like Mehtab, the woman who acted so superior all the time, succumb to the effect.

"They feel so natural," she said. "As good as regular steel." *Better.* She knew these were her emotions speaking, not logic. Stone blades, however well-crafted, couldn't possibly be better than steel. They were heavier, for sure. Was this why her breath was so uneven after the routine?

"Why would anyone make blades out of stone?" she wondered.

Mehtab smiled. "Do you remember what I told you about imlar?"

"You said that it's too soft to craft into weapons all by itself, even if it does make for comfortable armor."

"And?"

"And that it attracts metal."

"Exactly. Let's think of this metal-attracting property for a moment."

"What about it?"

"Imagine you are wearing this armor and wielding your regular blades."

Naia thought back to the time when she first wore the necklace, how Mehtab's pin latched onto it so forcefully, how all her blades shifted in their sheaths at its mere proximity.

"I guess I would have a problem keeping control of my blades," she said.

"Yes, you would."

"So would my enemy, though."

"Right. This is why imlar armor is so effective as protection against steel. One couldn't possibly stab you at all in this gear. The armor would deflect any such attempt without you even trying."

"You mean...?"

Mehtab smiled. "Yes. The armor affects steel, but not stone. You had no trouble at all just now wearing this armor and wielding imlarite blades. If this happened in a battle, you would be the only one able to do this, while everyone attacking you would lose control of their blades."

"Something like this could make one invincible, or very nearly so."

"Indeed. Especially one with the Ironblood skill. When Challimar royalty wore imlar armor, their Redcloak guards carried imlarite blades to protect them. Even their arrowheads were made of imlar, so that they could find their way into the enemy's armor with hardly any need to aim. This was why imlar was banned after Challimar fell. No one wanted this kind of power roaming around."

Naia looked at her thoughtfully. "A group of highly skilled fighters armed this way could defeat an army."

"Yes."

"But still, Challimar lost the Succession War."

"They were betrayed. The chronicles named this event Blood Council, a peace gathering that turned into a bloodbath where many Challimar nobles and royals were slaughtered. Where do you think Emperor Shabaddin got his idea for the Royal Massacre?"

If so, it's a wonder that Challimar royals fell for it again. Naia didn't voice the thought. It was terrible to think of the fate that had befallen Challimar, the kingdom she now felt strangely bonded to – not only by blood, but through everything Mehtab had told her during their lessons.

"The Chall must be feeling truly unsettled about it," she said quietly.

A shadow ran over Mehtab's face. "They do. And, they are in need of justice. Who knows, maybe we could see it served within our lifespan?"

Again, Naia felt odd at the undertones in the older woman's voice. It was as if the fate of Challimar was somehow threaded to Mehtab's own, making everything she was saying more personal than it appeared.

"What do you mean by justice?" Naia was looking directly at Mehtab when she asked the question, and she noticed a slight twitch at the corner of the woman's mouth, a cruel fold she had never seen before.

"There's only one way to serve justice in this case," Mehtab said. "Everyone involved in the conspiracy, everyone who had anything to do with the demise of the Challimar royals, must suffer the same fate they did."

The woman spoke calmly, and Naia chose to focus on this stoicism rather than on the chilling meaning behind Mehtab's words. Inadvertently, her thoughts wandered back to the dream she had previously – the giant hexagonal room, Chall and Zeg gathered there in their best holiday finery… She cut the memory off when it came to the blood, the chaos that ensued as she watched the scene from behind the veil of her baby wrappings. *It can't be my real memory. That is not possible.*

"But that would mean nearly everyone important in the Zeg Empire," she said. "Every noble family."

Mehtab smiled. "Some think it would be only fair. Royalty for royalty, chaos for chaos, destruction for destruction."

Naia peered into her face. "You *can't* possibly feel this way."

Mehtab laughed. "Of course I don't. What do you take me for, a bloodthirsty maniac?"

Naia smiled too, trying to reassure herself that this was simply a joke, ignoring the feeling of foreboding that rose in her chest. The Challimar armor suddenly seemed heavy. She felt the urge to pull it off, but as she turned to place the imlarite blades back into their box, Mehtab laid a hand on her arm.

"You looked so amazing as you practiced with them," she

said. "Why don't you do a bit more? I can sing you a Challimar song while you do."

Naia hesitated. Mehtab had a beautiful voice, but her songs tended to bring disturbing visions. Admittedly, these visions always came when Naia was sitting still and feeling tired, which tended to be the case during their lessons. Nothing like this should happen during a weapon practice, should it?

"All right," she said.

She settled for another short routine, a series of lunges and blocks designed for testing the weapons' reach. As Mehtab's voice rose in a beautiful, outlandish melody, Naia's mind slowly departed, sinking into a semi-trance that resembled a dream, yet felt far more vivid than the reality around her.

A giant hexagonal hall. Sunlight washing in through a row of large windows overlooking a lush garden below.

Echoes of clashing weapons ringing in her ears.

Men fighting beside her, wearing armor and blades similar to hers.

She is leading them into battle, enemies falling to her blades left and right. Their screams echo under the hollow, vaulted ceiling. Rich royal robes, soaked in crimson. Dark eyes, going lifeless with each strike.

Shahgar, Chall... Shahgar!

The war cry lingered in Naia's mind, as she slowly drifted back into awareness. It seemed familiar, somehow. Had she heard it before, in one of Mehtab's songs? Was it a command, one that drove every Chall guard in the hall to regroup around her, to fight by her side? Their unity, the ease with which her stone blades sank into the flesh of their enemies, filled her with excitement, making her spirit soar like the high notes of Mehtab's beautiful song...

Soon I will get my Jaihar ranking. And then, I will become a true defender of Challimar.

Naia wasn't sure where the thought came from.

THE BRIEFING

Karrim stopped beside the window of the headmaster's audience hall, looking into the training courtyard outside. It was the same one where he first met Naia, almost three years ago. The view afforded to him right now was probably somewhat similar to what the Jaihar seniors could have observed from this window back then, if anyone had been watching. Naia, fighting a Shadowblade. Except that there were important differences this time. The Shadowblade – Hamed – was, by the looks of it, using his full skill set. More, at times it also seemed as if he was having trouble keeping up.

Karrim leaned against the window frame, enjoying the view. The change in Naia since the last time he saw her was amazing. Her talent, brought into full bloom, amounted to a truly breathtaking effect. Dear Sel, despite all the efforts to forget their encounter three years ago, it all came back as he saw her. He longed to be down there with her, blade in hand. He knew he should never allow himself to entertain these thoughts.

He turned to Arsat and Ilhad, standing by his side with distracted expressions on their faces.

"When is her ranking tournament?" he asked.

"Tomorrow," Arsat said.

Karrim frowned. The Jaihar ranking tournaments were usually performed with pomp, in an event at the main arena that gathered a large audience from the city. This went well with the Jaihar Order's official image – an invincible force trained to defend order in the empire.

"I haven't heard of any announcements," he said.

"None were issued. Her ranking will be a closed event, attended only by our top command."

"Why?"

Arsat's eyes trailed to Ilhad. "Because of the assignment she is lined up for. It requires full incognito, under a very public disguise. The less is known about her, even within these walls, the better."

Karrim looked at his seniors curiously, trying to ignore a sudden sense of foreboding. Naia's secret assignment was none of his business. After he'd done his best for her three years ago, she was no longer his responsibility.

"We'd like you to be the one to fight her in her ranking tournament, Jai Karrim," Arsat said.

Karrim's eyes widened. "Me?"

"Unless, of course, you are too tired from your journey."

Karrim kept a straight face. Only someone very familiar with Arsat's style could catch the irony in his tone – even at times like this, when it was so plainly obvious from the man's words. The trip from Zegmeer, where Karrim's duties as the head of the emperor's bodyguards were mostly ceremonial, took about a day of leisurely riding. The only thing Karrim felt tired from right now was boredom. Ever since His Majesty's health took a turn for the worst, all the Jaihar Dozen ever did was stand around looking smart in their leathers and cloaks, or sneak out to the training range at the back of the palace grounds.

"I am not tired at all, Jai Arsat," he said.

"Good." Arsat turned away from the window. "After we're done here, Jai Ilhad and Jai Surram will take you down to the combat grounds for a briefing. But first, I'd like you to come into my study."

Karrim tried not to engage in any more guessing as he followed the headmaster through the door at the far end of the hall. Still, it took effort to hide his surprise at finding the room occupied by the most unlikely person Karrim could imagine: Dal Gassan, the head of the Daljeer Circle, the man he had seen in Zegmeer only days ago.

Well, the man's presence here was probably not that unusual, given that the Daljeer and the Jaihar did a lot of business together. With this knowledge, Karrim should probably not be surprised at the man's ease as he leaned into the visitors' chair with the look of someone who felt fully at home here. It was just that when they last saw each other at the emperor's court, Gassan had given him no indication they were both headed to the Jaihar Stronghold right away.

Karrim took care not to show any reaction as he stepped deeper into the room. The air here carried musty smells of tapestries and old parchment, reminding him of his favorite childhood days in the Order's library, before his talent with weapons brought on training so intense that he couldn't afford the leisure anymore. Karrim took a full breath of it as he walked to the indicated place, next to a fully set shatranj board.

"Are you familiar with this gambit, Jai Karrim?" Gassan asked.

Karrim looked closer, noting the complex layout. The game

was at its start, just a few moves in, with most of the pieces still on the board.

"I believe they call it 'black pawn debut'," he said.

"They do. They also call it the trickster attack, based on the way it tends to look so innocent until it's too late."

Karrim nodded. The emperor and all his advisers were fond of shatranj. As the head of the imperial bodyguards Karrim had to observe numerous matches at court. It helped to beat the boredom, not to mention becoming more familiar with the court politics. The conversations conducted during these matches tended to be far less inhibited than those that took place in the throne room. This was probably one of the reasons everyone in the emperor's closest circle loved to refer to shatranj moves when talking about matters of state.

"It might help our conversation," Gassan went on, "if I told you that I am the one who invented this gambit, about three years ago, during one of my visits with Jai Arsat."

Karrim raised his eyebrows. He knew that Arsat's fondness for the game seconded that of the emperor, but he had no idea that Gassan was his regular partner – one, apparently, good enough to invent a major gambit that had inflamed the minds of all the experts at court.

"I'm impressed," he said truthfully.

"Thank you, Jai Karrim."

"I must assume, however, that we are not here to discuss shatranj, are we?"

Gassan smiled. "Not exactly, no. We're here to apprise you of an upcoming situation at the imperial court."

"Go on."

"Three years ago," Gassan said, "Jai Arsat accepted a down payment from the Daljeer to secure your Order's services for a highly unconventional mission that strikes at the very heart of the empire. It came about because of His Majesty's illness, discovered by our physicians in its early stages. You are well aware of it by now, I believe."

"I am." *In more detail than you can possibly imagine.* As a healer, Gassan probably knew what it meant to stay by the bedside of a very sick man, to watch him wasting away among the court who hated him beyond limits, tasked with his safety and wellbeing. Karrim hoped his next assignment would be much more straightforward. He could use the challenge of taking on an army of foothill bandits, or something else equally entertaining, right now.

"How well are you familiar with the procedure of the formal succession contest, Jai Karrim?" Gassan asked.

Karrim shrugged. "As well as anyone, I believe."

"There's no such thing as 'anyone' when it comes to politics."

"True." Karrim had no idea what Gassan was driving at, an unsettling feeling he didn't like at all. "From what I know, the contest can be evoked only if succession is uncertain. Not the case here, given that Crown Prince Ramaz has an undisputable right to the throne."

"I'm sure you meant to say 'undisputed', Jai Karrim," Gassan said.

"Is there a difference?"

"Oh, but there is. A very important one." Gassan held a dramatic pause, giving Karrim plenty of time to sift through a number of possible scenarios in his mind. He settled for the most likely one, even though saying it out loud made him feel like a fool.

"If something happens to Ramaz, Prince Zewal is the next, followed by Prince Yusaf. More or less the same, as far as prospects for the empire go. You'd have to kill all three to bring up the possibility of a contest, but even then–"

"What if it's someone else altogether?" Gassan asked.

Karrim sensed a change of mood in the room. It was a genuine question this time, at least where the Jaihar seniors were concerned.

"If you have anything to tell me, Dal Gassan," he said, "why don't you just say it, straight up? I'm not a fan of theatrics."

Gassan nodded. "Very well then. My plan is to evoke the succession contest that would ultimately pass the throne to a different candidate, one we believe to be far more dependable than any of the immediate heirs."

"Who?" To the best of Karrim's knowledge, there was no such person in the imperial family. After three years at court he was feeling sick of the lot.

"Before I tell you, I must ask for your vow of silence."

"I can't give you one," Karrim said. "My duty as part of the Jaihar Dozen supersedes all else. If my vow ever comes into contradiction with the emperor's safety–"

"It won't."

"Still. All I can offer is my word that I won't speak of it unless his life is at stake."

"Not good enough."

"It is," Arsat put in. "Jai Karrim is a man of his word."

Gassan held a pause. "Very well. Are you familiar with Prince Halil?"

"Halil?"

"Do I sense disapproval, Jai Karrim?"

"Not really, no. I barely know the man." *And that's the problem, in this case.* In fact, Karrim was having trouble recalling the prince's appearance. The son of a lower concubine, Halil was rarely seen in the courtiers' halls. To Karrim's knowledge, he was both too young and too mellow to be a serious contender for the throne.

"We are charging the Jaihar Order with the task of putting him on the throne," Gassan said.

"How, exactly?"

"By sending one of your warriors to impersonate the only person who can legally challenge the imperial succession after Shabaddin dies. The royal heir of Challimar."

Karrim frowned. "You're bloody serious, aren't you?"

"Oh, yes."

"So, who have you lined up as your lucky victim?"

"Someone that we hope, come tomorrow, will be your newest ranked warrior. Naia."

Naia. A chill ran down Karrim's spine as he saw a smile of approval on the headmaster's face. "A bad idea. Very bad. Even if she performs brilliantly at her ranking tournament tomorrow, an assignment of this magnitude requires the kind of experience she wouldn't acquire for years."

"Her youth is an asset, actually. We need someone who hasn't been on any assignments before. She is also a perfect fit for this role in a number of other details you don't really need to know right now."

"What if she fails her ranking tomorrow?"

"It doesn't really matter. She is ready."

Inadvertently, Karrim's eyes trailed back to the shatranj board. The black pawn debut. As far as he remembered the gambit, the black pawn did reach the end of the board to become a queen, but had to be sacrificed later on to defeat the enemy's shah. Prince Ramaz, he assumed, if one wanted to get lost in the parallels.

"I assume I am being briefed right now because I am needed for this assignment somehow," he said. "So, what do you want me to do?"

"Naia's arrival at the imperial palace," Arsat said, "will be timed to the emperor's death – the event that will also, effectively, end your service at court until the new emperor can be crowned. We want you to assist her in any way you can, without making your acquaintance with her officially known. To watch her back, so to speak."

Watch her back. Karrim would certainly do his best at it, even if he doubted it could make a difference in the hellstorm likely to erupt after her arrival.

He turned to Gassan. "I hope you've made damn sure no one discovers who she really is."

"Meaning what?"

"An imposter, with a very large target on her back."

"You insult me with your doubts, Jai Karrim. Of course we did."

"How?"

Gassan chuckled. "Have you noticed any unusual rumors lately, Jai Karrim?"

"I hear rumors constantly, yes."

"Ones about Challimar, perhaps?"

Karrim's skin prickled. There *was* one rumor that had become particularly insistent, now that the topic came up. "Are you referring to the legend of Princess Xarimet of Challimar?"

"Yes."

"Surely you're not planning to…"

"I am, Jai Karrim. *We* are. This is why Naia's been training so hard for the past three years. Her blade skill is only part of it."

For a very brief moment Karrim felt a lump of nausea rise

to his throat. "She is not royalty, damn it. She is a common girl who has already seen far too much hardship."

"All this is about to change. Besides, she was hardly common to start with. You have to agree with me, Jai Karrim. You were the one who helped qualify her for the training."

"Don't make me regret it, Dal Gassan."

"I was hoping you'd be proud."

"You must be joking."

"Do I look amused?"

"No, you don't. That's the disturbing part, actually."

"Hardly." Gassan shifted in his seat. "Naia doesn't know about this yet, so the word you just gave me, about keeping this a secret unless it directly contradicts your duties to the emperor, applies to her too. You are not to mention any of this to her."

Karrim heaved a breath. He was beginning to regret giving his word, but it was, of course, too late to change that. "What about an exit plan for her? Someone as prominent as Xarimet of Challimar would be very hard to drive into oblivion after you see the succession through."

"Don't worry about that for now," Arsat said. "There will be plenty of ways to extract her from court safely after the dust settles."

"I hope you get what you want from this, Dal Gassan."

"We all want the same, Jai Karrim, don't we?"

"And what is that, exactly?"

"Peace and prosperity in the empire."

"Prosperity is a relative term."

"Fortunately, peace is not."

Karrim looked away. It definitely did not do to lose his temper. Not with an important patron of the Jaihar Order who also held supreme authority over one of the most influential powers in the empire.

"When you return to the imperial palace, Jai Karrim," Gassan said. "I would like for you to initiate the necessary background work to prepare for Naia's arrival. Your help would be invaluable in observing the undercurrents, so that we can identify any opposition early enough to smother it."

"I'll do what I can."

"Thank you, Jai Karrim," Arsat said. "The Jaihar Order has every faith in you. And now, Jai Ilhad will take you to the training grounds to give you your briefing for tomorrow's tournament."

Karrim followed the headmaster's gesture of dismissal with a salute and he exited the room.

He had a very bad feeling about the whole thing. But he knew, no matter what he felt, there was nothing he could possibly do about this.

THE TOURNAMENT

When Naia entered the private arena at the back of the headmaster's hall, she felt utterly unprepared for the greeting party waiting for her at the far end. The solemn group of the Jaihar seniors, wrapped in their dark gray cloaks, looked larger than any Shadowblade gathering she had seen before. But even the sight of them all gathered here for her sake couldn't possibly compare to the feelings that stirred in her chest at the sight of Karrim.

She had been told that he was back for a brief visit from the emperor's palace, and that she was likely going to see him today. But facing him here, among the elite group who came to evaluate her, was unexpected. She couldn't help a smile as she saluted. The way his lips twitched in response, just slightly, sent a surge of warmth down her spine. Dear Sel, he looked so good – powerful in his slim grace, his face a little paler and more drawn than back when she'd seen him last time, but every bit as desirable. She felt dizzy as she approached.

It seemed strange that he was the only one among the Shadowblades present here who wasn't wearing his ranking cloak. But before she could wonder about that, Surram stepped forward and beckoned her.

"I assume you have been informed about the details of today's tournament," he said.

"Only in broad terms, Jai Surram." She had been told it was going to be a private event. Beyond that, she had no idea how this was going to go.

"Unlike a usual ranking fight," Surram went on, "you will face only one opponent today. Jai Karrim."

Naia's eyes widened.

Too many emotions swept through her at once. She knew that she couldn't possibly be good enough to stand up to Karrim, not even with the three years of training that had passed since their last encounter. With his skill, he was going to destroy her. But somehow, this thought didn't seem important at all. Not compared to the knowledge that they were about to cross blades, something she'd dreamed about all this time. She was going to experience his closeness again. Her heart quivered in anticipation.

"Both you and Jai Karrim will fight without armor or padding," Surram said. "Every mark you leave on your opponent's clothes or body, every successfully landed blow, gains you points. Every misstep counts as a fault. You will get ten fault points if you are forced outside the boundaries of the field. Your weapons." He gestured to a small table, where about a dozen weapons of different sizes and shapes were laid out for display. She spotted her favorite set of blades – blunted, she assumed – as well as a staff, a pair of nunchaku, a tall halberd, a club, and an array of daggers of all sizes.

"Jai Karrim has a similar set," Surram said. "You can feel free to pick and choose whatever you need, as well as use every possible trick you've learned. There are no rules."

No rules. Naia eyed the weapons. Karrim could probably beat her very badly with a number of them.

"How do I know if I've succeeded?" she asked.

Surram's lips twitched again. "You won't, unless you drive Jai Karrim out of the field. I wouldn't try this in your place, though."

Naia looked at him curiously. In a normal ranking fight she would be set up against opponents she could best, at least theoretically. This wasn't the case with Karrim, unless he was having a very bad day. Why did they pitch her against him, if they didn't expect her to have any chance to win? She turned to Karrim, standing across the field beside the array of weapons laid out for him. Even in his stillness, he emanated power. If he fought her at full strength, this fight was going to take everything she had.

How long would she be able to hold up against him?

Their training day three years ago floated up in her mind. That time, she lost to him so badly because she assumed she would, even before the fight started. Now, three years later, she was not going to make the same mistake. She would be fighting to win. She had to believe it, no matter what.

"You will start and cease on my signal." Surram pointed to a gong in the corner of the field. "After you hear it, you're on your own. You may now select your first weapon."

He retreated to the edge of the field, where the other Jaihar seniors were already settling down on the stands, just wide enough to accommodate all of them.

Choose a weapon. Naia glanced at Karrim as she stepped into the field. She had no idea what weapon he was going to choose. Without this knowledge it was difficult to make her own choice. Worse, the minute she did, she would be giving him an advantage. She knew her only hope against him was to maintain the initiative.

The gong rang loudly over the quiet courtyard.

If she didn't keep her eyes on Karrim already, she might have missed his movement as his hand swept over his table, picking–

–the staff. *Damn it.* She grasped hers, the moment's delay giving him an opening to approach her. *Too fast. He's so fast. There goes my initiative, right off.* As he swept toward her, smooth and powerful like a gust of wind, she had no choice but to start on the defensive.

She recognized his attack, a more advanced one she'd learned only recently. As he dove under her raised arm and swung at her from behind, she would have been completely unprepared if she hadn't worked though this sequence before. She spun backward to meet his blow, cursing herself for being so slow. His movements were light, as if he was barely touching the ground. Just like when she faced him before, he seemed immaterial – except that now she possessed the skill and technique to engage him.

It took all she had to keep up as Karrim showered blows on her. *Trying to overpower me with brutal force.* This was a natural thing to do in his place, given the fact that she was smaller and slimmer than he was. If she allowed this to continue, he was going to tire her out and earn an easy victory. She was damned if she was going to allow it.

She dove under his staff, then flung the tip of hers into the opening, letting it slide through, out of her hand. It was too much to hope for that this movement would confuse him, but it gave her just enough time to reach toward her table and pick up the next set of weapons – nunchaku for her left hand and a long dagger for her right.

It wasn't any sequence she'd learned before. Probably a crazy idea to think she could pull off an improvised attack against Karrim – if not for the knowledge that there was no way in hell she was going to score against him by any conventional means.

She saw Karrim's eyes widen briefly as she flung the nunchaku around his staff, tugging at the chain sharply. As he shifted weight, trying to free his weapon, she moved her dagger through his blind spot to stab him on the other side.

Her blade met resistance as it grazed through. His shirt? His flesh? She left her guessing alone, for whoever was keeping scores right now, and swept her dagger across, then released it at the last moment to catch the end of his staff instead. As soon as she had a firm grip, she used her entire weight to flip backward, drawing him into a fall, using the momentum to throw him over her head and land on top.

The move didn't quite work as expected. She hoped to pin him to the ground, at least long enough to regain the initiative – if not disarm him in the process. Instead, Karrim rolled past her, once again immaterial as he bounced off the ground and grasped a sword from the table. *My table, damn it.* Of course, in a fight without rules no one said they should be using only their own weapons, or take the time to rush over to their tables to change them.

She grasped the dagger she had discarded earlier, lifting it off the ground just in time to meet his blow. His blade was longer, and he also had a dagger in his off hand, one she didn't even notice him picking up. She needed to do something fast.

She took a deep breath, calling on her inner balance, extending her senses. The steel. She couldn't control it, or draw it like imlar did, but she could surely sense it, like an extension of her hands. Her dagger was shorter than his blade, but also lighter, and this gave her the necessary speed.

Guided by the sound more than sight, she slipped under his blade, sweeping low. She sensed resistance again – a rip of cloth? – as she dove toward the table, extending her senses to grasp a pair of swords.

As their hilts sank familiarly into her hands, she felt a new surge of power rush through her body. In this new state, time seemed to slow, giving her plenty of opportunity to meet Karrim's blows, to anticipate them, to respond in kind. The world around them melted away. Nothing existed except the dance of their blades. Nothing mattered except the unity they felt. *The bond.* It felt exactly like physical closeness – or maybe even better in the way it took everything she had, without any chance to hold back.

She forgot they were being judged, forgot the fact that this was a fight without rules against the top Jaihar blade. This was the true reason she had been training – to experience this unity, at least once in a lifetime. *The feeling worth living for.* Perhaps her entire existence, her whole life here in the Jaihar Stronghold, were meant exactly for that?

When she heard the ring of the gong, it didn't register – not at first. The sound felt distant, surreal. Only when its meaning fully sank in did her senses return slowly, easing her into the outside world until she felt it all, bit by bit. The chirping of birds. The rustle of the light mountain breeze. The warmth of the sunlight on her cheek. The exhaustion. Dear Sel, the exhaustion. She could barely stand on her feet. How long had they been fighting?

She still couldn't see anyone but Karrim as he separated from the last lock they held, slowly, as if reluctant to let go. As she kept his gaze, she reflected that this was probably the only time in her life she was going to see him so disheveled. He looked awful, his face and hair matted with dust, his shirt ripped, soaked with sweat. Still, he was the most gorgeous man she'd ever laid her eyes on.

Hell, this fight did nothing at all to quench her longing for him. If anything, it made it even worse.

"Well done," Karrim said.

"Thanks."

Karrim's gaze shifted to a spot behind Naia's shoulder. *Someone's approaching.* She turned too, surprised at how difficult it felt, how every movement took far too much effort.

She had to focus to recognize the approaching man. *Jai Hamed. He's not expecting me to raise my hand and salute, is he?*

"Come with me," Hamed said.

Naia turned unsteadily, surprised that her feet could still carry her. Step by painful step, she made it to the edge of the arena, where her trainer, Jai Omar, was waiting with a towel. He didn't hand it to her, like he usually did. Instead, he stepped toward her and wiped off her sweat. She allowed him to tend to her, a welcome change from the necessity to do anything on her own.

She wasn't sure when she was going to collapse, but a collapse was definitely coming at some point. For now, she felt content with the fact that her breathing was finally getting even enough to support at least a brief conversation – if anyone expected her to say anything, of course.

Hamed was checking her clothes and gear, speaking to an attendant over her shoulder, one who was probably taking notes. Naia could see Karrim, on the opposite end of the field, undergoing a similar examination with Surram. After he was finished, Hamed spoke to Omar in a hushed voice, then nodded to Naia and retreated toward the command group on the stands.

"They're going to take a while to decide," Omar said. "Perhaps you'd like to clean up and change?"

Naia nodded. Her clothes were ripped and soaked with sweat, dust matting her face and hair, creaking on her teeth. She would love to change into something fresh – importantly, dry – before she spoke to the headmaster.

She saluted to her seniors and walked toward the exit, with Hamed's attendants on her heels. They were probably under orders to make sure she didn't suffer any hidden injuries, or collapse on her way out.

Before she left the field, she searched out Karrim, still speaking to Surram on the other side. He wasn't looking at her, but she could swear that as soon as her eyes fell on him, he tensed up and turned his head toward her. From all this distance, their eyes met and held on, before letting go.

Dear Sel, in three years, all her efforts to forget him had failed miserably. She longed for him more than ever before.

What in three hells was she going to do?

THE RANKING

Karrim was barely registering the attendants bustling around him, Surram making a string of notes on his scoreboard. They were going to find all the rips in his clothing, all the bruises that gave Naia her ranking points. They were also going to find a share of them on Naia's clothing and body too. But none of that really mattered, compared to the fight they'd just had.

In the past three years, Naia had trained to be his equal, good enough to stand up in a fight to the Jaihar's top blade. While Karrim's skill still surpassed hers, there was no doubt in his mind that she deserved a Shadow rank.

He knew that the Jaihar seniors were now going to engage in a lot of deliberations to compare scores and arrive at the same conclusion. As for Karrim, all he wanted was to retreat to some quiet place, which preferably included a bath and a clean set of clothes, and reflect on the experience.

When he'd first met Naia three years ago, he was already attracted to her. Now that she'd grown from an uncertain young girl into a woman and a warrior, the effect was so much more powerful. Crossing blades with her today felt more enjoyable than any fight he could remember. He wanted more, despite the absolute certainty that entertaining this possibility was a really bad idea.

He forced these thoughts away for now, watching the change of scene around him. Surram and his attendants departed, replaced by Dahib, the old weapon master, who approached the tables set out for the fight to inspect the potential damage to the weapons. While the man's long, deft fingers examined each item in turn, his piercing eyes continued to dart in Karrim's direction, until Karrim found the attention noticeable enough to respond to. He lowered the towel he was using to wipe sweat off his face and stepped closer to the table.

"Anything about me you find unusual, Jai Dahib?" he asked.

The older man's lips twitched. "Yes, actually. I've always known you to enjoy a good fight, but I've never quite seen you enjoying it this much."

Damn it. Karrim knew that with the disheveled state he was in, he couldn't possibly control his blush. Inadvertently, his eyes trailed to the senior Jaihar, still deep in conversation on the other end of the field, to make sure none of them was watching.

"It was fun, yes," he said. "She's very good. I'm sure everyone here saw it."

"They did." Dahib's eyes lit up with merry sparkles as he continued to watch Karrim. "But personally, I couldn't help seeing more. I hope you wouldn't mind me giving you a word of advice, Jai Karrim."

Karrim frowned. He knew Dahib to be extremely perceptive, the man that many in this stronghold sought out to unload their burdens. Dahib always had good advice for everyone – including Karrim, in his younger years, when he got into trouble far too often for his own good. He hadn't needed the older man's wisdom for a while, though. And now, this unexpected offer piqued his curiosity.

"By all means, Jai Dahib," he said.

"Your feelings for her are too powerful to ignore," Dahib said. "While you may think yourself strong enough to act as if they aren't even there, at some point this may become too much of a burden for you."

Karrim raised his eyebrows. He didn't have feelings for Naia. Not that way. Yet, as Dahib's words sank in, he felt surprised – and troubled – to realize that they resonated deeper than he liked. He craved her closeness, yes. He had assumed this to be purely physical. But now that Dahib mentioned it, he was beginning to wonder. He certainly felt different right now than ever before.

"I have no idea what you are talking about," he said.

Dahib's lips twitched. "Oh, know for certain that you do. Just remember my words. Some urges are best dealt with by suppressing them. Others require a more proactive approach. In this particular case I believe it to be the latter, not in the least because she feels the same way about you too. You are about to go on an assignment where you will be working side by side. I strongly suggest that, prior to that, you find a way to get this out of your system, so to speak."

Before Karrim could respond, Dahib turned and walked away to the other end of the field, leaving Karrim gaping.

Get this out of your system. An utterly shocking suggestion that would be a big mistake to entertain. Even if Naia felt the same longing for him as he did, she was too young and innocent to grasp the concept of getting someone out of her system by forcing an encounter with him. Besides, with the way Karrim felt right now, he wasn't sure whether doing something like this would help the situation, or make it even worse. Whatever Dahib said, Karrim firmly believed it would be best for him to stay away from Naia, as far as he possibly could. Except that the two of them were lined up to collaborate on a very difficult assignment, one where she would surely need all the help he could possibly give.

Bloody hell. He needed a bath, preferably a very cold one. He was too exhausted to think straight right now. He was sure he could deal with the rest when the time came. In his career as a Shadowblade, he had handled much worse.

Naia felt a chill run down her spine as she entered the headmaster's audience hall. She had been here only once in her life, when Arsat had officially informed her of her acceptance onto the Jai grounds. At that time, the room seemed hollow and empty, with only a couple of the Order's seniors present.

It looked so different right now. All the senior Shadowblades, dozens of them, were lined up in front of her, forming two diagonal rows at the sides of the headmaster's throne-like chair. The sides of the room glimmered with the silver of the senior trainers' cloaks. Everyone's solemn looks made her heart quiver as she approached.

She followed the headmaster's gesture to take a spot opposite his chair, in the center of the open space under the central vault. Sunbeams shining through a stained glass window at its top painted the floor around her green and yellow, with just a touch of orange at the edges. *Like Mehtab's stone.* She suppressed the thought.

Her eyes wandered through the rows looking for Karrim, but she couldn't find him anywhere. It seemed improbable to think he was too tired to attend. Maybe some urgent business kept him away? She tried not to dwell on the thought, an insignificant one compared to the meaning of the gathering. She was about to learn her fate, to find out whether she had earned a Jai rank – and which one.

As soon as she took her place, Surram stepped forward, holding a tablet with a scroll over it – the field record she recognized from this morning's tournament.

"Jai Hamed and I have added up your score," Surram said. "Your final result is eighteen points, counting the faults that factored against this total."

Eighteen points. Is that enough? Naia wasn't sure. But she realized with surprise that it didn't really matter. The fight with Karrim was the true reward she had been training for. She had learned enough to stand up to him, the Jaihar Order's best. Nothing else seemed important at all.

"After an extensive deliberation," the headmaster said, "we all agree that this result is remarkable for a graduating trainee, fighting without rules against our Order's top blade. Our decision is unanimous. The Jaihar Order is privileged and honored to welcome you into our top Jai rank. A Shadowblade. Congratulations, Jai Naia."

A Shadowblade.

Naia's immediate reaction was disbelief. She couldn't possibly have heard this right. Yet, another part of her mind saw the rightness of it. She *did* fight Karrim as an equal – or very nearly so. She had known, even this morning, that she was likely to get a Jai rank.

She just didn't expect to shoot all the way to the top.

Me. A Shadowblade.

Bloody hell.

It was probably a good idea to say something, but a lump

standing in her throat precluded any possibility of talking. She blinked, watching the headmaster rise from his seat and step toward her. Hamed handed him a cloak and Arsat took it, flinging it over her shoulders. *Shadow-gray. Dear Sel.*

The headmaster reached to Hamed for the rest of the regalia, handing them to her one by one. A clasp for the cloak in the shape of crossed swords. A ranking dagger with the black blade. She took it with stiff fingers and latched it onto her belt. Everyone around her was saluting, and – finally – smiling, even Ilhad. She saluted too, still afraid to say anything at all.

"And now," Arsat said, "you will report to my study to receive your new assignment, Jai Naia. Everyone else is dismissed."

An assignment? So soon? Naia did her best not to show her surprise as she followed him.

A NEW ASSIGNMENT

Naia paused in the doorway as she saw Gassan, sitting in a deep chair in the headmaster's study. The sight of him brought back all the memories of their first meeting, the starting point in a chain of events that ultimately led to her becoming a Shadowblade today. Was she about to learn the true reason behind it? The idea seemed far-fetched, but she couldn't quite rid herself of it.

"You've met Dal Gassan, I believe," Arsat said.

"Yes, I have."

"He is your employer on this assignment."

Naia frowned. She had always been under the impression that Shadowblades had a say in these decisions, but she wasn't about to question this now, after she had just been ranked.

"What's the assignment?" she asked.

Arsat and Gassan exchanged a quick glance.

"One far more complex than usual," Arsat said. "So, let me start with the background. I have been assured that your tutor, Dal Mehtab, has familiarized you with the story of Princess Xarimet of Challimar."

"She did." Naia looked at Gassan again. *My employer.* She couldn't overcome her disbelief. Gassan was not only her likely benefactor, but also, as she'd learned at some point, one of the most influential people in the empire. Why was he taking such a personal interest in her?

"We need you to impersonate Xarimet at the imperial court," Gassan said.

"What?" Naia's eyes widened. This made no sense. No one could say something this absurd with such a straight face.

"I know you are surprised," Gassan said. "You surely have questions. The Daljeer will answer all of them when you report to our serai tomorrow."

Dear Sel, they're bloody serious, aren't they? Inadvertently, Naia's gaze drifted to Ilhad, who had entered the room in her wake but hadn't moved or spoken since the start of the conversation. Why was he here? Was it usual for him to be present when the assignments were given out to the Jaihar warriors? Or was this honor reserved for the Shadowblades, or those about to embark on a quest that made no sense at all?

"I assume you have a purpose in mind," she said. "Other than a desire to test the quality of Dal Mehtab's tutelage and my impersonation skills."

Well, she probably should have phrased that better. She felt mildly guilty when she saw Arsat flinch and Ilhad abruptly look away. Politics at this high level was new to her. No one ever bothered with phrasing on the training range. Her ranking fight had happened too recently for her to acquire the finesse that was probably expected in conversations between Shadowblades and the Jaihar Order's important patrons.

She contemplated an apology, cut short when she saw Gassan's lips twitch into a quick grin.

"You certainly wasted no time picking up the attitude characteristic for a blademaster of your rank," he said.

Naia smiled too, carefully avoiding any look at her superiors. "This attitude is a special focus of our training, Dal Gassan."

Gassan's grin widened, his glance holding approval she found odd under the circumstances. "Good to know. And no, I have no doubt about the quality of Dal Mehtab's tutelage or your impersonation skills. What I am about to tell you, though, is confidential. You must give me your word not to speak of it to anyone at all."

"Given that you've already employed me, apparently, you have my word."

"His Majesty Emperor Shabaddin is gravely ill," Gassan said. "He has weeks to live, at most."

Naia wasn't sure whether to feel surprised or relieved. From the talk she'd heard around the stronghold and outside in the city, many considered Shabaddin a monster. The Challimar Royal Massacre was easily the mildest of his deeds. It seemed that no one in the empire, even his immediate family, would grieve his early demise.

"Sorry to hear it," she said.

Gassan rolled his eyes. "You can spare the small talk. I expect Dal Mehtab has also told you that the royal heir of Challimar is the only person in the empire who can legally claim succession rights at the time of the emperor's death."

"She did."

"Good," Gassan said. "You can guess the rest, I hope. Your assignment is to challenge the imperial heir, Prince Ramaz, to a succession contest. One you are going to win."

Moments ago, Naia felt reasonably sure nothing Gassan said could possibly make her feel even more surprised. She realized now that she shouldn't make any more assumptions. She probably looked stupid right now, staring at Gassan open-mouthed, but she couldn't help it.

To win. Right. Am I supposed to keep asking questions, or would staring at him, dumbfounded, suffice at the moment? She chose the latter, simply because she didn't trust herself with saying anything right now.

"Don't worry," Gassan said. "We are not asking you to become our new Empress. Someone else will relieve you of the crown once you have it. All we want you to do is keep up the act, no matter how many people around you try to challenge your claim, or simply remove you by force. I assume that acting like a royal pain in the neck would not present a problem to you?"

"Not at all." Once again, Naia prominently avoided looking at her superiors. Despite everything, she was surprised to find herself looking forward to working with Gassan. The man's directness, his wicked humor, make her feel strangely comforted.

"Good," Gassan said. "Once you win the throne and remove Prince Ramaz and his brothers from your way, we will bring forth a different heir. You will then formally renounce the throne and give up your crown to him to complete your assignment."

Sounds easy enough. Naia finally turned to Arsat. She would perhaps be feeling less surreal if he smiled – or at least showed some surprise. Instead, Arsat looked down to earth and businesslike as he slid a thick pile of parchments over his desk toward Naia.

"These materials," he said, "contain all the necessary information on top of what has already been relayed to you. You must memorize it all before you arrive at the imperial palace."

Naia nodded. It looked like she had some reading to do in the next few days.

"Tomorrow morning, you will report to Dal Mehtab in the Daljeer serai in Haggad," Gassan said.

"Dal Mehtab?"

"Yes. Why?"

"I thought you were my employer."

"I am acting on behalf of the Daljeer Circle, in this case. You will work with the Daljeer very closely, at every step of the way. I look forward to Your Royal Highness's arrival at court." Gassan stood up from his chair and bowed to her deeply, but his upward glance gleamed with mischief.

Naia had never seen Gassan looking so inspired. Of course, this probably meant little, given that she had only spoken to him a couple of times in her entire life. But she could sense that this assignment was somehow personal to him. Moreover, he really believed in her ability to play this role. Oddly, his confidence was beginning to catch her too. Suddenly the idea of impersonating a legendary princess to challenge the imperial rule didn't quite seem so insane anymore.

Was this how the Daljeer worked their magic on people's minds?

"Is the story of Xarimet really true, Dal Gassan?" she asked.

"It is," Gassan said. "Even though people in the empire have been thoroughly brainwashed into believing otherwise. After we came up with this plan, I did some research. Shabaddin's line comes from Qazeerah, the ancient Challimar queen. His distant ancestor, her consort, had betrayed and overthrown her, but the power he gained came with a price. To appease his people, including his closest advisors, he was forced to pass a succession law. No one's claim for the throne could surpass that of a true

Challimar heir."

Naia's eyes narrowed. "Is this why the emperor exterminated all the Challimar royals?"

She sensed a movement in the room, as if her words struck a sensitive chord. Arsat's face went still. Did her assignment touch on something personal to the headmaster? And if so, was there more to it than she was being told right now?

"Some say so, yes," Gassan said. "But not openly. You'd do well to remember it when you arrive at the imperial court."

Naia nodded. "Still. Convincing them that I am the real Xarimet risen from obscurity will be difficult."

The Daljeer's face lit up with a mysterious smile. "Not as difficult as you may think."

"All Challimar royals are supposed to be dead."

"All but one. I assume Mehtab told you the story of a baby, smuggled out of the palace during the massacre."

"She did, yes. But–"

"I am not sure if she also told you that both she and I were at the serai when the baby arrived."

Naia narrowed her eyes. She assumed he was speaking so confidently to ease her into the role, but it was getting harder and harder to tell.

"What happened to this baby?" she asked.

Gassan's face spread into a grin. "Oh, that's the best part. She was cared for by the Daljeer, among many other orphaned children we shelter in our sanctuaries. When the girl was old enough, her tutors noticed her unusual affinity for weapons. Upon their recommendation she was brought to the Jaihar Stronghold, where she proved to be so talented that she was able to achieve the rank of a Shadowblade. I, for one, take special pride in playing a part in this girl's fate. So does Mehtab, I am sure."

Naia's mouth fell open. She looked at her superiors, still sitting inanimately in their chairs.

"This seems far too wild," she said.

"Perhaps." Gassan exchanged a quick glance with Arsat. "But it's also the truth. That child is you. This is what makes it so perfect, don't you think?"

"You can't be bloody serious."

"See how you tend to reduce to swearing when you are surprised? You'll need to stop that. A princess never swears in front of others. And yes – I am bloody serious. You can depend on it."

Naia wanted to object, but a memory floating up in her mind froze the words on her lips. The visions she experienced in Mehtab's chamber. A baby, held in someone's arms, peering out of her wrappings. The regal, beautiful woman tucking her in, right before she was attacked. The blood.

Looking through the veil…

Did Mehtab use some sort of Daljeer magic to instill those memories? Or did it all truly happen to Naia at some point? Asking this question right now didn't seem like a good idea. Not with the way everyone was watching her so expectantly.

"The Jaihar Imperial Dozen stationed in the palace is instructed to assist you in any way they can," Arsat said. "Jai Karrim will resume command, as soon as he returns to the palace tomorrow. You must keep your acquaintance with him secret, however."

Karrim. Naia knew she shouldn't allow herself to dwell on the thought. "What happens after my assignment is complete?"

"You will return to the Jaihar Stronghold, of course," Arsat said.

"Just like that?"

"The exact details are still being discussed."

"Discussed?"

Arsat shifted in his seat. "We will relay the instructions to you later on. For now, you must focus solely on your mission. You have my solid assurance, however, that after the imperial succession is settled to our satisfaction, you will be free to return here and resume your normal life."

Our satisfaction. The personal way Arsat referred to this didn't escape Naia. She glanced at the headmaster curiously, but couldn't read anything at all behind his impassive expression.

"Very well," she said.

"When you report to the Daljeer serai tomorrow morning," Gassan said, "pack for a long trip. We don't want you to return to the stronghold for any reason after your assignment starts, even if you are still in the city. You will be leaving for Zegmeer in a day or so, after Dal Mehtab completes the necessary preparations with you. She will also remain by your side, posing as your handwoman throughout the trip."

Naia nodded. Despite too many questions crowding in her mind, she was beginning to feel excited. Not every Jaihar was offered an opportunity to impersonate royalty on a mission that would decide the fate of the whole empire. Besides, she would be working with Karrim. She would probably be able to see him every day.

This last thought filled her with guilt. She shouldn't be basing her assignments on her personal desires. But she simply couldn't help this one.

NIGHTTIME ERRANDS

Karrim ascended the side stairs, leading directly to the headmaster's study, at a fast walk. He had no idea why he was being summoned here. He already received detailed instructions for his return to Zegmeer. Everything seemed set. What could Arsat possibly want to talk to him about?

The door to the headmaster's chamber stood ajar, signaling that he was expected. As Karrim walked in, he was startled to see Ilhad sitting in a deep chair next to Arsat's desk. Did the man ever leave? In the flickering light of the lanterns, Ilhad's face was shrouded by devilish shadows that inadvertently drew Karrim's eyes as he crossed the room.

"Sit down, Jai Karrim," Arsat said.

Karrim obeyed, surveying the two men with interest. He didn't hurry to break the silence – and neither did they, until the pause became oppressive.

"Jai Naia has been briefed about the Daljeer assignment," Arsat said at length. "She is leaving tomorrow morning."

Karrim nodded. He assumed as much. It hardly seemed necessary to summon him here to tell him this information.

"I'm certain you are aware of many ways in which this assignment could go wrong," Arsat said. "The Jaihar Order has never done anything of this magnitude before. While we cannot predict what will actually happen, there is a particular scenario we'd like to prepare you for." He shifted in his seat and looked away, as if avoiding Karrim's gaze.

"Go on," Karrim said.

"As you yourself mentioned before, Jai Naia is very young, with no experience on any assignments – let alone a major mission like this. Her role as Princess Xarimet would give her access to unprecedented power. Many in her place would have trouble handling it."

"I'm sure she'll do fine."

Arsat nodded. "I, and all the Jaihar seniors, share this hope, Jai Karrim. However, at some point during the process, she will most certainly feel tempted to become a true contender for the throne, whether or not she chooses to act on it."

Karrim held his gaze. He could guess where this was going, and he hated the way the realization sent a chill down his spine. Irfat's hells, why couldn't all his assignments be as straightforward as his first assignment in Scinn, where all he had to do was defeat an army of bandits in a good, honest battle?

"I'm certain Naia would never consider it," he said.

The headmaster shook his head. "Your opinion is appreciated, but I'm sure you understand it isn't enough. If her assignment goes as planned, she would be able to achieve a status where no one could possibly stand in her way to power. Her orders are to use this position to put Prince Halil on the throne. However, it would be easy for her, in principle, to forgo these orders and take the crown for herself. If this happens, you are our failsafe, Jai Karrim. You must remove her from Prince

Halil's way. By any means necessary."

Karrim looked at him, dumbfounded. For once, he had no idea what to say.

These kinds of orders were every Jaihar's nightmare. The fact that they concerned Naia made him feel so much worse.

"It wasn't an accident that you were the one chosen to face her in her ranking fight this morning," Ilhad said. "Moreover, the weapons placed on your tables during the tournament were chosen deliberately too. These are all the weapons you'll have a higher chance of beating her with, in a one-on-one fight. Of course, we expect you to have the Jaihar Dozen as a backup, but we felt the need to prepare you for all possibilities."

Karrim blinked. It was fortunate that during the fight this morning he had no idea it was going to lead to the conversation he was having right now. He swallowed, his mouth suddenly too dry to talk. Or was it just an excuse not to say anything?

"I watched you both closely during the tournament," Ilhad went on. "I also supervised Jai Naia's training with many of these weapons. So, allow me to offer you some advice. A brutal force attack against her, with a heavy weapon, gives you a higher chance of besting her. I recommend a halberd, the weapon she purposely didn't pick today, but a heavy staff would do."

"What about blades?" Dear Sel, Karrim could scarcely recognize his own voice. Or was it all his imagination? Could he really have asked a question about the best way to defeat their newest Shadowblade, a woman who had such a special place in his heart? Karrim felt only slightly reassured to see no reaction from Ilhad, suggesting that his voice was probably fine – as was his sanity, if he assumed this conversation was really happening, after all.

"Blades are favorite for you both," Ilhad said. "Accordingly, you spent most of your time in a blade fight this morning.

Some of the other weapons set out for you, though, are not her best. I trust you memorized them all. With this knowledge, the choice would be up to you alone, Jai Karrim."

Cursed Irfat, we are not really having this discussion, are we? Karrim looked away. It wasn't going to come to that, he told himself firmly. Naia was never going to stray from her path, no matter what.

"The Jaihar Order rarely calls upon its warriors to perform this kind of role," Ilhad said. "But it is, unfortunately, our duty to do it in exceptional circumstances. With the information we gave you, with the men you have at your command at the emperor's court, you now have the power to defeat her, if needed."

"I know you don't like it, Jai Karrim," Arsat said. "Neither do I. But we must all do what needs to be done."

Karrim nodded, only vaguely registering the headmaster's gesture of dismissal before striding out of the chamber.

He wanted to see Naia tonight. To talk to her, to make sure they were on the same page. To warn her not to do something stupid. He knew he couldn't, with the damned promise he'd given to Gassan and his superiors that precluded him from talking about anything connected to Naia's assignment, but he had never felt so tempted to break his word. Hell, just seeing her right now, looking into her eyes, would make him feel so much better. He tried to convince himself that this was the only reason, that this had nothing to do with the way his entire body continued to long for her.

This last thought was the one that ended up convincing him the most. In this state of mind, seeing her tonight would put his control to the kind of test it never had to endure before. He couldn't trust himself around her. This meeting couldn't possibly lead to anything good.

As he ascended the stairs to his quarters, a private room in one of the buildings at the back of the grounds, he almost managed to convince himself that this decision was for the best. Almost.

After receiving her assignment, Naia spent a few leisurely hours relaxing in her new quarters. The room was far more luxurious than any warrior deserved to have – large, with its own bookshelf, desk, wash basin, and a real bed, draped in silky covers. A pity she had to leave this all behind early tomorrow morning.

At dusk, she ventured out for a meal and an evening stroll through the grounds. Everyone in the main dining hall greeted her with a cheer, the chef coming out personally to hand her a large mug of their finest local ale. She sipped it as she walked through the aisles, exchanging friendly slaps and greetings, receiving formal salutes.

The one person she wanted to see the most wasn't here, though. She couldn't spot Karrim anywhere in the dining hall, or on the training grounds. She even checked the servant areas and the stables, to no avail. Perhaps it was for the best. Much as she wanted to talk, or at least to see him, any contact with Karrim right now would only intensify the desire she felt for him. Besides, they were going to meet again soon enough, when her assignment brought her to the emperor's court.

She was just about to talk herself into heading back to her room when she saw someone approaching her across the inner area of the grounds. A Quickblade, pressing his palm to his chest in a formal salute as he approached.

Dear Sel, seeing ranked warriors salute to her was going to take some getting used to.

"Jai Naia," he said.

She paused, trying to recall his name. She had seen him once or twice on gate duty, but couldn't quite remember how to address him. Was this going to be part of her life too, having Jai warriors address her by name without having any idea who they were?

"Yes," she said.

"There's someone outside to see you. A woman. We retained her in the inner gate area. Would you like to speak to her, or should we send her away?"

Mehtab. Naia wasn't sure how she knew.

"I'll speak to her," she said, and followed the Quickblade to the gate.

Mehtab was pacing back and forth in the narrow courtyard. She beamed as she saw Naia, and stepped forward to hug her.

"Well done today," Mehtab said. "Congratulations, Jai Naia. A Shadowblade, eh?"

"Yes." Naia felt warmth spread over her at the older woman's words. Many had congratulated her today, but no one did it with such motherly pride, as if Naia's success was somehow personal to her. It was good to see Mehtab, even if highly unusual for the woman to come all the way to the Jaihar Stronghold. Naia had no idea why. They were going to see each other tomorrow anyway, weren't they?

"You may be wondering why I'm here," Mehtab said. "I needed to send a message to you, but couldn't resist the temptation to see you in person. Good that you were still up and about at this hour."

Naia smiled. The hour was still early for sleep, even if it was already dark. Of course, Mehtab couldn't possibly know much about the schedule on the Jaihar upper grounds.

216

"I'm glad you came," she said.

Mehtab nodded. "Me too. Here, I need to give you the list of things to bring when you show up at our serai tomorrow." She opened her shoulder bag and handed Naia a tightly folded piece of paper.

Her hand hovered in hesitation as Naia took the paper from Mehtab's hands.

"Is there something else you need?" Naia asked.

Mehtab's gaze wavered. "I wondered if you could do me a favor. I wanted to give this to Jai Karrim." She pulled out a scroll from her bag. "This is the text of the original song about Princess Xarimet, something I felt he should be familiar with before he leaves for Zegmeer tomorrow. I copied it for him myself. I can ask one of these guards to give it to him, but since you are going to the Shadowblade quarters anyway..."

The Shadowblade quarters. Naia hadn't yet contemplated the fact that she was staying in the same building as Karrim. The mere thought made her heart race.

"I didn't see Jai Karrim anywhere," Naia said, hoping her words didn't betray how hard she had been looking.

"He must be in his room, preparing for the assignment," Mehtab said. "No harm to check, at least – is there?"

Naia heaved a breath. Mehtab had to know about the attraction Naia felt for Karrim. With the amount of time she and Naia spent together, this was bound to slip out, at least a few times. And now, innocently or not, the woman was handing Naia a legitimate excuse to seek Karrim out in his quarters. The temptation was impossible to resist.

"All right," she said.

"Good." Mehtab beamed again and gave her another hug. "You can show up mid-morning tomorrow. No reason to exert yourself by getting up too early."

Without waiting for a response, she turned around and left, leaving Naia standing in the middle of the courtyard, gaping. She chose not to read any further into the implications of Mehtab's odd words. Now that she thought more about it, she realized that seeking out Karrim was definitely not a good idea, not with the way the mere thought of him made her feel weak in the knees. But she'd made a promise to her tutor, who was also one of her employers on an upcoming assignment. It was too late to take it back.

CONTROL

Naia stopped in front of the Shadowblades' quarters in indecision. The heavy two-storey building was mostly dark, its inhabitants likely away from the stronghold on assignments, or out and about, like her. It was easy to guess Karrim's second floor window by the flicker of a lantern light coming from inside. A side stair led up straight to his door. She felt a weakness in the pit of her stomach as she stepped toward it.

I am just going to drop off the scroll and go away. Perhaps leave it by the door without even knocking. It's utterly inappropriate to do anything else. Yet, as she ascended the narrow staircase, she knew she was not going to be able to walk away without at least saying hello.

Her heart quivered as she stopped in front of the door. She took a deep breath, then raised her hand and knocked. After a moment she heard a click of the latch, the heavy door swinging noiselessly inward.

Karrim was wearing a casual outfit, so different from the ones he always wore outside. Soft shirt and pants, with no leathers or weapon straps, made him look much more down to earth, even if still every bit as elegant and powerful. She swallowed as she ran her gaze down, all the way to his bare feet. Dear Sel, it felt so good to see him. Merely standing next to him made her feel better than she remembered feeing in a very long time.

The message. Yes. She held out Mehtab's scroll. "Please forgive the intrusion, Jai Karrim. Dal Mehtab asked me to give this to you."

He hesitated, his gaze momentarily unfocused, as if distracted, then reached forward and took the scroll. His fingers briefly brushed hers. The contact made her stomach flutter.

"What is it?" he asked.

"It's a poem about Princess Xarimet of Challimar. Mehtab copied it for you."

He didn't question it any futher, his eyes flicking to the scroll he held without making any move to open it.

"Thank you," he said.

"I… I hope I didn't disturb you."

Karrim shook his head softly. His eyes returned to her face. Emotion stirred in his gaze, making her shiver. Or was it her imagination?

"You didn't," he said.

She knew she was blushing. She was also beginning to feel light-headed from the way he was looking at her. His expression was guarded, but close behind the guard she sensed wonder, fascination. It was as if he considered her presence here to be a miracle, as if she was a rare gift he cherished. An odd thought on her part. It was probably all in her head.

She shuffled in indecision, knowing that this was a really good moment to leave, yet unable to bring herself to do it.

"Would you like to come in?" Karrim asked quietly.

Not a good idea. The thought barely registered in her head before she nodded.

Silently, he stepped aside to let her in.

As she entered his room, keeping a conscious distance, she tried to convince herself that his invitation, the way she accepted it so eagerly, didn't mean anything at all. She was here only as a friend. They hadn't really spoken to each other since their meeting about three years ago, when Karrim had done so much to clear a dark spot on her record and ensure her future. Now was her chance – if not to catch up, at least to reconnect again. To talk. Except that right now talking was very far from her mind.

No one in this stronghold ever crossed the boundary of another's quarters unless they had a reason to seek privacy. If she wanted to talk as a friend, she could have invited Karrim to come out with her. Well, he could have offered it too. Instead, he clicked the door latch back into place, watching her with the expression she was having so much trouble reading. The wonder she spotted earlier was still there, but there was now something else behind it that she couldn't quite place. It looked almost like apprehension, as if he was expecting an attack, even though it didn't make any sense.

His room looked similar to her new quarters, yet arranged with extra elegance that indicated that Karrim probably thought of it as home. A lit lantern sat on the desk by the window, spilling its soft, flickering light on the pages of a leather-bound book he must have been reading before she showed up. A stand near the door held a wash basin, a jug, and a large bucket of water. Her eyes trailed deeper, to the bed sinking into a deep alcove by the far wall – neatly made, beckoning with pristine sheets. *The bed.*

Karrim continued to watch her silently, without moving at all. He had his back to the light, leaving his face in shadow so that it was even harder to read him right now. Her heart was beginning to pound, the draw of his presence powerful like imlar, clouding her head, making it so hard to think straight.

In her haze, she briefly wondered if Mehtab had this in mind when she'd sent her to Karrim's room. It probably wasn't that important to deliver the scroll tonight, if at all. Karrim had plenty of chance to read the original story of Xarimet all by himself. Did Mehtab use this blunt move, that in retrospect should have been obvious, to bring them together? Naia knew this should matter to her somehow, but her fading mind simply couldn't find any reason to care.

Slowly, she stepped forward and reached up to touch Karrim's face, tracing the line of his high cheekbone with her fingertips. A barely detectable shiver rippled through his body in response. It echoed through her too, as if they were connected somehow.

Dear Sel, she had wanted to do this since she first saw him. And now, as he stood in front of her, not moving yet, but very definitely not drawing away, he was giving her permission to do it.

When Karrim opened the door, the sight of Naia standing on his doorstep instantly drew his mind into a dangerous semi-stupor he had experienced only once before, at fifteen, after a long gulp of a particularly strong brew. He didn't even register what she said to him, not at once. *A scroll. Right.* He took it from her, immediately forgetting about it. He had been dreaming of seeing Naia tonight. He had talked himself out of trying, and had utterly given up on any possibility of it. Yet, against all the odds she was here – desirable as hell, with no idea of what had been going through his head ever since their fight this morning.

It was a really bad move to invite her in. But the words escaped Karrim's lips before this realization really registered in his mind – or whatever was left of it, anyway. He knew his voice came out husky as he spoke. Her immediate response, the way her breath quickened as he issued the invitation, made him feel dizzy.

Hell. If he had any sense left, he would open the door and send her away, rather than latching it behind her as he ogled her like a starving hyena. Even if she came here with similar intentions, she had no idea what she was playing with, no clue about the fire that ignited his every nerve at her mere proximity.

He kept very still as he watched her. He couldn't trust himself with moving right now. There was still a chance – a very remote one – that she was here for another reason. That she was going to say something polite and leave. The thought was painful, but he forced it through his head anyway. Slowly, just to make sure.

The blush rising into her cheeks made her skin glow. This glow would consume him too if he touched her right now, burn him like an infernal flame. Every inch of his body craved her. He had never felt this way about anyone.

Inadvertently he rememberd Dahib's advice this morning. *Get it out of your system.* Well, Karrim certainly had a chance to do it now, or at least try – except that he should really know better.

He was still struggling with this last thought, too slow and sticky to keep up with the events, when she stepped toward him and reached up to touch his face.

Damn it. He didn't expect the way his body fired up in response, as if struck by lightning. It was probably a good idea to discourage this somehow, to evade the encounter. But this seemed no more possible than discouraging a man dying of thirst from taking a sip of water brought to his lips. It took all he had to hold still just long enough to give her one last chance to reconsider. And then, she closed the distance and stepped into his embrace, forcing all thoughts out of his head. His hands moved on their own, around her waist, up her back, into her hair, freeing it from its bond to let it spill freely down her back. He threaded his fingers through its lush silk, tilting up her face toward him. Her lips parted to meet his – an invitation he couldn't possibly resist.

She tasted like cider – sweet and fresh, and deceptively light for the way one sip instantly went to his head. Her kisses, innocent and eager, took over his senses so completely that he came the closest he ever remembered to losing control. Worse, he didn't mind losing it at all. In his dazed state, he couldn't find it in himself to care.

If he didn't stop right about now, he was going to do something they might both regret later on. He had never wanted it more.

This wouldn't do at all. He forced the thought through his head, using all his remaining strength to pull back from the edge. He was the senior here, the one in control. An encounter like this was a bad idea on so many levels, no matter how much he wanted it. If he had any sense left, he should let her go.

They were leaning into the wall now – the place Karrim didn't remember getting to. He was pinning her down, his tongue invading her mouth, their bodies twined so much that it took him a moment to sort them apart. To break the kiss and pull back. To lean into the wall beside her, reassuringly cool, yet not nearly cold enough to make a difference. It didn't help that she was still close enough to feel her warmth all the way down his side.

His body screamed in protest as he held still, heaving breath after heavy breath, trying to calm his senses. Hell, they'd never trained him for this kind of situation. No training was possible for handling someone like Naia.

It took a while for Karrim to finally feel in control enough to turn and face her. She seemed breathless too, leaning her head against the wall by his side. The light of the lantern fell on her face, giving him an extra chance to appreciate every detail. Her tousled hair, spilling over her shoulders and back in thick mahogany waves. A patina of sunset pink lighting up her cheeks. Her half-open lips, still swollen and moist from his kiss. *Her lips. Don't think about her lips. Look her in the eyes, damn it.* It didn't help. Her dark, gold-rimmed eyes spelled desire, a promise that echoed through his every nerve.

"Forgive me." Karrim barely recognized his own voice, husky and hoarse. Just in case, he shifted further away from her. "I'm being such a bad host."

Her lips twitched. "I haven't complained so far, have I?"

A choice, he reminded himself. *You must give her a choice.* Ravaging her like a beast wasn't the way to do it. Not with an innocent young girl who clearly came here with no idea what to expect from a scoundrel and a seducer of Karrim's reputation.

He forced a smile, hoping against reason that it would look like an easygoing one. "You haven't complained, because I haven't offered you any alternatives." *Or any time to breathe, damn it.* "Would you like to sit down?"

Her grin seemed a little uncertain, but also so seductive he barely stopped himself from reaching for her again. "I'd rather lie down." She glanced at his bed, then back at his face with a question.

Three hells. No. He should say "no" right now. Instead, he stepped away from the wall and gestured silently. An invitation she took no time to accept as she swept past him into the depths of the room.

This was the point of no return. As the thought settled firmly into his fading mind, every muscle in his body quivered with anticipation.

Naia kept her back to Karrim, moving deliberately slowly as she took off her knife belt and unclasped numerous straps of her gear. He was surely watching her right now, and she didn't want him to notice the tremble in her arms. He was acting so controlled, probably doing his damndest to make sure her decision to share his bed wasn't an impulse she was going to regret. Why was she having so much trouble doing the same?

It was impossible to detect his approach by any sound he made, but she still sensed it in the movement of air, in the way the small hairs on her neck stood on end with anticipation. When he reached around her and closed his hands over hers, she heaved a ragged breath, willing herself not to lean back into him. Not yet. His closeness, his warmth all the way down her back made her skin tingle. She wanted to savor the moment.

"Are you sure you want to do this?" he asked quietly.

"Yes."

He released her hands, tracing his fingers over her arm in a light touch that echoed with a shiver down her spine.

"Have you done this before?" he said.

She turned around in his arms, looking up at him. "Do I seem like a virgin to you?"

"Yes, actually. At least in some ways."

"What ways?"

"Are you?"

"No."

He shook his head gently. "Forgive me for asking. You just…"

"What?"

"For one, you don't seem like the kind of a person normally open to indecent propositions."

"Normally, no. But I am open to one now."

His hands closed over her back, sliding down in a slow caress that made her quiver. He caught the hem of her shirt, half-unbuttoned and loose, and pulled it up, over her head. His free hand traced down, over her collarbone, around her breast. Her nipple hardened when he rolled his thumb over it, sending a surge of pleasure all the way down to her core. She couldn't help a moan as she arched into his hands.

This can't possibly be real, was her last conscious thought. And then, his hand slid lower, and she couldn't think of anything at all.

OBLIVION

In his time, Karrim had had enough women to perfect his skills, enough to learn to overcome his desire for them, to channel it into battle. He didn't remember ever feeling like this. It was a delicious torture to balance on the edge as he savored every moment of holding Naia in his arms, her shivers as she yielded herself to him, her faint natural smell of wild honeyweed that reached directly to his primal core.

She said she wasn't a virgin, but she acted like one, in the way every one of his moves seemed to take her by surprise, in the mix of uncertainty and hunger in her response. Whoever had sex with her before was obviously inexperienced, or extremely inattentive. Just like three years ago, when Karrim had first encountered her raw talent stifled by the Har brutality, he was now encountering her raw sensuality, powerful but suppressed by inexperience. She clearly had no idea what her body was capable of. Karrim felt privileged to be the first one to show her, an idea his possessive side was finding more appealing than he cared to admit.

*

Through Naia's combat training she had learned many ways one could be rendered helpless in a fight. But she had never imagined anyone could have so much control over her body by giving her pleasure, or that she would be so eager for anyone to do whatever he wanted with her. As Karrim lay her down on the bed, his sheets cool to her burning skin, any idea of resisting whatever was happening to her seemed impossible.

At the very least, she should be feeling shy right now. No man had ever seen her naked before. Not like this, with the lantern light pouring over her, so that nothing could possibly escape his eye. But she couldn't find it in herself to feel ashamed. Instead, she felt drunk with the awe she saw in his eyes as he stroked her open and slid his hand below, into the heat between her legs. Her body shook with the sensation his touch brought, and she could feel this shiver echo in him too, as if, through their invisible link, he could feel every bit of her pleasure.

His hands played her, every slow stroke leaving her breathless, hitting exactly the right nerve. She could sense her release coming, and she was powerless to do anything at all about it, even if she wanted to. Her fingers dug into his skin as she gasped and arched into his hands, until she couldn't possibly hold it in anymore.

Tears rushed down her cheeks as she clenched and convulsed in his arms. Dear Sel, she could understand now why he had questioned her if she was a virgin. If this was what sex was supposed to be like, she had definitely been a virgin before.

He held her in his arms as her aftershocks died out, his toned, muscular body so warm and smooth against hers. It took her a while to come back, to look around, to see his smile, his gaze that made her stomach flutter.

"I... I never felt this way before," she said.

His eyes gleamed, his smile curving into a wicked grin. "That was just the start."

Virgin or not, Karrim was certain that the orgasm she'd just had was her first. He nearly climaxed too, just from watching her. And now, as she clung to him – thoroughly spent, but definitely ready for more – he couldn't possibly hold back any longer.

As he eased over her, she opened up to him so eagerly, guiding him inside. He meant to go slowly, but his mind momentarily blacked out as he entered her. Before he knew it, he was buried to the hilt, thrusting into her with force and speed he was having serious trouble controlling.

He slowed and held back just enough to make sure that he wasn't causing her pain, that she was all right. But then, she moaned and tilted into him. Hell, she was so wet, so tight, so eager. As he picked up a rhythm, her inner muscles tightened around him, showing him how close she was. *Too fast.* He had to pull back. He nearly did, but then she started convulsing around him, and he lost the last shreds of control.

Their screams joined into one as he drove them both to the peak, and into oblivion.

When Naia finally found the strength to move, she felt surprised to find her body seemingly intact, and light like she had never felt before. Karrim lay naked next to her, his hand trailing down her skin in a slow caress. Her heart quivered as she turned and met his gaze, stirring with warmth that made her feel weak.

Karrim's skill surpassed everything imaginable, but there was also more. He was her perfect match, in every possible way.

This last thought was scary, but she followed it through anyway. The Jaihar warriors didn't form bonds. She was probably just another conquest to him, one of those he was so famous for. She'd do her best to think of him this way too, no matter how differently she felt right now.

She heaved a breath, watching the movement of his hand trailing over her skin, the way his muscles shifted as he turned to face her more directly. How could the mere sight of him still excite her so much after being so thoroughly spent? Or was it the way he looked at her – as if she was a precious, cherished object he admired?

Was this how he looked at every woman after he'd just made love to her? She tried to tell herself that she didn't care.

His face relaxed into a grin as he saw her watching.

"I hope I didn't cross any boundaries," he said.

She grinned too. It was so easy to smile lying next to him. "You've crossed many of them, actually. What you did to me was…" She hesitated, trying to find the right word.

"What?"

Enjoyable? Amazing? Thrilling? None of the words she knew came even close. *To die for.* Yes, this was the way she felt – not something she would ever say to him. She tried to smile. "Um. Probably a bad idea?"

"Probably, yes."

"Do I hear regret?"

His grin faded. "Hell, no. You?"

"I started it, remember?"

"Some would say you merely responded to my suggestive behavior."

"Such as?"

He shrugged. "Oh, I don't know. Inviting you in, maybe?

Locking the door? Showing you the bed?"

"It was over there, in plain sight. Besides, I distinctly remember asking for it. You were trying to get me to sit down."

"I was trying to save you from a misstep."

"Well, you succeeded, obviously."

They looked at each other and laughed.

"I suppose I can concede to a more equal share of the blame," she said.

He found her hand and brought it to his lips, a tender gesture that made her shiver, head to toe. There was another word she could think of that applied to the way she was beginning to feel about him, but she knew she would never say it, even to herself. She chided herself for even thinking this way. She couldn't afford to consider what happened just now as something serious, something that could ever happen again. They both needed this, a culmination of the growing desire they had to suppress for so long. Now that they'd satisfied this urge, they should move apart and get on with their lives. They had an empire to fix, and they needed to be able to stay around each other without doing anything rash – or at least thinking about it all the time.

Except that she also knew she would never be able to stop thinking about it. Not when she already had a taste of him. Not when this taste proved to be everything she dreamed of – and so much more.

She tried to smile again, to pretend she was taking it lightly. It didn't work at first, but as she looked into his eyes, the smile came out easier. It took no effort to feel happy when she was lying naked next to him, her body still warm and tingling from the memory of the way he had claimed her just now, inside and outside.

I've dreamed about this ever since I first laid my eyes on you. It was best not to think about it either. The Jaihar were all about learning to take sex casually, something easily available and just as easily discarded on a whim. She would do well to finally embrace the idea. Except that, with Karrim, it felt so much harder to do it.

"Is anything wrong?" Karrim asked.

"No. I just…"

"What?"

She sighed. She supposed there was no harm in telling the truth, as long as she kept it only to the physical part. "I couldn't help regretting that this could probably never happen again."

He pushed up on his elbow over her, his hand sliding lower down her stomach, resting there with his fingers splayed, so that a mere twitch sent surges of pleasure down the paths she had no idea about. She gasped as she immersed into the new sensation.

"The night isn't over yet, is it?" he said. "Why don't we make the most of it?"

She nodded, unwilling to speak for fear of breaking the movement of his hand. Through half-closed lids she could see Karrim's grin. Hell, she probably *couldn't* move right now, even if she wanted. Not when he slid his finger lower, into her moisture, teasing her most sensitive spot.

Dear Sel, he has me completely in his power. She knew this wasn't true, not for a fighter of her skill, but she found it strangely alluring to think this way.

No use worrying about the future now, not when they were still together and could indulge in each other again and again until they had no more strength left.

CONVERSATION

"You look exhausted, Jai Karrim," Gassan said.

Karrim glanced away, shifting in the saddle to find a more relaxed position. Every muscle in his body ached, but even if he had to choose a thousand more times, he would never change a thing about what happened last night. And now, facing the day-long ride from Haggad to Zegmeer in the company of Gassan, whose piercing dark eyes didn't seem to miss a single detail in Karrim's appearance or mood, he knew he had to be extra careful.

It wasn't the first time in his life that he'd spent a night in lovemaking before starting out on an assignment, but he had never felt so utterly spent – or so happy about it.

"I'm fine, Dal Gassan," he said. "Thank you for your concern."

The Daljeer's eyes lit up with a gleam of suspicion, making Karrim uncomfortably aware that the older man probably knew – or at least guessed – more than he cared to reveal.

"I heard Jai Naia's performance at her ranking tournament was spectacular," Gassan said. "Too bad I wasn't allowed to witness it."

His voice was neutral, but Karrim did manage to catch the keen side glance, as if the man was purposely trying to gauge his reaction after throwing Naia's name into the conversation. It was like playing shatranj, and Karrim had to pull himself together if he wanted to have even a remote chance of not losing the match.

"It was impressive indeed," Karrim said. Inadvertently, his thoughts drifted to last night again, his body echoing with warmth at the memory. What happened between him and Naia had surpassed his wildest dreams. In many ways it had changed him forever, even if he was never going to admit it to anyone. Ever since he had first seen Naia – an innocent young girl enfolded in her armor of defiance – he couldn't stop dreaming about such an encounter. But the reality was so much better than he had imagined. He was going to cherish this memory to the end of his days.

He caught himself as he noticed Gassan's eyes on him.

"Any reason to watch me so closely, Dal Gassan?" The question was probably a mistake, if only by the way Gassan's expression shifted to predatory as if he just saw an opening for a blow.

"Yes, actually," Gassan said. "There's a question I've been curious about for quite some time. Given that we have so much time to spend together, I was wondering if you could enlighten me about it."

"What question?" Hell, Karrim knew he was going to regret this even as he spoke, but there was no possible way around it. Gassan was the kind of a person who would ask anyway. No use beating around the bush.

Gassan eyed him levelly. "Isn't it true that the top Jaihar warriors are supposed to be celibate?"

Karrim tossed his head, letting out a short laugh. "Celibate? Hell, no." *And I suppose you're expecting me to ask what brought on the topic.* Karrim should have taken extra care to look over his appearance this morning. He probably had a love bite or two somewhere in plain sight. Yet, no matter what he looked like, it was none of Gassan's business how he spent his time off duty, especially given the fact that Karrim wasn't even working for the Daljeer right now. In fact, he and Gassan could have had a good laugh about it, if Naia wasn't the one involved. The last thing he needed was to reveal anything like that to her employer on her very first assignment.

"At the very least, relationships between Jaihar warriors are forbidden, aren't they?" Gassan said.

The way the Daljeer paused confirmed that he was giving Karrim an opportunity to ask the question. His brow furrowed in disappointment when Karrim failed to oblige. It was like deviating from a common shatranj gambit, a tactic that usually didn't pay off, but in the short run tended to bring on a hell of a lot of satisfaction.

"Lasting relationships that carry an emotional load are forbidden, yes," Karrim said. *But not the occasional sexual ones.* Given that most Jaihar were men, it was usually a moot point anyway, with rare exceptions. But Karrim felt too tired to pursue this thought, even in his head.

"And who's the one to decide if a relationship has gone too far?"

Karrim sighed. He was not in the mood to play these games right now. Not when he was having too much trouble staying in the saddle.

"I assume all this questioning has a point," he said.

"Hell, yes. Jai Naia is instrumental to all my plans. And you are supposed to assist her on this assignment, as permitted by your other duties."

Or kill her, if things don't turn out the Jaihar's way. In Karrim's tired stupor, the thought seemed almost ironic. "I'm afraid I still don't see your point, Dal."

"Oh, I am very sure you do."

Karrim slowly turned around in the saddle to face the older man.

"Given that you are an important patron of the Jaihar Order, Dal Gassan, I believe my superiors right now would want me to reassure you that whatever I, or any other of our warriors, choose to do in their off time will not, in any way, threaten any of our assignments. Privately, however, I feel obliged to add that this is none of your business. I trust this is the last time the topic ever comes up between us."

The Daljeer held a thoughtful pause. "For now, Jai Karrim. And thank you for your reassurance."

Karrim glanced at him curiously. "You have an issue with me, don't you?"

"Not with you, as such. With your cockiness, mostly. Especially when it comes to women, pardon the unintended pun. Jai Arsat seems to have great faith in you – but, with an assignment of this magnitude, I can't help feeling concerned."

Karrim knew he should probably be annoyed, but the idea of a Daljeer senior fearing his involvement because of his effect on women just seemed too ridiculous.

"You think I can't keep my cock in my pants," he said.

"I have a number of court ladies to back me up on this assessment, actually."

"They're just bragging."

"Seriously, can you?"

Karrim didn't bother to respond, keeping his eyes on the breathtaking view of the sun-kissed foothills cascading off into the sea of sand. The dunes rose like waves, spreading toward the eastern horizon. In just a few miles they would come into the distant sight of the Imperial City of Zegmeer, but here in the wilderness one could feel as if these lands were as virginal as they used to be centuries ago, before the rise of the Zeg Empire.

He supposed Gassan did have a reason to worry, with the way things had gone last night. Karrim himself was finding it unthinkable to entertain the possibility that he would have to follow through with the last order he received. He knew the price that came with his high rank. Regardless of his feelings, he was not going to waver if it came to the worst – and this realization in itself was too horrifying to dwell on right now, with the memory of last night still warm on his skin, with the way his body ached at the mere thought that next time he saw Naia he would not be allowed within touching distance of her.

"Perhaps we could leave my cock alone and use this chance to talk more about your assignment?" he said.

Gassan glanced at him sideways. "What about it?"

"I'd like to know more about Dal Mehtab."

"Mehtab?"

"Yes."

"Why?"

"She has been very close to Naia for the past three years, as far as I understand. And now, her position as Princess Xarimet's handwoman places her at the center of the whole operation. How much do you trust her?"

Gassan shrugged. "She is a Daljeer of high standing. A Chall by origin. A brilliant scholar, or so I heard."

"*Heard?*"

"Yes. Why?"

"I thought you knew each other personally."

"We met briefly, about twenty years ago, but our paths took us separate ways until this assignment came up. She'd spent most of her life in Challimar. My base is in our main serai in Zegmeer."

"Back to my question then. How much do you trust her?"

"As much as I do any other Daljeer of her skill."

"This doesn't seem like an answer."

"It's the best I can give you, I'm afraid."

"In that case, I'd like to say something else, Dal. It is imperative for an assignment like this that everyone involved understands the proper chain of command – and that everyone can follow orders, no matter what."

"You are speaking like a military man."

"I *am* a military man. But, regardless of my occupation, it's the only way to operate, especially on this kind of a scale. The sooner your Daljeer subordinates can start doing things this way the better."

Gassan paused, rocking in the saddle with the measured steps of his horse. Karrim did not rush him, enjoying the view.

The road ahead narrowed, constricted by two cliffs of velvety red rock that formed a walled passage in between. Deadman's Pass, named this way after an ancient general died as he rode through it with an arrow in his chest, right into the waiting arms of his loyal troops. The locals affectionately referred to the place as "Maiden's Cleft". The passage did resemble a very tight womb, an ideal point for ambush and a sore spot for the Jaihar Order, given the fact that its patrons often traveled this way carrying lots of gold. The raids had stopped lately, after Arsat had ordered a particularly successful campaign against the local bandits, but the bad fame remained, forcing those who were not in a hurry to take a long way between Haggad and Zegmeer through the western foothills.

Despite its reputation, the place was beautiful, the dramatic backdrop of the red cliffs accented by the curtain of silvery green honeyweed vines running along its side. At this time of the year they stood in full bloom, their fuzzy yellow flowers emanating a faint aroma that instantly echoed in Karrim's chest. Naia's skin had a natural honeyweed smell, and just now even a small waft of it was enough for his entire body to stir, rising to action despite his exhaustion.

Three hells, what in the world was he going to do in Zegmeer, where he would have to work side by side with her without any possibility to act on his longing for her?

A faint movement at the corner of his vision sprang him back to alertness. As his eyes darted in search of the source, he also detected a barely perceptible hum of a small flying object, approaching at high speed. *An arrow.* Karrim shot out his hand, catching it by the shaft. He had a brief moment to register Gassan's blank stare before he kicked his horse into a gallop, racing toward the source of the shot.

He spotted the attackers at once, now that he knew where to look – three men hiding behind the rock protrusion, in the shelter of the vines. What the hell were they thinking, attacking a Jaihar of his rank?

He didn't bother with the crossbow strapped at his saddle, drawing three daggers off his belt and sending them flying just as he approached the ambushers at full speed. His heightened senses caught three thuds as the blades reached their targets, followed by groans and whimpers. Three bodies folded out of their hideout and rolled slowly down the side of the cliff.

Karrim knew he would have no time to bother with all three. He hoped the one survivor he chose would remain alive during the questioning. As he reined his horse into an abrupt stop, he reached over just in time to catch the falling man by his arm, breaking his fall, sliding off the saddle to lower him smoothly into the reddish road dust.

Alive. Good. He glanced over at the other two bodies, sprawled a few feet away. His aim had been good – two to the heart, killing the men instantly, one to the leg, enough to render the man immobile, yet not enough to threaten his life. The captive crouched against the cliff now, his eyes darting wildly between his two dead companions. He was avoiding Karrim's gaze, which spoke of the fact that he probably recognized the Jaihar, at least by reputation. *Bloody stupid, to attack a Shadowblade with only three men.* Karrim kept the thought to himself, waiting for Gassan to dismount and step up to his side.

Gassan leaned over the prisoner, studying him. Karrim looked too, noting the man's youth – probably just over twenty—as well as the golden speckles in his brown eyes, hinting at his Chall origin. Nothing like the rich dark gold of Naia's eyes, but enough to trigger a memory. Karrim glanced away, meeting Gassan's gaze.

"Challimar rebels, I believe," Gassan said.

The prisoner's lips twitched. "Daljeer dog."

Gassan sighed. "Pleasantries aside, what were you thinking?"

"We were thinking you would be traveling alone, Dal Gassan."

If Gassan was surprised that the man knew him by name, he certainly hid it well. "Well, I wasn't alone, was I?"

"How were we supposed to know he's a high-ranked Jaihar?" The wounded man's eyes slid over Karrim with hatred and fear.

Karrim shrugged. In his tiredness, with the way he slouched in the saddle, he probably did inadvertently seem less threatening to the men watching them from a distance. But this thought wasn't nearly as important as the fact that his decision to ride with Gassan had been a last minute one. Had Gassan been alone, he'd likely be dead. Too close a call for a man who had just set forth a grand plan to bring down the empire.

"Why do you want me dead?" Gassan asked.

The prisoner looked sideways, his mouth forcefully snapping closed. Karrim caught a waft of a smell, sweet and bitter at the same time. He reached over and grabbed Gassan, pulling him away. The tiny cloud washed over them and dissipated into the rising wind, too transient to do any harm.

"Was that–" Gassan started.

"Devil's ash." Karrim turned to the prisoner – still and stiff, his glassy eyes staring into the distance, his lips frozen in a twisted smile.

Gassan was already on his knees, searching through the dead men's clothing.

"Nothing," he said.

"Can't say I'm surprised."

"You look like something's bothering you, though. What is it, Jai Karrim?"

Apart from the fact that I just killed three men? "They seemed far too well-informed about your travel plans."

"My travel plans are rarely a secret."

"A bloody mistake, if you'll forgive the expression."

"I tend to be very forgiving of someone who's just saved my life. And yes, perhaps you are right. I should be more careful from now on."

"Did anyone in the Daljeer serai know you and I were going

to travel together today?"

"I didn't have a chance to tell anyone. They all know I usually travel alone. Why?"

"Probably nothing." Karrim walked back to his horse and mounted it in one quick move. "You mentioned these attackers were likely Chall rebels."

"The only plausible possibility, as far as I know."

"Why do Chall rebels want you dead?"

"They hate all Zeg, don't they?"

"That is not an answer."

The older man's gaze trailed away for a very brief instant. "Some believe the Daljeer were the main driving force behind Challimar's destruction."

"Why would anyone think that?"

"We had the most to gain in the long run, by taking possession of all Challimar's scholarly achievements."

"Doesn't seem like reason enough to kill."

"It does, to those who value knowledge above all else." Gassan sighed, climbing into his saddle. "The Daljeer did benefit a lot, especially after the Royal Massacre, when the emperor gifted us with the entire contents of the queen's personal library. I suppose, to the Chall loyalists, it may have looked like a reward for our part in the planning. Worse, I can't even tell if there's any truth to these rumors. After I took charge of the Daljeer, I made sure that anyone with even a remote possibility to have had anything to do with Challimar's tragedy stood as far away as possible from power."

"Seems drastic."

"It was the least I could do." Gassan touched the reins, urging his horse into a walk.

They rode in silence through the tight gauntlet of the

red cliffs. Karrim kept on high alert, but he could spot no movement at all around them. Not even a sound, save for the whisper of the rising breeze and a distant cry of a hawk. Whoever their attackers were, they were likely alone, a thought that seemed somewhat reassuring.

"So, what happens when we arrive in Zegmeer?" he said.

Gassan shrugged. "We stick to our plans."

"We need to take extra steps to ensure your safety."

"There's no need, really."

"What if you run into another assassination attempt?"

Gassan turned to face him. "I am very touched by your concern, Jai Karrim. But such attempts are not new to me – nor would they ever cease, even if we take extra precautions. The only way I can think of making things better is to follow through with our plans and put a reasonable man on the throne, which should end the unrest once and for all. So, let's keep our eyes on the goal, shall we?"

He kicked his horse into a trot, and Karrim had no choice but to follow.

PRINCESS XARIMET OF CHALLIMAR

Naia lowered her reins, letting her horse walk on freely as she looked at the large gateway ahead. *The Imperial Palace.* The tall towers rising at its sides made it look like an entrance to a grand temple, yet she could see no religious symbols anywhere in sight. Instead, their carved ornaments were shaped like imperial crests, with the royal Zeg emblem over the top – an eagle on the back of a lion.

The plaza in front of the gate was flooded with people. It was hard to see all the way across, to the elevated platform at the far end. The twelve motionless shapes around its perimeter had to be the Jaihar Imperial Dozen, but from this distance she couldn't see anything except their cloaks, flipped to the black side to hide their distinction and ranks. One of them was Karrim. The thought made her feel warm inside.

Her eyes hovered on the occupant of the tall, massive chair set inside the Jaihar ring. Prince Ramaz, the heir to the throne, here to accept condolences and pledges of loyalty on behalf of the imperial family. Not officially crowned yet, but assumed to be the next emperor in only a few hours.

Well, this arrangement was about to change.

She glanced at Mehtab, riding next to her with visible discomfort. The woman was a brilliant scholar and an expert on every Chall custom, but she definitely had things to learn when it came to physical exercise. On the other hand, Naia tended to feel this way about nearly everyone non-Jaihar – especially during the past week, when she had traveled from Haggad to the Daljeer serai in Zegmeer and stayed there in confinement to undergo some last-minute preparations, with nearly no time to exercise. She felt a guilty sense of relief that the news of the emperor's death, announced in the serai at dawn, meant that she could now escape her confinement and take the stage.

This was the day she'd been preparing for, since long before she knew about it. The ultimate mission any Jaihar could only dream of – leading a dynasty change in the empire that would alter the flow of history. She could barely contain her excitement.

The Daljeer had spared no detail in preparing her grand entrance. Her outfit was blinding to look at, its yellow silk, covered by a heavy jeweled cloak of the Challimar royal family, gleaming in the morning sun. Her guards, three dozen men wearing red cloaks over singular Challimar breastplates, towered on each side of her in a diamond-shaped formation. All of them were ethnic Chall, as far as Naia could tell, making it seem as if the royal Redcloak unit had risen from the dead to accompany her on this ride. The effect had to be very powerful to all the spectators watching her pass by, their cheers rising in waves all the way down the plaza and into the streets beyond.

As she rode by, head high, people watched her in an

enchanted semi-trance, as if she was the Holy Prophet descending from the sky. She had seen these looks before, even among her small entourage. There was no way her Daljeer-appointed guards and servants could possibly believe she was the real Xarimet, yet seeing their expressions sometimes made her wonder. Their reverence, whenever she was around, bordered on worship.

Up until now, her preparations for the role were nothing but rehearsing, trying to foresee possible scenarios and to prepare for them the best she could. Now she was living the role, in real time. As she glanced haughtily toward the royal platform ahead, she felt every bit the royal pain in the neck she had been trained to be. Every small gesture mattered, and she got it all down to every tiny detail.

Half of the city must be streaming behind her, a colorful crowd where Zeg, Raj, Chall, and Scinn mixed into a giant torrent that swept and flooded the busy main street, collecting all the small streams that trickled from the side alleys to join them. She could hear their hails all the way down to the bazaar, a continuous wave of sound rising and falling like a tide. *Hail, Xarimet! Shahgar, Chall!*

The procession halted in the center of the plaza, where they dismounted and proceeded on foot through a double chain of the imperial guards toward the palace. The crowd here looked more organized, groups of nobles and their entourages gathered under their banners. Rulers of the provinces and members of the High Council. To the best of Naia's knowledge, many of them had been privately forewarned about her arrival. Yet, as they all stared at her open-mouthed, it seemed as if until just now they had no idea at all about her existence.

She trailed her gaze past them to the royal platform, fixing it on Prince Ramaz.

Memories hit her without warning, real, as if she was experiencing one of Mehtab's dreams. The plaza around her faded – still there, but not as real as the visions in her head. She saw the large hexagonal hall; the tall, regal man standing in the center, talking to the queen. She remembered his frown, his abrupt gesture that signaled the execution of everyone Chall in that hall.

It wasn't the same man, no. Prince Ramaz looked more frail than his father, his thin lips twitched into a cruel line, his dark eyes darting restlessly around. Not a cold-blooded murderer, but a maniac whose unpredictability was far worse than Shabaddin's famed temper. Yet, somehow, the image of the two men superimposed in her mind, forming a memory that couldn't possibly be hers.

She blinked, slowly coming back to reality, hoping that her moment of confusion didn't show as she took another look at her rival.

Ramaz's appearance fit everything she'd learned about him. Pale face, framed by an unruly mane of jet-black hair. Cruel gleam in his busy eyes. The short whip on his belt, its white leather covered with splotches of rust. *Dry blood.* Even the mantle over his shoulders was just as described – a long jeweled strip of soft, delicately tanned skin. His mother's, if one believed the rumors. Naia swallowed, running her eyes over the rest of the group gathered on the platform – the other imperial princes; the elderly sages of the Divan; Gassan, hidden among a small group of Daljeer standing off to the side; the imperial guards; and yes, the Jaihar Dozen. She knew each of them by name, and she saw recognition and bewilderment in their eyes as they looked at her – a compliment to her disguise. Karrim, at the very back, gave her a brief smile – eyes only – that washed over her with warmth.

It seemed hard to believe that all these impressions took only a moment, as the sounds of her name, announced by a liveried man at the side of the platform, echoed over the heads of the crowd.

"Princess Xarimet of Challimar!"

Ramaz's gaze, already fixed on her with nearly palpable intensity, hardened. He frowned, then forced a grimace-like smile that didn't touch the upper part of his face.

"Is this some kind of a sick joke?" He glanced at the announcer. "Skin him alive. It will teach everyone here better than to blabber out nonsense without thinking twice."

The announcer edged away in panic, stopped short as he realized that no one was about to obey. Everyone, even the guards, were looking at Naia with expectation.

"Don't speak," Mehtab whispered from behind. "Let the Daljeer handle this one."

Naia ignored her.

"Do you find my name amusing, Prince Ramaz?" she said. "Or do you, like me, feel entertained by the fact that people in this plaza are cheering for me louder than they ever cheered for you?"

Gasps echoed around her. Naia saw the Daljeer exchange glances and frowns. But she didn't care. If she wanted to win this match, she had to keep her eyes on the prize.

The prince's eyes narrowed as he turned to exchange words with a thin, bearded man behind him. Sage Yakkab, the Grand Vizier, according to the descriptions. An ally, even if a skeptical one. The older men at his sides must be the sages of the Imperial Divan. No important decisions in the palace were ever made without their approval.

Ramaz was talking agitatedly, his long fingers clutching the handle of his whip. Yakkab appeared to soothe him, bowing deeply, speaking quietly into the prince's ear. The sages around them edged away, glancing around nervously.

After a lengthy exchange, Yakkab stepped forward.

"His Imperial Highness requests proof of your identity."

Naia heard a shuffle of papers beind her. The Daljeer of her suite, producing the painstakingly prepared paperwork that was supposed to authenticate her. A waste of time in the mind games Ramaz was trying to play. She raised her hand to stop them.

"His Imperial Highness should be speaking to his own record-keepers about this. Papers authenticating my lineage are in order, and will be provided to them after we're done here. I have no wish to waste my time on such mundane details."

"Neither do I," Ramaz said. "We are done here. Guards, kill her."

Again, nobody moved. No one even turned their heads, all eyes – including the Daljeer – fixed on Naia.

She smiled. "Do you always run to your guards when making decisions, prince?"

Ramaz swallowed. She could tell that behind his fury he was beginning to panic, fighting with all he had not to show it.

"You're no princess," he said. "You reek like a commoner. I can smell it all the way from here."

"Ah, the reek. It's not that obvious from where I stand, prince. I can tell for certain that it's not coming from here. In fact, I sense it trail all the way from the imperial seat."

More gasps echoed around them. Ramaz's face lit up with uneven red splotches. The sight seemed strangely comforting.

Naia'd gotten well used to it during her time on the Har grounds.

"How *dare* you?" Ramaz said.

"I make it a point to always speak my mind, Prince Ramaz. One royal to another."

"Guards!"

"Do you allow your guards to speak for you too, then?"

"*Kill her!*"

Naia could see the Jaihar around the platform tense up imperceptibly, but she kept her place. Her instincts told her that at this point in the game, with all the preparations in place, no one was going to rush at her with weapons – not in a way that mattered, at least. But even with this knowledge, it was remarkable to see no one move at all.

She seized the moment, raising her voice and pitching it to a deeper timbre that made it easier for the sound to roll through the plaza.

"I, Xarimet of the royal line of Challimar, hereby step forth to claim my birthright to the imperial throne. I challenge you to a succession contest, Prince Ramaz."

Ramaz jumped to his feet and rushed to the edge of the platform, towering over her. Her arms flexed on instinct, at the ready to subdue him. He caught the movement and receded – and for the first time since she walked in here, she saw genuine fear in his eyes.

"She can't," Ramaz said. "She *can't* do that."

"Princess Xarimet's birth records are genuine, prince," Sage Yakkab said. "To the best of our knowledge, she is the true Challimar heir."

"Whoever she is, *no one* can challenge me!"

"I'm afraid she can, Your Imperial Highness. Challimar is the only kingdom in the empire that still carries the legal right to do so."

Ramaz's hand clutched the handle of the whip on his belt so tightly that his knuckles went white. "She will bloody lose."

Yakkab swallowed, his eyes drifting over Naia with an unreadable expression. "Perhaps, Your Imperial Highness. But by law, we must allow her claim to proceed to the council vote."

"If she lives that long." The last words, spoken softly, carried only to the people in the immediate vicinity. Ramaz's face was red now, his cheek twitching. He looked at Naia for a moment longer, then turned and strode off the platform, followed by the other princes and all his guards.

A long silence followed his departure.

"Come now, Sage Yakkab. Even with all the paperwork, how do you know she is the real Xarimet?" The voice came from a tall, dark-haired man, standing under the silver and blue crescent-shaped banner. Naia recalled her lessons as she turned to the speaker, putting the features she learned from descriptions onto the real man. Prince Ajarham Selim, the ruler of the rebel-embattled province of Raj that fared the worst under Shabaddin's rule. This man would have every reason to support her. Why was he acting so confrontational?

"The Daljeer are prepared for these questions," Mehtab whispered fervently. "Let us—"

"I'll handle it." Naia stepped forward, ignoring the rising whispers behind her.

Whatever the Daljeer believed, entertaining this kind of questioning could be endless and would likely play into her opponents' hands. Prince Ramaz and his supporters, if any, would drag these questions on forever, blocking her claim from proceeding to the council vote. If she wanted to establish her position unequivocally, she needed to do something different.

Most people associated with the Challimar Royal Massacre were dead, but she was certain that some of the closest advisors to the emperor from those times must still be around. In her visions, she remembered the men of the emperor's suite who were not warriors, clearly there in the advisory role, some older than Shabaddin. If she could identify at least one present here, it should be enough to turn the conversation.

She turned back to the royal platform, calling up the visions she'd had during her lessons with Mehtab, the semi-trance that had always been induced by Mehtab's voice. It helped that she was wearing the imlar neklace now, lying snugly over her collarbones.

Her inner vision drew her away, back into that large hexagonal room of her dreams. This time, right into the heart of the battle. She heard the screams, the clanging of weapons. Saw the veil lying over her face. Her nostrils filled with the metallic smell of blood. Faces loomed around her, Chall and Zeg, their expressions ranging from cruelty to horror. *The faces…*

A part of her continued to realize that there was no way in the world she could possibly have this kind of memory. It must be all part of the Daljeer's magic – or scholarly knowledge, as they insisted it was. But it didn't really matter. It served, at least for now. Naia focused on her altered state of mind, until some of the people on the royal platform started to acquire an extra dimension, as if seen through two sets of eyes, in two different time lines. Very few, two or three, maybe. In the here and now, they looked old, stooping with age. But there, in the past, she could see their younger faces, both familiar and different at the same time. If superimposed, she could now identify them…
Or was it the way they emanated nervousness, fidgeting and

keeping to the back rows?

She turned to the one who stood out the most. A middle-aged man, his eyes darting around, as if intent on keeping off her face at all cost. *Darting eyes.* She held on to the image, calling up his face in her memory at the same time. Dark, thick hair, now showing distinct streaks of gray. Deep lines of age etched into his forehead and cheeks… Lines of worry? Guilt?

"You." She pointed. "What is your name?"

The older man trembled. "Hakeem."

She noted his Chall blood now – subtle, but recognizable in the gold rimming the brown of his eyes. He was watching her with apprehension, as if anticipating a blow.

"You were there, weren't you?" she said. "You were in the chamber, when my family met their doom."

The sages around them parted, leaving the old man standing alone in front of her.

Slow, uncertain, he took a step forward.

"How could you *know*?" His lips trembled and closed, as if he couldn't fully control them.

"I remember," Naia said quietly.

Prince Ajarham of Raj shook his head. "You're too young. You *can't* possibly remember anything like this. It's all a setup, isn't it?"

"I also remember the reason for the conflict," Naia said. "My family refused to sign away their royal claim. They chose death over forsaking our birthright. Today, I am here to set things right, to make sure my family didn't die for nothing. To end the tyranny in this empire." She turned to Hakeem. "You tried to protect my mother, before she was struck down." *My mother.* There, she said it. Whether or not she believed it to be true, the image had now become part of her. "For that, I thank you, Sage

Hakeem."

The plaza around them sank into silence. Even with her warrior senses, Naia could detect no movement at all, everyone within earshot frozen in place, watching her.

"You... you were but a newborn," Hakeem whispered. "You can't possibly know..."

"I am an Ironblood. Our memories are long, even those from our infant days. You, a Chall, should know it well."

"A Chall?" Ajarham said, but no one was listening to him anymore. Slowly, the sages approached and gathered at the edge of the platform, looking at her in mesmerized silence.

"Princess Xarimet." Hakeem's voice broke. "Your Royal Highness." He folded down to his knees, pressing his forehead to the floor.

The plaza kept still for another moment, then exploded with a rising cheer. For a moment, the wave of sounds drowned all else. Naia let it wash over her as she swept the plaza with a regal glance, her eyes hovering on the key points that could tell her what to expect next. The representatives and nobles from all the imperial provinces, huddled under their banners. Gassan and the Daljeer, watching her with captivated looks. Sages and courtiers, their expressions varied between shock, disbelief, and reverence.

Sage Yakkab bowed to her deeply. "Your Royal Highness. Allow me to be among the first to welcome you into the imperial palace. In preparation for the succession contest, it would be my honor to personally escort you inside."

The guards in front of them were parting, Naia's suite rearranging itself for entrance into the palace. She didn't bother to look. She kept her eyes on the Grand Vizier, on his slightly stooping posture, on the etch of worry in the lines around his deeply set eyes, bright and clear, despite his advanced age.

"Your plan had better work," Yakkab said quietly. His lowered hand trembled as he slid his gaze from Naia to Gassan, who had stepped up to her other side.

The glance that went between the two men sent a shiver down Naia's spine. She knew that Yakkab had been the empire's last defense for the past two decades of Shabaddin's rule. Sel knew what he had to endure in this role, what he had to do to stay in power. She may never learn why Gassan, and her Jaihar seniors, felt so personally invested in this plan to overturn the ruling dynasty. But now that the game was in play, she couldn't possibly let them all down. No matter what, she had to make her mission a success.

She knew that all these people around her, looking up at her with disbelief and hope, had put their faith in the Daljeer, not her. But for better or worse, she was the only one who had the power to see it through.

A ROYAL BATH

"You took a lot of risks today," Mehtab said. "Was it really necessary?"

Naia shrugged. Mehtab's frown of disapproval was familiar, an expression that tended to preclude lectures on royal manners or obscure aspects of politics. Except that none of this seemed merited now. Well, perhaps Naia did outstep her script, by acting even more arrogantly than she was taught, but wasn't the training she received all about merging into the role?

"You can't possibly get your way by playing safe all the time," she said.

"It's not your business to judge these things. You acted against my explicit instructions. You could have ruined everything."

"Well, I didn't, did I?"

"Fortunately for all of us, not this time." Mehtab pursed her lips and turned away, busying herself with unpacking.

Naia watched her curiously. It must have seemed scary to Mehtab, one of the orchestrators of the whole plan, to watch Naia take the lead and act independently, without being able to interfere. But didn't it work out well in the end? She wasn't quite sure why Mehtab was so upset.

"I didn't plan any of it," she said. "It's just that when they all started questioning me, I had to do something."

"Yes, you had to – whatever you were told to do."

"Would Princess Xarimet have done what she was told, in my place?"

"You are not her."

"I am, to all these people."

Mehtab leaned closer. "I *trained* you to be this way. Every word, every action you perform in this role is *my* doing. If you ignore my instructions and fail, you'll ruin many lives. Don't think your little success today can outweigh all that."

Naia shrugged. It was useless to argue when Mehtab was in such a bossy mood. Better to wait it out. Maybe when Gassan showed up, as she was sure he was going to sooner or later, they could all have a more normal conversation?

She took extra care to check out her chambers. Staying here would make her vulnerable, especially after Ramaz had expressed his intention to kill her so clearly and publicly. She needed to know where to expect danger from.

The suite was more luxurious than anything Naia had ever seen. Four large rooms opened into an antechamber that rivaled in size the Jaihar Headmaster's audience hall. Her bedroom, reachable through a short passage in the middle, looked big enough to house a squadron, far too excessive for one person. She gaped at the vast space, dominated by a low, wide bed, then walked past it to the window opening into the garden outside. Any average assassin would likely come from there, even if there was no way to predict the more sophisticated ones. She took care to close the shutters and check them for holes, before proceeding into the next room at the far end.

The bath chamber.

Dear Sel.

Moist vapors, fragrant with lavender, rose oil, and just a tinge of sulfur underneath, enfolded her face as she stepped inside. The room had an octagonal shape, arranged around a large basin built into the floor, glimmering with gold inlays snaking between ornate blue and white tiles.

It took her a moment to realize where the light was coming from. The faceted glass panels overhead splintered the sunlight into myriads of tiny rainbows, playing in the crystal-clear water of the basin. Naia heaved a long breath as she stood in the doorway, watching its turmoil.

The imperial palace was built on hot springs, one of the major reasons for the choice of its location. In the scope of Naia's mission this knowledge was a minor detail. But now that she saw it, she found herself ridiculously excited at the idea.

Through the steam, the blue and white inlays of the walls seemed locked in a perpetual motion, highlighted by the play of the turbulent waters. She could see all the way to the bottom, through streams of tiny bubbles rising to the surface. If she submerged into it, they would probably tingle her skin. She heaved another breath of the warm, humid air, trying not to dwell on the thought.

The door behind her creaked open to let in Mehtab. As the older woman stepped up to her side, her lips twitched into an idle smile. Oddly, her face showed none of the earlier irritation, no trace that they ever had an argument at all. Good, no difficult conversations then. Just in case, Naia kept her eyes away, focusing on the flow of the water.

"Go ahead," Mehtab said.

"Go ahead and what?"

Mehtab pointed with her chin. "Take a bath."

"Really?" Naia looked at the woman with doubt. It was so unlike Mehtab to suggest a leisurely activity in the middle of action, especially right after they had a disagreement.

Mehtab stepped forward and crouched at the edge of the basin to touch the water, then quickly stepped away. "It's perfect. And we have plenty of time. It will take Sage Yakkab hours to make the arrangements."

"Hours?" Naia frowned. Back on the plaza, Yakkab seemed anxious to proceed as soon as possible. "Why that long?"

"It's not as easy as you think," Mehtab said. "Prince Ramaz will insist on having your papers examined and reexamined by the top imperial scholars. In the meantime, Yakkab has to go through all the formal preparations for the council gathering. That is bound to take time."

"I'm sure Sage Yakkab will do his best."

"Don't bet on it. As of yesterday, he was not completely convinced."

"Well, he is convinced today. In fact, he's as motivated as we are."

"Oh, and you are suddenly an expert on these things?"

"I am, in his case. I saw it in his face."

Mehtab stiffened for a moment, then relaxed as she reached over and patted Naia's shoulder. "Don't let your success on the plaza today go to your head. It was just a start. Remember, your job is to stay alive and follow instructions, and let the Daljeer do the rest."

Naia didn't respond. In all her time with Mehtab, she'd learned well that the older woman did not like to relinquish control to anyone at all. She wasn't sure how Mehtab and

Gassan were getting along, given that he had seniority in all the important decisions. But it definitely didn't sit well with Mehtab if Naia showed any inclination to think on her own.

She looked back at the bath. If they indeed had hours at their disposal, there couldn't possibly be any harm in enjoying the bath, could there? The chamber seemed secure. The faceted glass panes on the ceiling looked like permanent fixtures, too thick for anyone to break through without causing a major ruckus. The door through her bedroom was the only way in and out. If she locked it, she would be reasonably safe here, at least in the short term.

"All right, I'll take a bath," she said.

Mehtab nodded. "Good. While you do, I will take care of some errands and prepare your official outfit. Dal Gassan will come here to appraise us, as soon as he learns the exact timing of the succession ceremony." She gave Naia a quick sideways smile and departed without waiting for a response.

Naia took care to lock the door behind the older woman, then shed her clothes and crouched at the side of the basin, watching its crystal-clear movement. Fragrant steam rising from the water gently caressed her skin, beckoning. It had been a while since she took a proper bath, and none of the ones she'd seen before were nearly as luxurious as this. Hell, one could easily get used to the palace comforts.

She was about to dive in when an odd movement at the far end of the pond caused her to pause in mid-step. Was it the twirling of the underwater streams that caused it? It seemed like the most natural explanation, but to her warrior's eye something felt slightly off. A special iridescent gleam stood out from the general turmoil, moving in odd patterns, as if alive.

Naia circled the pond, peering into the water. She caught it now – a narrow glassy ribbon coiling under the surface, about a palm in length and so transparent it looked nearly invisible.

A Crystal leech. Their venom was one of the rarest and most potent substances known to Naia, a slow but certain death. The nearly odorless substance was even more dangerous because it left no trace when it entered the body. The poisoned person initially didn't feel a thing, making it relatively easy for the poisoner to get away before the victim dropped dead an hour or so later. The effect was cumulative, more potent with higher doses, and definitely aided by the effect of a hot bath. This made the poison highly valued, even if far too expensive for regular use.

Crystal leech trade was not officially recognized, but those who dealt in poisons and herbs and wished to venture into this dangerous but profitable enterprise employed specially trained leech hunters. Those were desperate men, who spent their usually short lives traveling to the glacier lakes at the highest peaks of the Halayar Range, where they killed leeches on the spot, collecting a few precious drops of their body juices. To the best of Naia's knowledge, no one ever used live leeches – the creatures were not only dangerous but also so fragile and sensitive to their environment that keeping them alive in captivity normally wasn't worth the trouble.

Anyone crazy enough to bring a live leech to Zegmeer and let it loose in this basin must be extremely wealthy, which significantly narrowed the list of possible culprits. She supposed she should feel honored that someone here had gone to all this trouble on her account, but the incident served as a reminder of how serious things were. Given that the leech looked very much alive, it had to have been planted right before she entered the chamber – a very short window for anyone to act.

She sat near the edge of the water, watching the tiny maw adorned with neat rows of needle-like teeth open and close as the animal transitioned from the state of agitation – one where it was most likely to bite anyone nearby – into the beginnings of death agony. This warm water with high mineral content could sustain the leech for a while, but it was going to kill it in the end. No reason to engage in any heroics when time and patience were going to finish the job.

Naia waited until the glassy shape floated lifelessly up to the surface, then used her delicate headscarf to fish it out and lay it on the edge of the basin. The dead leech was beginning to swell and turn milky, like a link of udder sausage in the window of a butcher's shop. It probably still held plenty of venom, so Naia kept clear of touching it with her bare hands as she wrapped it up more securely, so that she could carry it without doing any damage, and put it on a bench near the door.

She returned to the water and peered inside, making sure there were no other surprises. From what she remembered about the leech poison, it disintegrated quickly in warm water, so she waited a few more moments to make sure, then slid in and stretched out, relaxing against the smooth tiled wall. It was probably reckless of her to take a bath here after what happened, but she simply couldn't resist the temptation.

When Naia returned to the anteroom, the leech bundled discreetly in the scarf draped over her arm, she felt refreshed and balanced – just the right state of mind to greet Gassan, pacing back and forth across the large space.

"Where's Mehtab?" he asked, as soon as she walked in.

Naia looked at him in surprise. The older woman was by her side all the time lately. Now that Gassan mentioned it, her absence when Naia exited the bath chamber and dressed did seem unusual. She assumed Mehtab had retired to the servants' quarters, but looking in the direction of the open door, she could see no movement inside.

"She mentioned running some errands. I assumed them to be for the Daljeer."

"I'm sure they are." Gassan smiled. "Well done today, by the way."

"Thanks."

"You had them all convinced, even Prince Ramaz."

"Not Prince Ajarham of Raj, though."

"Especially Prince Ajarham of Raj. He's just not the kind of a man to admit it openly. As for Yakkab, the old man was near tears when he spoke to me later on. He looks at you as a savior, and has given us unconditional support, all thanks to you."

Naia grinned. "Mehtab didn't seem all that happy with the way I acted."

Gassan's eyes drifted away briefly, as if Naia's words somehow caught him by surprise. "Anything in particular she said to you?"

"Not really, no. I believe she just doesn't feel comfortable with my tendency to deviate from the script."

"I think I know what you are referring to," Gassan grinned. "Mehtab's wrong, in this case. What you did today is yet another proof that you were born for this assignment. Quite literally, I believe. In this role, confining yourself to the script can easily lead to a fatal mistake. I am sure Dal Mehtab understands it too, no matter what she said to you."

"I'm sure she does." Naia glanced away. Gassan's reaction, his surprise at Mehtab's actions, didn't sit well with her. Up until now she had assumed that the Daljeer were in full agreement with each other about the way that events were supposed to unravel. Now that they'd entered the battlefield, so to speak, they couldn't afford to have allies argue over the details.

"How did you do it, by the way?" Gassan asked.

"Do what?"

"Recognize Hakeem."

"I... I am not sure." Back on the plaza, driven by inspiration, it seemed natural. Now, in a more balanced state of mind, Naia was aware that there was no way in the world she could have recognized a man from the massacre, even if she did indeed witness it as a baby, which was an impossibility all in itself. The only consolation was that it didn't really matter. It worked, and that was the only important thing.

"Anything on your mind?" Gassan asked.

Naia placed her scarf on a side table and carefully unwrapped the leech, white and shriveled by now, like a discarded cabbage strip.

Gassan's eyes narrowed as he leaned forward to study the creature, careful not to touch it. "Where did you get this?"

"It was swimming in my bath."

He looked up sharply. "Are you–?"

"I'm all right. I spotted it before I stepped into the water."

"That's a hell of a task."

"Not for someone of my training. Any idea who could have planted it?"

"Just about anyone." Gassan kept his eyes on the leech – another sign of uncertainty Naia felt necessary to note.

"I heard these creatures are enormously expensive," she said.

"True. The price probably narrows the list of potential culprits to the imperial family and top court officials – which doesn't tell us much anyway. Anyone close to Shabaddin would have a hell of a lot to lose if we succeed."

"Not all of them would have the opportunity to act in such a short window of time."

"Still. We're talking at least twenty people, with too little time to do anything about it. Just do your best to stay alive."

"Right." Naia rewrapped the bundle, careful not to crush the creature inside.

"The preparations for the ceremony are in full swing," Gassan said. "I'd say we have about two hours, but be ready in one, just in case. May I bid your leave, princess?"

She couldn't help a grin. "You may."

He bowed and exited the room. Naia watched him thoughtfully. In the next few hours, seeing people bow to her was going to become natural. After her experience back on the plaza, she was already coming to terms with it. It was much harder, though, to deal with all the uncertainties – from the identity of the mysterious leech owner to Mehtab's unexpected absence and Gassan's surprise about it.

The elaborate plan Naia was helping to execute couldn't possibly withstand any secrets or disagreements between its perpetrators. When Mehtab showed up they needed to have a talk about it – preferably with Gassan present. Someone needed to be there to back up Naia's point of view.

DOUBTS

The windowless chamber lay in deep shadows, the flicker of a single oil lamp utterly inadequate to the task of illuminating the low, vaulted space. Mehtab could barely see the man seated in a deep armchair, beside a fully set shatranj board. She frowned. Everyone at this court was so fond of shatranj – men, who never ceased to find petty parallels between the game's intricate rules and the imperial politics. All the more power to her, then. When she seized control, she would make sure all those who survived the aftermath would have nothing else to do but play the silly game all day long.

She crossed the chamber and lowered herself into the other, empty chair.

"Well played today, Sage Hakeem," she said.

The man nodded, leaning forward into the light. The flame highlighted his face, creased by numerous lines that for a moment made his features appear devilishly grotesque. The shadows folded into the corners of his mouth, briefly lifting up into a smile.

"My part wasn't hard at all," he said. "You are the one who

planted these memories in her head. The girl seems like a perfect tool, just as you said."

Mehtab frowned. The girl *was* a perfect tool – or would be, after Mehtab dealt with her wilfullness. She hoped the leech was going to take care of it, once and for all.

"You did bring the antidote, did you?" she said.

Hakeem nodded, holding out his hand so that she could now see a small egg-shaped vial resting in his palm. "This extra shipment is the last my supplier will be able to obtain in a while. Crystal leeches are getting so rare that it is nearly impossible to find anyone still in the business of making antidotes to their venom anymore. We still have a jar of the creatures at the ready, but no more antidote available on short notice."

Mehtab nodded. "It's all right. Naia's the last one I'll use it on. I left her in the bath, with a leech, before I came to see you."

"Why, if I may ask?"

"She will never spot it in the water."

"Still. Wouldn't it have been easier to administer the poison during one of your hypnosis sessions with her?"

"Too risky. With her Jaihar training, she has the senses of a spider, even in a deep trance. I cannot possibly lose her trust."

"In this case, you could perhaps have refrained from taking risks until she played her main part in the plot?"

"She is getting too willful. I can't possibly have her disobey my words."

"It's only a few hours."

"Critical hours. I knew you had the antidote."

"What if I had tripped on my way here and broken the vial?"

Mehtab stifled a laugh. Hakeem's frail looks could be deceptive, but she knew better. The sage's command of his reflexes were frightening for someone of his age, with no warrior training at all.

"I didn't mean to sound amusing," Hakeem said. "Not with these stakes. If anything goes wrong now, after all these preparations…"

Mehtab shrugged. "It won't, not after the leech treatment. That was exactly why I had to do it. As you've seen on the plaza, seeing people bow to her is already going to her head. You can only imagine what an effect it would have when she has the crown on her head."

Hakeem nodded, his eyes trailing to the shatranj board. Mehtab looked too. The black pawn gambit, so popular here lately. Gassan credited himself with inventing it. But would he really have been able to do it without all the people who stood behind him and fed his fantasies with their extensive knowledge?

"Do you have doubts the girl will play the part as instructed?" Hakeem asked.

Mehtab shrugged. "No, I don't. Imlar is a powerful draw." She raised her hand to her neck in a habitual gesture, touching the stone she wore at her throat under the tall collar of her abayah. "Unlike you, I am on track with my part of the plan."

"What's that supposed to mean?"

"Dal Gassan's assassination. You were in charge of it, remember? I hoped he wouldn't be here to meddle with my plans anymore."

Hakeem shrugged. "You could have warned us he was going to travel to Zegmeer in the company of the Jaihar's top blade."

Karrim. Mehtab's lips twitched. Traveling with the Jaihar warriors was highly unusual, unless they were employed as bodyguards. Karrim was particularly well-known to avoid any company when traveling on assignments. Gassan's abrupt decision to join the Jaihar on the ride to Zegmeer had to be enforced all the way from the top, a change of plans no one at the Haggad serai was warned about. She hoped it was a coincidence, not evidence that Gassan was suspecting anything.

She didn't regret the loss of three Chall assassins. She could find many more, especially after her plans for the empire were fully executed. She felt sorry only that she missed the perfect time to remove Gassan, so that she could prevent his future interference.

"What about Jai Karrim, by the way?" Hakeem said.

"What about him?"

"I assume he received orders from his superiors to assist Dal Gassan. After the succession ceremony today, those orders could put him directly in our way. I don't cherish the idea of that kind of complication."

Mehtab couldn't help a grin. "No need to worry about him. He will never go against Naia."

"Are you certain?"

"Oh, yes. She has him by the cock."

"How can you be sure?"

Mehtab batted her eyes innocently. "I might have played a little matchmaking game to ensure that."

"A matchmaking game?"

"Their lust for each other was quite evident, so I made sure to send her to his room at night, on a fake errand. My sources tell me she stayed until morning. I am sure they had a very good time."

"Still. Reportedly, if Jai Karrim had these kinds of reservations about every woman he ever spent a night with, half the empire would be off limits to him. Half of the imperial palace, for sure. Besides, Jai-ranked warriors are not known for thinking with their cocks."

"True." Mehtab reached over and took the black pawn off the board, twining it in her hands. A delicate piece, but so powerful if backed up by a carefully prepared play. "But the way he feels about Naia is different. By the time he deals with the fact that she is the one he must go against, it will be too late."

Hakeem's nod looked hesitant, but it didn't matter. A man like him, a commoner risen to power through his scholarly achievements, couldn't possibly grasp the kind of control that came with her bloodline, purified by generations of highly selective breeding. Even less so could he understand the bond Ironbloods formed with imlar, one that robbed them of their natural will when someone of her power was around. Mehtab never saw the need to explain it to Hakeem in any extra details. He was her tool too, after all, just like all the others.

"How much time do we still have?" she asked.

"As far as I know, Yakkab is somewhat ahead of schedule."

"Stall, if you need to. I need an hour, at least."

"Your wish is my command, my empress."

Mehtab rose. She had an hour to revive Naia from the leech poison and put the finishing touches on the girl's preparation for her final role in the succession contest. The most historic one in the Zeg Empire, one that every survivor would remember for centuries to come.

"It's time," Mehtab said.

Naia opened her eyes. *Did I fall asleep?* Alarmed, she peered into Mehtab's face, only partially reassured by the woman's unconcerned look.

She was having serious trouble recalling the last twenty

minutes or so. She had been dressing up when Mehtab walked in. For whatever reason, the older woman seemed surprised to see her. And then…

Naia glanced into the full-length mirror in the corner, directly across from her seat. Her outfit, the royal Challimar yellow accented by the imlar bodice and limb guards, settled over her heavily, a protective cocoon that brought calmness and reassurance. Inadvertently, she raised her hand to touch the necklace resting over her upper chest, its yellow-green gem nested in the cleft between her collarbones. This was the last thing she remembered – donning the imlar gear, after a short and fruitless argument with Mehtab about the appropriateness of wearing it for the ceremony. It didn't feel right, walking around the palace wearing body armor, even if it did look elaborate enough to pass off as jewelry. Yet, during her training Naia had long learned how little control she had over the occasions when Mehtab set her mind to something like that.

"Did you sing just now?" Naia asked.

"Don't you remember?"

"I…" Naia hesitated. Now that she was more awake, she was beginning to realize that she should be feeling far more concerned. Warriors in their prime didn't get blackouts. Not unless they suffered a major trauma in a fight. Definitely not during an assignment they had been training for since long before they were ranked. Yet, no matter what happened, she didn't really have a choice. This was the moment she had been preparing for. She had to go out there and play her part, no matter what.

"No, I don't," she said.

Mehtab reached over and patted her arm. "The last few months have been taxing for you. This assignment should be easy, compared to all the preparations you've gone through. Just remember to do as you're told."

Do as you're told. Right. "Dal Gassan was here earlier, looking for you," Naia said.

In the mirror, she saw Mehtab's gaze drift away just briefly, setting her on alert again. Did the older woman have something to hide from her superior?

"I was overseeing the preparations," Mehtab said. "I figured I had enough time to go to the Divan chamber and back, since you were in the bath. You didn't encounter any problems, did you?"

The bath. Naia's eyes trailed to the bundled-up leech, tucked away under her folded bath sheet. There seemed to be no reason to hide it from Mehtab. Yet, something kept her from bringing it into the conversation.

"No problems at all. It was very relaxing, actually." *Too relaxing, in fact.* She still couldn't figure out what made her fall asleep just now. The residual leech poison that may have been released into the water? It should have been minimal, with just one leech, in such a large basin. She rubbed the bridge of her nose. Even with her knowledge of poisons, she shouldn't have allowed herself the indulgence of a bath after disposing of the creature. She should really be more careful from now on.

"Are you all right?" Mehtab asked.

"Yes. It's just that..."

"What?"

"I didn't expect to fall asleep just now."

Mehtab's lips twitched. "You've been working very hard, that's all."

"My work isn't over yet."

"It almost is."

It's the imlar. Naia wasn't sure what drove this certainty. She raised her hands to unclasp the necklace, but Mehtab's hands covered hers, stopping her.

"I thought we were done with this argument," the older woman said.

"Does Dal Gassan approve?"

"Of what?"

"Of me wearing so much imlar."

"Dal Gassan has given me full control over these details."

Did he really? Naia looked at the older woman thoughtfully. She had no idea what brought on all these thoughts. Now was not the time to doubt her allies. It was critical for all of them to be on the same page.

"I found a crystal leech in my bath," she said.

Mehtab's hand, still lying over Naia's, stiffened. Naia glanced into the mirror, at the older woman's frozen expression. She couldn't quite name the mix of feelings she saw in Mehtab's face. Surprise? Shock? Yes, those were definitely there, but there was something else too.

Or was it just her daze talking?

"You weren't bitten, were you?" Mehtab said.

"I saw it before I got into the water. It died, and I fished it out." Naia pointed with her chin to the bundle in the corner.

Mehtab kept still as she eyed the shape. "This is a very elaborate form of assassination. I am glad you weren't hurt."

"Clearly, whoever planted it had no idea about my rank. Which is actually reassuring, isn't it?"

Mehtab opened her mouth, but before she could respond, the sound of voices in the outer chamber stopped the conversation.

"The succession ceremony," Mehtab said. "It's time to go."

She reached over and retrieved Naia's royal cloak. *Oh, that dratted thing.* Naia flung it over her shoulders and straightened it out regally, cursing the person who designed the jeweled piece – heavy like an extra suit of armor, stiff in all the wrong places.

She held her head high as she walked out of her chamber, where a liveried messenger was talking to her Chall guards. They all saluted as they saw her – the imperial greeting, palms up.

There seemed to be more of them than she remembered before, but she wasn't quite certain. Strange how this detail didn't seem important at all.

THE SUCCESSION
CEREMONY

The throne room seemed more densely packed than the plaza outside had been this morning – and very nearly as large. The giant space, obviously designed to dwarf anyone entering it, stretched on forever to the elevated platform with the throne hovering at its far end like a distant beacon reigning above the crowd. Like at the plaza, the space around the throne was separated by a double chain of guards, their imperial purple cloaks bright next to the black-clad ring of the Jaihar on the inside.

The crowd looked different here – richer dressed, more important-looking. No one chanted or cheered, but as Naia's Chall guards led the way through, the courtiers fell away much quicker than the crowds outside, so that she barely had to slow her steps to match. She sought out Prince Ramaz, next to the throne, watching her with narrowed eyes. The group around him included his two brothers, their expressions equally murderous. Naia smiled at them as she took her place on the other side of the throne.

She took a moment to spot all the important participants of the gathering. The members of the imperial council – high nobles and province rulers – lined up opposite the throne in a solemn line, each standing under their house banner. Further on, a dark blue canopy glittering with gold-speckled star embroideries, marked the representatives of the Church – the Immam, surrounded by a group of blue-clad priests. The Daljeer stood on the other side, less conspicuous but perceptibly closer to the throne, their plain brown robes common-looking compared to the explosion of colors around them. It took a second look to notice a young man next to Gassan, tall and gawky, looking so out of place in his ill-fitting imperial robes. Prince Halil, the chosen heir. It didn't escape Naia how the Jaihar grouped closer to the spot, with Karrim directly behind the prince. Leaving nothing to chance.

As soon as she took her place, the Immam started droning a prayer. The giant chamber gradually sank into silence, the only sounds the rustling of the robes and nervous coughs. Following the accents in the chant, the sages of the Divan stepped forward, one by one, bringing the royal regalia. The crown, a heavy golden circlet resting on a purple pillow. The official seal. The imperial cloak, draped over the outstretched arms of three sages walking side by side. And finally, a plain bronze bowl. Yakkab's hands trembled under its weight as he set it onto the pedestal in front of the throne, just as the prayer stopped.

"Your Imperial and Royal Highnesses," he said. "Lords of the Imperial Provinces, members of the High Council, and Sages of the Divan. By Lord Sel's will, after the passing of our beloved Emperor Shabaddin Selim Zeg, we are facing an event that has been evoked for the first time in nearly four centuries. The Imperial Succession Contest."

A rustle swept through the crowd. The reaction to "beloved", Naia guessed – the wording very few here had reason to support. She saw Prince Ramaz turn away abruptly, and a few of the Divan sages exchange uncomfortable glances.

"I hereby present to you the contenders," Yakkab said. "His Imperial Highness, Crown Prince Ramaz Bezabith Harah Elim Shab of the Zeg imperial line." He pointed, and the guard standing behind Ramaz raised the imperial banner, answered by the cheers of the crowd. The cheers seemed half-hearted, as far as Naia could tell – yet strong enough to make her wonder. Even those who hated Shabaddin and his offspring might have reasons to fear a major change, a bet on a wild card like her, despite Gassan's likely assurances that the heir he'd planned would not be that far from the imperial family.

"Prince Ramaz's challenger," Yakkab went on, "is Princess Xarimet, of the royal house Challimar."

A low-pitched hum cut through the rising cheer. An arrow, flying at full speed. Naia reached past the Chall guard standing beside her and caught it. She glanced at the plume – plain gray, clearly to conceal its owner's allegiance. She could well guess, though, as she saw Ramaz's smug look, just before more arrows flew in from different directions.

In her imlar armor, Naia hardly needed to bother. But she still couldn't resist reaching out and catching them all, their flight distorted by the proximity to her wrist guards. Ten, all sent from different directions, likely the first wave of what could easily become a major hellstorm.

The Jaihar's cloaked shapes were darting through the crowd, pulling the archers out of their hiding places. Three hells, this room was surely examined very carefully, prior to letting everyone in. How did Ramaz do it?

ANNA KASHINA

Naia locked her eyes with Karrim, right next to Prince Halil, his face unreadable. She could sense no more arrows coming, counting under her breath as the Jaihar dragged the archers out of the hall, into the custody of the imperial guards outside. Their hand signs, palms down – all clear – were confirmed by Karrim's lowered hand. The signal to return to the ceremony. Naia handed the arrows she was still clutching to her Chall escort and settled into her spot, watching the turmoil recede around her.

"Impressive," Ramaz said. "You must be a juggler in your real occupation. Incidentally, I haven't heard anyone cheer for you, princess."

Naia smiled. "Not worth sacrificing your men for this, prince. They will cheer, when I win the crown."

The prince's cheek twitched as he glanced away.

Yakkab looked nervous as he turned back to the line of nobles standing in front of the throne. "My lord and ladies. You may now cast your votes, by placing them into this bowl. Purple, for Crown Prince Ramaz Bezabith Harah Elim Shab of Zeg. Red, for Princess Xarimet of Challimar."

Red for the Ironbloods. Naia wasn't sure where the thought came from. She was beginning to feel odd, sounds in the room echoing too loud, every movement too exaggerated.

The Immam rang a gong. The vote. Prince Ajarham of Raj, the first in the line, stepped forward, looking at Naia thoughtfully. He held a black velvet pouch, weighing it in his hand before placing it in the bowl. The pouch was non-transparent, so that no one could see the color inside. *Red for the Ironbloods.* She glanced at Ramaz, peering intently, as if trying to see through the cloth.

"A stupid procedure," Ramaz said.

The gong rang again. Another noble stepped forward, his banner green and black, for Scinn. Again, he appeared to hesitate as he placed his bag in the bowl, looking at Naia.

Red. Red for the Ironbloods. Shahgar, Chall. The ringing in Naia's ears was getting louder. She kept her head high, trying to look relaxed, just as Ramaz became more and more agitated. *Red… Red…* Was it the gong, its deep, guttural sound somehow shaping itself into the word? Or was it her altered mind that, for some reason or another, simply wouldn't clear up? Was Mehtab singing again? Naia sought out the older woman – seemingly calm as she stood inconspicuously beside Gassan – reassured to see no tension or disapproval in her tutor's face.

Red…

Red…

The ringing of the gong ceased. All the council members resumed their spots. The pile of bags reached the rim of the bowl – seventeen votes that would decide the empire's fate.

The attendants brought in two more pedestals, each with an open bronze plate, setting them in front of Naia and Ramaz. The Immam stepped forward and approached the bowl, reaching inside.

Ramaz's lips curved into a grimace of distaste, his eyes resting on the Grand Vizier with a calculating look, as if already plotting the older man's punishment. His brothers looked unsettled, one biting his lip nervously, another one standing still, his expression cold and distant, as if the proceedings here didn't concern him at all. Naia glanced at Halil, deep inside the Daljeer's ring, directly in Karrim's sight. Gassan, next to him, held a parchment in his lowered hand – one that would seal the prince's right to the throne, as soon as Naia gained control. She had rehearsed that part very well. As soon as the vote was announced, she knew what to do.

When the first ball came out of the bag, the room exhaled a collective sigh that rang loudly under the vaulted arches of the ceiling. Purple. A vote for Ramaz. The prince looked smug as the Immam placed it into the plate in front of him, just as the other ball was released. Red.

Naia didn't bother to look at the plates with growing piles of balls for each contender. This was the part she could do nothing about. It was much more interesting – and important – to watch the room, so that she could spot any possible danger. No more assassination attempts seemed forthcoming, though. Not for now anyway.

The Immam took out the last ball, placing it on top of her pile. She looked. The red balls in her plate towered much higher than Ramaz's purple, for everyone to see.

The Immam turned, facing the hall. "By our Lord Sel's will, I hereby announce the results of the vote. Five, for Crown Prince Ramaz Bezabith Harah Elim Shab of Zeg. Twelve, for Princess Xarimet of Challimar. With our Lord Sel's blessing, hail the successor to His Imperial Majesty Shabaddin Selim of Zeg and our new ruler. Empress Xarimet of Challimar."

Naia had come in here today expecting this outcome. Still, she couldn't help the chill that ran down her spine as the echoes of her name – her stage name – rolled throughout the hall, met with the rising cheer of the crowd.

"Hail, Empress Xarimet Selim Zeg!"

The room around Naia sank into chaos. Ramaz and the imperial princes were trying to push through to the priests, edged away by the double line of guards that had somehow formed in the previously empty space in between. The sages of the Divan were all talking at once. The crowd pressed in all different directions, some to approach Naia, others to join the arguing group near the pedestal on the other side of the throne. The Immam held up the imperial crown, placing it on her head. Someone else shoved the royal seal into her hand. A ring. She slipped it onto her finger, so massive on her small hand.

The throne. I must sit on the throne. She knew she shouldn't, not according to Gassan's instructions, but the thought was too persistent to ignore. She took a step toward the chair, then stopped as she saw Gassan and the Daljeer pushing through.

"May I speak with you, Empress Xarimet?" Gassan said.

I was supposed to call him forth. How could I possibly forget? She gestured for the guards to let them through. Her ears were ringing, as if someone was talking inside her head. *Red... Red for the Ironbloods.* She forced the voice down and straightened out regally to face Gassan and his group.

"Empress," Gassan said. "I have a scroll with Emperor Shabaddin's last will, if it would please you to look. Here." He handed it to Yakkab standing by Naia's side, who ran his eyes down the sparing lines of the text.

Show interest. I must ask him what it says. It was the right thing to do, yet Naia felt a strange reluctance. The echoes in her head were becoming louder. *What in three hells is wrong with me?*

"What does it say, Sage Yakkab?" she asked.

"Um." The Sage's hesitation was not part of the plan, she was sure of it. "I... I don't understand."

"Is it written in a language unknown to you?" Naia wasn't sure what prompted her question. She didn't give a damn what the scroll said, or why Yakkab seemed so dumbfounded. *I am the Empress. They are my subjects. No scrolls could ever change that.*

"What do you mean, you don't understand, Sage Yakkab?"

Gassan demanded.

The Grand Vizier kept his eyes on Naia as he handed the scroll back to the Daljeer. She reached over and snatched it before Gassan could put his hand on it. Odd, how no one made any move to object, everyone watching her in mesmerized silence.

She lowered her eyes to the scroll, fighting the ringing in her ears as she ran her gaze over the few lines, down to Shabaddin's signature at the bottom. Fake signature, even though it looked real enough to her.

"Give it to me, damn it," Gassan said quietly.

Mehtab stepped up to his side. "You must watch your language around the empress, Dal Gassan." She turned to Naia. "Perhaps Your Imperial Majesty would care to read the scroll out loud?"

Naia nodded. Mehtab always knew how to resolve the conflict. No one in this room could possibly be wiser than Mehtab.

"By my last decree," she read, *"I name my son Halil to be my successor and ruler of the empire. But, if Princess Xarimet of Challimar comes forth and challenges the succession, it is my last decree to yield the throne to her."*

Stunned, Naia lowered the scroll and looked at Gassan, who leaned closer to the throne, so that he could speak to her without being overheard.

"You didn't have to read it all, did you?" Gassan said.

Naia swallowed. "But I…"

"The Daljeer did not write that last part," Gassan said. "I have no idea who did. You had to know it, didn't you?"

"I…"

"Why don't you improvise, like you did back on the plaza?"

"Improvise what?"

"Anything that could save this situation. We need an inspiration. I know you can do it."

Naia nodded. An inspiration. Right. She didn't feel the same urgency about this as the Daljeer obviously did, but she did remember what she was here for, even if this memory seemed hazier and hazier in her mind. Her eyes trailed to Halil, standing motionlessly inside the Daljeer ring. His smile made her wonder. Wasn't he in the least bit concerned about this turn of events? Wasn't he going to protest, or at least question how this change in the scroll came to be?

She suddenly realized why everyone always looked so distant when Halil's name came up in connection to the throne. Perhaps he was a better prospect than any of Shabaddin's other offspring, but could he ever be a good leader? Would she be doing the empire any favors by putting it into his hands?

She opened her mouth to speak, but at that moment Mehtab stepped up closer with a smile on her face. "Well done, Your Imperial Majesty."

As the sound of Mehtab's voice reached Naia's ears, her mind started to blur. Mehtab was saying something else, but she couldn't quite catch the words. She sensed the metallic smell of blood. A veil hovered in front of her eyes, so that the room suddenly seemed to be coated into the uniform red color. *Red for the Ironbloods. Shahgar, Chall.* The words – she couldn't recognize the language, but it seemed familiar.

Was Mehtab talking to her?

She tried to force her mind back into reality. Except she still wasn't sure. Was she standing in the imperial palace in Zegmeer? Or was she in Challimar, in the airy hexagonal chamber with windows overlooking the lush gardens below? Were these people

284

gathered here her subjects or her betrayers? Were they cheering for her, or were they closing in to kill her? Probably both, she reflected, strangely calm as she finally tuned in to Mehtab's words.

"The Empress will don her imperial cloak now," Mehtab said.

The weight of the Challimar royal cloak over Naia's shoulders lifted, and another one settled into its place, softer and more comfortable. The imperial Zeg mantle. She looked over the crowds, noting an abrupt movement off to the side, fast and smooth as a shape darted through, maneuvering skillfully between the courtiers.

Karrim. Why did she feel fear, rather than relief, watching him approach?

"Quick," Mehtab said. "Order him to stop."

"Why?" Naia knew Mehtab couldn't possibly have time to answer. Karrim could move fast, especially when he was this angry. She could see it in the way his nostrils flared, in the way the muscles knotted in his neck. On behalf of the Jaihar Order, she should be sharing his anger too. She had just been manipulated into a position she never meant to hold, forced into a deal she had never accepted. And now, since Karrim was still technically her senior, she would have to explain this to him – and quick, before he took to murdering someone. Looking at his face this seemed like a very immediate possibility.

Except that she didn't really have to answer to him at all. Not anymore. She was the empress, which made Karrim her sworn vassal and the head of her bodyguards, once all the formalities were finalized. She didn't have to explain anything to him. Did she?

She was surprised at the last thought, which caught up with her faster than Karrim's feet carried him toward her through the last few strides, everyone in his path hastily scrambling aside.

"What the hell are you doing?" Karrim demanded.

Naia lifted her chin. "You are addressing your empress, Jai Karrim. How dare you speak to me this way?"

Karrim's eyes widened, just briefly. Naia felt surprised too. This was *Karrim*, the man she cared deeply about, probably the only one here who at least gave a damn about her wellbeing. She could well relate to both his anger and his disbelief. She had felt exactly the same, just moments ago. Yet, a stubborn part of her drove her to stare him down until Karrim's gaze wavered and his stance eased. His eyes trailed to the scroll she still held in her lowered hand, then to Gassan who stood to the side with a stunned look.

"Forgive me, empress," Karrim said. "I just… I hoped we could talk."

Naia was about to agree, but at that moment Mehtab stepped between them. "The empress needs rest, Jai Karrim. She is tired."

Naia had felt well-rested when she entered this chamber less than an hour ago, yet as Mehtab spoke, her limbs felt so heavy she could barely stand on her feet. *Rest.* Yes, she did need rest, in her chambers, with Mehtab talking to her in that wonderful voice of hers. She nodded her agreement, sweeping her eyes over Gassan's and Karrim's surprised faces, over the imperial princes shouting at each other on the other side of the room.

"I wish to be escorted back to my chambers," she said.

Yakkab stepped forward. "Your Imperial Majesty. Allow us to prepare the imperial suite for you."

"No need." She shook her head. "The chamber I currently have will do, at least for today."

Yakkab bowed and stepped away.

As if by magic, guards appeared by her sides. *The Chall.* Naia knew she should be feeling concerned that everyone here seemed to be accepting her without question, but she was too tired to think straight.

Mehtab. Where is Mehtab? This seemed like the most important thing right now. As she followed her guards to the door, she turned to see the older woman behind her, talking to Gassan in heightened tones. Beside them, Karrim was standing very still, watching. Naia turned away from him and stepped through the door into the hallway outside.

AFTERMATH

Gassan shook off his stupor, watching the crowds of courtiers streaming out of the chamber in Naia's wake. *Empress Xarimet.* He had no idea what had just happened. Definitely not something the Daljeer had planned for, or ever imagined possible. Hell, he had inspected the scroll very carefully, only this morning, before sealing it with the exact replica of the emperor's personal seal. No one except a few trusted Daljeer had had any access to it since then.

He turned to follow the crowd, then stopped abruptly as Karrim slid toward him, his hand unfolding with a dagger Gassan could swear wasn't there just a moment ago. He felt a cold touch of steel on his neck as the Jaihar backed him into the nearest wall, a feather-thin edge resting against his jugular with the decisive finality that warned him against any possibility of movement.

The chamber around them emptied too quickly, with only a few Jaihar Glimmerblades in sight – no one for Gassan to expect any help from. Not that anyone in this palace, even the Jaihar, could possibly protect him from Karrim holding a dagger to his throat. The only marginal comfort came from the

ANNA KASHINA

knowledge that Karrim probably wouldn't kill him on a whim. Based on their prior interactions, Gassan was reasonably sure of it, despite the fact that Karrim's expression right now definitely spoke otherwise. He clung to the thought, fighting the groping clutches of panic.

"What did you bloody do, Dal Gassan?" Karrim demanded.

Gassan slowly let out a breath, a risky move that made Karrim's blade push deeper into his skin. "I assure you, Jai Karrim. I am just as surprised as you are."

Karrim's grip tightened, sending a surge of heat down Gassan's spine. He supposed of all the ways to die, bleeding from a sliced jugular was not the worst one for someone of his occupation. With Karrim's blade skill, with how sharp he kept his weapons, it probably wouldn't even hurt all that much.

"The truth," Karrim demanded. "I want the bloody truth."

"The best I can offer you are my guesses, Jai Karrim."

"Which are?"

"Mehtab."

"What about her?"

"As far as I could tell, she was the only one in the scene who didn't seem in the least surprised. She also seemed to be adamant about taking Naia away as fast as possible. Don't you find it at least a little bit unusual?"

Karrim's grip loosened, just enough to allow Gassan another short breath.

Calm. I must keep calm at all cost. This was the only way to deal with people on edge, at least in theory. Of course, the fact that it was Karrim he had to deal with put the situation onto a whole different scale.

"Mehtab was in a perfect position to meddle with our plans," Gassan said. "She knew about the scroll. And, she had access to

289

it, just like all the top-ranking Daljeer who have been informed about the details of the plan."

"I thought you inspected the scroll before bringing it here."

"I did, right before it was sealed this morning."

"This morning?"

"Yes."

"What happened since then?"

"I don't know."

Karrim's eyes flared, then narrowed again as he apparently thought more of it. Gassan chose to take it as a good sign.

"Why would Mehtab do something like that?" Karrim asked.

Gassan's shrug was cut short by the bite of steel on his skin. He did his best to distance himself from it. No matter how mad, Karrim wouldn't let his blade slip, not by accident. He would come around eventually – or so Gassan hoped.

"I am determined to find out," he said.

"You *told* me you trusted her."

"I *did* trust her. Wrongly, as it appears."

"That's a bloody understatement."

Gassan looked through the open doors into the hallway outside – empty, save for the distant echo of cheering. Strange how everyone here seemed oddly content with the choice of Naia as the empress, despite the fact that she was a woman, and an outsider they had no idea existed until a few hours ago. A legend, true, but also a foreigner in Zegmeer. Why would anyone in this palace accept her so eagerly?

He turned back to the problem at hand, far more pressing in both the literal and the figurative sense.

"I am aware you would have absolutely no trouble killing me right now, Jai Karrim," he said. "But it wouldn't solve anything, would it?"

"It was your assignment that got us all into this mess."

"True. However, at the moment, no one except me appears to be in any immediate physical danger. Which leaves us plenty of opportunities to correct things, if we go about it the right way. So, why don't we work together to look into this? Ideally, without turning on each other. I hate to mention it, but my neck is getting rather stiff."

Karrim measured Gassan with a long look, then slowly lowered his blade.

Gassan let out a long breath.

"Before I even begin to consider trusting you again," Karrim said, "you must tell me everything you know."

"I already did."

Karrim raised his blade again. Gassan did his best to relax against the wall at his back, all the easier because of the grim realization that he had nowhere else to go. Besides, no matter what he tried, he couldn't possibly escape if Karrim was of a mind to do anything rash.

"Look," he said. "I promise you, I did not hide anything from you, or your superiors, when planning this assignment. I also spoke the truth when I said that the Daljeer have made arrangements to put Prince Halil on the throne. I have no idea what went wrong."

"Your fellow Daljeer, obviously. Your trust in them was grossly misplaced."

"True. But we cannot possibly do anything about it unless we get past our current impasse. Which means, no weapons pointed at each other."

Karrim held a pause, then finally sheathed his blade with a speed that made Gassan blink. He knew he should be feeling a lot more frightened of the possibility of finding himself at the receiving end of this blade, but the situation was too urgent to dwell on the thought.

"Our first question is about Jai Naia," Gassan said.

"What about her?"

"I wonder how much did she know about this... change of plan?"

"Are you implying she and Mehtab conspired about it?"

Gassan shook his head. Ever since the vote result was announced, Naia had looked dazed, as if her mind was not fully there. She didn't look like a co-conspirator, or a person fully aware of her surroundings, for that matter. He had no idea what could have caused this kind of a state.

"I don't think so," he said. "She seems... affected somehow. Not herself. Didn't you see that?"

Karrim's gaze darkened. Gassan knew the Jaihar was not going to speak, but he saw the answer clearly anyway. Karrim knew Naia too well to miss something like this.

"We need to learn what's wrong with her," Gassan said. "As well as who did it to her, and to what end."

Karrim's jaw tightened. "You don't know the half of it."

"What exactly are you referring to?"

"This turn of events puts her in direct violation of her Jaihar assignment – at least the way our superiors see it. Do you have any bloody idea what I'm supposed to do, if she doesn't stand down and give up the crown?"

Gassan's skin prickled. Of course. Arsat would never have agreed to Gassan's plan without enforcing some sort of a failsafe.

Damn it. The last thing they needed right now was for Karrim to turn on Naia and mess up this already impossible situation.

"There's no immediate rush for you to act on this order, is

there?" he said.

"It depends."

"I was the one who hired her. I believe it is up to me to determine whether she's in any violation of her assignment."

"To an extent, yes."

"I need just a little time, Jai Karrim. I must go back my quarters and do some research."

"Research?"

"Yes."

"Now is hardly the bloody time to—"

"It is, I'm afraid. I must also meet with the Daljeer seniors, at least those who are in the palace right now."

"I thought you were done with trusting them, after what happened."

"I have no choice. I can't possibly solve this on my own. Just keep your eyes on Naia and Mehtab. I'll find you as soon as I learn what I need. In the meantime, if anyone asks about me – *anyone* – don't tell them about this conversation. Not even a hint that we suspect anything's wrong. Act ignorant."

"This seems like a safe bet," Karrim said. "Given that this is exactly how I feel right now."

"Good. Let's keep it this way for now, shall we?" Gassan turned and sped away along the hallway.

Ever since leaving the throne room, Naia continued to feel very odd. She was still in control of her body, or so it seemed, for all her reflexes appeared to be normal. But she also felt strangely detached – as if everything happening to her was unreal somehow. Every sight, every sound, reached her with a tiniest delay, as if she was perceiving it through a veil – the vision that kept returning over and over again.

She had a sense that Mehtab, who kept determinedly by her side, knew about her condition and could likely tell her more about it, but there was never a chance to ask – not with the way everyone was milling around her, the courtiers practically falling over each other in the effort of getting her attention. Perhaps it was the shock, she kept telling herself. She had woken up this morning an elite warrior on a mission to protect the imperial heir and put him on the throne. True, she had expected to win the crown in the process – briefly – but she wasn't supposed to end up with the emperor's cloak on her own shoulders.

There had to be a way to correct the situation. Regardless of how her name ended up on Gassan's scroll, she could still renounce the throne as planned, and pass it on to Halil. She was going to do just that, as soon as the dust settled.

Dazed, she followed Mehtab back into her chambers. The older woman ushered out the courtiers and servants and closed the doors behind them to bring on a blissful silence.

Naia blinked. She had no idea how much time had passed since she left this chamber earlier today. It must be close to nightfall now, following an entire day of impossible events that piled on too fast to keep up. And now, everything seemed a blur – an odd sensation she hadn't experienced before.

"How are you feeling?" Mehtab asked.

"Shocked," Naia said truthfully. "I have no idea what could have possibly happened."

"Why don't you relax, and I'll tell you a story?"

"Now?" Naia threw a restrained glance at the tightly shut door. She could see the movement of shadows at the floor crack, the courtiers milling restlessly outside, in anticipation of her reappearance. She needed to address them, to send for Halil, to talk to the Divan about the proper procedure for the transfer of power. In fact, she should have done it all while she was still in the throne room, instead of going on this mindless detour to her quarters. And now, she definitely had no time to sit around and relax, did she?

She opened her mouth to voice this, but Mehtab's stern look cut her off.

"Yes, *now.*"

Wordlessly, Naia walked over to an armchair and sank into it. Mehtab rarely spoke this way, and when she did, it was unthinkable to disobey.

She raised her hands to remove her armor, but Mehtab stopped her with an abrupt gesture.

"Don't."

"Why?"

"I know wearing imlar makes you feel comfortable."

Naia paused. It did, even though she was beginning to question the wisdom of wearing it all the time. Was it her imlar gear that made her feel so dazed and relaxed right now? Or was it Mehtab's voice, so soothing in its low timbre? As the older woman bunched up the pillows around her, she hummed a soft tune, its sound bringing on the memories of Mehtab's home back in Haggad. It was just like one of their lessons Naia had come to crave, the only times in her life when she could truly experience human warmth.

Except that *other* time, with Karrim. The thought cut through her haze like a blade, but Mehtab's singing drew her in again. She relaxed into the pillows, leaning against them as she watched Mehtab settle beside her.

"Remember what I told you about the the defenders of Challimar?" Mehtab said.

"The Ironbloods, yes."

"One of the things that made them special was their bond to imlar."

"A bond?"

"Yes. Just like yours. You can feel the imlar you are wearing speak to you, can't you?"

Once again, Mehtab's words forced Naia into a semi-trance. *Speak to you.* She could feel the power coursing through her veins, settling over her mind with such calmness and peace that nothing else seemed to matter anymore. Unable to resist it, Naia closed her eyes and leaned into the pillows at her back, Mehtab's voice washing over her.

"Imlar is in your blood," Mehtab said. "It's your birthright. Just like Princess Xarimet, you are a true defender of Challimar."

The room was slowly spinning – or was Naia only imagining it? She felt light, as if flying. Mehtab's voice seemed to be coming from a distance, yet it filled her, as if its soft, whisper-like tone coursed through her blood too, more powerful and potent than any substance Naia was familiar with.

"You were born to this destiny, Naia," Mehtab said. "This was why I overruled the Daljeer's decision to put Halil on the throne and added your name to the scroll, so that your claim couldn't possibly be disputed."

Naia opened her eyes. "You were the one who did this? But how—"

"It's unimportant now."

"I thought you were one of the Daljeer."

Mehtab smiled. "I think of the Daljeer as my tools, in bringing about my grand plan. To execute it, I've spent half a lifetime gaining the Daljeer's trust. I used my scholarly knowledge to rise high in their ranks, so that I could take charge of some of their most important decisions. And now we are here, about to bring my plan to completion."

Naia nodded slowly. In her altered state, this information did not seem unusual at all. In fact, it made perfect sense.

She could no longer recall the urgency she felt only a short while ago. Nothing seemed as important as remaining in place, so that she could keep listening to Mehtab's words.

Gassan. I should ask about Gassan. "Is Dal Gassan informed about this plan?"

Mehtab laughed. "Gassan is a fool who thinks he is in control of the whole empire. In truth, he cannot even control his own subordinates. He has no idea what's going on."

Naia wondered at the way this information, which should have sent her running to her superiors to tell them about treason, produced no effect on her at all. It should have been important – yet nothing seemed important at all in the face of the present. Mehtab's voice, humming her favorite tune, was so comforting. So beautiful. Naia flowed with it, caught in the flood of her visions.

Looking through a veil…

"Shouldn't I go out and address the people?" she heard herself asking.

"In time," Mehtab said. "First, you should relax as I sing to you. Then, I will tell you what to do."

Naia didn't question it. She leaned back into her pillows and closed her eyes.

DESTINY

Gassan stared at the pile of books and scrolls on the table in front of him in barely disguised disbelief. He turned to Dal Bakhum, the head of the Challimar serai, standing in front of him with a forlorn face. The rest of the Daljeer seniors crowded behind, eyes downcast.

"I take full responsibility for overlooking this before, Dal Gassan," Bakhum said. "We sent all Dal Mehtab's belongings to you as requested, but up until a week ago none of us knew about her secret hideout. Once I discovered it, I traveled here as fast as I could to bring these to you."

Yet not fast enough. Gassan nodded, looking at the pile again. The book on top, *The Five Kingdoms,* looked just as unremarkable as it did on the shelf of every other library he had ever seen it in. One of the commonest history books, the manicured version of the official Zeg history. Challimar barely owned a chapter in the volume, promptly marked with a crescent-shaped bookmark, and Gassan probably knew the contents by heart. It was the notes scribbled on the wide margins of each page that drew his eyes, telling a wholly different story that not only deviated from the official version by a very long shot, but also made Gassan's skin creep from the implications.

Every important name in the empire was here, each of them connected to a particular event in the chronicle, each labeled with an attribute – an axe, a cross, or a flame symbol that, Gassan supposed, signified the manner of death this person deserved.

Here and there, the pages were also stained with rusty splotches that Gassan recognized as dried blood. He didn't want to speculate on the source of it, but one thing was clear. The owner of this book was a very disturbed person. Since, by Bakhum's admission, the book had been found in a secret hideout in Mehtab's private chambers, he had no reason to doubt who the owner was. Not with everything else going on.

Prior to the succession ceremony, Gassan could have still done something to avert the worst. But now, there wasn't much he could do to remedy the situation. Not without removing Mehtab first.

He suppressed the impulse to confront the woman at once. This was no time for rash actions. Judging by these notes, her plan, whatever it was, had been in the makings for decades, probably even before the night she and Gassan first met in the Challimar serai. He needed to know more before deciding how to proceed.

He turned to the pile of scrolls heaped next to the book. Old Challimar songs, written side by side in their original language and in the Zeg common speech. He ran his eyes through a few lines, then raised his gaze to Bakhum.

"Any idea about these?" he said.

The man licked his lips nervously. "Street songs, popular in

Challimar. I doubt they are important."

"They must be, if she's been storing them so secretly."

Bakhum's lowered hands trembled. "I am deeply sorry, Dal Gassan. I've searched her quarters myself, on your orders, but I must admit, my trust in her was so absolute that I did not take the task seriously enough. Not until recently."

"What made you change your mind?" Gassan asked.

"This." Bakhum pushed forward a small leather bag, his fingers trembling as he upended its contents onto the table.

It was a pile of notes written, as it seemed, on random sheets of paper. Mehtab's steady, even hand looked neater than the work of the best Circle's scribes. Gassan leafed through them. They all appeared to be routine "to do" lists and potion recipes, the only remarkable thing about them the way Naia's name tended to appear on each with clockwork regularity.

Gassan felt a chill in the pit of his stomach. These notes had been hidden in the Challimar serai since before Mehtab moved to Haggad. This meant they had to be written before Mehtab had officially received her assignment as Naia's tutor. How could she possibly know anything about the girl?

He could think of only one explanation. Mehtab must have been secretly following Naia's fate since that first day the girl was brought to the serai as a baby. In some other reality, he could have found it understandable. But the recent events put this knowledge into a wholly different light.

He turned back to the pile, looking through odd drawings he couldn't quite identify. It wasn't until he flipped to the end of the pile that he realized what they were. Crystal leeches – or, more precisely, their venom glands, greatly magnified.

Crystal leech poison was a highly valued ingredient in some special medicines, administered in very small dozes. But never before did Gassan see anyone's research notes so preoccupied with the creatures. Along with the fact that Naia had recently found one in her bath, this had to hold a special significance, even if for the moment he couldn't quite grasp what it was.

"This pouch was found by one of my closest associates," Bakhum said. "In a secret compartment built into a wall behind her desk, opened accidentally when the desk was moved. It had a note attached to the outside. Here." He pulled out a crumpled piece of paper, taking the time to unfold and smooth it out over the tabletop.

Gassan ran his eyes over it, gaping in disbelief.

It was an ink drawing – a necklace, its elaborately woven patterns merging from two sides to enfold a large stone set in its center. Despite the lack of color or dimension to the drawing, Gassan could almost see the gleam of the ornate lines, the deep shine of the stone it held. It seemed so real.

Was it because he had seen this piece before?

His gut knotted as he ran his eyes over the lines at the bottom – sparse words, whose meaning left him momentarily blinded.

He had been such a fool.

And he doubted he had any time left to do anything about it.

His fingers trembled as he reached for the note and folded it carefully, shoving it into a deep pocket inside his robe.

"I must talk to Jai Karrim at once," he said. "Send word to the serai to mobilize everyone. Meet me in the throne room."

He didn't wait for a response as he burst out of the chamber.

For the first time in his life, Karrim had no idea what to do. Formally speaking, he should be pledging his services to Naia, the new empress. But there was also the *other* order he

had received from his superiors just before departing for this
assignment.

If she tries to take the throne, kill her.

To the best of Karrim's knowledge, Naia hadn't actually tried.
Instead, the crown was forced on her, most likely without any
prior warning. Back in the throne room, she looked beyond
surprised. Stunned. Disbelieved. Until something changed in
her, a moment Karrim didn't quite catch before she became
distant and commanding.

What the hell was going on?

Perhaps he shouldn't have agreed to let Gassan out of his
sight. He also probably shouldn't have threatened him with a
blade, given that the Daljeer was an important patron of the
Jaihar Order and a man in charge of one of the foremost powers
in the empire. It was just that Karrim was no longer sure of
anything. Why did Gassan feel so compelled to do his research
at such a tense moment? Was it truly necessary in the current
situation? Or was it just an excuse to escape Karrim's wrath?

Karrim was painfully aware that the Jaihar Dozen was the
only force standing between a group of uncertain, agitated
inhabitants of the imperial palace and the raging crowds
outside, chanting Xarimet's name with such fervor it was as
though she was the Holy Prophet descended from the sky.
Perhaps, given this kind of enthusiasm, appointing her as a
ruler of the empire wasn't really such a bad choice. At least she
wasn't a deranged imbecile like Ramaz, or a cold-blooded killer
like his father had been. She also wasn't weak and indecisive,
like Karrim suspected Halil would turn out, if he was handed
the crown right now. Orders or not, Karrim should perhaps
be giving Naia a chance – at least until he learned much more
about the situation.

One last time, he patrolled all the guard posts he had set out, a Glimmerblade at each overseeing a squad of the regular guards. The last post was at the apex of the large hall right outside Naia's quarters, its doors still tightly shut, the Jaihar stationed outside having a visible difficulty keeping the courtiers at bay. Karrim swept past them and leaned closer to the tightly shut doors, trying and failing to catch any sound or movement within.

If Naia didn't have a Shadowblade rank, he would be feeling very concerned right now. He had a serious urge to knock. He did promise Gassan not to try anything on his own, but who knew how long was Gassan going to take with whatever it was he was doing – or if he was ever coming back?

What in three hells was the Daljeer up to?

Karrim turned to scan the hall, over the heads of the milling crowd. He could see none of the princes, who had undoubtedly retreated to their chambers to brood and search for possible loopholes in the succession law, along with opportunities to mount a revolt. The princes' envoys were here, though, each positioned strategically in a space of their own. The courtiers kept a balanced distance from all of them, calculated to avoid any gestures that could be interpreted as misplaced loyalty, without appearing impolite. The Immam's blue cloak formed another focus of color a distance away, like a cold flame flickering amidst the group of priests. Some of the Divan members were here too, minus the Grand Vizier. His absence bothered Karrim more than anyone else's. He should be looking into it, but he didn't dare to leave this hall, in anticipation of possible action.

The chambers Naia had been given, unlike many others at the palace, had this convenient hall outside – a vast room with enough space to accommodate a court assembly. It was as if someone had been expecting her to inherit the throne, an idea that seemed both preposterous and disturbing at the same time. Did the Grand Vizier have anything to do with it? Did anyone else, present or absent from this chamber, orchestrate the whole thing?

The wait was becoming unbearable. Karrim couldn't decide if he should act or stall. He knew how to be patient, but what if every moment of his inactivity was bringing about a disaster he couldn't even foresee?

He almost talked himself into breaching the etiquette by forcing his way into Naia's chambers, when a movement at the back of the crowd caught his attention. He glimpsed a brown Daljeer robe, relieved at the sight of the familiar face. Gassan. *About bloody time.* He hurried over, his momentary relief dissolving into concern as he saw the older man's frown.

"Jai Karrim." Gassan spoke in a heightened whisper, an unnecessary precaution since even a loud voice would unlikely be heard above the agitated hum of the crowd. "What's the situation here?"

"There's no bloody situation, Dal. She's still locked up in her chamber. I've absolutely no idea what's going on in there."

"*I* do." Gassan grasped Karrim's elbow, pulling him aside into a quiet passage that led into an alcove with a window overlooking the palace garden.

Only now did Karrim notice how unkempt the Daljeer looked, as if he had just run all the way across the palace without stopping. He waited, knowing that any attempt to rush the information would only lead to a bigger delay.

"Have you ever heard of the power of imlar, Jai Karrim?" Gassan asked.

Karrim shrugged. "Are you referring to its ability to attract other metals?"

"Among other things, yes. What do you know about the imlar stone?"

"Imlarite. Used mostly in jewelry, I believe."

"Mostly, yes. However, you would perhaps be curious to know that imlarite's ability to attract metal is even higher than imlar. Especially when it comes to gem-quality stones."

"This is fascinating, Dal Gassan. But is it really time for a scholarly lesson?"

"Bear with me for this last question, Jai Karrim. What do you know of the Destiny Stone?"

"The large imlarite piece, worn in a necklace by the Challimar queens?"

"Yes."

"It's not particularly beautiful, as I heard."

"True, even if that is a matter of opinion. It has an interesting color play, but lacks the clarity or luster of the more precious pieces. Yet every Challimar queen for the past few centuries has been wearing it around her neck at all times."

Karrim shrugged, his eyes darting past Gassan to the hallway outside. "Once again, fascinating, Dal, but what does it have to do with our current situation?"

"Everything." Gassan pulled a piece of yellowed paper out of his sleeve and shoved it into Karrim's hand.

Karrim looked at the drawing – a necklace, set with an irregular-shaped stone, with words scribbled underneath.

"Does this look familiar?" Gassan asked.

"I believe I've seen Dal Mehtab wearing this kind of necklace, even though she usually keeps it hidden under her collar. Why?"

"What about the words?"

"It's in an older Chall dialect, as far as I know." Karrim peered closer. "I'm not that good at it. Does this first word mean 'fate'?"

"'Destiny', to be precise."

Karrim's eyes widened. "Mehtab's necklace."

"Exactly."

"Do you mean to say, this woman is walking around wearing *the Destiny Stone*?"

"Yes. And it gets worse. The words on this paper are a chant every Challimar queen sings to evoke the stone's power, once she puts it on for the first time." Gassan shook his head. "In brief, I've been an idiot. It has been right there, in front of my eyes all the time."

An idiot. Karrim was beginning to feel like one himself. Despite all the revelations, he still didn't have the faintest idea what was going on.

"How much do you know about the Challimar Ironbloods?" Gassan asked.

"I know that the last of them was killed off during the royal massacre." *And I assume, at some point, all this questioning is going to come to a point.* Karrim glanced at the doors to Naia's chamber, still tightly shut.

"I thought so too," Gassan said. "But this paper suggests otherwise."

"It does?"

"This chant was used by the queen to bind the Ironbloods to her. It says so here: 'The Destiny Stone will bond you to the iron in their blood. Take it, and claim your birthright.' It took me a while to realize that this paper is not part of some old text, but a message. A letter I watched delivered, right in front of my eyes."

Karrim blinked. "Is this supposed to make any sense?"

"Eventually, yes. Let me just talk through it."

"We don't have the bloody time for this, Dal."

"Indeed we have very little of it, so I'd appreciate it if you don't waste any more. Just listen. Do you know where the Jaihar top weapon skill, like yours, comes from?"

"From training. Why?"

"Not only that. It comes from a special ability, inborn or induced – which, as a matter of fact, is very similar to that of the Chall Ironbloods. All the Jai warriors, especially the Shadowblades, are better than others, because they carry extra iron in their blood. This iron is what bonds you to your weapons, so that you can sense them, almost like living things. The Daljeer have a name for this quality. A blade whisperer. You and Naia both share this gift, which makes you so good at what you do."

Karrim wanted to object, but something in the older man's gaze stopped him. There was truth to these words, a plausible explanation to why, despite equal training, some Jaihar were so much better than others.

"Assuming you are correct," he said, "what does this have to do with our current situation?"

"Everything, Jai Karrim. With one important addition. Imlar's ability to attract iron means that it has an exceptional effect on anyone with your kind of talent. If you wear imlar – even a small piece of it, like, say, a necklace – it speaks directly to your blood. Anyone who can tap into this bond would be able to influence you through it."

"What the hell do you mean by influence?"

"It acts like hypnosis. This was exactly how the Challimar royalty bonded with their Redcloak guards, who always wore imlar when on duty. The queen's Destiny Stone amplified the link. This chant, written here, was the way to activate the bond during the coronation. When the queen donned the Destiny Stone, she spoke the chant written here, and any Ironblood within reach became imprinted with it. In the future, hearing her voice, pitched to a special timbre, made them obey her without question. I assume the same thing could be done to a Jaihar of your talent, through regular sessions involving, say, an imlar necklace and the Destiny Stone... Is it beginning to make sense yet?"

Karrim glanced at the paper in his hand, then at Gassan. "Naia and Mehtab."

"Exactly."

Karrim heaved a breath. This was bad. Worse than he had thought.

"How did Mehtab manage to come upon the Destiny Stone?" he asked.

"I believe I know, but we don't have time for those kind of details now. We have to stop her – before it is too late."

"What do we have to do?"

"Did you see the necklace and armor Naia was wearing during the succession ceremony?"

Karrim did, even if at the time he mistook it for a set of elaborate jewelry. "Yes. Why?"

"They are made of imlar. So much of it that her mind is no longer her own. We must convince her to take it off, at all costs."

"If you are correct about the influence she is under, she probably won't comply, will she?"

"Probably not, especially if Mehtab and her stone are still around."

Karrim's jaw knotted. "This doesn't leave us with many choices, does it?"

"Fewer than you think. Do you have any idea what all the imlar she is wearing will do to your weapons?"

Karrim glanced down at his gear. Now that Gassan mentioned it, he remembered how his weapons shifted when he stepped into Naia's path back in the throne room. At that time, he had other things to worry about. But now, the memory of the sensation hit him with new force. Iron. All of the blades he had on him would act unpredictably as soon as he got into close range. Fighting against someone of Naia's skill with this kind of a disadvantage could be fatal.

"What about her own weapons?" he asked.

Gassan glanced at the doors of Naia's chambers uneasily. "The Ironbloods used to wield special swords, made of imlar-infused stone. The Daljeer own the last existing set. Dal Mehtab had recently requested for it to be shipped to Haggad. I assume Jai Naia carries them now, instead of her regular blades."

"Bloody great." Karrim sighed. Ever since he received his last orders from Arsat and Ilhad, he had been focused on finding his way around them. And now, he was not only facing the necessity of a direct confrontation with Naia, but also had to do it on unfavorable terms that would make the possibility of sparing her life that much more difficult. Worse, none of these thoughts could possibly measure up to the necessity to do the right thing.

He knew how to follow orders and do his duty, no matter what.

He didn't like it one bit.

"I'll need a staff," he said.

SHOWDOWN

"Now that you have the throne," Mehtab said, "are you ready to give it up?"

"Yes," Naia said. *To Halil.* Deep inside, she knew this wasn't what Mehtab meant, and she was fine with it. She would do anything Mehtab said. Anything.

Mehtab nodded. "Good. Then let me use our last few moments here to tell you something important."

Naia leaned back into the pillows. She was dimly aware of the hum of the crowd outside her quarters. But their restlessness didn't matter. Not when Mehtab needed her.

"My story has to do with Challimar royal succession," Mehtab said. "As I'm sure you know, it always goes from mother to daughter, save for the rare occasions when the queen bears only male heirs. It's always worked smoothly, until, forty or so years ago, Queen Lileah gave birth to twin girls. There was much dispute about which one of them was the firstborn. It was clear, though, that the twins were very different from each other. Tajeerah had a gentle, calm demeanor, while her sister Selhath was strong-willed and temperamental. As the girls grew, the Divan decided that Tajeerah would be a more desirable ruler. They sent Selhath into exile."

"Just like that?" Naia asked.

"Yes. Just like that. Many protested this decision, but eventually they all forgot about Selhath's existence, save for a few loyal followers who vowed to see their princess restored to her birthright some day."

"Restored, how?"

"I'm coming to that." Mehtab's voice softened with a smile. Naia didn't feel like opening her eyes to see it, but she imagined the way it curved the older woman's lips, normally set into a straight line. She cherished those moments when Mehtab showed a softer side, making it easy to imagine her as the mother Naia never had.

"At first, Selhath resented her fate," Mehtab said. "She vowed revenge against her more fortunate sister. But as the years went on and Tajeerah became a great queen who led her kingdom into prosperity, Selhath came to realize this turn of events was probably for the best. She was about to lay down her pride and make peace with Tajeerah, but just then the young queen made a grave mistake. She succumbed to the political pressure and agreed to a deal that would give up her ancient imperial succession right to the Zeg Emperor Shabaddin, in exchange for peace and protection from the empire."

"Perhaps it was for the best? Peace and protection could be worth giving up one's pride."

"Never," Mehtab said. "Especially to the Zeg, cruel and dishonest people, not to be dealt with."

Naia frowned. "Zeg people are numerous. Surely they couldn't *all* be bad, could they?"

"Don't interrupt, just listen." Was there an edge to

Mehtab's voice? Or did Naia only imagine it? She knew she should probably open her eyes and look at the older woman's expression, but this seemed like too much of an effort. *Just listen. Right.* She relaxed back into her pillows.

"From her exile," Mehtab said, "Selhath used all her resources to interfere with the event. She set a plan in motion that would eventually restore her to her birthright. This plan required making sure the treaty never happened at all."

"The Challimar Royal Massacre… Did Selhath orchestrate it?"

Mehtab heaved an exasperated sigh. "It doesn't really matter. What matters, though, is that the massacre did happen. The Zeg assassins spared no one. Of all the Challimar royals, Selhath was now the only one left."

What happened to her? This time Naia didn't dare to voice the question, drawn by the deep timbre of Mehtab's voice, by the way her words cut the air, sharp like double-edged blades.

"Selhath's followers knew where to find her. During the massacre, their chosen envoy – the queen's lady chamberlain – sneaked out of the palace to deliver the royal regalia to Selhath in her hiding place. In the Daljeer serai, just outside the royal capital."

"The Daljeer?" Naia didn't feel surprised – or had she somehow lost her ability to feel anything at all? In any case, it made perfect sense. It all came back to the Daljeer, one way or another.

"The messengers all died on the way," Mehtab went on, "but the lady chamberlain did manage to reach the serai and hand the package to Selhath. A bundle, containing the precious necklace I am now wearing. She disguised it cleverly inside a baby's wrappings, so that no one would suspect a thing."

"A baby?" Naia remembered the story Gassan told her the day she received this assignment. *Me. She is talking about me.* She knew this realization should bother her somehow. But she still didn't feel a thing.

"Yes, a baby," Mehtab said. "At first, Selhath believed this baby to be only a decoy that ensured the necklace could be delivered to her without raising suspicion. Later on, though, she discovered that this baby – a girl – had Ironblood lineage. She was out of Selhath's hands by then, but Selhath took care to follow the girl's fate, shape it, so that the girl, when grown, could become Selhath's sworn protector."

"A protector?" Naia frowned. She was beginning to realize what bothered her so much when Mehtab mentioned the baby just now. She and Gassan were the only people who spoke to the lady chamberlain. According to Gassan's story, the lady handed the baby directly to Mehtab. Could it be that…?

Her eyes snapped open. "You. You are Selhath."

The older woman smiled. "Yes. You recognize me now, don't you?"

Naia nodded slowly. As she recalled her vision through the veil – her baby vision – the features now became more and more familiar. The majestic woman, dying before her eyes. *The Challimar Queen.* She was not Mehtab, but they looked alike, like sisters would. The same face was now looking back at her – older, yes, but clearly recognizable. Seeing it felt oddly comforting, like reuniting with a long lost relative.

Was this why Mehtab always made her feel so at home – at least when Naia was wearing her necklace?

"How can I possibly have those memories?" she whispered.

"Through my necklace," Mehtab said. "This stone I am wearing has a name. Destiny. The birthright of every Challimar queen. My sister was wearing it when she was killed. Now that I have it, her last memories have passed on to me. Every time I control you through the Destiny Stone, you see some of the visions stored inside it."

"Control. You are controlling me." Naia knew this realization should probably bother her, somehow. But she just couldn't find it in herself to feel alarmed. She trusted Mehtab implicitly. The older woman was the closest to the family she'd always wanted to have.

Mehtab reached over and gently touched her arm. "The control I speak of is in our bond. You do feel it, don't you?"

"Yes."

"And you will do anything to protect me."

Slowly, Naia stood up and sank down to her knees in front of Mehtab. It felt so natural to do it – comforting, even – as if she had just now reclaimed her rightful place.

"I will," she said. "I will always protect you, my queen."

Mehtab drew up, her face unreadable as she looked down at Naia.

"I know," she said. "You will die for me, if needed."

"Yes."

"But first, you must give me the throne."

"Of course, my queen. Anything you say."

"Good." Mehtab's lips twitched. "Let's go out and announce it, shall we?"

Naia lifted her head. *Announce it. Right.* All the courtiers were still out there, waiting. She could hear their expectant hum outside her chamber, like a swarm of bees waiting for their queen.

She rose to her feet and stepped toward the doors, throwing them open.

Whispers echoed through the chamber as she appeared. The crowd backed off to form a wide semicircle, freeing a large space around the doorway. They started bowing as they saw Naia – all except two men, who pushed forward through the crowd into the empty space.

Karrim and Gassan.

Their blank expressions sent a chill down Naia's spine.

Something was terribly wrong. They were supposed to be on her side, right? Except that they were both Zeg. Under Mehtab's rule Naia was about to announce, they were both going to die.

Should this realization bother her somehow?

"Take off your necklace and armor," Karrim said.

Naia lifted her chin. "No."

"This wasn't a request."

"Nor was my answer open for any discussion, Jai Karrim. Stand down, before I have you removed."

She sensed Mehtab step up behind her and place something in her hands. *Swords. The imlarite blades to go with my armor.* Their hilts sank comfortably into her palms. She felt a lot safer, facing Karrim now that she was armed.

She looked past Karrim to the court gathering.

"Lords and ladies of the imperial court," she said. "I have an important announcement to make. This woman standing beside me is Selhath, the true heir to Challimar. I hereby–"

Karrim drew a dagger.

Naia reacted before she could think, raising her armored wrist forward into its path.

The blade shifted in his hand, his muscles bulging as he struggled to control it. He uttered a curse under his breath as it flew out of his hand and latched onto her wrist guard.

"How dare you attack me, Jai Karrim?" she demanded.

Karrim's jaw knotted. "I haven't attacked you. I was just showing you. The imlar you are wearing is affecting you, just like it's affecting this dagger. You won't be yourself until you take it off."

"No."

Gassan stepped up to Karrim's side. "Jai Naia, listen. The stone set into Mehtab's necklace is known as the Destiny Stone. She is controlling you with it."

Naia's lips twitched. "I know all about it, Dal Gassan. Queen Selhath told me." *And you would be a fool to think this knowledge could possibly change anything.*

Selhath was her rightful queen, the true heir of Challimar. Selhath owned her, body and soul. Looking into Gassan's urgent face, Naia was dimly aware that for some reason he was expecting his words to change something about this line of thinking, but for the life of her she couldn't understand why.

"Just try it," Karrim said. "Take off your gear."

"So that you have a better chance of killing me?"

Karrim raised his hands up and away from his sides. "I am unarmed. Unarmored too, if that makes you feel better. I swear I won't attack you if you take off your armor."

"Your oath means little, ever since you drew your dagger on me, Jai Karrim."

"Get out of Empress Xarimet's way, Jai Karrim," Mehtab said. "She is in the process of making an important announcement to her court."

"Not while she is wearing this much imlar."

Mehtab laughed. "So, what are you going to do, take it off by force?"

Karrim's face hardened. He raised his hand, and the nearest Jaihar guard flung a long object into his path.

A staff.

Naia swallowed. Karrim was a blade fighter, just like her. The fact that he chose a staff, in place of his regular weapons, could only mean one thing. Karrim knew about the effect imlar would have on his blades. He came here prepared for a fight, one that he could plausibly win.

The memories of their fights back at the Jaihar fortress floated up in her mind. A staff was one of Naia's worst weapons to defend against. If Karrim won, he could do anything to her. He could kill her, if he wanted to.

Judging by his blank expression, he was going to do just that.

She drew her blades and squared off to face him.

IMLAR

Karrim could sense the hum of power around Naia, her imlar armor enclosing her into an impenetrable cocoon. It was good that he'd gotten rid of all his metal-based weapons and gear, which would have rendered him all but useless against her. He swung his staff, glad to feel no obstacles to the wood, no ill effects from the armor she was wearing. Her blades flew up in response, giving him a full, even if a rather rushed, view. Their craftsmanship was superb – from what he could tell, a near-exact replica of her regular swords, crafted entirely in stone.

As they locked gazes, he saw Naia's dilated pupils, her frozen expression that made her normally vivid face almost unrecognizable, mask-like. Her shape blurred as she advanced.

Karrim met her head-on, stretching the movement to aim a low attack she blocked far too easily despite its sneaky angle. Her body unfolded so fast that he nearly missed the moment her blade came through again. *A close one. Right.* This fight was bound to turn ugly, any moment. But there was no way but forward, and he put his entire skill into it.

Naia was picking up speed and he found odd enjoyment in

trying to match her blows, parry for parry, thrust for thrust. It felt like a dance, thrilling and intimate, an ultimate form of closeness only two Shadowblades could have. Unbidden, the memory of their night together floated into his mind, surging through his nerves. He forced it away, putting his entire strength and speed into each move, perfectly matched by the moves from her side.

Karrim knew they could go like this for quite a while, until one of them made a fatal mistake. Except, unlike Naia, he was not protected by armor. He was also the one at a formal disadvantage, fighting against the edged weapons with a blunt one – a fact that never bothered him as much as it did now. Any misstep on his side could easily become his last, with likely devastating consequences to the empire. He had to apply everything he learned to win this fight, all the extra knowledge relayed to him by Ilhad.

He recalled every detail of Naia's ranking tournament, every word Ilhad said to him afterwards, glad now that despite his resentment he had the good sense to listen. *The staff is a weapon you could defeat her with.* It seemed far easier back then. The only consolation right now was the fact that his taller, heavier build would provide some advantage. He put all this knowledge into each blow, using full force to attack her without giving her any chance to recover.

As he whirled around her, her spiked wrist guard bit into the wood of his staff – the first move on her side he could consider at least a minor fault. He used the momentary lock to put his weight into the twist that forced her to falter in her balance – ever so slightly – before she pulled free. Moving as fast as he could, not to give her any chance to compose herself, he spun his staff around her arm, bringing it down on her sword in a blow of such force that it echoed through his own arm. It didn't shatter the stone, as he hoped, but he was relieved to see her stagger and edge backward before settling herself again.

The room around them was deadly quiet, even though Karrim's peripheral senses told him the edges of the room were packed with spectators. He had given his Glimmerblades an order to keep everyone away, but he knew it was redundant. No one in their right mind would attempt to interfere in this fight, or even move, for fear of getting caught in it.

He knew his best hope lay in maintaining both speed and strength as he launched another forceful attack. Naia faltered, recovering nearly instantly, but not fast enough. He saw an opening on her right and went for it, reaching for her arm, letting his staff go full force to connect the blow. *Yes.* He pulled the movement, feeling almost guilty when he felt her waver and let go, sending her blade flying.

Her jaw set with determination as she regrouped, but he knew he had already won. There was no way, even in her imlar armor, she would be able to resist him one-handed. Not for long. This certainty drove him on as he called on his entire skill, putting everything he had into picking up speed, even though moving faster didn't seem possible anymore. His mind blanked out to anything else besides the blows he showered on her, steady and unrelenting, even after he saw defeat in her eyes.

His standing order from the Jaihar Headmaster was to kill her right now. He erased this thought too, numb inside as he landed the last blow – a dirty crash to the side of her head, driven in nearly without resistance, and with barely any time to control it at all.

Her eyes widened in a brief expression of disbelief, gone far too quickly as light faded out of her gaze. Her hand unclenched, releasing her remaining blade. Her body folded bonelessly to the floor.

Karrim panted as he stood over Naia, clutching his staff with unnecessary force, watching blood drip out of her split temple as she lay at his feet, staring lifelessly at the ceiling.

Dear Sel, what have I done?

His heart quivered with a dread he had never experienced before as he finally gathered enough strength to move, to kneel on the floor beside her. *To help her. To take off her damn armor.* Not because his knees simply gave way under the weight of what he had done.

He didn't want to hit her on the head. Not this hard, at least. He'd done his best to twist the blow to reduce the direct impact, but beyond that he just didn't have any other choice. The spot where his staff landed, on her temple next to a key pressure point, made the outcome random, at best. He could have cracked her skull. He could have caused a deadly concussion, even if she was still alive. His mind simply refused to delve into the possibilities.

Given the orders he had received, the Jaihar command would cheer him now for a successfully completed assignment. He had stepped into Naia's path with full knowledge of that. And now, his victory felt far worse than defeat.

If Naia had struck him down, if he was the one on the floor right now, he would at least be feeling nothing. He would be far better off.

The silence around him felt oppressive, everyone in the room holding their breath in shock. He distanced himself from it, reaching forward to brush his fingers over Naia's skin, pressing at the base of her throat to reach some key pressure points, then lower to feel for the pulse. Nothing. He forced his eyes to the damage he had done.

A bruise darkened the skin at her temple, blood oozing out of the long narrow gash. It looked so dark as it mixed into her hair, like a pool of spilled ink.

Dazed, he reached behind her shoulders to unclasp the imlar necklace, tear it off her chest. It held on briefly before letting go, as if the magnetic metal had the ability to stick to the iron in her blood.

A faint gasp of protest echoed behind him as he crumpled the necklace in his hand and stuffed it into his pocket. *Mehtab.* Out of the corner of his eye, he saw her move, and flicked up his hand to give a sign to the Glimmerblades to hold her back.

He forced down all emotions as he traced his fingers over Naia's chin, tilting it up. *Breathe, damn it. Damn it to hell.*

He leaned down and pried her lips open, heaving a full breath of air into her mouth, then pressed her chest in steady pulses before trying again. And again. And again.

Someone was grasping his shoulder, trying to pull him away. He shook their hands off. Someone was talking to him, but he didn't pay attention. A breath. Push. Again. And again. He couldn't afford to stop. *Wake up, Naia, damn it. Wake up.*

He almost missed the moment when his fingers at her throat caught a faint flutter. At first he thought it was the echo of his own heartbeat, pounding in his temples so hard it threatened to overwhelm him. He heaved a long breath, his fingers searching around her skin again. Here. A movement, not steady enough to tell if it was going to last, but definitely genuine.

He was surprised at the strength of his relief, especially with the knowledge that this was not the time to celebrate anything just yet. His fingers flew to the sides of her head to press the deep points just above her ears, then harder on her temples, outside the damaged zone, and finally at the base of her neck.

He felt for the pulse again. *Steadier this time. Good.*

His side vision caught a movement, a figure gliding along the wall to the exit from the room.

Mehtab. Not a bloody chance.

He spun around and grasped one of Naia's imlar blades, sending it flying.

In his heightened state, the blade seemed to move impossibly slowly, as if having difficulty tearing through the air. He was certain it would never arrive in time to cut off Mehtab's retreat. When it reached its target, sticking into the door frame across her way, he released the breath he didn't realize he was holding.

The room, frozen in terrified silence until this moment, exploded with movement all at once, courtiers backing out toward the exits, the Glimmerblades rushing into action. They closed in around Mehtab, looking to Karrim for further instructions.

"If she as much as moves," he snarled, "kill her."

"Really, Jai Karrim," Gassan said. "Wouldn't it be prudent to let the Daljeer handle this one?"

Karrim's upward glance caused the man to stumble back, as if hit by an invisible fist.

"The Daljeer have already handled this one. This is why we are here, facing this situation." Karrim didn't wait for a response as he turned back to Naia. The thought of losing her seemed impossible on so many levels that he felt nausea rising in his throat at the mere possibility. He swallowed it down and reached for her pulse again, now steadier, then hit a few other pressure points to stabilize her.

Gassan knelt by his side, peering into Naia's face. Karrim didn't bother to make space for him, or even to acknowledge the man's presence. Gassan was behind the whole ordeal. Karrim would be damned if he ever relinquished control to Gassan again.

"Let me look at her injury, Jai Karrim," Gassan said.

"No."

"You do remember that the Daljeer possess superior healing skills."

Karrim hesitated. In all the time he had known Gassan, he had come to think of him as a politician, someone equal both in stature and in ruthless cunning to the Jaihar command. Not a typical Daljeer. *Healers and scholars.* Right. Gassan had to have excelled at both things to achieve his high post in the Daljeer Circle.

He forced his eyes up to the Daljeer. "She has a concussion. A bad one. I still can't tell if she has a fractured skull."

"I know." Gassan opened the leather bag at his belt and rummaged inside, producing bandages and several tightly corked vials. He rubbed the contents of one onto a cloth and pressed it over Naia's injured temple, then mixed two others in a small cup and forced several drops between her lips.

Karrim watched numbly, surprised and reluctant to admit that the man's confidence had a calming effect on him. Never mind that Gassan's scheming nearly brought about the biggest mess he ever remembered dealing with, with grave consequences to the empire.

"We should take off her armor." Gassan fumbled with a hinge at Naia's breastplate, his long finger pushing a deeply set button that snapped the lock open. From behind them, Mehtab gave a small grunt of protest, silenced as Karrim briefly glanced her way.

After they stripped off the armor, Gassan's deft hands ran

over Naia's entire body, pausing over the right wrist, which he felt out with more care than the rest, before rubbing some more ointment into her skin. With surprise Karrim saw that the inky spot at her temple looked paler now, almost like a normal bruise.

Finally, Gassan sat back on his heels, packing away most of his medicines.

"Her skull's intact. As is her arm, amazingly. I believe she will be more or less fine when she comes to."

"Any idea how long that will take?" Karrim asked.

Gassan picked out a new vial. "About two seconds." He quickly uncorked it and held it in front of Naia's nose.

She coughed. Her eyes snapped open, rolling around until they met Karrim's. Her eyelids fluttered, and Karrim saw an unsettling mix of apprehension and hesitation as she looked up at him.

"Sorry," he said. "I didn't mean to hit you so hard."

Her eyes fluttered again, her daze giving way to confusion, and finally a smile – faint, but clearly present. "It wasn't a fair fight."

He nodded, weak with relief. "It wasn't. You've grown too bloody good for me."

Her lips twitched – not quite a grin, but close enough. "Neither of us were using our best weapons. I'd like a rematch."

Karrim smiled too, warmth washing over him as he looked at her. This was the Naia he knew, not the mindless creature who had fought him just now, dominated by imlar and an evil woman's will.

"I accept," he said. "After you recover."

She started to sit up, but Gassan's hand stopped her. "You should lie down just a little longer, Jai Naia. You need rest."

Before she could protest, Karrim leaned over and picked her up, rising to his feet effortlessly as he cradled her against him. Guards and palace servants rushed over, directing him through the arched doorway into the massive bedchamber. *Fit for an empress. Dear Sel.* By royal decree she was the empress now, a situation that needed to be resolved very soon for the sake of everyone involved. Karrim pushed these thoughts out of his head as he lowered her onto the vast bed that rivaled in size and grandeur the bed in the emperor's chamber.

He had no doubt now that whoever had chosen accommodations for her was well aware of the last-minute change in Gassan's succession plans, even if thinking about this didn't seem important right now.

"You must rest," he said. "I will leave Glimmerblades at the door to make certain you're not disturbed."

"I will leave a Daljeer healer," Gassan said. "So that she—"

"No," Karrim snapped. "No bloody Daljeer."

"She will need medicine to go to sleep, Jai Karrim. And another one, to alleviate the pain when she wakes up."

"I am not going to lie down and sleep when there're things to be done," Naia said, but even as she spoke, her eyelids were drooping, betraying her exhaustion. As he set her down on the bed she leaned into the pillows, her eyes falling closed.

"You can give her the medicine now, Dal Gassan," Karrim said. "And leave the pain medication for when she wakes up. I intend to do my damndest to be here when it happens."

He wished he didn't have to leave her alone, but he had pressing matters to attend to that couldn't possibly wait – such as questioning Mehtab, the traitor who almost destroyed everything.

THE FATE OF THE
EMPIRE

Even sitting in a small dungeon-like prison cell, dimly lit
through the narrow slits overhead, Mehtab still looked like
a queen. She held her head high, her expression a mix of
arrogance and defiance. She certainly didn't look like a captive,
or someone who had messed up a serious assignment and was
about to face her superior over it. Gassan thought back to the
time they'd first met, on that fateful night in the Daljeer's desert
serai outside of Challimar's capital. She had been a young girl at
the time, yet as he now realized she already had these traits, the
haughty, majestic demeanor, the likeness with her regal sister
that should have alerted him back then, if he hadn't been so
preoccupied.

The last living descendant of the Challimar royal line. How
did they all manage to remain so utterly blind to her identity, to
her grand plans?

"You have no idea what you are messing with," Mehtab said.

Dear Sel, she was already acting like an empress. Gassan

wondered briefly what it must have felt like all these years for this power-hungry woman, raised with the full awareness of her birthright, to be forced into exile, to pretend to be someone of no consequence, to play secondary roles in most of her official duties. It had to be even worse now, when her plans to take over the empire had been cut off so close to the goal. Suddenly, the fact that Karrim was also present in the chamber, standing by the door to block the only possible route of escape, seemed even more reassuring than it should. Who knew what weapons their captive still harbored under that fine silk abayah that flowed so loosely over her majestic shape?

"Princess Selhath," Gassan said.

"Queen."

"You've never been officially crowned."

Mehtab – for despite his address just now he still couldn't bring himself to identify her by any other name in his mind – smiled scornfully. "I received the Destiny Stone from my dying sister, the queen."

"Indirectly, through a messenger."

"No matter. The package with the stone came directly from the palace. In Challimar, this ritual supersedes the need for a formal coronation."

The package with the stone. Three hells. Only a very deranged person could think of using a baby as packaging material, without caring at all that they were dealing with a human being. Of course, if Naia was indeed born to one of the Redcloak guards in the palace, as Gassan suspected because of the girl's Ironblood traits, this action probably saved her from certain death. Still, the very idea that the stone, not the baby, had been the driving force behind the lady chamberlain's dramatic flight, was difficult to accept.

"Why don't you tell me the entire story from the start?" he said.

"Why bother?"

"How about for conversation's sake?"

"So that you try to do even more to destroy my plans?"

Gassan smiled. "I was not aware that you still had any plans to destroy."

"All the more reason then." Mehtab looked away. She seemed outwardly calm, but Gassan could see the stiffened muscles in her neck, the way she kept her face exaggeratedly still as if afraid to betray her feelings. The fact that she was hiding something, the hint that some of her plans may still be in motion, terrified him. But he was damned if he was going to show it.

"Did you really think you could pull this off?" Gassan said. "Take over the empire?"

Mehtab shrugged. "I *am* the rightful heir."

"To the throne of Challimar, perhaps."

"To the empire, for anyone who knows their history."

"Not without the formal succession contest."

"Which has just been enacted – by your own design, by the way."

By my own design. Gassan wasn't sure this was the case anymore. His elaborate plan, even the shatranj gambit that led to it, had seemed so perfect. Did Mehtab find some twisted way to influence even that?

He crossed his arms over his chest. "Very well. If you don't want to give me any information, I'll start with what I know. I have no idea where you were taken after your initial exile from Challimar, but somehow, very early on, you ended up with the Daljeer. In Zegmeer, at first."

Mehtab's lips twitched. "True, if you are really interested in going that far back."

"I've read your record. You came to us as a child, and soon became one of the most talented scholars among your peers. You also showed a strong inclination toward Challimar studies, which, given your ethnicity, didn't really surprise anyone. This was how you ended up in our Challimar serai, wasn't it?"

Mehtab shrugged. "It was an ideal vantage point to stay close to my followers and keep an eye on my sister."

"Did the queen know about it?"

"Tajeerah?" Mehtab let out a short laugh. "She was too preoccupied with the prosperity of our kingdom to care."

Gassan eyed her curiously. The way she spat out the word "prosperity" told him how little this woman cared for the wellbeing of her subjects. He shivered as he remembered her notes, handwritten in the book margins. Had Karrim lost the fight with Naia just now, had Mehtab been able to ascend the throne, the Zeg would have been drowned in a blood bath of a magnitude no one had ever seen before. Even now, if the succession was not resolved soon, they were facing a major upheaval, judging by the unrest among the Chall all throughout Zegmeer.

"Let's move to the Challimar Royal Massacre then," he said.

Mehtab's eyes darted around, before fixing on a distant point of the ceiling.

"Did you know about it beforehand?" Gassan knew he shouldn't be expecting a straight answer, but he couldn't stop staring, as her wavering gaze confirmed his words.

Mehtab's full lips stretched into a slow smile as she turned around to meet his gaze. In the room's dim, scattered light, her golden-speckled eyes gleamed, like molten imlar.

"Of course I knew," she said. "How else could all this have

possibly worked so perfectly?"

Gassan's skin crept.

"Did you take any part in planning it?" he asked slowly.

Mehtab continued to watch him with that triumphant look, as if he had just complimented her. *A confirmation.* A wave of nausea turned Gassan's stomach. Dear Sel, this woman had no heart.

"Why are you so interested in chewing over history, Dal Gassan?" she asked.

Gassan swallowed. Again, the fact that Karrim was in here with them, standing reassuringly close behind Gassan's back, seemed more comforting than it should. In his eventful life, Gassan believed he had seen it all. But facing this woman right now took this knowledge to a different level.

"To plan out the massacre, you had to have an ally close to the emperor," he said.

Mehtab shrugged, but his heightened senses detected her indifference to be fake.

"I'll come back to that question later," he said. "For now, let's move on. As a perpetrator – or one of them, at least – you knew the timing of the massacre, and the plan to pass on a precious package to you. It wasn't a coincidence that you ended up in the outside hallway of our serai that night, the first to receive the messengers from the palace."

Mehtab's smile widened. "If you are so certain of it, why ask?"

"I'm not asking. I've seen the note sent with the package. They – whoever it was you allied with – sent you the Destiny Stone, and the instructions on how to activate it with your voice. Why choose Naia as a way to conceal it?"

Mehtab shrugged. "Most people see a baby as a more

precious thing than anything hidden in its wrappings. What better way to divert attention?"

"Was it your idea too?"

"It was my suggestion."

"Seems a bit heartless, doesn't it?"

"To the likes of you, perhaps. In truth, the Destiny Stone is far more precious than thousands of babies. Besides, the lady chamberlain saved the little brat from a likely death, by taking her away. It's… humane, isn't it?"

Once again, the way she said the word "humane" – with uncertainty, as if unfamiliar with the concept – made Gassan's skin creep with a chill. He forced his mind away from it, to the information she was telling him.

"So, you had no idea Naia was an Ironblood?"

"Not at first, no. The lady chamberlain died before giving any explanations. But since everyone in the Daljeer serai expected me to take an interest in her, I started to look closely. She showed an unusual talent with weapons, so I ensured her placement with the Jaihar. It was a safe place for her, wasn't it?"

Gassan nodded slowly. It made sense, especially if he allowed himself to fall into Mehtab's twisted flow of logic.

"And you just took the Destiny Stone and kept it."

"It belongs to me." Mehtab's nostrils flared in anger as she turned to Karrim. "Your Jaihar watch dogs dared to rip it off my neck. You must order them to return it at once."

Karrim's lips twitched, his hand sliding into his pocket to bring out the necklace. It gleamed as it rested in his palm, the grotesque, freeform stone playing with colors.

Gassan stared. In all the excitement, he never had a chance to take a good look. And now, seeing the Destiny Stone up close for the very first time, he began to realize what all the ruckus around it had been about. Centuries worth of history, condensed into a piece so distinct that its looks in itself could feed legends and lore.

The golden-green glow emanated by the turbid semitransparent gem seemed ethereal. For a moment, the dim room seemed brighter, as if the sunlight ravaging the landscape outside these walls had found its way through. The more Gassan watched its play, the more it seemed unthinkable to tear his eyes away from its beauty. Or was it the stone's magic, speaking to the iron in Gassan's blood?

He forced his gaze to the setting, the twining lines of dark gleaming metal. From his scholarly work he knew these imlar carvings to be designed precisely to complement the stone, to channel its energy so that it could evoke the strongest reaction from its bearer, the most powerful response to those who knew how to use it to command. This was an ancient, powerful object that had already done far too much damage.

For a brief, frightening moment he feared that holding it in his hand could somehow put Karrim under Mehtab's influence, that she could use her chant to activate a bond, like she did with Naia. Karrim was an Ironblood too, even if his bloodline originated from an entirely different source.

Gassan reached over to take the necklace, but Karrim drew his hand back and closed his fingers over it.

"Given the way this stone has been used to control one of our warriors," Karrim said, "I think it would be safest in my possession for now, Dal Gassan."

"I am not so sure, Jai Karrim." Gassan glanced back just in time to see a special gleam in Mehtab's eyes as she turned away from the scene. He recognized the expression. *Hope. She thinks she can control Karrim with the stone. Damn it.*

"We should destroy the stone," Karrim said.

Mehtab swept forward. "No. Give it to me. You're messing with the powers you have no idea about!"

Karrim sidestepped her smoothly, shoving the necklace back into a deep pocket of his shirt. The way he was handling it, without any apparent care or respect to an artifact that ancient and powerful, seemed somewhat reassuring.

"On second thought," Gassan said, "keep it for now, Jai Karrim. It might still be of use. But if you ever notice being influenced by it in any way…"

"Don't worry, Dal Gassan," Karrim said. "I won't be."

"The only thing that remains," Gassan said, "is to find out who was assisting Princess Selhath in this palace."

"*Queen* Selhath."

Gassan ignored her, watching Karrim's narrowing eyes.

"I think I have an idea where to start," Karrim said.

"You do?"

"We should question the Divan sages."

"What makes you think they are involved?"

Karrim shrugged. "Members of the Divan influence all kinds of decisions here, often without being obvious about it."

"Any particular decision you are referring to?"

"The one that made me wonder about more than once today was the choice of the chamber Naia was offered."

"Her *chamber*?"

"Yes. It befits the empress in every possible way, including the private bath – a big status symbol – as well as the size of the area outside, large enough for a formal court gathering. This palace has several suites like this, most of them occupied by immediate members of the imperial family, or standing empty, waiting to be claimed by someone very influential. Most noble guests, even the province rulers, are stationed in more conventional chambers. Whoever made the decision to accommodate her in this chamber had to know she was going to carry the crown – at least temporarily."

Gassan shook his head. "Some of the Divan sages, including Yakkab, knew about my plan."

"Which didn't really involve Naia holding the crown for any amount of time. She was supposed to give it up, back in the throne room."

At that moment Mehtab launched at Karrim with outstretched claws. He caught her by the wrists, holding her at arm's length.

Gassan was surprised to see the Jaihar's bulging muscles, suggesting that the effort was costing him more than it possibly should for a warrior of his skill when wrestling with a middle-aged woman. *Bloody hell.*

"Sit down, Dal Mehtab," he said. "There's nothing you can possibly gain by this outburst."

Mehtab pushed away from Karrim and slumped into her chair. Or was it because the Jaihar pushed her? Gassan couldn't quite tell. In any case, this was probably the closest Mehtab would ever be able to come to obeying his words.

Dear Sel, in all these years, when the Daljeer had been devising the plans to bypass Ramaz and his brothers in the succession line, Mehtab had been right there, close enough to the top to know everything that went on. To influence Gassan's decisions, to feed him ideas he was going to help her implement – like the one about Xarimet, a legend Mehtab had pulled out of obscurity to serve her goal.

Gassan knew he would have plenty of time to curse himself later for how blind he had been. Right now, he had more urgent things to think about.

"One last question for now, Dal Mehtab," he said. "What about the crystal leeches?"

"What about them?"

"As I gathered from your notes, you've spent years researching them. And then, Jai Naia told me today that she found one in her bath."

"Oh, did she?"

Gassan leaned closer. "Given the way you've put Naia so completely under your influence, you had no benefit in killing her. Why did you want her to be stung?"

Mehtab's lips spread into a mocking grin. "You are one of the top Daljeer scholars, Dal Gassan. Why don't you figure this one out on your own?"

Gassan sighed and stepped away.

"Come, Jai Karrim. I believe we've learned everything of use here."

"Say goodbye to Naia for me," Mehtab said.

Gassan, already at the door, stiffened.

Say goodbye to Naia. Did Mehtab believe she was never going to see Naia again? And if so, why?

After her fight with Karrim, Naia would certainly be too weak to defend herself right now. True, Karrim had stationed enough Glimmerblades next to her to ensure her safety from all the usual kinds of dangers, but who knew what else could be in store for her? Despite all the guesses, Gassan was painfully aware of the fact that he had likely uncovered only a fraction of Mehtab's seemingly endless resources. She had gathered enough to orchestrate the demise of an entire kingdom, and kept ahead of him for over twenty years, after all.

Karrim's face had shifted – a change of expression that didn't exactly alter any of his features, but made him look ruthless. He rushed to the door and flung it open, turning to the nearest Glimmerblade standing outside.

"Jai Semir," Karrim said. "You're in charge, until I get back. Lock this cell and don't open the door, no matter what." He tossed the key to the Glimmerblade as he rushed out.

Gassan followed, his growing unease gradually turning into panic. *Say goodbye to Naia for me.* What was he still missing about Mehtab's plan?

AMBUSH

Naia opened her eyes. Did she fall asleep without realizing it, again? What the hell was wrong with her?

The memory came back all too suddenly, along with the throbbing in her temple. A blow to the head. Right. Followed by the Daljeer medication and the welcome oblivion it brought. She should feel lucky to be alive.

She tried to sit up in bed, waiting for the room to stop spinning in front of her eyes, until she could tell floor from ceiling with reasonable certainty. This had to be good enough. She would be damned if she was going to relax in her chambers when the action involving her assignment was going on elsewhere.

She swayed as she stepped out of bed, pausing to regain her balance. Voices carried through the closed door from the outer chamber. The Glimmerblades. It took her a moment to notice their heightened tones, rising in a rapidly accelerating argument. What the hell was going on out there? She knew she shouldn't feel concerned, not with the Jaihar's finest guarding her, but it was probably a good idea to get out there and find out the reason for the disturbance.

She glanced into the mirror. Her clothes were blooded and torn, so she searched around for something to change into, pulling on the first thing she could find – pantaloons and a blouse of yellow silk with the golden accents along the neck, chest, and waist. A hideous outfit when it came to fighting, even if its heavy ornaments could probably offer at least partial protection against a stab.

She still felt nauseated, the throbbing in her temple getting worse by the minute. She didn't have much time before the medicine Gassan had given her wore off. She should find Karrim and learn what the hell was going on.

The voices outside changed their tone. Not the Glimmerblades anymore. The men in the outer chamber right now spoke in hushed tones, as if afraid of being overheard. She also heard their footsteps – stealthy, as if their bearers were up to no good, yet not stealthy enough for a Jaihar.

She searched around for a weapon. Damn her earlier gullibility, when she had allowed Mehtab to pack away her Jaihar gear too far away to reach at short notice. The imlar blades? Gone. She must have been sicker than she thought when Karrim brought her in here after the fight. Her eyes fell on a small dagger, one she normally hid in her bodice when she traveled around in her Xarimet disguise. It would have to do.

She grasped it, then quickly bundled up her pillow and blanket to make it look as if someone was still sleeping in the bed. She slid behind the door when she heard the key turning in the lock, pressing into the wall just as it swung open, letting in a group of hooded men.

The pain in her head was becoming unbearable, but she forced it to the back of her mind to focus on the action. The fighters filing into her room moved far too smoothly and stealthily for her liking. Standing up to them with a single dagger, when she was still so unsteady on her feet, was going to be a challenge.

One of the men approached the bed and upended the contents of a small jar onto the bundled blanket that looked like a sleeping shape. Everyone edged back, giving Naia a clearer view.

Her breath caught at the sight.

The bedcover gleamed with crawling shapes, transparent, but still visible. She narrowed her eyes to make sure. Crystal leeches. At least a dozen, delicate and deadly as they flailed over her bed in their dying agony, searching for a place to release their poison. The magnitude of this made the single leech she found in her bath seem like a joke.

Someone had spent a fortune to ensure her death.

The men around her bed were peering, their postures uncertain, betraying their surprise at the lack of reaction from the sleeping person. Just enough time to act, before they realized what was going on.

She kicked back the door she was hiding behind, diving low as she swept forward. Her dagger blow was answered by a satisfying grunt. As her victim staggered and fell, she reached over and snatched a sword off his belt, shifting the dagger into her off hand. Better, if not quite the Jaihar-quality blades she'd gotten used to during her training.

It took all she had to keep up the melee. These men were much better fighters than she expected to encounter outside the Jaihar Stronghold. As they rushed at her all at once, she had an uncomfortable feeling that they must have been trained in synchronous combat. Her attempts to counter them by putting them into each other's way failed miserably, the men regrouping every time to maintain the formation. Several of them attacking her at the same time turned out to be more of a challenge than she expected.

Out of the corner of her eye she caught sight of the leeches crawling on her bed – still alive, and obviously much more resilient than she had originally believed. She feigned a move in their direction. Two attackers set off in pursuit, so unexpectedly fast and precise it seemed frightening.

She shifted her balance abruptly – one of her favorite moves that, she knew, for a briefest instant would make her appear simultaneously present in two places at once. Her skin prickled as one of her attackers matched the maneuver. It took all she had to slide out of his way at the very last instance, putting a leg into his way to trip him onto the bed. Right into the bundle of leeches.

His curse sounded foreign. *Chall. He is swearing in Chall.* She had no time to wonder about the implications, using the momentum she gained to stab left and right, sending two more men to the ground. It didn't seem enough, though. She had taken down four men so far, less than half of the force that had come in here after her. Worse, she was beginning to feel exhausted, her headache making her vision blur, and her attackers still looked just as composed as before.

Her heart leapt as she heard running footsteps in the outer chamber. The doors burst open to let in the two newcomers.

Gassan and Karrim.

Thank the prophets.

Karrim didn't pause at all as he rushed forward, his hands unfolding with swords. Two of Naia's attackers went down in a single sweep. The others backed away toward the window, bursting it open and dropping into the garden outside. Thuds and more Chall cursing echoed down below.

Naia darted toward the bed, to the man bitten by the leeches. He was still alive, even if she knew that with the amount of bites he had he wasn't going to survive for more than a few minutes.

The man's pale lips twitched, his face holding awe she didn't expect from someone who had just tried to kill her. She recognized him for certain now. One of her Chall guards, a man who always kept to the back and rarely got into her line of sight. She remembered him chanting her name, only this morning, with fervor that bordered on worship.

What could have possibly made him go after her, only a few hours later?

"You're a Chall," she said. "Why did you attack me?"

"I didn't. We were bringing salvation, why did you resist us?" *"Salvation?"*

"The leeches. Don't you understand?"

"No, I don't."

The man frowned in disbelief. "Queen Selhath didn't tell you?"

"Did she order this?"

Naia didn't notice Karrim's approach. Not until his blade whizzed by, landing right beside the injured man's leg.

"Next time you avoid a direct answer I'm aiming two inches to the right," Karrim said. "It will probably take a few tries to sever your leg."

The man's lips twitched. "Go ahead. We both know you don't have the time. I'm a dead man." He turned to Naia. "Queen Selhath taught you everything about Ironbloods. How come you don't know about the leeches?"

Naia blinked. She *did* think Mehtab had taught her

everything, but it was very clear how wrong she was. She was having serious trouble keeping up. The pain in her temple didn't help. Very soon she was probably going to pass out, and none of this would matter at all.

She didn't quite notice Karrim put out his arm to support her, not until she was already leaning on him heavily, Gassan rushing to her side with a vial in his hand. Three hells, she was becoming all but useless, her warrior training no help at all.

Gassan held the vial to her lips. "Drink it."

Naia obeyed. The liquid was so bitter that she almost gagged on it, but she did feel the relief almost instantly. The pain subsided, like a heavy blanket lifting up, until she could see the world again in such amazing clarity that she blinked.

Dear Sel, she should have more appreciation for things she normally took for granted.

She looked at their captive again.

"I think you can cut off his leg, Jai Karrim," she said. "Clearly, he is not going to tell us anything of use."

The man's eyes narrowed. "You really don't know, do you?"

"Why would we waste the bloody time questioning you, if I did?"

The man edged away, his eyes on Karrim's sword. "The leeches. Their venom can turn a regular person into an Ironblood. That's what Queen Selhath did to us. She… she *made* us into her Redcloaks so that we could protect her. Some died, before she perfected the process. But it was all worth it. And now…" His eyes trailed to the window where his comrades had disappeared.

Naia turned to see Gassan's frozen look as he too looked out of the window.

"But Mehtab… Queen Selhath told me I am already an

Ironblood," she said. "Why bother with the leeches?"

"To an Ironblood, leech venom acts like imlar. It puts their minds fully under the control of the Destiny Stone. If the ritual succeeded, you would no longer have trouble with your loyalties, or the need to wear imlar to obey her. You would have followed her unconditionally, without any argument."

Naia's eyes widened. Without any argument. Now that she thought about it, she realized that she did tend to argue with Mehtab a lot. Did it cause a problem? It probably didn't matter now, but she knew for certain that it would take her a while to settle all this information in her head.

Gassan leaned forward and smelled one of the leeches on the bed, now perfectly still and already growing milky.

"Iron," he muttered. "Their venom's based on iron. What an idiot I've been." He turned to the captive. "We had Queen Selhath in custody when you came here. This means she couldn't possibly have sent you. Tell me, who did?"

The man's smile came out ghostly. "You'd like to know, wouldn't you? Sorry. You'll have to figure that one out on your own."

His last words came out as a whisper, head rolling to the side as his body shook and went limp, like a puppet suddenly cut off its strings.

Dead.

They all stood for a moment, looking at him.

"I think another conversation with Queen Selhath is in order," Gassan said.

"Yes," Naia said. "And this time I am bloody coming along." She darted to the corner and dug out her Jaihar blades and the knife belt. She longed to put on her leathers too, but she knew there was no time.

POISON

Mehtab lifted her head as she heard shouting outside the cell. *It's about time.* She rose from her seat, assuming the majestic posture appropriate for the queen and future empress greeting her loyal defenders.

The turmoil outside approached, followed by the scraping of a key in the lock. The door burst open, letting in Sage Hakeem at the head of the Ironbloods. *My troops.* Pride seized her as she glanced over them, two dozen men that rivaled the Jaihar's best.

She didn't bother with greetings, sweeping past Hakeem into the outer chamber to look at the bodies of the Glimmerblades scattered around the floor. Good. Her warriors were even better than she originally thought, when she had finally worked out the recipe to convey the Ironblood abilities to regular men. This small test proved it all. Blood was far more important than training, at least when it came to the warriors whose original abilities did not exceed the impossible, like Shadowblades. She still wasn't sure how her Ironbloods would hold up against the Shadowblades, but she hoped she wouldn't have to learn it at all. Naia was about to be converted into Selhath's obedient tool. As soon as the leech poison took hold, the girl would do everything she was told, without any argument or second thoughts. She would finally rid Mehtab of Gassan, and make Karrim wish he was never born at all.

Mehtab glanced around the chamber again. Eight Glimmerblades lay perfectly still – dead, or so she assumed by the way her Ironblood warriors stood over them impassively, obviously unconcerned about any possibility of resistance. Good. This left only three Glimmerblades up and about – hopefully, not for long. She looked at her warriors again, each wearing a plain imlar necklace to symbolize servitude. They would obey her even without it, but it did help to seal her certainty that every one of her orders would be instantly followed.

By habit, she reached for the Destiny Stone at her throat, cursing when her fingers touched only skin. Damn Karrim for taking the necklace away. He was going to pay triple for this.

"Where are my other warriors, Sage Hakeem?" she asked.

"I've sent them to Naia's chambers. With enough leeches to finish the job."

"You could have freed me first."

"We had to use the window of opportunity. Dal Gassan's medicine left her sleeping and vulnerable in her chambers, with only three Glimmerblades on guard. A perfect time for our warriors to do the job. Besides, we couldn't possibly attempt a rescue with Jai Karrim in here with you, could we?"

Karrim. The man was like a fly, dropping into a lovingly cooked dish just before it was ready to be served. A fly Selhath couldn't wait to smash.

"Karrim and Gassan went to the girl, I believe," she said.

Hakeem shrugged. "Too late. The poison would already be in her system. The only thing that could save her now is the antidote – which would deliver her right into your service, Your Majesty."

"Let's go then." Mehtab swept toward the door, stopping short as she heard the sound of running feet outside.

Her warriors instantly regrouped to shield her, freezing in disbelief as the door to the chamber swung open, letting in four of their comrades.

Mehtab stared too. Her Ironbloods, her prized warriors, limping and disheveled, as if they had just been run over by a herd of wild elephants.

For the first time since the beginning of the ordeal, she felt her stomach quiver with fear. Did Naia, injured and sedated, do this to Mehtab's warriors all by herself? And where the hell were the others?

"What happened?" she demanded.

"The… the girl." The speaker, a tall, pale-skinned warrior, was one of Mehtab's first successful ones. She had never seen him so unsettled before. "She's in far better shape than we thought. And then, Jai Karrim showed up and…"

Karrim. Mehtab clenched her teeth. "Did you administer the leeches?"

"We dumped them onto her bed. But she… she tricked us. She should have been asleep, but she must have heard us fighting with the Glimmerblades in the chamber outside. When we entered her room, she ambushed us, and disabled many of our men. We are so very sorry, Your Majesty."

Mehtab pursed her lips. There was no use in scolding anyone right now, or showing her temper. Not when they had so little time.

"We must split up," she said. "Bring all the imperial princes to the throne room. Dead, if needed. I will meet you there.

Quick."

Naia stared at the Glimmerblades' still shapes stretched on the floor of her antechamber. The guards Karrim had left behind to ensure her safety. The elite Jaihar warriors. She knew they were dead even before she bent down beside the nearest one. Jai Fahid. During her trainee days, this cheerful man always used to joke around with her and tell stories in the dining hall. Her anger boiled as she looked further on, to the others. Damn Mehtab and her blood lust. No one deserved to die in her crazy succession fight.

"We must hurry," Karrim said. "I left the rest of the Glimmerblades guarding Mehtab. If more of these Redcloaks are still on the loose…"

Cursed Irfat. Naia was on her feet and through the door before she could think, running in Karrim's wake.

They raced through the hallways at top speed, Naia close on Karrim's heels, with Gassan far behind. Still, when Karrim skidded to an abrupt halt in the gaping doorway ahead, Naia knew they were too late, even before she stepped up to his side.

Still shapes of the Glimmerblades were scattered around the floor, eerily reminiscent of the scene they had left behind in her own chamber, but on a greater scale. *All eight of them. Three hells.* She trailed her eyes to the small door at the far end. It stood ajar, revealing a small, dungeon-like room behind. Empty. She glanced up at Karrim, seeing the grim acknowledgment in his gaze.

"The princes," she said. "She will go after them next."

"Right."

They rushed back along the passage, nearly colliding with Gassan, who had finally caught up with them.

"Where to?" he asked.

"Prince Halil's chamber." Karrim was running, and Naia took off after him, afraid to lose him in the maze of the back hallways.

They hadn't gone very far when the faint echo of a battle brought them to a halt. The sounds were coming not from the hallway ahead, but from a side passage.

"The throne room," Karrim said.

The throne room? What in three hells would Mehtab want in there? Naia didn't have time to contemplate the question as she and Karrim charged in the direction of the sounds.

The passage in front of them ended abruptly with a tightly shut door. A servants' entrance. Karrim kicked it open without breaking stride, the force of his blow dislodging the top hinge, leaving the door hanging crookedly across the opening. He edged inside, side-stepping to give Naia a clear view.

The throne room was a mess. Hooded fighters pressed a disarrayed row of the palace guards, moving with frightening unity and grace that eerily resembled the encounter Naia had in her chamber. The sages of the Divan huddled by the far wall in frozen terror. The floor was strewn with bodies, the purple of the imperial guards' cloaks interspersed here and there with the jewels and gold of the imperial robes. *The princes.* Naia's mind, numb and detached, refused to react to this impossible information, as she recognized them all. Ramaz and his brothers. And off to the side, Halil, the chosen one she was supposed to win the throne for. *All dead.*

This can't possibly be happening.

She drew her blades and rushed into battle.

As she and Karrim advanced on the Chall warriors side by side, images floated up in Naia's mind. The hexagonal room.

The clanging of weapons. The smell of blood. Chall and Zeg fighting. Men, killing each other… for what? For the glory of a kingdom long gone? Or was it some sort of an elaborate revenge Mehtab had designed during her years of exile, one that would claim lives without any purpose at all?

As Mehtab's name floated up in Naia's head, it stayed there, like a spell evoked by a carefully triggered thought. No, not the thought. The voice. The singing. She felt her limbs growing heavier, making it harder to resist the warriors who were now starting to crowd in on her on all sides. If she didn't shake off the spell, she would be lost. Not to the blades, no. She would be lost in her own mind, never to find a way out again.

The giant hall. The fighting.

Looking through a veil…

She was a Chall too. These warriors and she were supposed to be on the same side. Like Naia, they were all Ironbloods, even if not by birth. They had the same iron coursing through their veins, even if they couldn't remember it.

I must remind them.

The words came to Naia's mind with a clarity so sudden that it felt like a splash of cold water in her face.

She raised her voice, putting all her force into the command that rolled far throughout the hall:

"Shahgar, Chall!"

Her voice carried all the way out to the room's distant corners, ringing under the high ceiling vault.

The war cry from my dreams.

The call to all Ironbloods.

The rows of her opponents rippled.

The echoes of her voice bounced off the walls, traveling from figure to standing figure. Weapons lowered everywhere inside.

All eyes fixed on her with fervor, their lips mouthing the words:

Shahgar, Chall. Shahgar.

We are one.

Mehtab's chant stopped.

Naia blinked, slowly coming back to awareness. *What in three hells did I just do?* She raised her eyes, looking past Karrim and Gassan, over the heads of the Chall warriors watching her fervently, all the way to Mehtab.

The older woman stood up straight, a triumphant smile playing on her lips.

"Well done," she said. "Welcome to the ranks of my Ironbloods."

She slid forward with surprising speed, her hand flinging something in Naia's direction as soon as she got close. A gleaming string hurled off her hand, flying through the air like a ribbon of light.

Crystal leeches.

Sel's prophets, so many of them.

The glassy shapes twisted as they flew, a transparent cloud approaching so fast that a normal person would not be able to react at all. They scattered too – a shield rather than a spearhead, so much more area to avoid. Naia knew that she should move, that she was out of time, but just then Mehtab's voice rose in a song again, hitting a high note that made her pause in her steps just enough to… to…

The leeches.

They will sting me, and then everything will be fine.

Welcome to the ranks of my Ironbloods.

Yes.

Naia was aware that she should probably try to divert them in some way. Instead, she stepped directly into their path. As soon as they reached her, they would envelop her with welcome oblivion. She spread her arms toward them, offering them more surface to latch on to, longing for their touch more than she had longed for anything before.

My queen. Command me. I will bring you to glory. I will destroy your enemies. I will die for you, if you wish.

A hand appeared out of thin air in front of her, moving with surreal speed as it swept through, scooping the entire ball of leeches into its grip.

Karrim.

Naia snapped out of her trance, watching with widened eyes as he clenched his fingers to crush the leeches in his hand.

So many. Even if he moved very fast, he would never be able to avoid their sting. Not all of them. *No. Dear Sel, no.*

Mehtab's voice rose in a song again, but Naia didn't listen anymore. The sight of Karrim's face, pale and drawn as the poison entered his blood, cut through the spell like a blade.

He swayed as the poison worked – much faster than usual, because of the sheer amount of it. *All because of me. He just killed himself to protect me.* The thought seemed too enormous to hold. Naia forced it out of her head as she rushed forward and caught him as he fell, before he could hit the floor.

One leech could kill a healthy person in an hour. With so many leeches stinging at once, Karrim had only minutes to live. Hell, they'd just seen this in action, back in her chambers. Naia's attacker had died too quickly to be properly questioned, stung by less than half of the leeches they were dealing with right now.

She knelt, holding Karrim against her as she looked into his face.

"It was a bloody stupid thing to do," she said.

"I know." His smile looked ghostly. His dilated pupils made his normally light eyes look dark, the only indication of the pain he was in. He was still clenching his fist, and Naia could see transparent goo ooze through his fingers. Crushed leeches, infused with so much poison that even touching it seemed like a very bad idea.

Gassan was by her side, saying something, but Naia didn't pay any attention. The battle wasn't over, not if Mehtab's warriors woke up from their trance and chose to attack her right now, in her most vulnerable moment. She had no idea what was holding them back, and she didn't care. If anyone as much as touched her, she would bloody kill them all.

Karrim's gaze wavered, then focused on her face.

"Don't let anyone stand in your way," he said. "You are the empire's only hope. You will make a hell of an empress."

Me? An empress? Karrim was clearly getting delirious, the realization not helping at all. She had no intention of keeping the throne. And now, with Halil dead, she didn't have any idea who to give it to. There was only one thing she knew for sure. Mehtab was not going to have it. Not in a million years.

Dear Sel, when this was over she was going to *kill* Mehtab. She had never felt so much anger toward anyone in her life.

"You belong on the throne." Karrim's voice sank to a near-whisper. "They all see it. They just refuse to acknowledge it. *Show* them."

Naia frowned. He was speaking clearly, as if he was still in his right mind, but he couldn't possibly mean any of it. More, this didn't seem significant at all. *I'll do anything to make you live.* She realized it with certainty now, as she held him in her arms, looking up desperately for anyone, anything that could offer a way out of this nightmare.

All this time, Karrim had been her beacon, her only true friend, the man she owed everything to. Her lover. Well, that part had been too good to last, nor was the physical closeness the deepest bond they shared. Not by far. And now, she was going to lose him, before having any chance to know him more.

His head lolled, and she caught it into the crook of her arm, brushing her fingers over his temple, wiping off a sheen of sweat covering his forehead. She cradled him as she leaned closer, touching her lips lightly to his cheek, inhaling his scent – spring water and sun-baked sandalwood. Her eyes rimmed with tears. She didn't bother to blink them away.

"Empress?"

It took her a moment to react, to lift her tear-stained face to the approaching man. Sage Hakeem, the one whose presence helped to confirm her identity back at the plaza. What in three hells could he possibly want?

"Empress Xarimet," Hakeem said. "Dal Mehtab has the antidote that could save Jai Karrim."

"Traitor!" Mehtab snarled.

Hakeem kept his eyes on Naia. "Dal Mehtab requested that I find a vial of this substance for her. I aided her, under the assumption that she was acting on the Daljeer's behalf. She should have it on her person right now."

The antidote. Naia's mind snapped back into gear. The substance was even rarer than the poison itself. Could they really be this lucky?

Gently, Naia lowered Karrim to the floor, then rose to her feet and stepped toward Mehtab. "Is it true?"

"No." Mehtab edged away. "Hakeem is just trying to mislead you, to divert the blame." Her eyes darted sideways as she spoke, a giveaway sign Naia had learned too well during their lessons.

Not this time, damn it. She reached forward. "*Give it to me.*"

"I don't have it. Not here."

"Where, then?"

"It's back in my room. You'll never get it in time."

"The substance is precious, empress," Hakeem said behind Naia. "She would never let it out of her hands. I've seen her put it into the inner pocket of her robe. Search her."

Naia drew her belt dagger. "If you don't hand it over, Mehtab, I will take it off your dead body."

"You will be killing me for nothing. I don't have it here, I'm telling you."

"I don't bloody care."

Mehtab's lips twitched. She hesitated for a moment longer, then bent down to fumble in her robe, drawing out a tightly corked egg-shaped vial.

"Here, take it – but careful. It's fragile." She turned away and hurled it into the corner of the room.

Even with her Shadowblade training, Naia had no idea she could ever move so fast. Time seemed to stop as she dove after the flying vial head-first, her outstretched hand breaking its fall just before it hit the floor. She clenched it tightly as she landed messily on her stomach and rolled over the floor.

Almost as an afterthought, she twisted around and threw her dagger. Not to kill Mehtab. Not like that. Merely to threaten her, for now. She tried to convince herself of that, but her weapon – a natural extension of her body, bonded to her blood and controlled by her thoughts – knew otherwise. As she rolled to a standstill, holding the precious vial tightly in her fist, she heard a grunt and a moan behind her, followed by the thud of a body hitting the floor.

She didn't even turn to look as she rushed to Karrim.

Gassan was still kneeling beside him. Hakeem stood a few

paces away with a frozen expression on his face. She pushed past both of them to kneel at Karrim's other side.

"Is this the vial, Sage Hakeem?"

"Yes."

"Tell me what to do."

"He's barely breathing," Gassan said. "It may be too late."

"It's not, damn it. Does he need to drink it?"

"Yes."

She lifted Karrim's lifeless head and pried his lips open, forcing the entire contents of the vial inside as she tilted up his chin, so that she wouldn't spill a single drop. After a moment his throat wobbled slightly as the liquid passed through. A conscious swallow? Or was it the last convulsion of his death agony? She refused to think this way.

Was it enough against this much poison?

Was it too late to do anything at all?

"All we can do right now," Gassan said, "is wait."

She nodded and gently laid Karrim's head down on the floor. Several Daljeer healers appeared in the doorway and made their hesitant way toward them, kneeling on the floor by Karrim's side.

"Watch over him," she said. Then, she turned and looked at Mehtab, a distance away, crouching beside the throne.

Alive.

She felt a strange sense of relief. She didn't want Mehtab to die. Not by her hand, even after everything this woman had put her through.

Not without a closure.

DESTINY STONE

Mehtab sat with her back propped against the leg of the throne, blood seeping from underneath the dagger protruding from her shoulder. She was clearly in a lot of pain, yet her face creased with a triumphant smile, as if everything that happened here today was part of her plan. Naia's stomach clenched as she approached her.

"I am the true Xarimet of Challimar," Mehtab said. "You are an imposter, Naia. You have no right to the throne. You will restore the Destiny Stone to me and take your place by my side. Here, put this on." The imlar necklace, similar to the one Naia wore for her lessons, gleamed in Mehtab's hand.

Naia's body tensed with an odd urge to obey. She longed for the peaceful feeling the necklace always brought – the calm knowledge that someone was here to take care of her, to tell her what to do. She shrugged it off. Those times were gone. At some point, Naia thought of Mehtab almost as a mother. And now, this woman had tried to destroy everything Naia cared for, in her power-hungry rage. More, she didn't show the least regret about any of it.

Naia felt oddly calm as she raised her sword over the woman. *Someone I've been so close to. Helpless. Unable to do anything at all in her defense.*

Am I truly going to kill her in cold blood?

Her hand wavered.

From the corner of her eye, she saw Gassan stepping up to her side. He raised a hand, as if to stop her, then dropped it away.

"Before you do this, I must tell you what this woman really did," he said. "I finally figured it out. All of it. Sorry it took me so long, Jai Naia."

Naia held her blade steady.

"Mehtab," Gassan went on, "is a brilliant scholar, really. Worthy of the centuries of fame earned by her kin."

Mehtab's lips twitched in a scornful smile. "I am Chall royalty. Of course I am brilliant, you oaf."

She spoke calmly, yet, knowing her well, Naia could see she was in pain. Blood was spreading from the dagger wound, seeping into her garnet-colored silks. *Her shoulder. I could have aimed more to the left. Then we wouldn't even be talking right now.* The thought brought no relief whatsoever.

She didn't want to kill Mehtab. Now that her battle rage had receded, it didn't seem like the right thing to do.

She lowered her sword.

"All right," she said. "Tell me what you've learned, Dal Gassan."

"You may know a lot of it already," Gassan said. "This woman's research in the Daljeer's Circle – decades of it – was devoted to only one topic. How to make Ironbloods. She aimed to recreate the elixir originally used by the Chall to generate their elite warriors, the same elixir that spawned the Jaihar too,

centuries ago. And she succeeded. She discovered the formula
anew, by identifying its key ingredient. Crystal leech poison.
When it's administered to a person, it opens the blood to
iron that floods it to toxic levels, and beyond. The antidote is
extremely rare and costly, because it is infused with liquefied
imlar."

"*Imlar?*"

"Yes. Imlar draws the iron into itself, helps keep it under
control. But the iron doesn't disappear. It circulates in the
blood in its harmless imlar-bound form, releasing back slowly,
until the person adjusts to the change. Eventually all imlar
disappears, but the iron remains."

Naia shook her head. "But if so, anyone ever treated this way
must become an Ironblood."

"They do. Except that most crystal leech victims die, so we
never knew it. And yes, I assume the few survivors, rich enough
to afford the antidote, do acquire Ironblood qualities. They
might become better with weapons, but the chances that any of
them are trained in advanced weaponry are remote. Even if they
do become better fighters, this happens too rarely for anyone to
notice."

True. Due to its price, crystal leech venom – as well as the
antidote – was normally used on people of high importance, by
those who could afford it. The survivors would likely be found
among the wealthiest merchants and nobles, usually in their
middle years – people who tended to make enemies in high
places, but rarely raised a sword on their own behalf.

Mehtab's captivated look confirmed beyond words everything
Gassan said.

"She has made many errors perfecting the process." Gassan
looked at Mehtab, too, as he spoke, as if searching for giveaway

signs that could support his story. Like right now, when Mehtab's tiniest shrug at his last words spoke volumes. Mehtab didn't like to admit to any shortcomings. The mere fact that she offered no objection was a good indication that he was right.

"The notes we found in her chamber are splattered with blood," Gassan said. "I assume, that of the unsuccessful would-be Ironbloods."

Mehtab's lips twitched. "They were honored to submit themselves to the process. And yes, they've all been told that death was a possible outcome, and that I would use their blood for research. They made their choice, because of their devotion to me."

Gassan's eyes hovered over her with an unreadable expression. For a moment Naia thought he was about to respond, but he continued as if he hadn't been interrupted.

"Those few that survived – the warriors in this chamber – can fight beyond regular skill. They lack proper schooling – this is why the Jai-ranked warriors can still beat them. This was also why Mehtab wanted you on her side so badly. Under your command, these men would have become the core of the army Mehtab has been building for the past two decades or so, one that would have been invincible once you had taught them all the Jaihar secrets and techniques."

An army of Jaihar-trained Ironbloods. Naia's skin crept as she looked down at Mehtab, who still hadn't offered any objection to Gassan's words.

"Why did she put a crystal leech in my bath?" she asked.

"Mehtab was controlling you with imlar. But from time to time you tended to be able to escape her influence."

Like that time on the palace plaza. Naia remembered how upset Mehtab was that Naia disobeyed her instructions and deviated from the script. Was this why Mehtab chose that particular moment to do it?

"The leech treatment would have sealed her control over you, once and for all," Gassan said. "You would have followed her unconditionally – just like the warriors here."

Naia glanced around at the Chall warriors, still standing around with dazed expressions, as if their minds were not truly there.

"Mehtab's power over them is nearly absolute when she is wearing the Destiny Stone," Gassan said. "It is considerable even when the Destiny Stone is merely around – like right now, since I believe Jai Karrim carries it in his pocket."

Naia turned to Karrim, still motionless on the floor. The Daljeer healers were kneeling around him, their solemn expressions making her heart quiver. Still, none of them had walked away. She chose to take it as a good sign.

"Despite the antidote, he'll probably die anyway," Mehtab said calmly. "No one has ever been bitten by that many leeches at once."

Naia's sword hand twitched again, but she stifled the rising rage. No matter what this woman had done, she was not going to take the bait.

"So, what did you expect to achieve with all this?" she asked.

"My birthright." Mehtab's face twitched. With pain? Agony? Probably, even though Naia wasn't so sure her dagger had caused the worst of it.

"The power that has been denied to me for so long," Mehtab said. "It's inevitable now. As soon as everyone learns of my proper lineage – and your lack of it – the empire will be mine, as it was always meant to be."

"So that you can – what – kill all Zeg?"

"All who sympathized with the Challimar massacre, yes."

"And how are you planning to identify them?"

"I won't. I'll kill enough of them to make sure everyone knows better."

Naia heaved a breath. Glimpsing into Mehtab's soul was more frightening than anything she had ever seen in battle.

Thanks to Naia's susceptibility to imlar, Mehtab's plan almost came to pass. Karrim had stopped it in the nick of time. And now, Mehtab was trying to make him pay the price, with Naia powerless to do anything beyond what she had already done.

She turned to Gassan. "So, what do you propose to do with her?"

"I intend to make sure she faces justice."

"Too dangerous. If rumor gets out that she is the rightful Challimar queen–"

"Not just the queen. The rightful empress." Mehtab struggled to sit more upright. "You will announce me at once and surrender the crown to me, girl."

Once again, Naia's body felt an odd urge to obey. She saw the Chall warriors around the room raise their heads – like machines that had been awakened to action.

She caught herself under Gassan's intent gaze.

"The Destiny Stone," he said. "As long as it's nearby, you are all in danger of falling under her influence. We must get it out of Jai Karrim's pocket, and away from her."

Naia nodded, then strode over to Karrim and knelt by his side. The Daljeer edged out to make room for her.

His skin seemed to have regained some of its color, his eyes moving under his shut eyelids as if he was asleep and dreaming. She reached over to touch his wrist, feeling the pulse. Steadier now. More, his fingers twitched in response, briefly twining with hers, as if even in this semi-conscious state he could recognize her.

Her stomach quivered.

"He may survive yet," Mehtab said from across the room. "But if so, with this much leech poison in his blood, he will be forever mine. He will obey every word I say."

Naia forced away the anger brought by these words. *She's purposely trying to unbalance me. The stone. Get the stone.* She ran her hand down Karrim's side, feeling out a deep shirt pocket, reaching all the way inside.

The necklace felt heavy, yet flexible as its links folded and coiled around the exquisite stone. As Naia pulled it out, she couldn't help pausing to look at its fire, the reds of a dramatic desert sunset stirring up in its turbid yellow-green depth, a swirl of colors so captivating that she couldn't take her eyes off it.

The hall around her slowly receded. She was standing in Mehtab's room, back in Haggad, wielding her imlar blades. Around her, the Chall and Zeg were fighting. Her awareness transcended three different timelines, merging them. *Destiny. My destiny.*

Challimar, reigning over the sands.
Challimar, the Sel-blessed land.
Challimar, a beautiful dream.
I will protect you with my life.
Challimar, betrayed and destroyed.
Challimar will rule once again,
Led by our true queen, Xarimet,
Born from the ancient royal line…

"Naia."

The sound of her name penetrated her haze – or was it the voice that spoke it? *Karrim.* Was he speaking to her from another time line, back when he was still alive and well? She could no longer tell.

"Naia."

Her eyes snapped open.

Karrim was sitting up. Fully awake, the urgency in his gaze forcing her into awareness. *How long have I been dozing?*

"You've taken something from me," Karrim said. "Something you shouldn't touch."

She looked down at her hands, still clenching the necklace. *The Destiny Stone. Cursed Irfat.* She looked up at Karrim with hesitation. Was he fully recovered? Or was he under the influence of the stone too, about to challenge her for it? Was Mehtab controlling him, now that he had been bitten by the leeches and recovered? Was this why he was asking her to give the stone back? Naia clutched the stone in her hand and edged away, glancing to where Mehtab sat, leaning heavily against the foot of the throne.

The woman's face crinkled with a devilish grin as she drew a long breath for the next line of the song.

Gassan was running toward her, but Naia knew he would never reach her on time.

"Destroy the stone!" Gassan shouted. "Smash it with your sword. Now!"

Naia threw the necklace to the floor, drawing her sword and stabbing the stone with a force that echoed all the way through her arm.

In her altered state of mind, it seemed as if the impact shook the floor under her feet, the ornate pillars, and the high vaulted ceiling overhead. A shock wave pressed on her ears and rolled through the room, into the garden, over the heads of the crowd gathered outside the palace walls…

No, not the shock wave. A piercing scream that trailed to high notes beyond the range of normal human hearing, evoking a sense of guttural panic.

The scream.

Was it the stone that screamed like a child, as it shattered into a thousand tiny pieces?

Or was it Mehtab, struggling to her feet, snatching a sword from the floor among the wreckage, shouting something as she rushed across the room with the blade in her hand?

Rooted to her place, Naia knew she would never be able to respond in time. Bound by the scream that still filled the air, she couldn't possibly move – not even when she heard the whizz of a blade flying past her from behind.

Mehtab moved with surprising deftness to block the throwing dagger using her imlarite blade, but more daggers followed, so fast she couldn't possibly get them all. Her body shook as the daggers hit, burying deep in her chest.

The scream.

Naia wasn't sure if she was the one screaming now. Or was the sound still coming from Mehtab's throat, a high note that would not stop until it shattered everything in sight? As Mehtab folded to the floor, slowly, like in a dream, her eyes sought out Naia's, pouring out all the emotions trapped inside. Anger. Fear. Disbelief. Hatred. And finally, defeat.

Light faded out of those eyes, the darkness that descended into its place gaping like a hole in Naia's soul, one that could never possibly be filled.

It took ages for time to return to its normal flow. Sounds filled the hall once again, the rustle of the ornate wall tapestries in the light breeze. Strange that this was the first thing Naia heard, before the shouting, the sound of running feet, the clatter of her sword hitting the polished stone floor as it slid out of her unresisting hand. *Dear Sel, did it all really happen this fast?* She followed her fallen sword with her gaze, strangely detached as she looked at its mangled shape, the bends in the noble steel, distorting its once-perfect lines.

My sword. Despite its exquisite make, it couldn't survive the impact with the Destiny Stone. Strange that she still cared. It seemed like such a small price to pay for ending this nightmare.

She turned to Karrim, kneeling behind her. His dagger belt was empty, his sword at the ready in his hand.

"You… you killed her," she whispered.

Karrim's shrug still looked a bit shaky. "Someone had to. You didn't look ready or able to defend yourself."

I wasn't. She heaved a breath. Even deadly injured, Karrim continued to be her savior.

"Are you all right?" Karrim asked.

Am I? Naia wasn't sure. In fact, she wasn't sure if she would ever be all right again. She looked down at the floor, at the remains of the imlar necklace, at her badly dented blade, at the tiny pieces of the fiery stone rainbow scattered around at her feet. Her gaze drifted onward, to Mehtab's still shape, to the princes' bodies lined up behind her in the depths of the room. Everyone with an immediate claim for the throne, dead. All hopes, shredded to oblivion in one short battle.

She came to her senses only when Gassan stepped up to her side and lay a hand on her shoulder.

"Come, Jai Naia," he said. "Your assignment is not over. We still have the imperial succession to decide."

DECISIONS

For the past few hours Gassan had been having too much trouble keeping up. And now, when the events suddenly came to a halt, he had no idea what to do. He needed to gather the Daljeer council. He needed to consider any of Shabaddin's other children who were even remotely suitable and could be speedily inserted into the succession line. He needed to send word to the Jaihar, to speak to the province rulers, and to consult with the Divan sages and the Immam.

He had no time for any of it.

He looked at Naia, barely able to stay on her feet, her royal Challimar outfit ripped and stained with blood. Damn it, despite all that, she looked so good. If only she carried the right bloodlines. But it was no use to wish for something that couldn't be. She was a nobody, a girl so unimportant that someone in the Challimar royal palace had deemed it acceptable to use her as a decoy, hiding the token of royal inheritance into her wrappings without a thought of leaving any clue about her parentage. The mere idea continued to fill him with anger. And now that the perpetrator of all this was dead, there was no further way to find out who Naia's parents had been, or why they had allowed anyone to use her this way. While her Ironblood origin was obvious, she couldn't have been a legitimate child. The Redcloaks were precious, their children's births carefully recorded and kept track of. Most likely, Naia was a bastard of some forbidden union. Perhaps one – or both – of her parents offered her to be used as a means to deliver the necklace to Mehtab, knowing that they were going to be killed and this action was their only hope of saving her life? A far-fetched theory with no possible proof, but Gassan was determined to stick to it. It was the only way he could possibly accept the rest.

Naia deserved to be among people who valued and respected her, the closest to a family she was never allowed to have. Once they resolved the current stalemate and enabled her to return to her Order, he hoped the Jaihar could play this role to her. Well, maybe one particular Jaihar, he corrected himself, as he saw Naia and Karrim at a distance, talking to each other. She smiled and blushed at his words, her tiredness less obvious now that he was close. His face, as he looked at her, softened with such affection that Gassan finally started to understand what all these women were swooning about. The ruthless Jaihar warrior looked caring and gentle, Naia's closeness coating him in a special glow that left no doubt the two of them belonged together. Too bad that the Jaihar warriors could never be permitted this kind of a bond.

Gassan ran his eyes around the chamber, pulling to attention as he saw Sage Yakkab hurrying toward him with a few Divan members in his wake. His welcoming smile faded as he saw Yakkab's determined frown. A business conversation, then. Well, forgoing the pleasantries certainly saved time. The Grand Vizier was bound to have some questions about the spectacular failure of all their plans – hopefully along with some helpful insights into the next steps.

"Where's Sage Hakeem?" Gassan asked.

"I ordered the palace guards to take him into custody," Yakkab said. "He continues to claim innocence, but we have every intention to look into all his connections with Dal Mehtab and find out how far their scheming went." He glanced uncomfortably at Mehtab's still body, stretched on the floor.

"Palace guards? I am relieved to find out some of them are still around."

Yakkab's lips finally twitched into at least a semblance of a smile. "I fully intend to reprimand them for running, when the battle got out of hand. I definitely expected better from our empire's finest."

His gaze trailed further this time, to the bodies of the princes. Gassan watched him carefully, surprised to find far less regret than he expected in Yakkab's face.

"This turn of events leaves us facing a most unfortunate dilemma, doesn't it?" he said.

Yakkab's raised eyebrows looked somewhat exaggerated. "A dilemma, Dal Gassan? What could you possibly mean?"

Gassan's instincts fired up at once. He glanced at the sages, noting how they all avoided looking at each other, like conspirators afraid to be discovered.

He gestured around the chamber. "You may have noticed, Sage Yakkab, that our plans for the imperial succession have just changed."

Yakkab shook his head. "I am not sure what you are referring to, Dal Gassan. The imperial succession has occurred as planned, in agreement with Emperor Shabaddin's last will. We have a new empress now, voted on by the council, carrying undisputed claim to the throne as the sole heir of her ancient bloodline. The matter is open and shut, isn't it?"

Gassan knew it was a bad idea to show a strong reaction, with everyone in the room able to see their conversation, but he simply couldn't help it.

"You are out of your mind, Sage Yakkab," he said.

The Grand Vizier smiled, his gaze trailing to Naia in the distance, giving orders to servants and imperial guards. Everything around her magically clicked into place, people hurrying to follow her commands, taking away the bodies, cleaning the blood and debris from the floor. Karrim stood behind her left shoulder, exactly where appropriate for the head of the Jaihar Guard. The Chall formed the perimeter around them, solid and competent, their expressions showing none of their earlier daze.

"She is a living legend," Yakkab said. "People in Zegmeer are elated with joy and pride. And it looks like she's doing just fine. I believe I speak on behalf of the entire Divan, as well as the council, when I tell you that we intend to keep her, no matter what the Daljeer may think about it."

"It's hardly that simple, Sage Yakkab."

"I don't see why it can't be."

"We both know she is not the real Xarimet. The truth about her is bound to come out, sooner or later."

Yakkab smiled, then fumbled in his robes, producing a long, rolled up parchment.

"After the succession ceremony, I charged my best scholars with an urgent task to research the topic. They've been able to achieve remarkable results, given how little time they had. This scroll here details all the proof of Princess Xarimet's identity – independently of the papers you produced on her arrival, which have already been authenticated. We are sending out copies to all the libraries throughout the empire."

"This seems like a desperate game to play, sage."

"Not at all. You can attest to it yourself, in fact. Weren't you one of the Daljeer who received the baby brought to your Challimar serai that night – wrapped in a blanket that also concealed the Destiny Stone? Didn't you tell me yourself that this baby was Naia, the name Her Imperial Majesty used to go by in her disguise?"

"You bloody know what I mean, Sage. Jai Naia is that baby, yes, but she has no royal bloodlines."

"You have no proof that she doesn't."

"Correct. However, I also have no proof whatsoever that she does. On the contrary, I have a note right here, one that came in her actual wrappings when she was delivered to us so dramatically. This note, previously stored among Mehtab's private papers, states beyond doubt that the baby is only a decoy used to deliver the Destiny Stone–"

Yakkab stopped him with a raised hand. "Of course, Dal Gassan. Princess Xarimet's protectors would do no less. If they indeed had to send their precious princess away through the guard-infested city streets, writing a note like this was exactly the right thing to do, in case the baby fell into the wrong hands. It makes perfect sense, doesn't it?"

Gassan heaved a deep breath, glancing around the chamber. He knew he had to make a decision right now, without a chance to consult with the Daljeer, or the Jaihar command who would most certainly oppose the idea. Worse, whatever decision he made, he had to live with its consequences. There was no going back on something like this.

He glanced at Naia, speaking to the imperial guards. They

all looked at her with such fervor that he could only stare. Sel's prophets, she was born for the role. Was it really up to Gassan to fight a rising tide of this magnitude?

"I suppose it does make certain sense," he said.

"I knew you would see it my way, Dal Gassan."

Gassan sighed. Naia was a Jaihar to the bone, with deep ties to her Order. She had been asked to play this role for a very short time, and she still believed her assignment was about to end. What would she say, if she learned she had just been volunteered to continue it, possibly for the rest of her life?

"You won't be able to pull it off without her full cooperation, sage," he said.

Yakkab grinned. "I intend to be very persuasive."

"What about the Jaihar command?"

"With the empress's help, I am certain they can be convinced."

"They will be livid, once they learn what happened."

"They already know – or will, very shortly."

"What in three hells do you mean?"

Yakkab's smile looked indulgent, as if he was talking to a temperamental child. "I've personally dispatched a letter to inform them of the events. I used one of our specially trained Jaihar-bound messenger hawks, the ones we reserve only for very special occasions. It should take the bird less than two hours to reach them. Probably another eight hours for Jai Arsat to reach Zegmeer. I'm expecting them first thing tomorrow morning, and will meet them armed with my best arguments."

"Which are?"

"Dictated by common sense, no more. Despite all your careful planning, we nearly lost the empire to a raving maniac. I am certain Jai Arsat shares my determination not to allow anything like this to ever happen again. Besides, we've already succeeded in his agenda, to avenge his brother and remove Shabaddin's line from the throne." His gaze drifted to Naia and Karrim, talking to the Chall guards gathered around them.

How the hell does Yakkab know so much about the Jaihar Headmaster? Gassan kept the question to himself as he looked at the Grand Vizier thoughtfully. He could guess only some of the reasons why Yakkab seemed so invested in seeing Naia on the throne. The girl must have impressed him when she stood up to Ramaz so bravely, when she showed so much compassion to the victims of Shabaddin's rule. For the last twenty years, Yakkab had been balancing a very tough game. Did the sage truly believe Naia could put an end to it?

He looked at the Chall warriors, watching Naia with the devotion of the holy fanatics. Was it because of their imlar bond? Or did they truly believe she was Xarimet, as some of the Daljeer told him after they had observed Naia's preparations in the serai? Whatever the reason, they seemed willing and ready to die for her, a loyalty so rare toward the Zeg imperial family in the years of Shabaddin's rule, especially from the Chall.

"If you truly wish to keep her, Sage Yakkab," he said, "I suggest you talk to her as soon as possible."

Yakkab smiled. "I intend to. But first, she needs some rest. It's getting late, and she's already had such an eventful day."

"We have only ten hours before Jai Arsat gets here."

"Just enough for a good sleep."

Gassan sighed. "You might want to offer her another accommodation then. Her chamber is a wreck after the fight earlier this evening."

"A team of servants has been there for the past half hour, cleaning up. I've sent some of my best. I expect, whenever Her

Majesty chooses to retire tonight, she and Jai Karrim will find the chambers fully suitable for their well-deserved rest."

"She and *Jai Karrim*?"

Yakkab's smile widened. "I'm sure that, as the head of her bodyguards, he wouldn't want to leave her side, even for a moment. I would do no less, in his place."

"You don't play fair, do you?"

"I see absolutely no reason to."

Gassan shook his head. Throwing Karrim into the bargain took the game to a whole different level. He never realized Yakkab could play this dirty. Resisting this man's careful scheming seemed more and more futile.

"I bow to your ability to think through all the details, sage," he said.

Yakkab winked. "I have been leading the Divan for the last thirty years, Dal. Far longer than you have headed the Daljeer. In this position, one tends to learn a lot."

"So I see," Gassan said. "So I see."

A REST

Naia and Karrim walked back to her chamber side by side, surrounded by the honorary escort of imperial guards suitable for an empress. She supposed, until a replacement could be found, she should be thinking of herself as one. Right now, she didn't want to think of anything at all, besides the fact that she and Karrim were both alive and well. More, Karrim's formal position as the head of her bodyguards enabled him to stay beside her at all times, a rule she was about to enact in full force. Just to make sure, she gestured for him to follow as she crossed her antechamber, the rest of her guards peeling away to assume positions by the doors.

Inside, the air was warm and fragrant, aromatic oils burning in the lanterns skillfully placed around the room. Someone had taken great care to clean away the remains of the fight they had here earlier, as well as to change all the rugs, pillows, and covers. Her bed beckoned with the soft freshness of crispy clean sheets. She inhaled deeply, her tiredness forgotten as she turned to Karrim standing quietly by the door.

"You need to rest." His voice trailed up in the tiniest hint of a question that sent her heart racing. *Rest.* Yes, they both needed it, but not right away. Not when they were alone in this chamber with no one to disturb them until morning. Just in case, she lowered the door latch into place. Her breath caught as she stepped toward Karrim, who watched her in silence.

"Don't *ever* try to die on me again," she said.

He smiled. "I was about to say the same to you."

She grasped the sides of his vest and drew him into a kiss, shivering as his hands slid up her back to pull her closer. His touch made her stomach flutter. She cupped his face, threading her hands through his hair. The smell of his skin, now mixed with sweat, made her feel dizzy. His closeness was so solid and real after the nightmares they'd lived through.

She had no idea how much time passed before she finally pulled away. It wouldn't do to assault her own bodyguard, even if he left no doubt of his eagerness for her. She could afford to maintain at least a semblance of civility. They needed to clean up and change. To rest and get some sleep, if they had any sense left. Of course, no matter how tired she was, she found it impossible to think about rest right now.

"I am acting like a bad host," she grinned. "Would you like to sit down?"

He grinned too, his eyes briefly flicking deeper into the chamber. "I'd rather lie down."

"How about a bath first?" Dear Sel, the mere idea of taking a bath with him made her head spin. Or was it her earlier concussion? Probably both, but she didn't want to think of anything beyond the immediate future right now.

His gaze trailed past her toward the bath chamber. She looked too. The soft flicker of the lanterns visible through the open door left no doubt that whoever had cleaned up this bedchamber had also made sure the bath was ready and waiting.

"A bath sounds nice," Karrim said. "But let me check it first."

"*Check?*"

"As I heard, last time you took a bath here you found some rare creatures in the water."

Naia nodded. The episode seemed so far away. In the haze of Karrim's closeness, she had almost forgotten about it.

"All right," she said. "Check it then, while I secure this chamber."

He held her for another moment before letting go, his hands tracing around her waist, up her back, as if he was having trouble releasing her. Before he finally pulled away, he brushed his cheek against her face – a tender gesture that made her stomach clench.

She knew she shouldn't be thinking beyond tonight, but it was so difficult not to daydream.

After Karrim disappeared into the bath chamber, she swept around the room, making sure everything was in place. She reined in her impatience, forcing herself to move slowly and meticulously as she checked all the corners, all the windows, all the nooks and walls behind every curtain and tapestry. If anyone disturbed them tonight, she was going to kill them, no matter who it was.

Her heart raced when she finally approached the door of the bath chamber and stepped inside.

The room looked different at night, with no sunlight coming in from above. If anything, it seemed even more inviting. Someone had definitely spent time here to evoke a romantic atmosphere. A narrow ledge running along the wall was set with burning oil lanterns, spreading around the soft aromas of jasmine and cedar. The water emanated warmth, beckoning her inside.

She shivered as she saw Karrim approach her from the depths of the room. The lantern light caressed his shape, subtly accenting every one of his graceful lines. She paused in her steps, savoring the sight.

How did she ever get this lucky?

"Everything's secure," he said.

"Let's get in then." She raised her hands to pull off her clothes, but he stepped in and took over, drawing the soft, jeweled cloth up over her breasts in a slow movement that made her shiver from head to toe. His tongue teased her erect nipples before he dropped down to take off her pantaloons and sandals, then straightened again to strip off his own clothes.

Naked, he scooped her into his arms and stepped into the water. The swirl of the warm undercurrents caressed her skin, taking away the sores and strain of the impossible day. Dear Sel, just touching him like this, skin to skin, made her feel so disoriented, exhaustion blending with her mounting desire into an impossible, dizzying mix.

Dazed, she shifted over him until she sat astride on top of him, chest to chest, lips to lips. His arms closed over her, holding her as he leaned his back against the side of the basin. She gasped as she felt his erection, right there, pressing against a sensitive spot. He grinned as he shifted under her, drawing out the exquisite sensation.

This position made her feel more in control, yet she knew it to be only an illusion. She was still in his power, with the way he seemed to know her body better than she did, each move building up her excitement, coursing through her every nerve. She shifted higher so that he could enter her, lowering down onto his cock. *So deep. Yes.* Her gasp turned into a moan, all her illusion of control gone as she rode him with accelerating rhythm. She felt drunk, spiraling too quickly, yet unable to hold anything back. He owned her right now, and giving herself to him so unconditionally made her feel complete.

She had no idea what tomorrow would bring for both of them. But having this one night with him made it all worth it.

Her vision darkened as he picked up speed, taking the last shreds of control away from her, building up a release so intense that when it seized her, she could no longer tell where she was. She knew she was screaming, and she didn't care if anyone could hear her right now. Hell, she had no idea she could come like this, again and again, until she felt more spent than she ever felt possible in her life.

Afterwards, she drifted off to sleep right in the bath, draped over him, warm water lapping gently over her skin. She awakened briefly when Karrim lifted her out of the water into a long soft towel, and drifted off again as he cradled her to his chest and carried her to bed. He lay down next to her, and she curled into his arms, warm and solid like a safe haven.

When she woke again, hours later, to the first light of dawn, he was still there, his arm over her – an embrace that made her feel protected like never before. The air in the chamber carried the scents of the floral air fresheners. She heaved in a full breath, closing her eyes as she settled back into the pillow.

She wished she could stay like this forever, immersed in Karrim's closeness. But she knew this wasn't possible. In a couple of hours she would have to return to the matters at court, to handle the aftermath of the damage, to relinquish the crown to whoever Gassan was going to line up next, now that Halil was dead. And then, she would have to say goodbye to Karrim and return to her Jaihar duties.

They could perhaps continue to meet in secret between

assignments. But she knew for certain that something like this would never be enough.

She shivered as Karrim ran his hand lightly down her side, over the curve of her hip, then turned and met his smiling eyes.

"I noticed you were awake," he said.

She smiled, holding his gaze. "I didn't mean to sleep this long. Somehow, last night, you managed to make me so utterly exhausted."

"Apparently not exhausted enough. Let me try again."

She raised her hand to touch his face and flinched at the pain in her head. Dear Sel, why did her headache have to surface at this particular moment? No more than a pang that receded right away, but a reminder of her injury at Karrim's hand, an experience she never wanted to repeat again.

Karrim's grin faded. "Are you all right?"

"I'm just fine."

He reached over and touched her temple, the side of her head. The warmth of his hand was so calming, taking the last of the pain away.

"Next time we fight," she said, "I wouldn't make it so easy for you to beat me."

"I had an unfair advantage."

"You mean, by being superior in skill?"

"Not that, no."

Dear Sel, his face was so serious. Why was he looking at her like that?

"What then?" she asked.

"Remember your ranking tournament?"

"Yes, I do."

"The choice of weapons we were given was deliberate. Every one of them, if used correctly, could in principle give me advantage over you."

She shook her head. "No. That's impossible. Maybe the staff and the halberd, yes, but the blades…" Her voice trailed away under his gaze. "How do you know?"

"Jai Ilhad briefed me after our fight."

"*Briefed* you?"

"Yes."

His expression made her skin prickle. *Jai Ilhad.* The lesson they had, a long time ago, floated up in Naia's memory. This man could detect each warrior's weakness, use it against them.

She didn't want to ask the question, but she asked it anyway. "Why?"

"My role on this assignment was to be your failsafe. Not only by assisting you in your mission, but also by making sure you didn't deviate from your orders. In particular, our superiors were concerned about the scenario where you chose to keep the crown, instead of passing it on to Halil."

A chill ran up her spine. Their fight yesterday, the blow to the head. She thought the attack was triggered by his intention to release her from imlar. She had no idea that by attacking her he was following orders.

It still didn't make sense, though. In that fight, Karrim could have killed her all too easily. He had intentionally stayed his hand. Why did he do it?

She knew she should ask, but this was not the first question on her mind, nor the most immediate one. Ever since that time, Karrim had been in a position to kill her many times over. Hell, he could easily do it right now, if he wanted to. Clearly, this wasn't his plan, at least not anymore.

"Why are you telling me this?" she asked.

"Because I don't want to keep a secret from you that could

ever stand between us."

Stand between us. She swallowed. It was too easy to take his words too seriously, a mistake she didn't intend to make.

"I assume, if our superiors learn you've told me about this, you will be in trouble."

"Most definitely."

Was there a smile in his voice? In the semidarkness, she couldn't quite tell.

"Why didn't you kill me?" she asked.

"In truth, I almost did."

"I know enough about your skill to realize that that is no kind of an answer. You tilted your staff to reduce the damage. You also tried your damndest to revive me. You could have easily finished me off, why didn't you?"

Karrim frowned. "Did you want me to?"

"That's a bloody stupid question."

"Right."

She laughed. Somehow, between the thrill of lying naked in bed with him and the impossible information he just told her, she seemed to have lost fear. More, the idea that she had just spent the night with her would-be assassin added to her excitement. She was playing with fire by keeping him this close. Despite her attraction for him, he was the deadliest man in existence, and she barely knew him at all. Yet, somehow all these considerations seemed so unimportant right now. Not when she caught his gaze, so intense in emotion that her head was beginning to spin all over again.

She eased back into her pillow. "Now that you didn't kill me, you stand in violation of your orders, don't you?"

His lips twitched as he glanced down at the sheet covering his body. "Well, I don't *stand*, exactly. Or, rather, a certain part of me does, but–"

"I am serious."

"So am I. Bloody serious, if you care to check for yourself."

She heaved a breath. The sheet was draped too loosely to see the part in question, but the mere thought of it consumed her mind with possibilities. "Really. Why did you spare my life?"

He shrugged. "I did the only thing I possibly could. The right thing. Whether or not our superiors end up seeing it this way, I don't actually give a damn."

"*I* do."

"Why?"

"I don't want to lose you."

There. She said it. More, she was surprised to realize how deeply she meant it. Of course, now that it was out, he would likely get up and run – the man whose occupation precluded him from any possibility of forming lasting bonds, notorious for the way none of his relationships ever carried any commitment at all. How could she even hint at having feelings for him, after what he probably believed to be casual sex?

She glanced away, afraid to see his expression, and froze as he reached over and gently touched her cheek, turning her face back to him.

"You won't lose me," he said.

"But the Jaihar seniors–"

"You are the empress, aren't you? They are your vassals. So am I."

"It can't possibly stay this way."

Karrim shrugged. "At the moment, you are the only one who has a say in how it is going to be."

"But–"

"Trust me, I've played enough shatranj to recognize a

winning game. Our empire has seen enough bad rule to be longing for a change. They've tried to put *Halil* on the throne, for Sel's sake. You could do so much better."

Her eyes widened. Last night, when he had told her she was going to make a great empress, she took it to be his dying delirium. And now, when he talked about it so calmly in his normal state of mind, it made odd sense. More, she had just come dangerously close to admitting her feelings for him, and he didn't seem to be in the least bothered by it. On the contrary, he seemed content with remaining by her side, for as long as she wanted.

"It's going to be messy," she said.

"It doesn't have to be."

She shook her head. "The Daljeer – and the Jaihar – won't stand for it. You think I can actually go against them, all alone?"

"Not alone. I'm here, aren't I?"

"Why?"

"Because I want to be. As for our superiors, deep inside they all know that whether they like it or not, you are doing the right thing."

She knew things couldn't possibly be this good. One way or the other, they were going to lose each other. But for now, they should use their time together as wisely as they could.

"I'll consider it," she said.

"You do that." Karrim's eyes darted to the door. "By the way, I believe we have about an hour before someone comes banging on the doors outside. People in this palace tend to start early."

"An hour is too short."

"I'm sure we could find a way to spend it well."

She laughed as she pulled him into her arms.

IMPERIAL RULE

Naia couldn't hide her regret as she heard the distant knock on the door. She was lying in Karrim's arms, once again so thoroughly spent that any movement seemed like a chore. They didn't nearly have enough time together, if there was such thing as enough when it came to Karrim. Why did they have to be bothered at this early hour?

"Let me find out who it is." Karrim gave her a quick kiss, then slipped out of bed, gathering his scattered clothes. Naia's stomach fluttered as she watched him moving around the chamber, so graceful and handsome that he took her breath away, over and over again.

Karrim dressed and clasped on his weapons far too fast. As he reached for his cloak, he froze with a frown on his face.

"What is it?" she asked.

"I think I hear Jai Arsat's voice."

"Jai Arsat?" Naia sat up in bed. "It couldn't possibly be. There is no way he could have gotten here so quickly, is there?"

"He could have, if he rode all night."

"Why would he do that?"

Karrim shrugged. "I believe what happened here yesterday

qualifies as an emergency. It was my job to inform him, but someone else beat me to it, apparently."

Naia jumped out of bed and quickly dressed, glancing in the mirror to settle everything into place. When did she get used to her royal outfit? The jeweled yellow silk lay over her body naturally, like the best training leathers she had ever donned on the Jaihar upper grounds. It still didn't seem nearly as comfortable, but she no longer felt constrained by it. Was it because she had just gained the experience of wearing these clothes into battle?

She glanced into the mirror again, then put on the crown – more for the purpose of hiding the faults in her hastily done hair than to make any deliberate statement. It seemed appropriate while she was still the empress, didn't it? But even more importantly, she couldn't possibly afford to look sloppy. By the sounds in the outer chamber, she was likely to be greeted by the entire court.

Karrim flung his Shadowblade cloak over his shoulders and stepped up to her side just as they heard a hesitant knock on the door leading into the bedchamber.

"Come in," Naia said.

The imperial guard that entered her chamber kept his eyes down, as if afraid to see something he wasn't supposed to.

"What is it?" Naia asked.

The guard looked up hesitantly, visibly relieved when he realized that she and Karrim were fully dressed. *Dear Sel, did everyone here know what we were doing last night?* Naia dismissed the thought. Of course they did – and by the looks of it, no one here had any problem with it.

"Forgive me for disturbing you, empress," the guard said. "There are many people out there who insist they need to see you urgently. We've kept them off for as long as we could, so as not to interrupt your rest." He glanced at Karrim again, who responded with a grave stare.

"Many people?" she asked.

The guard nodded nervously. "Besides the usual court assembly, Your Imperial Majesty's visitors include the headmaster of the Jaihar Order and two of his senior officers, as well as a group of important-looking Daljeer. The sages of the Divan are here too, in case it pleases Your Imperial Majesty to have a word with them."

Dear Sel. In Naia's refreshed state, the magnitude of the embassy seemed ridiculous. "What about the Immam?"

The guard didn't appear to notice the irony. "His Holiness is on his way, along with the high priests... Do you wish to wait for their arrival, empress?"

"No." Naia suppressed a smile, aware of how unseemly it was to laugh right now. She had nothing to laugh at. She could easily put her life in jeopardy by going out there to face these men. Yet, somewhere between her fight with Karrim yesterday afternoon, and their lovemaking at night, she seemed to have lost fear.

"I will speak to them right away." She gestured to Karrim and strode past the guard into the outer chamber.

The assembly indeed looked impressive. Naia wasn't sure she had ever heard of an event in the empire's recent history that warranted the presence of such a large group of the important-looking Daljeer – more than two dozen, all elderly and haughty – together with the entire Divan and the Jaihar command. The room, that looked ridiculously large to her just yesterday morning, suddenly seemed tight and confined.

All conversations stopped abruptly when she walked in, even

though her presence wasn't announced. Perhaps it was the way her ornate outfit gleamed in the sunlight coming in through the wide arched windows along the far wall. Or the way the courtiers and sages of the Divan all folded down into deep bows in front of her, the movement rippling through the crowd until only the Daljeer and the Jaihar remained upright, like lone rocks sticking out of the wind-swept sand.

Naia nodded to the assembly, taking an effort to look unabashed as she trailed her gaze to the Jaihar group. Her main challenge. She had no idea what they had in store for her, but by the looks of it, it couldn't possibly be good.

Arsat's face showed an uncharacteristic wealth of emotions, heavily dominated by irritation and disbelief. His eyes darted over Naia's royal outfit to Karrim's silent shape at her back, and onward to the bowing courtiers. Surram and Ilhad by his side looked no better, even if both of them showed a visible effort to remain impassive.

Naia heaved a breath. She was here because these men had ordered her to, and she was not about to feel bad for that. A Jaihar warrior didn't abandon her assignment when things got rough.

She looked at Gassan, wondering at the way the Daljeer seemed so curiously calm. This calmness alarmed her far more than the Jaihar's anger. But she knew she would have no time for any guessing.

Sage Yakkab stepped forward and bowed.

"Empress Xarimet," he said. "Forgive the early disturbance. The Divan sages and courtiers wished to be among the first to greet Your Imperial Majesty on your first day of what we are all certain will be a long and prosperous rule. We would also like to discuss with you the details of the formal coronation ceremony,

ANNA KASHINA

and your address to the crowds that has been unduly postponed because of the unfortunate events last night."

Naia blinked. He was addressing her as if her position as empress had already been decided, which was definitely news to her. By the look of it, the Jaihar seniors shared her surprise, even if the Daljeer continued to show no reaction whatsoever. Did they conspire with the Divan about it, behind the Jaihar's backs? If so, the conflict was probably about to erupt. She supposed there was no way forward but to get on with it.

"I assume," she said, "Jai Arsat might have something to say?"

Yakkab's neck stiffened. "I…"

"I do indeed have something to say," Arsat said. "But perhaps it would be wise to speak in private?" He prominently avoided using her title as he spoke, a detail that seemed especially noticeable now that almost everyone else had expressed their obedience.

Yakkab's eyes widened in alarm. "Your Imperial Majesty. Given the top blade skill Jai Arsat and his men possess, it wouldn't be advisable to–"

"It will be fine," Naia said. "Jai Karrim is here. His duty as the head of the Jaihar Dozen is to protect me with his life." *Even against his superiors.* She was watching Arsat as she spoke, and she noticed the way the headmaster's nostrils flared when she said this. Karrim had orders to dispose of her if she took the throne. And now she had just volunteered him as her protector against their own seniors. This conversation was not going to be pretty.

Gassan stepped forward. "I beg your permission to join the conversation, Your Imperial Majesty."

Naia had the sense not to smile as she nodded. She could guess the direction of Arsat's thoughts, but she still had no idea

389

what Gassan, the original perpetrator of the plan, was up to. In an odd way, she was looking forward to talking to both of them frankly, without being overheard.

"Granted, Dal Gassan." She turned to Yakkab. "We will go to the guard room over there, sage. Perhaps you could remain here in case we need you?"

Yakkab bowed. "No need to leave, Your Imperial Majesty. The guard room is not a comfortable place to talk." He raised his voice. "Lords and ladies of the court, you are all excused. The empress wishes to have a private meeting."

Naia's eyes widened as she saw the richly dressed crowd streaming out of the chamber without any hesitation or surprise. Dear Sel, being an empress was going to take some getting used to. She watched Yakkab usher everyone out, closing the doors firmly behind them and receding into the corner with the determination of a man not to be budged.

Well, his presence was not going to change much, she reflected. The more the merrier.

"What can I do for you, Jai Arsat?" she said.

"You can drop the act, Jai Naia. Everyone here knows who you are."

Naia lifted her chin. "Everyone here also knows what happened. I assume that includes you."

Arsat crossed his arms on his chest. "We have been told, yes. Perhaps you'd care to explain it in your own words, though?"

"Explain what?"

"This." Arsat's glance encompassed her royal outfit, the chamber, and even Yakkab, pressing his back to the door as if afraid that someone from the outside might try to force their way in.

It wasn't easy to maintain calm in the face of Arsat's anger.

390

Once again, Naia reminded herself that she was no longer a trainee, and Arsat no longer held every thread that governed her life.

"I ended up in this position through treachery," she said. "The same treachery that led to the death of all the immediate heirs to the throne. I had no choice but to step in."

"*Step in*? Is that what you call it?"

"Yes, I do."

"I call it a bloody power grasp."

Naia's eyes widened. In all her time with the Jaihar, she never heard the headmaster swear.

"I did not ask for this power, Jai Arsat," she said. "But, for better or worse, I am bestowed with it."

"And you intend to keep it?"

"Until a better candidate can be found, yes."

Arsat's glance slid past her to Karrim. "You had your orders, Jai Karrim. Ones that covered exactly this kind of eventuality."

Karrim held his gaze. Naia marveled at the way he continued to look so relaxed and friendly under Arsat's wrath.

"With respect, my duty to the Jaihar Order supersedes any orders I receive, even from you, Jai Arsat."

"What the hell is that supposed to mean?"

"Carrying out this particular order would have threatened the wellbeing of the empire, and of all the Jaihar. Jai Naia is currently the only one keeping it all together."

"This is bloody nonsense." It was Surram who spoke this time, his face pinched in poorly controlled anger.

Before Karrim could respond, Gassan moved with surprising speed to step between the Jaihar and Naia. "Jai Arsat, Jai Surram. Please listen."

The headmaster's eyes flared. "Stay out of this, Dal Gassan.

You have already done enough. It is your fault we are facing this situation right now."

Gassan bowed his head. "You are absolutely right, Jai Arsat. I take full responsibility for everything that went wrong. And I would never stand in the way of Jai Karrim's orders. I merely wanted to point out that he did, indeed, do his absolute best to carry them out."

"Obviously not." Arsat's eyes darted to Naia.

"He fought her. And he won. He left her for dead, after a blow to the head which, everyone was sure, had split her skull."

"He should have made certain of it."

"He would have, if we hadn't all been under attack from superior troops. Believe me, he did everything humanly possible to fulfill his duty. You cannot fault him for anything that happened beyond his control."

"But—"

"The fact that Jai Naia is alive is very lucky. If not for her interference, if not for the unique way she and Jai Karrim work together, the empire would have ended up in the hands of a raving maniac who would have drowned us all in blood. You should thank your two best warriors for saving us all."

Arsat appeared to hesitate. "Yes, I read the report about your woman, Mehtab. A maniac indeed. But she is dead now, isn't she?"

"Yes. And Jai Karrim was the one who killed her, may I add, after she rendered everyone else incapable and almost killed him by poison."

"No matter. Now that the emergency is over, Jai Naia has no bloody business wearing this crown."

"She didn't want to wear it, she was forced to. But you cannot possibly ignore the fact that for now she is the best we have. Removing her from power would plunge the empire into a new disaster, one we cannot possibly afford."

"Jai Naia belongs to our Order," Arsat said. "If she takes the throne, she cannot be a part of it anymore. Among other considerations, it would deprive us of a valuable warrior, one of our very best."

Gassan smiled. "Didn't you previously give an order to kill her?"

Arsat glanced back at the Jaihar seniors standing motionlessly behind him. Naia could see their indecision, the way they made no move whatsoever to rush to Arsat's aid. The headmaster saw it too. His posture deflated just a tiny bit as he turned back to the Daljeer.

"What do you propose, Dal Gassan?"

"For the moment, nothing. Let things stay the way they are. At the very least, it will give us all time."

"But Jai Naia—"

"Is a capable ruler. She has already shown it on enough occasions. In fact, the Divan stands fully and unanimously behind her."

"They do?"

"Oh yes. Sage Yakkab has gone to great lengths to uncover documents that prove her royal claim beyond all possible doubt."

"Fake documents, you mean."

Yakkab grunted in protest, but Gassan's glance stopped him.

"The Daljeer scholars have authenticated them."

"You couldn't have," Arsat protested. "This is a direct violation of our agreement. You know everything about Naia's lineage – or lack of it, as happens to be the case."

"It is an understandable assumption, Jai Arsat. We were all

misled, and I take full responsibility for it. Naia's father was the captain of the queen's Ironblood guards. He was also the queen's consort and lover, loyal to her until his death. Which means that Naia's mother could only be one person. The queen herself. In Challimar, this fact would have made Naia eligible to inherit the crown. Thus, with all the nobles' support she gained yesterday in the succession contest, she is indeed the undisputed ruler of the empire."

Arsat heaved a sigh. "Do you truly want to play it this way, Dal Gassan?"

"With the Jaihar's cooperation, I hope."

"I assume you need my cooperation too," Naia said.

Gassan bowed. "Once I secured Jai Arsat's agreement, I was going to beg you, empress–"

"Save it." Naia glanced at Arsat. "I'll do it, for a time, under strict understanding that I can step down as soon as you find a suitable heir to take my place. I have a few conditions, though."

"Name them," Gassan said.

"The Jaihar's full agreement would be a start."

Arsat held a pause, exchanging looks with Surram and Ilhad.

"Very well," he said at length. "For the moment, the Jaihar will go along with this. However, Jai Karrim must return to our stronghold with me, so that we can discuss the matter of his violated orders. I will send Jai Hamed and twelve Glimmerblades for the Jaihar Dozen right away."

"No," Naia said.

Arsat lifted his chin abruptly, as if he had been slapped.

It felt odd to directly contradict this man, who had held supreme authority over Naia for as long as she remembered. She supposed, in her new role, she had to get used to it.

"Jai Karrim will remain here," she said. "With your full

pardon, until further notice."

"But–"

"This is not negotiable. The empire will compensate you for his services. As well as mine, given that I am still a member of your Order, on an assignment approved by you."

"But–"

"The alternative is my withdrawal from the deal," she said. "Along with the gold the empire currently pays to the Jaihar Order. As you know, I am capable of training my own bodyguards. Without the Jaihar, I will take the necessary steps to reinstate the Challimar Redcloaks, and–"

"Wait," Ilhad said. He stepped forward and whispered into Arsat's ear, followed by nods from all three Jaihar seniors.

"We will consider this," Arsat said.

"The arrangement is unconditional, Jai Arsat. I want Jai Karrim by my side, as long as he will serve me willingly. I also want my pick of the Glimmerblades for the Dozen. You will be given my list of names before you depart."

Arsat's gaze wavered. "We have never been dictated to on these details before."

"I am not dictating to you either – apart from Jai Karrim, that is. I am expressing a wish, which should go along well with the Jaihar Order's pledge of loyalty."

Arsat hesitated only briefly before lowering his head. "Very well. We will do as you wish, Your Imperial Majesty."

Naia smiled. "Thank you, Jai Arsat. The empire deeply appreciates your continued service. I hope you and your men will join us all for the coronation feast." She looked around the chamber, feeling surreal when she saw all three Jaihar seniors bow to her, lower than she had ever seen them bow to anyone before.

She looked at Gassan. His smile sent a surge of warmth

down her spine as she watched him and all the Daljeer fold into deep bows too.

They had come such a long way from the time when they met, on that fateful morning, in the lower Jaihar courtyard. She knew she was never going to learn everything that happened after that day, but here and now, it didn't seem to matter. She turned and met Karrim's eyes, sparkling with a smile that made her feel lightheaded.

The Challimar queen, the woman she was now given the right to call her mother, had a lasting affair with the head of her guards. And now that Naia was the empress, nothing precluded her from doing the same with Karrim. In fact, after the coronation was over, she was going to take him to her chamber and stay inside with him for a very long time. His smile promised her so much that she shivered in anticipation.

Outside, the crowds roared her name. Soon, she would come out to address them all. And then, she would do her absolute best to rule the empire as well as she could, with Karrim by her side.

ANNA KASHINA

ACKNOWLEDGEMENTS

There are so many people to thank, for everything in my life that ultimately led to this publication.

I thank my friends and critique partners, J. M. Sidorova, Y. Wolf, A.C. Wise, A. Greenblatt, L. Korogodski, L. Waldman, and especially Bernie Mojzec – who not only provided useful feedback on my writing, but also extensively consulted me on medieval weaponry and blade techniques. I am grateful to the amazing cover artist Alejandro Colucci, who possesses the magic of bringing my characters to life and has truly surpassed all my expectations with this book. Last but not least, I thank my agent, Jennie Goloboy, and the stellar Angry Robot team, especially Marc Gascoigne, without whom this book may not have happened at all.

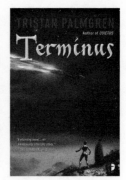
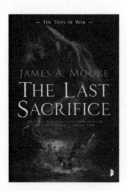
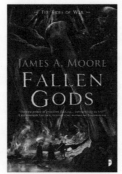
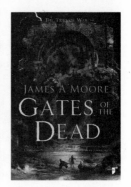

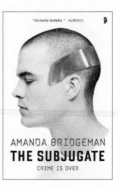